ZARRIN

Also by David Briggs

The Direction of Our Fear
The Claim
Reflections

ZARRIN

DAVID BRIGGS

Red Door

Published by RedDoor
www.reddoorpress.co.uk

The right of David Briggs to be identified as author of this
Work has been asserted by him in accordance with sections
77 and 78 of the Copyright, Designs and Patents Act 1988

ISBN 978-1-915194-00-8

A CIP catalogue record for this book is available
from the British Library

Cover design: Kari Brownlie
Typesetting: WatchWord Editorial Services
Printed in the UK by CPI Group (UK), Croydon

To the memory of all refugees,
and their bravery and suffering

Where I Am From

I am from my early memories
From lovely friendship and harsh separation
I am from the three days that I spent in the war
    with deserted streets
From shoes mixed with blood, with music of warplanes

From the dark black nights and sound of hungry dogs
I am from the morning when my dad asked a man
    who's ready to shut down his shop and leave
the country, "Do you have kuboos? Even if it is old?"
Believing that one day the sun will rise up again and light
    this persecuted city
I am from the beautiful neighbourhood and the nice people
From my grandma's house and pomegranate trees
I am from the smell of summer rain and fresh air
Birds singing and the wind dancing with the trees

I am from Nova and Muhammad Ali,
Where both of my grandpas live in heaven
I am from the wing on the branch of a fig tree
From the grapes hanging from the pergola
I am from my early memories and full life of dreams.

Anonymous

1

Escape

On the sixth or seventh day, in a wadi somewhere, where she rested for a while, waiting for the road ahead to become safe, for a truck that might take her on, she sat in the shade of a pistachio tree and watched as a kestrel hovered above a small rock outcrop, head down, intent on some invisible lizard or vole or hamster that busied itself amidst the crevices. Long minutes it hung there, a star of brown against the blue, wings fluttering, tail bending to the wind, and all was silence. Then, with no warning, the bird fell like a stone, down, straight towards the Earth, as if all levitation had suddenly been lost and gravity had reclaimed it. In the silence, she thought that she could hear its body, as it carved the air aside.

Then, a wing's width above the ground, it twisted, banked, and with a careless slash of a curled claw swept up its prey; shrieked its victory.

In that same moment, she saw, or sensed, for the movement was too fast, another trajectory. A dark arrow-flash. An eagle owl or buzzard, perhaps. It came from upwards and right, from some other stratum in the sky, too high for human vision. It swooped, not in a tangent line but following a perfect arc – a parabola, the sweep of a swan's neck – and, even before the kestrel had completed its cry, smashed into it. Feathers scattered, gobbets of bloody flesh spattered on the ground. The bird wheeled away, dangling the lifeless kestrel in its talons. And all was silent again.

Only a single feather remained, floating, this way then that, in a parody of flight. Then it, too, yielded, and sank to the sand.

It seemed apocalyptic, though she couldn't quite read the message. Perhaps it told of the layers of power and retribution in the world. If so, she needed that, and it gave her comfort of a sort.

Where she was, at that moment, she had no idea. She'd travelled without a plan, without a map. The land she'd walked through had been alien and uninformative. No signs, no names; few people, and those she did see shied away from her when she approached. She must have been here before, she thought. In her childhood, she'd journeyed the length and breadth of Syria with her father as he pursued his interests – chasing suppliers or creditors or potential customers for the products of his woollen mill – or when they went to visit relations, scattered around the country from Al Hasakah to Kobane, as far west as Hama and Homs, for the roots of the Kashlan family spread far and deep. Since her marriage, she'd travelled in more style with Mahmet. To social events or business dinners and meetings with dignitaries and politicians, businessmen, imams, leaders of this faction or that. Though in those more recent years she had been consigned to the back seat as befitted a married woman; and from the luxurious cocoon of the air-conditioned car, behind tinted windows, the world outside had seemed remote and uninteresting.

But today, as she walked, as she sat there alone in the grey desert, she cursed her inattention. Her failure, too, to pick up a map.

Whether one existed at home, she didn't know. What use had they for maps? They had drivers who took care of such concerns: how to get from here to there, which road to take. And time had been against her. She'd left on the spur of the moment when the chance arose. Other than her shoes, she'd had no time to change, had left in what she was wearing. All she'd managed to snatch was a bag that she'd hastily filled with food from the kitchen – water, bread, dried fish, fruit – a comb (why that?), a shawl. Her ID card and wallet. Then, almost as an afterthought, she'd gone to Mahmet's study, yanked at the drawer where he kept his money, taken it out.

She'd stood for a moment looking at it. A small wad of notes. Not local currency but US dollars. The currency for business that needed to be conducted privately, unseen. Deals and personal contracts and bribes. Sometimes, she knew, there might be four or five thousand dollars there. Now, though, there was less than three hundred. He must have drained the cache recently on a transaction of some sort, she thought, regarding it in disappointment.

Then she realised the obvious truth. It was the contract on her. Payment for Rohat's men.

The money felt even more soured and sordid than it had seemed before, and she almost dropped it in disgust. But common sense took hold. She stuffed it into her bag, fled.

Outside, she'd crept through the garden. Mercifully it had been empty, for it was just after noon, hot, siesta time, and no one would be looking for her yet. Even so, she'd kept to the shadows beneath the bougainvillea and vines; at the servants' door in the back wall she had looked around to check that she was unobserved before slipping out. In the street, she'd glanced about her again, still nervous, then hastened away. She had kept her head down, cloak drawn around her, fearing every moment that she would hear her name or heavy feet running behind her, feel a hand on her shoulder, a restraining grip. Each second that she remained unmolested seemed like a gift, and she muttered her thanks for it.

She'd headed north, out of Deir ez-Zor, not because she had any plan or that seemed the right way to go, but because it was the way the road took her. But then she'd had a fright: a black car, its interior impenetrably dark, had oozed past. She imagined the faces inside, observing her, expected it to stop, the doors to be flung open, Mahmet, or his brother Rohat, or Rohat's men, to leap out. She wanted to turn away, yet dared not in case they caught her unawares.

Perhaps her hijab saved her. Perhaps the men inside were paying less attention than they should. Perhaps it wasn't them. For whatever reason, the car moved on. Afterwards, though, she took the first turning that she could, into the back streets and alleyways, the narrow lanes. They felt no more welcoming. Women watched her from the doorways; the few men around regarded her with hostile eyes. She didn't belong there. Her clothes, the way she walked, the fineness of her features were evidence of her difference. Too rich, too proud. In far too much of a hurry. But there were no cars, and the alleys were a maze, and for the moment she felt safe.

Soon, though, she was lost. In the shadowless lanes, beneath the midday sun, she had no idea which way was which; every street looked the same. Repeatedly, she found herself in blind alleys, had to turn back. She became convinced that she was walking in circles, like a mouse in a cage. Her feet were already sore. Her bag felt heavy on her shoulder; her body ached. Her mind was ragged from lack of sleep, the torment of what had happened; her fear. She couldn't think, had no point of reference, jumped and jibbed at every sound.

But slowly the buildings began to change. White-painted stucco was replaced by bare breeze-block, rough red brick. The streets became narrower, the houses crowded in. She pushed between lines of grey washing strung from wall to wall, tripped on rocks, slipped on the water that leaked from a broken tap. She had to shoo away begging children, inquisitive dogs. At the corners, black refuse bags were piled up, ready to be torn open by the cats and rats. Sewage washed down the gutters, gathered in green algal pools. The air was thick with the stench of ordure and wood-smoke and rot.

And then she was out of it all. She stood in a landscape of thorn-scrub and fields, rocky ridges, terraces, tumbledown walls, hills that shimmered in the sun.

For some moments, she remained there, feeling released, and surprised by the fact. She'd not believed that it would happen. They would find her, she knew. They would take her back. What had happened already would happen again, and would go on happening, for ever, for as long as she lived.

Just there, in the brightness of the afternoon, a donkey watching her from a field, its mane trembling against the mob of flies, its ears alert, such fears had seemed unreal. Yet in the instant of thinking it the notion was banished. From away to her left there'd been the roar of a vehicle, then others in its wake. Diesel fumes made a dark smudge against the land. Out of a cutting came a convoy of trucks, army vehicles, camouflaged, a government flag – red, white and black, with two green stars – fluttering on each one. Although it was nothing unusual, nothing to do with her, she had felt a wave of panic, wanted to hide. As soon as they had gone, she'd hurried away, into the scrub.

In that moment, too, a plan of sorts had taken shape in her mind. Less a plan, perhaps, than a simple goal. Something, somewhere to aim for. The north. The border with Turkey. Another country. A place she might be safe. For she wasn't safe here, and never would be. Injured honour does not heal with time. Family honour especially.

For the days that followed, she'd travelled north. She avoided the roads, kept to the farm tracks and donkey trails. Roads felt dangerous: she might be seen; even now Rohat and his men were probably looking for her. She feared the police and the army, too, for since the street protests had started, since the rumours of civil war had taken hold, anyone alone, behaving strangely, looking out of place, would attract attention, might be arrested. And women like her did not walk alone.

She clung to the hills and the edge of farmland, skirted villages when she could, moved out of sight when she heard vehicles or people approaching.

The going was harder than she dared believe. The tracks were rough. Here, beyond the margins of the Euphrates, the land was raw and cruel. The farms were small. They huddled in the valleys, or around an oasis, near any water they could find. The sky was unforgiving: a lid of pale blue in which the sun blared white, searing anything that moved. The wind came from the desert, dry and laden with grit. She turned half into it, away from the main highway and the towns where she'd be seen, where her pursuers might find her. Into the blistering heat, the biting sand, her cloak pulled to her mouth for protection. She walked through days of thirst and hunger, fear. Sun and dust. Dust and sun. Days that died into nights of coldness and despair; nights in which she huddled in search of her own scant warmth, and measured the slow passage of time by the circling blizzard of stars, and *Feresu'l-a'zam*, the winged horse, as it crept across the horizon.

Yet, amidst it all, she found small kindnesses. By contrast with the world around her, they came like acts of huge moment and generosity. In a scatter of houses somewhere, a woman came to the door, offered her milk from a bowl. A young girl, five years old at most, walked with her for a while, holding her hand. An old man, working in a rough, walled field which might once have been an orchard, called to her. When she hesitated, he beckoned urgently: come, come. As she reached him, still uncertain, he pointed at the tree beside him, half-withered, its broad leaves ragged and pale. 'When the plant knows it is dying,' he said, 'it makes fruit for the next generation. See.' On the stems, in what shade was left from the leaves, were clusters of figs. 'Take some,' he said. 'Take them with you. For what it doesn't know is that there is no future any more.'

On other days there was nothing. She would walk for hours without seeing anyone. The houses were silent, doors and shutters closed. The fields were untended. Out on the hills there was no sign of cattle or sheep or goats. The sky was empty. Her only company would be the carrion crows that mocked her from the bare trees, and the vultures that gathered around her whenever she stopped. On days like that she yearned for some sound, some sign of life, for she seemed to be journeying through a world that was abandoned and dead. She might be the only one left, the only one living. It was a state that bore down on her, frightened her, more even than death.

In the daylight, as she walked, what had happened felt remote, as though it had been done to some other woman in some other world, some other version of herself. But, at night, the pictures and the pain and the fear returned. The hatred, less of them than of herself, for what they had made her. The curse she would carry for ever more. In her dreams, as she fought against them, she heard herself scream and, knowing it was a dream, struggled to wake for fear that she would attract attention, bring them back to her. But she could not wake, couldn't find the exit from her suffering, so it continued, unremitting. Only when the sun came did her dreams retreat and the men slink away, like demons afraid of the light. Yet, as they went, they taunted her with their promises. *We will return.*

On another night, after a day in which the whole world seemed to be shifting, reshaping itself, sifted in the wind, she found shelter in the lee of what once must have been a farm truck, and tried to sleep. The fizz of the sand, the gathering cold, nagged at her. She dipped into and out of dreams, each one another torment against which she had to fight. She stared at the endless sky, made fuzzy by the dust, and tried to pick out the constellations, as if seeking old friends. She dozed, her hands crossed in front of her, then woke with a start, feeling a sudden strangeness, as though despite everything she was no longer alone. Allah was with her, she thought. Or *shaitan*, or some other god. Whoever it was, they were welcome, for they made the night seem worth surviving, gave the day ahead a purpose of some sort.

How many days she walked, she couldn't have said. A dozen, fifteen, maybe more. The only change she noticed was that, towards the end, there were others with her on the dry and dusty land. Families, small groups of men, women like herself, now and then a group of children. She'd see them walking towards her, obliquely across the bleak plateau, moving slowly as if at the end of their strength; or parallel, half a kilometre away, until they dropped into a wadi, disappeared from sight; or picking their way through the rocks and scree from the cliff-line above. Sometimes, when she stopped at night, she could hear their murmuring voices from the darkness or a child crying, or would catch the slow tramp of feet moving past on the rough road.

At first, she assumed that these people were an indication that she'd entered a more populous area of the country, and she tried to avoid them, imagining that amongst them might be people who knew her, or agents of her husband or his brother, sent to find her and bring her back. But gradually she realised that they were people like her, though fleeing from something that she did not know. Poverty perhaps, or drought. Or the revolution, and the war that would inevitably follow. She came to accept their presence, and she learned to follow them, for they seemed to share the same vague notion of where they were bound.

So it was that one morning, on a day she couldn't name – all sense of time gone – she found herself in what seemed to be a gathering place for the hungry and lost and homeless, each one a piece of flotsam discarded by the world.

After the long days alone, the sudden presence of others crowding around her came not as a relief but an assault, like a wave breaking over her, too strong to hold. She felt she would drown. They brought with them the realisation of how close she remained to the world she'd tried to flee and to the brutality it contained. As she stood amidst the crowds, trying to make sense of the noise – the shrieks of children, the keening cries of babies and mothers, the shouts of men in uniform, women in white coats – she felt afraid, wondering: would they be here, Rohat and his men, waiting, watching, knowing that she would come?

As if in answer, someone grabbed her arm. She gave a cry. 'This way,' she was told. 'Come with me.'

Dazed, she let herself be steered between the press of people, too tired to resist.

'There,' the man said. 'Stay in line.'

Where she was, why she was here, she had no idea, and did not ask. The world had a purpose of its own, and it wasn't hers to know. She merely did as she was told and stood in the queue, shuffling forward one step at a time as the women ahead of her moved and the sun dawdled on its trek across the sky and blazed its hot stare at them.

At some point a man appeared beside her, dressed neatly, as if he were an official of some sort. He demanded to see her wrist. She held it out, and he steadied it with his own hand, holding it firmly, then branded it with a small stamp, inked from a pad. When she looked at the mark, she saw that it was a number. '17-04-11'. Was that what she was now, she wondered: just a number? But then she thought: perhaps that was the date.

And later, two young men walked down the queue handing out water. And later again, as the sun sank, they were all told to lie down, get what rest they could.

For long hours, she lay there, awake, listening to the murmuring voices around her, the occasional cry of children, the slow pad of soldiers walking by. And little by little, in those hours, another realisation dawned. She'd reached the border. Somewhere in those endless plains and hills, or in a waterless valley where the fields were crusted and bare and no one any longer lived, she must have crossed it. She was in Turkey. She'd found safety, of a sort.

The next day, just before noon, she received the confirmation she hoped for. She found herself standing in front of a fold-up desk, while a bored official worked through his list of questions, ticking boxes as he went, never looking at her, scarcely waiting for her replies.

'*Hawillya?*'

She handed him her identity card.

'Is this information correct?'

'Yes.'

'Zarrin Sinjari?'

She tensed. Did he recognise the name? 'Yes.'

'From Deir ez-Zor?'

'Yes.'

'You're Syrian?'

'I was born there, yes – but my family was Iraqi.'

'Kurdish?'

'Yes.'

'Your age?'

'Twenty-two.'

'What other family do you have?'

She hesitated, wondering how much truth she could afford to give.

'I don't know. My mother and father are dead. There is no one else.'

The man regarded her, his eyes distrustful. 'Married?'

'I was. My husband died.' Another lie.

'Your family name?'

'Kashlan,' she said.

The man wrote it down.

'You'll need to be examined – you know that.'

'Yes.'

When he'd finished, he gave her a form, directed her to a tent, then, as she turned to go, said in a dull, mechanical tone, 'Welcome to Turkey.'

In the tent, a nurse examined her. She did so perfunctorily, looking into her mouth, at her ears, eyes, hair; running her hands across her body, breasts, stomach.

'You aren't pregnant? No?'

'No.'

'You're sure?'

'Yes.' Though after what had happened, how could she know?

She was waved through, directed to another queue, and after that through a high, barbed-wire gate into a fenced compound. There, the process was repeated, one more interrogation, this time in the only common language they could find, English. The same questions. Where was she from, was she married, was she pregnant, was she sure?

Then another examination, gentler, but more intrusive, so that she stiffened, flinched. The nurse frowned at her. 'Did something happen?'

She nodded, said nothing.

'Do you want to tell me?'

She shook her head.

'Soldiers?' the nurse asked.

Again, she nodded. It was the easiest thing to do. It was not really her story, but safer that way: let someone else decide.

'I'm sorry.'

Another nod.

'They'll take care of you in the camp.'

'Thank you.'

The nurse wrote on a form, then looked up. 'You're from a good family, aren't you?'

She shrugged.

'I can tell. You're in good health. You have good skin. Your English is good. And I have heard of the Sinjaris.'

Zarrin froze. How much did the woman know?

'My husband is dead,' she said, repeating the lie.

'I'm sorry. Do you have money?'

'I am not what you think,' Zarrin told her. 'I am poor.'

The nurse smiled. 'I don't want anything. But if you have money it will help. It will be your only way out of here. But it is dangerous. People will try to steal it. Do you want to leave it with me?'

'I am poor,' Zarrin said again.

The nurse regarded her for a moment, nodded. 'I understand. Take care.'

The camp was large, crowded, frightening – though most things frightened her now. She was put in the single women's section. It had its own fences, was patrolled by armed guards day and night. Whether that was as protection against the outside world or from the men in the adjacent compound, Zarrin was not sure, but she found comfort in the fences and gates and guards.

She shared a tent. Her partner was an old woman, bent and shuffling, gap-toothed. The woman's breath rasped, and she had a cough that rattled in her throat. At night she muttered to herself in her sleep, words that Zarrin could never quite catch, yet which seemed to fit together, almost to rhyme – a prayer, perhaps, or a poem or song in an ancient dialect. But after a month or so she died, and Zarrin was alone.

But not quite alone, for in her sleep that feeling returned – that sense of another, of a unity that she couldn't quite grasp. As though someone, or something, accompanied her now, guiding her life.

Then sickness came. After two or three days she asked to see a medic, found herself in front of the same nurse who had examined her when she arrived.

This time she introduced herself. 'I'm Dr Schreiber,' she said. 'We met before. Remember? I'm glad to see you looking so well.' Then, later, when the examination was complete, 'You're pregnant. Didn't you know?'

Zarrin shook her head, dumbfounded. But she remembered the growing sensation she'd had as she travelled – of someone else with her. Perhaps she had known after all.

Dr Schreiber smiled. 'I had my suspicions before. When was it, do you think?'

She counted back. 'Two months ago,' she said. 'A bit more.'

'You seem sure now.'

'I am.'

Dr Schreiber nodded. 'I understand.'

Did she, Zarrin wondered; did she understand? Could anyone?

'We will look after you. Don't worry.'

Yet how could she not worry? The child brought no sense of motherhood or hope, promised nothing but trouble. And she knew its origins, how it had been conceived. She didn't want it, wanted to rid herself of its presence, the memories it held. She wanted to flee the camp, escape, be on her own again. But what choice did she have? She was weak from her journey, from the change in her body, the child, she imagined, gnawing at her from inside. She knew that out there, beyond the fence, she would not survive, that the child would kill her. Here, at least, there was some small chance. Perhaps the child would die within her, or at birth. Or, if it was born, would be taken from her, disposed of in some way.

She stayed. Through the summer, into the winter and then for two months more she remained there, though life was never easy. In the summer the sun was unrelenting, and there were no trees, no shade in which to hide. The wind was from the desert, and carried just heat and dust. The winter, when it came was cool, wet. At night, the air felt tautly stretched, and in the morning the skin of the land was white. For days at a time it rained, grey clouds rolling in from the west. Water dripped through the seams of her tent, gathered in pools by the doorway; dampness crept into her clothes as if seeking a home. The ground outside was churned to brown mud.

And yet she found she could bear it, and was able to resign herself to wait. She was anonymous here, safe. Or as safe as was possible any more. The dangers that existed – disease, an assault by someone who believed that she had money or jewellery worth stealing, the unwanted attentions of a guard – might happen to anyone, were not hers alone. And there was food of a sort, shelter, people around to help. It gave her time to recover, for the wounds to heal. A hard scab to form over the memories.

Time, too, for the child inside her to grow.

2

Turkey

During those months, her moods and her intentions swayed. She was irritable with others, irritable with herself, didn't seem to know her own will any more. Her thoughts about the child were the same, always changing. There were times when she imagined it with fondness, and seemed to cradle it there, within her. There were moments when it felt fragile, as though it might break if she so much as moved. There were other times when it felt like a talisman, protecting her against the world, and she couldn't hold back a sense of fondness and gratitude. But at other times it felt like a curse. A burden deliberately left for her to carry by the men who had raped her; a germ that they had planted and which would one day burst out and infect the world.

By way of distraction, she dwelt on the past. Lulled by the simple rhythms and sounds of the camp, she would sit in the doorway of her tent and let her thoughts wander. Away from the meanness and tedium of the place, away from the dust and heat, back to the life she'd known before. A life that seemed to tease her with its innocence and intimacy, yet no longer felt like her own. A story-book life, where the sun shone kindly and she was surrounded by comfort and family and friends. Lambent scenes from her childhood, where she felt wanted and loved. Lounging beside a tinkling fountain, a tiny lizard in her hand, watching as the creature put out a tentative yellow leg, a flickering tongue, and began to explore her wrist. Alone in the shadows, where the scent of jacaranda and the flowering ash made a plasma around her, and the flames from the fire danced across the shoulders and faces of the adults who huddled in its glow. Hearing her name, called from the house – 'Zarrin, Zarrin' – yet willing herself to ignore it, so that she could continue whatever game it was she played; then running, running, running down the flagstone path into her mother's arms.

Each memory a moment of peace and tranquillity, sealed. Always at her home, or nearby, or with her parents in attendance. Safe times, happy.

With a little more effort, she could recall other times, later. When she was twelve or thirteen, the look she sometimes received from a boy she passed in the street, or met at one of the family gatherings. A glance that seemed to follow her, and made her tingle with some strange electricity that she could not name. Seeing her own body once, reflected in the mirror of her room, and feeling for the first time as though it was not just some representation of her, out there, unattached, but the person she was, her real self. Something that could own her, command her, give her pain or pleasure as it willed; something that would one day take her over and determine her fate.

Was that what had happened? It seemed so. For now, those times had gone. Brought to an end not just by the progress of time, but by the fierce tide of her own body and life. Adolescent desires and dreams, family obligations and marriage, the absurd foolishness of love.

Ended too, she now realised, by the yet more over-powering forces that were sweeping the world. The armies and the planes and the bombs. War, destruction.

She heard about them from the people in the camp, saw evidence in the growing numbers of people who arrived there, each more desperate than the last. Occasionally she found herself confronted by the consequences: a boy on crutches, one leg amputated at the knee; a woman with her face scarred and deformed by acid or fire; covered stretchers being hurried towards the makeshift hospital that had been set up just outside the compound. The scream, now and then, of jets overhead. The cries of a parentless child.

When that happened, it released within her another conflicting tide of thoughts. Pity and loathing, each of equal measure. For the world, for herself, for the small life inside her. How could she inflict that on any child, wanted or not – all that hatred and horror? How could she ever counter it? What chance did either she or the child have? Then, she would touch the broad swelling of her body, imagine the child there, see it crouched, already a refugee from the tumultuous world. But in a moment her thoughts would twist again, and it would seem not helpless but evil, like the larva of some repulsive parasite wasp, growing fat and bloated on her organs, waiting for its time to come, and she would loathe it. When those thoughts came, she would toy with notions of how she might rid herself of it, and break the cycle of malevolence it implied; she drew back from them, not from any fear of the hurt they might cause to herself, but only from that deeper instinct. That tug of motherhood. Inherited, perhaps, from her parents, or ingrained within her by those years when she would watch her grandfather tending the sheep, lambing them, struggling to save even the weakest. Pity or compassion or the simple imperative of life.

*

The birth was the worst. It ravaged her, raked her, was like the unwanted conception all over again. It was as if she and the child were at war with each other. She shouted and sweated and swore. The child resisted every step of the way. She raged and sobbed, until at the end of too many hours to count, hours that bled into each other and became another lifetime, the pain and the child seemed like one – a wild ocean too wide and hateful to cross.

Then two doctors came and stood by her bed, talking urgently in French. She couldn't understand what they said, but their voices soothed her. She imagined being borne away by the sound, by a music of unknown words. A paper was thrust in front of her, and a pen pushed into her hand.

'*Signez! Signez ici.*'

She scribbled her name. As the pain came sweeping back once more, wave upon wave, an angry storm, she was wheeled away. The sound and light and pain seethed, and she imagined herself being torn apart, body and limbs separated, tossed aside, left raw in the sun. Meat for the desert dogs that constantly circled her.

But, when she woke, the pain had gone, and the dogs. The baby, too.

And, in that torment, a darkness flooded in to take their place. It seemed to fill her, draw her into itself, irresistible, so that with a final cry of fear and despair she let herself go.

When the pain came back, when she woke again, it had changed. A deep pulsing hurt, like a saw, tearing at her loins and guts.

Yet the baby changed that as well. He was brought to her by an African nurse – a heavy, shambling woman, who wheezed as she moved.

'Boy,' she said. 'Lovely son.'

Zarrin turned away, feeling no interest. It was out of her. She neither wanted it nor hated it, just wanted it gone. But the nurse insisted, and laid it down on her chest.

'Here. You take. Your son.'

For a moment the bundle did not move, and Zarrin felt she might ignore it; that, if she did, it would crawl away, or just shrivel and disappear. Then it stirred; made a noise. Instinctively, she cupped the body to her. When she held it to her breast, it was as though it belonged there, had come home. When it suckled, her pain eased, was replaced by something that felt like relief or release, oneness. And, slowly, a strangeness grew within her, a feeling she could not recognise, almost feared in case it devoured her, was death creeping in. After so long expecting exactly that – death dressed up as a hungry animal – almost yearning for it, she found herself fighting to push it away. Not now! Not when she had this small promise of life in her arms, at her breast.

It came anyway. Not death, but contentment. Peace.

When he slept, she listened to his breathing from the cot beside her, and yearned to lift him to her, hold him again. When he fed, she reached down to him and kissed his head. Sometimes, she looked into his eyes, and saw her own reflection there – the mother, within the child – and that felt fitting, like an answer to it all.

She named him Elend, for it meant the first rays of the morning sun, and that was what he seemed to be. A new day starting.

She was allowed to stay in the hospital block for two days. As she left, the African nurse thrust some money into her hands. Zarrin tried to refuse, but the nurse wouldn't yield. 'No. For you. For baby Elend.' Zarrin blinked. Though she had screamed in the hours of birth-giving, and called to her mother and her god and blasphemed, she had not cried. Now the tears came.

*

When she was released, Zarrin returned to her tent, but the nurse came each day to check up on her, give her advice. Her bleeding stopped; her new wounds healed. The baby grew strong.

During the following weeks, Zarrin began to plan. She could do that now, had an obligation to do so, for the future was not just hers but Elend's. She needed to move on, to escape somehow and start a new life in the world that waited outside.

What sort of world that was, she couldn't imagine. All that she saw of it, heard of it from people newly arrived or from the camp staff, was that it was a world of confusion and fear. More death, more destruction. A world that was filling with refugees. It contained, as well, more personal terrors. Rohat and his men. No place for her.

And yet for Elend there was no choice. He could not live here, confined. His only world was the one out there, and somehow he must enter it, learn to grow up in it, find a role and make a life for himself. She could not deny him that.

There were other reasons to go, and soon. The heat of summer was coming. If she didn't leave before then, she would have to stay until the autumn, when the weather would cool. And life in the camp was changing, becoming harder, more complex.

In the months she'd been there, the compound had grown to the size of a small city. It stretched around her as far as the eye could see. The fences that had partitioned the camp into family, men's and women's quarters had long been removed;

in their place, zones based on different criteria: religion and ethnicity and influence. The haphazard patchwork of tents had given way to rows of wooden huts and metal containers, in neat blocks each with its number and code. Makeshift churches had been built, like a sentinel for each zone. Next to the hospital, simple schools had been set up. In every area – one for every thousand or so people – water pipes had been laid to standing taps. Latrines had been dug, and the waste was carted away and used somewhere, or perhaps just dumped in the desert. On the western side, upwind from the stench and the scentless, invisible waft of disease, a military camp had been established, where soldiers drilled, ready for deployment should the need arise.

And with the growth came something else. A complex structure and symbiosis of power and influence and need. Leaders and followers and servants, wealthy and middle-class and poor, lenders and debtors, sellers and buyers of every sort. Men sold their protection, women their bodies, children anything they could find or steal. There was a sense of turmoil in the place; it was never quite at rest. Rumours flared and spread like fire. Vendettas brewed. There was drinking and drugs. Fights broke out between Shia and Sunni, Christian and Kurd, men of families that knew each other from generations before and still had matters to settle. There were outbreaks of typhoid, measles, leishmaniasis – what was known in her homeland as Aleppo Evil, bringing angry sores, permanent scars. Zarrin did not want Elend exposed.

She feared, too, that amongst them – the refugees, the fleeing rebels and soldiers – would be spies and agents. Rohat's men, or members of the criminal gangs that had always worked in Syria, doing the dirty deeds that the rich and ruling families required. Men who might know about her, be looking for her, and know what price had been put on her head.

She feared what might happen. That the army would move in, break up the camp; that she and Elend would be sent back. Better, she thought, to take their chances alone.

She tried to imagine where she would head for, what her goal would be. England, she thought: the place where all refugees seemed to want to go. And why not? To her, the country seemed to offer everything she wanted, not just for herself but for Elend too. Get there, and she could start a new life, safe from Mahmet and Rohat and from everything that had happened. She could forget, learn how to live again. Perhaps, one day, she might find a father for Elend, so that he could have a full and proper life as well.

She began to ask around: how did you get out, who could help, how much would it cost?

A man who claimed to be an agent came to her. 'I might be able to help,' he said. 'How much money do you have?'

'Some,' she told him, avoiding his eyes.

'It's not cheap,' he said. 'And the further we take you, the more it will cost. Do you have enough?'

She had no idea, but nodded.

'Dollars?' he asked. 'That's what you'll need.'

Another nod.

'I will see what I can arrange. I will contact you when I have news.'

The next day, she was called to the medical hut so that Elend could be examined. It was Dr Schreiber again. 'I hear that you are hoping to leave,' she said, as she felt Elend's stomach.

'Who told you?'

'Many people tell me many things. Am I right?'

'One day, perhaps.'

'Don't go yet,' Dr Schreiber said. 'Wait another month or two. The weather in the mountains will be bad.' She nodded at Elend. 'He is strong. You have done well.' Then she dropped her voice, spoke almost in a whisper. 'Be careful. Don't trust the agents. If you plan to leave, arrange it yourself.'

Back in her tent, Zarrin stood feeling uneasy, suspicious. Something in the exchange with Dr Schreiber felt false. She tried to dismiss the thought, but it dogged her, making her restless. She thought of checking her money, hidden in a small hole she'd made beneath the bed, safe, she hoped, until she needed it. But she knew that each time she looked, each time she lifted the soil, it added to the chances of it being found. Someone would see her; the disturbed soil would give her away.

The next day, the message from the agent came. 'I have news for you,' it said. 'Meet me by the eastern gate at noon. If I'm not there, wait.'

She went, taking Eland with her, waited as instructed. She stayed there for two hours, talking to Elend as she held him, one hand protecting him from the sun; telling him about the journey they would make, and the life that lay there at journey's end. A life like her own childhood, perhaps, though transplanted to England.

But the agent never came. And when she returned to her tent it was to find it ransacked. Her clothes and other possessions were scattered across the floor. Her bed had been stripped, the mattress torn open, Elend's cot the same. The place where she had hidden the money, beneath the bed-leg, just inside the wall, had been dug open. The hole was empty, the tin, the money, gone.

Zarrin pushed the meagre stuffing back into Elend's cot, laid him down. His legs kicked, his lips moved as he watched her, anticipating his next feed. She clucked at him, soothing him, as she tidied up. She picked up her cloak, the one she'd been wearing when she arrived. The seams had been ripped apart, as if the thief had expected the money to be hidden there. She smoothed out her bed, turning the thin mattress over to cover the tear, replaced the bed. Her mind felt dead. Without money, she had no hope. Elend's future, too, had gone. She'd heard enough stories from the older refugees, the ones who'd been here from the start. They were trapped, had no means of escape, hoping against all their expectations for Turkish policy to change, for Europe to step in, for the Americans to save the day.

Who had done it, she wondered: the agent? Someone else who knew of their arrangement and had used a false message to lure her away? Dr Schreiber? She remembered the invitations: leave your money with me. The advice: don't go yet. The interest in her affairs. Was it her? She tried not to believe it, yet couldn't shake the notion away. It seemed right, now, to think the worst.

She fed Elend. As it always did, the action soothed her and put order into the world. What else was life for, other than for him? For the child, for the next generation. For those who would surely make the world a better place.

Eventually she slept, with Elend in her arms.

In the morning, she was woken by a call from the doorway of the tent. It was Dr Schreiber.

'I've brought you this,' she said. She held out the tin in which Zarrin had stored her money. 'It's all there.'

Zarrin rubbed at her eyes.

'I don't understand.'

'You must forgive me,' Dr Schreiber said. 'I removed it. Or rather, I had it removed. As I told you, people tell me things. I heard what would happen. I know how these things work.'

For an instant anger flared. 'Why didn't you tell me?' Zarrin demanded. 'And save me all this.'

The doctor smiled, shook her head. 'Would you have listened? You didn't when I first warned you. But I'm sorry. I'll do what I can to get your things repaired. Though you understand, it's not easy.'

Zarrin's anger melted. 'I know. It doesn't matter. I should be thanking you instead.'

'There is no need for thanks. But please, take one piece of advice. If you really mean to leave, talk to Umal Amir. He drives one of the waste trucks. He will help. And until then, the money would be safer with me.'

*

She took Dr Schreiber's advice, waited a month, then sought out Umal. He was easy to find. He had a personality that announced him from two hundred metres away, even without the aid of his booming voice. He seemed to be filled with good humour and confidence, and had ample room for both, for he was tall, heavy-chested, large-bellied. He wore a bushy moustache, greying at the edges, smoked without stop. 'That's what you pay me with,' he said. 'Cigarettes. Cigars better.'

He asked her what she wanted.

'I can get you out of the camp,' he told her. 'That's all. After that, you are on your own.'

She nodded. 'When?'

'Two, three days.'

She was lucky. Umal had organised things well. Most people went in with the food waste and slurry, he told her, but for her it was *de luxe* class – a half-empty truck laden with piles of old bedding. 'Just you and the fleas,' he said, with a laugh.

She crouched in a small space he'd made for her in the centre of the load, Elend clutched against her, smothering any risk of sound. At the gate, they stopped. The driver and guard talked for a moment; she heard someone clamber onto the tailboard, saw the pile of bedding beside her move as it was prodded. 'OK,' a voice said. The gears crunched and the truck jerked forward.

They drove for almost an hour, bumping along a rough and pitted road. When at last they halted, Umal called to her to get down. She clambered out, blinking in the sunshine as she looked around. They were parked at a junction, where the dirt road they'd been travelling on crossed a larger highway. It stretched away in either direction, hazy in the heat, deserted.

'Istanbul that way,' Umal said, pointing. Then he nodded back down the road. 'Other way just border. Old life.'

He seemed to see her doubts.

'Don't worry. I find you first lift.'

As she waited beside him, she took out fifty dollars from the deep pocket she'd sewn in her cloak, handed it to him. He waved the note away. 'For your cigarettes,' she said.

'Too much,' he said. 'And anyway, cigarettes no good. Make me cough. Helping better. Get me place in heaven maybe, or better seat in other place.'

After about fifteen minutes, a truck appeared, grinding along the highway. Umal flagged it down and spoke to the driver in a local dialect that Zarrin couldn't understand.

Negotiations seemed to be difficult, and several times the driver shook his head, spat. But then Umal called to her.

'Fifty dollars,' he said. 'No more. He take you to Istanbul. He treat you good.' She handed over the money. Umal helped her into the cab. For a moment he stood, regarding them, then reached up and chucked Elend's cheek with a finger. 'Look after baby now. He nice baby. Grow up big man, like me.'

She looked in the mirror as they pulled away. Umal stood on the roadside, watching. Then he turned, went back to his own truck.

They drove on in silence. The driver sat, hunched forward, arms crossed over the steering wheel, chewing on something, *khat* perhaps. His eyes were narrow, almost closed, and Zarrin kept glancing at him to make sure that he was awake. The cab was hot; the engine cowling beside her legs burned if she touched it. Diesel fumes permeated the air, seemed to form a film on her lips, so that when she licked at them, trying to moisten them in the stifling heat, she could taste the sourness. Elend soon became restless. She hugged him to her, trying to pacify him, afraid that if he cried the man would take offence, perhaps order them out. The baby's hand went to her breast, pummelling it in the search for comfort. Surreptitiously, she opened her cloak, moved him inside, allowed him to suckle. The driver glanced at her, seemed to ponder, then looked away.

The day wore on.

Zarrin wondered where they were, how far they had to go. Once, she ventured the question. The driver shrugged, said something she couldn't understand.

Later, he got out, peed into the dust, then drove on.

The road was straight and featureless. Ahead of them were mountains, yet they never seemed to get nearer, nor to grow in height. Zarrin tried to look at the speedometer to work out how far they might have travelled. It was broken. The needle swung from zero to a hundred or more and back.

She dozed.

She was woken by a change in the sway and vibration of the vehicle. She looked out, half-expecting to see houses, streets. Istanbul? Instead, the land was bare. They were driving on a dirt road. Thorn-scrub, sand, shadowed rocks stretched to the horizon.

The sound of the engine changed; the truck slowed. They bumped to a halt. The driver sat for a moment, staring ahead. He turned, looked at her. His lips were parted, and there was a dark smudge of whatever he'd been chewing at the corner of his mouth. 'Down,' he said.

'Why?'

'Down now,' he repeated.

'No. We're going to Istanbul. You have to take me the whole way.'

He reached past her, clicked open the door. 'You go. No more sit there.'

'No. We have a deal.'

For a moment he stayed there, his face close to hers, his arm stretched across her breast. She could smell his breath, musty, stale. She cringed back, fearing his assault.

Then in one swift movement, he snatched Elend from her lap.

Zarrin screamed, tried to grab him back. Elend cried. The driver turned, held him out of the window. 'Baby fall,' he said.

'Alright. I'm going.'

She clambered down, ran around the cab, held up her hands, beseeching. He thrust the child into them.

'My bag,' she said.

The engine clattered as he forced it into gear. He threw the bag out.

'I need water.'

He spat.

She stood, clutching Elend to her as the truck pulled away. She watched it trundle along the road, trailing a plume of dust and smoke. She picked up her bag, plodded in its wake.

Ahead of her, the dust settled. The air became clear. They were alone on the flat, dry plain.

3

Istanbul

For an hour Zarrin walked, following the way the truck had gone. When it had left her, she had assumed that she'd been dropped on one of the cut-off corners from the old road, and that, if she followed it, she would soon rejoin the main highway. But, an hour later, the road continued, straight and relentless. The land on either side seemed barren, no sign of livestock or crops or tillage. No buildings in sight. When she'd set out, the sun had beat down upon her, relentless. But as she walked it lowered, painting the sky with gold and offering relief at last from the heat. Then a breeze stirred, making devils of the dust, and she felt the chill of the evening to come. She tucked Elend more deeply into the sling that she had fashioned from her shawl, pulled him closer.

More than once, doubt assailed her and she stopped, looked back, wondering whether she was being led ever further from civilisation, out into the wilderness; whether the road might even trick her, and lure her southwards, across the border, into Syria again. Yet, each time she stopped, the thought of that long and purposeless trek back to where she'd started, perhaps for another hour or more beyond that, was too much to face. She turned again, walked on.

Elend whimpered. He was hungry, she knew. She wanted to feed him but dared not pause. There was no sign of habitation, no shelter; if she were benighted out here, where would they sleep?

To calm him, she began to sing. 'Nami, nami', a lullaby that her mother had taught her, and must have sung to her when she was too young to remember:

Sleep, sleep, my baby,
lie down on the rug,
sleep in the dark until it is gone
and the sun returns
to brighten the world around you.

Her voice, she knew, was cracked and rough, and wavered from the tune. But, as always when she sang, it seemed to soothe Elend and weave a magic over him. He quietened, stilled, and she felt the same stillness settle in herself.

She sought in her mind for other songs, found tunes with words she couldn't remember and improvised with words of her own; when those failed, the all-purpose sounds of lullabies – 'hulum, hulum'.

Engrossed in her singing, in Elend's brown eyes gazing back at her, his eyelids closing, she didn't hear the cart coming. It was the snort of the donkey that alerted her and made her look around. Even then, the man on the cart showed no sign of slowing, nor offered a greeting of any kind. He simply drew alongside her, the wheels of the cart grating on the ground, chassis creaking, the steady clop-clop of hooves counting the distance gone. She stopped, watched as it moved past her. The cart was empty save for a small pile of sacks, yet the thought grew sluggishly in her mind: why does he not offer me a lift? But then, as if of its own accord, the donkey halted. The man remained hunched on the bench seat, didn't turn. She walked after him, stood looking up.

'Please. Will you take me?'

He gave a small flick of his head. Get in, it seemed to say. She did so. Without any word from the man, the donkey plodded on.

After twenty minutes or so, they turned onto a small side-track, little more than a worn scar in the land. Ten minutes later and the ground dipped into a shallow wadi. Compared to the land she'd been travelling through, it seemed verdant and homely. Nestled on the far side was a scattering of barns and a small cottage, within which a lamp burned. The cart drew up outside, and the man got down, signalling to Zarrin to wait. He entered the cottage. A few minutes later his wife came out, beckoned her. She followed the woman indoors. There, through a mixture of odd words and sign language, she was told to wash, then given a cup of warm milk, which she drank at the table in the kitchen while the woman prepared a meal.

Watching her, Zarrin asked if she could feed Elend, made a gesture of lifting him towards her breast to indicate what she meant. The woman smiled, spoke to her husband, who nodded and dutifully lowered his eyes. Zarrin opened her cloak, slipped Elend beneath it, felt the child twist, reach, suckle. The woman said something that she couldn't understand, but the expression on her face, smiling, nostalgic, was warm and empathetic. Zarrin smiled in return, love for her child, gratitude to these people, bringing tears to her eyes. And later, as they ate together – thick stew, hot, sweet coffee – the baby became a sort of language between them, reaching past the barriers of the words they spoke, drawing out laughter and sighs of contentment.

After a while, the woman fetched pictures of her own children and showed them to Zarrin, passing them back to her husband afterwards so that he could see and give a brief nod of remembrance. There were three of them, two boys, one girl. From what Zarrin gathered, they didn't work on the farm, but lived far away in the city. And perhaps they never came back now, for later, when she was shown to the only spare room in the house to sleep in, Zarrin saw that apart from the single bed and a small table it was bare: no sign that anyone ever used it any more.

The next day the man drove her in his cart further along the sandy track, down the wadi until they reached the tarmac road. There, he handed down a bag containing bread, apples, a plastic bottle full of water from his well. She tried to thank him, but he brushed her tributes aside. Instead, he reached beneath his jacket and lifted a string over his head, dangled it in front of her. Hanging from it was a wooden bead, painted with two concentric dots, in white and blue. An eye-bead, she knew – *nazar* – worn here, as they were at home in Syria, to protect against evil and to bring good luck. She regarded it, uncertain what she was expected to do, and he signalled her to hold out a hand. She did so, and he laid the pendant in her palm, gently closed her fingers around it. Then with no other words, he clicked the reins of his cart and drove away. She stood, holding the pendant, watching him, but he did not look back.

*

She reached Istanbul after five days. During those days, every step of the way seemed like a saga, and might have merited its own book. Later, though, they merged into each other, became inseparable and lost their drudgery and sting. For one day she hardly travelled at all, sheltering from the scorching sun, the blistering wind, in the ruin of an old farmstead. The air tasted of dust and salt, and the wind sang a mournful song of the distance it had travelled, the sorrows it had seen; death and despair. At some point a van stopped and she was invited to get in. The driver was middle-aged, ugly. He babbled at her in Turkish as he drove, took her as far as Kayseri, where he held open the door for her, helped her down, as if she were royalty. In Ankara she was ordered off a bus, though she'd bought the ticket: not valid, she was told, meaning 'we don't like refugees' – or Kurds perhaps, or just 'women like you'. At other times, she stood for long hours beside the road, or simply walked, singing to Elend in her low, crooning voice, more remembered songs from her childhood that her mother once sang to her, a thin thread of connection across the generations.

Istanbul shocked her and assailed her with its fumes and noise. Since her marriage, she'd lived in a city, albeit in the plusher and more spacious parts, and had visited both Damascus and Aleppo often with Mahmet. She knew that, until you understood them, cities could seem chaotic and unsettling places. But this was urban drama on another scale.

'Fourteen million people,' the truck-driver who brought her there had told her, as she marvelled at its size. 'That's what people say. And growing every day.' He gave her a glance, making it clear what he meant. Then he spat out of the window. 'Three million of them Kurds.'

That first night, she found a room in a small hotel, not far from the highway where the driver had dropped her. She did so reluctantly. Her small supply of money was already dwindling, and every dollar she spent hurt. But Elend was tetchy from the journeying, and she was tired, and she knew that her milk would be slow.

The next day, she made her way to Sultangazi. It was the Kurdish quarter. She'd been told about it by Kurds in the camp, who regarded it as a place to aim for, a destination where you could be amongst people of your own sort. She'd learned about it, too, at school, heard it discussed by the men in her family – uncles and grandfather – in bitter tones. A place of both haven and exile for those driven out of their homelands by persecution and war. In the 1950s, from rural Kurdistan, by the atrocities of government troops; in the 1980s, when the revolution occurred, and in the guerrilla war that followed. In the years since, as revolt and suppression and economic decline laid waste to their lands. In the early years, the place had been settled informally, as a *gecekondu bölgesi* – a shanty town, thrown up overnight. But over the years since then, as if in acknowledgement that life there wasn't temporary any more, the buildings had been converted into more solid homes and the whole area acknowledged with a name.

Getting there took most of that day. It was on the other side of the city, in the northern fringes, and no one of importance needed to go there; even roads seemed to shy from it whenever they could. She dragged herself through the hot and dusty town, fighting against a continuous tide of traffic, which clogged the roadways, piled up at the intersections, spilled onto the sidewalks and areas of wasteland, filled the whole place with its fumes and clamour – its roars and growls and burps and farts and perpetual tooting of horns. When she tried to escape from the busier thoroughfares, she lost herself in the maze of tiny streets, had to ask for directions, was directed or misdirected, got lost again, but arrived at last in the early evening. Her feet were sore from the unyielding concrete and cobbles, her clothes clung to her body, her mouth was sour from smoke and sweat; Elend was fretful in her arms.

Their arrival brought disappointment. She had expected the place to announce itself with a flourish of Arabic script on the street signs and shops, the sounds of her Kurdish language spilling from the houses. But it seemed no different from the other suburbs she'd plodded through. Poorer perhaps, the roads more pitted and potholed, the houses more neglected, paint flaking, more chaotic, so that they leaned towards each other across the narrow streets as if in some secret conclave. The only Arabic she saw was on an old drinking well, and that long since abandoned, the stonework cracking and claimed by weeds. There, and on the graffiti and posters that plastered the walls – and most of those had been defaced.

She scrounged some food from a kiosk – stale bread, a few ends of meat – stealing dinner, she guessed, from the countless dogs that roamed the area. A small group of them gathered opposite her and watched, sullen, silent, muzzles flecked with sputum, as she ate. Then she found a place to sleep for the night: a scratched-out depression in the soil beneath an overhanging plinth that once, perhaps, had carried a statue or memorial of some sort. She fed Elend, curled in her small space with him held against her breast. Her sleep was fitful. Through the night, into the dawn, the cats screamed from the darkness, and the police sirens wailed from the city beyond, and her own thoughts crowded around her, as she imagined the dogs were doing, waiting for their chance to pounce.

In the days that followed, she explored the area, trying to find a niche within it where she could survive, where she and Elend might be accepted. It was not easy. The place was too poor for refugees. It had no surplus in it, no scraps or crumbs that the dogs and cats did not eat. And the people could tell that she did not fit. It was not just because she was an outsider, a new arrival with the dust of the road on her clothes, and the creases of travel and trouble on her face. It was because of what she was within, her own brief history. Her education, the wealth she had known. The way she spoke, the confidence she bore. She betrayed it with her eyes.

Yet the place teased her, for below the hard patina of imposed Turkishness she caught glimpses of the culture that she had once known, and yearned to grasp it. She heard it in the voice of the *muezzin*, calling from the mosque, and of the man – a tray of the traditional round buns balanced on his head – walking down the street, shouting out his wares: '*Simitçi, simiitçi, simiiiiitçi...*' In the sound of a *saz* being played from an upstairs room, its music rippling out into the street like cool fresh water, like the fluttering wing-beat of doves, like the twist and turn of children dancing. More than anything, that was what reminded her of home. Of her old home, before she fled, before she was married, before she grew up, became betrothed to Mahmet, found what she thought was love. Before her family disavowed her. The innocent home of her childhood.

But as she got to know the place she discovered, too, some of its complexities and dangers. As in the camp, there were layers and factions, customs and rules, allegiances and enmities that she did not understand, yet which she sensed ran deep. There was power, too. Imams and *ulama*, whose words were treated as law. Men with new-made wealth, and the influence that money could bring. Silent armies that served them; people who watched. Messengers who carried information where it needed to go. Hirelings, freebooters, who did whatever else was necessary.

Perhaps it was inevitable, she thought, all this hierarchy and fissility and graft; just part of being Kurdish. Perhaps it was everywhere, but until now she'd simply been too privileged to see it. Or perhaps it was just the natural consequence of people being forced together in this way, into *varoş*, ghettoes. Especially displaced people such as these, with all their seething fears and resentments, their jealousies and ambitions, their suspicions of the world around.

And amongst them, of course, might be the people she feared. Agents of the Sinjari family. Mahmet's men or Rohat's. People who were paid to keep them informed on matters of possible interest to a rich yet precariously balanced family in Syria: the state of the PKK, the emerging leaders and activists, the politicians who might be blackmailed or bought, the price of guns and drugs. The whereabouts of a missing wife and sister-in-law, soiled by shame.

It seemed too plausible; it felt so inevitable. For all her fleeing, she was just one border away, five hundred kilometres at most. Of course they'd be looking. Of course they'd be searching. How could they not?

The notion troubled her, haunted her at night, made her try to shrink into the shadows during the day, seek anonymity. Yet the only place for that was amidst the prowling dogs and cats, and she did not fit there, either. And gradually she came to realise the paradox of her situation. For safety she needed to be hidden from those who might be seeking her. To survive – to win pity and the occasional gift of alms – she needed to attract attention to herself. Here, though, everything was in reverse. She was too obvious to any of Rohat's men, yet invisible to everyone else – just another poor Kurd in streets full of people the same. After two weeks, she knew that she had to move on. She left Sultangazi and made her way back down the hill into the Turkish areas, and sought there places that better suited a refugee and beggar like her. Areas which were fluid, and where people came and went. Small shopping malls, suburban parks, outside tram and railway stations away from the centre of town. Places through which people with money – shoppers, commuters – strode with urgent intent; but within which others, like herself, could float unnoticed, until, with a smile, a touch, a beseeching gaze, they jabbed against a ready sympathy.

When it could be done without obvious risk, that was what she did – beg. Clutching Elend against her, arm extended, she sat on the pavement, stood outside shops, moved from car to car at road intersections, eyes always alert for the police, ready to slip away. It worked. Between the insults, the spittle that was aimed at her feet, sometimes her face, the subtle kicks at her ankles, people were kind. It surprised her how many. Not one in ten, nor even one in a hundred, but, in a city of millions, enough to allow her to survive. Most offerings were small: five liras, ten, occasionally a small handful of loose change. But once, a man – a businessman from the way he was dressed – beckoned her to follow, and took her into a shop; made her choose the food she wanted – a tin of sardines, sausage, dried fruit, bread, milk – and filled up a bag for her, and paid for it. When there was nothing else, she rummaged in waste bins, found what she could.

Occasionally she stole. Bread from a market stall. An apple from a display outside a shop. A carton of milk. Each time she muttered a prayer: *forgive me for what I do*. She tried to absolve herself with the knowledge – *it's not for me, but Elend* – then pushed the thought away. How could she load the blame on him?

At night, she slept where she could. In a park, by the river beneath a bridge, with a group of others in a safety cave in a road tunnel, ignoring the acrid air that burned her throat and the angry roar of the trucks. For three nights, until a group of youths returned and claimed it for the use it had always had, she made a nest in a hollowed space beneath a dense cluster of Judas trees, lulled by their scent.

Always, she held Elend close. Not just a son but a talisman too. More than that, a purpose. When he needed feeding, she would find somewhere hidden, enclosed, and loosen her cloak, nestle him to her. Then she would feel him fill her again with that sense of wellbeing and trust. It made the hardship that pervaded the rest of her days seem bearable.

In those minutes when they were conjoined like that, mother and child, he feeding from her, their pulses and breathing in instant synchrony, she tried to observe him as if from afar, and fit him into her life. Who was he? The half that wasn't her – what was that? Who would he become – the mother or the father, or some jumbled combination of the two? And if either of those, father, or half-father, then what sort of boy would he be, what sort of man?

Would the part of him that was not her, and which she didn't know, break out one day, wilful or malicious and wild?

That thought disturbed her, and if it ever happened she knew she'd have to do whatever was needed to excise it, for she wanted him to be kind and gentle and good. There was only her, she told herself. That was all he had to protect him against the world, and against himself, and whatever legacy his making had left. It was she alone who could shape him and give him life.

And as the weeks turned to months, it seemed that maybe she was making progress in that endeavour, for despite the

41

deprivations he stayed well, began to put on a little weight, grew stronger again. Once, an elderly woman paused as she was passing, and looked down at him in Zarrin's arms and said, 'What a lovely child. You've done so well.' And she bent forward, and kissed the top of Elend's head.

As their lives settled into a routine, she used the time to wean Elend, though fighting her emotions as she did so. She knew that she would miss those moments with him, the special bond they implied. It felt like a link between them broken. Children grow and leave you from the moment they are born, she thought, as she fed him for the last time; each step another unit of separation. But when, at nine months old, Elend said his first word, she felt a flare of success. Not 'mama', for to him there was only her, so why should she need a name? But 'cuddle', or a sound that she could interpret as such – the prize she was always promising him for his patience, his strength, his goodness; for her own comfort, too.

With Elend weaned, growing, she started to look for more reliable ways to make a living for them both. She looked for jobs, but quickly found herself thwarted. No work was available, not for someone like her, without valid papers, with a child that she could not leave. But, roaming the streets, she realised how untidy the public areas were, and an idea germinated in her mind. She used some of the money she had gained by begging to buy a brush, and adopted a square in the tourist quarter of Sultanahmet, and swept it clean, and made a small sign that she leaned against the wall where she sat: *The cleanest square in Istanbul – Elend and I made it for you*. People smiled as they passed. Some dropped money onto her mat. Others gave her their litter – drinks cans, sweet wrappers, unwanted leaflets that had been thrust into their hands. She bought a plastic waste bin, and set it beside her, and when she accepted contributions asked for five liras as a disposal charge. Most obliged, and thanked her for the service she was providing. Her takings increased.

From her vantage point, she observed life in the square. It wasn't large, perhaps fifty metres across, but on the opposite side was a café where people would sit outside, drinking coffee or beer, smoking. In the evening, there was sometimes music, and she could smell the sweet, bready smoke from the pizza oven, the tang of grilling meat. Sometimes, in the late evening, the café owner would bring her food.

In the centre of the square was a plane tree, and around its trunk a circle of bench seats. People rested there from the sun and read their newspapers. Mothers rocked their infants, in buggies and prams. Children clambered onto the seats, jumped off, laughing. Lovers met. Deals were sometimes done. When she swept the area in the evenings, after the last users had gone, Zarrin seemed to feel the warmth of the place, as though, as well as their sweet-wrappers, their cigarette butts, their tag-ends of betting slips and receipts, an occasional coin, people had left some remnants of themselves. A memory, a smile, an unused kiss.

One evening, something glistening in the dust beneath the benches caught her eye. She picked it up. It was an earring. A single drop-pearl, set on a silver chain, the hook ornamented with fine filigree. She wondered who had lost it, tried to remember the women she had seen during the day, sitting in that spot.

The next morning, she noticed a woman searching by the seat. As she turned, looked around, Zarrin beckoned her across.

'Are you looking for an earring?' she asked.

'Yes. Have you found one?'

Zarrin reached into her pocket and took it out. 'I found this, last night when I tidied up.'

The woman laughed, showed her its twin, thanked her effusively. 'You're wonderful,' she said. 'They were my mother's. I couldn't bear to lose them. Here. Let me thank you properly.' She handed over a fifty-lira note.

As the woman left, her earrings gleaming in the sun, Zarrin mused on the strange value of things. It's not for themselves that they're special, she thought, but for their relationship to people's lives.

Soon, she had a small parallel industry established. She separated out the cans and bottles that she collected, and once or twice a week, when she had enough, took them to a recycling plant a kilometre or so away and sold them for a few liras. Now and then, she found or was given more substantial things that retained some life in them: a book, a shawl that was too hot to wear, a child's toy, an umbrella, a buggy, even a bicycle. She kept the buggy for Elend, but the other items she cleaned up, and set them out along the wall behind her, with a discreet notice saying: *For Sale*. Eventually everything sold. For everything has value to someone.

She had positioned herself, without any intent, in the corner of the square, beside a small and rather plain Catholic church. It had been the most obvious place to sit. She was out of the way, for there were no shops or steps or seats there that anyone else would need, and the door to the church was around the corner, in the adjacent wall. But it had other advantages. It gave shelter on hot days, protection from the wind. People entering or leaving the square couldn't help but see her. And a small proportion – those going to or coming from the church – found themselves confronted with one of the parables they knew so well, and felt obliged to act accordingly.

The location had another benefit, too, for when services were held there they could hear the sound of the organ and singing from inside. Elend would gurgle and wave and kick when he heard it, and Zarrin, too, felt strangely soothed, even though it wasn't the music of her religion. What her religion was, she was no longer sure, for she seemed to have left her God in some other life, or He had left her. That frightened her at times, that sense of abandonment. It made her feel further away from her family and her past, even more lost and alone in the world. Yet she was not alone any more, she thought, for she had Elend.

There was nowhere to sleep in the square. It was too open and the benches beneath the plane tree didn't feel like hers to claim. At night, therefore, she took her belongings around the corner, and slept beneath a flight of steps that ran down to the basement of a shop.

As Christmas approached, the music from the church changed, and a decorated tree appeared beside the door. The people who came to sing and worship there changed, also. It was a time of giving. The tin tray that she used to collect the money people offered jangled with the sound of coins, glistened in the light from the tree.

But she knew enough of Christianity to realise the irony of the situation she was in. Trading beneath the church walls. Would Jesus turn up one day and overturn her stall, condemn her?

In its way, that happened. Though the Son of God, in this case, worked for the council. He came in the week before Christmas, in a neat suit, brown leather shoes. He stood in front of her. What she was doing was illegal, he said. She had to stop at once. He waited while she packed up her belongings in her blanket, loaded them onto Elend's buggy and left. She returned, but a few days later it happened again. Once more she returned, and this time the man did not reappear. The square, it seemed, was hers. Or Elend's perhaps, for people would stop and take photos of him as he lay on the mat, or crawled and played with the toys she'd salvaged from the materials that she'd collected. The star attraction.

After a while, though, she learned that other desperate people had taken up her idea, and other squares elsewhere were being cleaned and maintained in the same way. Soon after that, she was approached by a man who told her that he was co-ordinating the scheme – which was now called *Şehir Temiz*, Tidy City – and she would have to pay a fee to continue as a member. She refused, and two days later, when she returned to her place, she found that the square had been despoiled with bags of rubbish, newspapers, garden waste, ordure. She spent the day tidying it up, but that evening watched as a group of youths dumped new offerings, and scrawled a message on the wall where she usually sat: *Shit Square*.

The next day, she changed most of the modest stock of money she had made during her time in Istanbul into euros, and left.

4

Journey North

Once, long ago, before Elend was born, or Zarrin, before even her mother and grandmother, there was a young man. Where he came from, or who his parents were, he didn't know. So he roamed the world, seeking the place where he belonged. For years he travelled like that, across dusty deserts and flat and endless plains where the wind could fell a horse and blow a man away; through high mountains where the thunder crashed like falling rocks, and rocks rumbled like thunder, and the lightning was like the flashing eyes of angry gods; over wild seas with waves as tall as the tallest mosque and where, if a man drowned, his body would sink for a thousand years before it settled, lifeless, on the ocean's lightless floor. And in all those years, he never found anywhere that felt like home, and where he believed he might stay.

Sometimes people would ask him, 'Why do you travel so far? What is it that you seek?' And he would explain – that he was searching for his homeland, and the place where he belonged. Now and then, someone a little wiser would ask, 'What kind of place is that?' and he would reply that he did not know, for he had never been there, and did not have any family so there was no one who could tell him from what sort of place he came. And once or twice, someone even wiser asked, 'How will you know when you find it?' and, after a little thought, he would shrug and say, 'I will know because the place will know me.' Then he would walk on.

One day, he stopped to talk to an old woman who stood leaning over a gate beside the road. 'Where are you going?' she asked, and he told her: to find the place he belonged.

'Where is that?' she asked, and he answered,

'I do not know.'

'How will you know when you find it?' the old woman asked him, and the man replied,

'I just will, because it will know me.'

At which point, the old woman laughed, showing gapped yellow teeth.

'Why do you laugh?' he asked.

'Because that is what everyone says – all the wanderers and searchers who pass this way. For a hundred years, I have stood here and I have given them all the same advice, and they have all ignored me. Sooner or later, each one of them has come back, still searching.'

'What advice is that?' the man asked.

The woman laughed again and said, 'Do you really want to know?'

'I do,' the man replied.

'And if I tell you,' the woman asked, 'will you heed my advice.'

The man nodded. 'I will.'

The woman regarded him with piercing eyes, testing the truth of what he said. Then she beckoned him to her, and kept beckoning until he was so close that he could smell the sourness of her breath.

'You are looking for the wrong thing,' she said quietly.

'What should I be searching for?' the man asked, 'if not the place that I belong.'

She beckoned him to come even closer, until his ear was against her mouth. He could hear the rattle of her old dry throat, and feel the brush of her breath against his skin. Then quietly, so quietly that he could hardly hear it, she whispered one word. 'Love.'

The man thanked her for her advice, and walked on, and the woman stood for a long time watching as he faded into the distant haze. And she has watched out for him ever since, but he has never returned. And she is content. For he, at least, must have taken her advice and found what he sought. Not a place to live, but love to claim him – for, with that, he could live anywhere.

This is the story that Zarrin tells Elend, and which she tells herself as she makes her way westwards, out of Istanbul, towards Greece and the huge and unknowable continent that lies ahead. She tells it as they wait and as they walk, and when she lulls him to sleep at night. Whether Elend understands the words, she doubts, but he seems to recognise the meaning in her voice, and is soothed by it, just as the story soothes her. For it is a story she has been told by her grandmother, and she by her mother before, and back before that for generations. It is probably no longer the same story; it must have changed in the years of retelling, for Zarrin knows that sometimes she changes it herself. But, in every telling, it seems to connect her not to any place but to all the people who have been before and heard and told the story. And it gives her the same message that it must have given them. Hope.

*

But there is another story.

On the banks of what in ancient times was known as the Evros River, a group of travellers wait. The have come from many different places, by different ways, but now they are one. They have been brought here by people-smugglers, bundled across Turkey in two windowless white vans. Europe lies ahead. Only the river separates them from their goal. It is dark and shapeless in the night. A Stygian tide that seems to lure them and repel them in equal measure, so that each of them, as they wait there, feels trapped.

Minutes stretch out into hours and nothing happens. They talk in low whispers. Children whimper, and are hushed to silence. Sometimes a small light briefly flares – a mobile phone or a longed-for cigarette. The river's voice never changes, the same slurring song, like an old woman crooning, keening.

Then, at last, a new shape forms in the darkness. It is a man, heavily built, clothed in black. He approaches the group and announces himself as their guide. Instructions are given, in Greek, passed on to those who do not understand and clutch at the neighbours, muttering, in Arabic and English. As the people realise what is meant to happen, there are gasps or muted cries of alarm. Someone starts to weep. But reluctantly the people pick up their belongings, form into a ragged line. They follow the man along the bank, between the trees, stumbling on the rough ground, tripping against roots. An old woman slips, has to be helped to her feet. Within a few minutes they reach a small, sandy bay cut into the river bank, and draw to a halt.

As they stand there, two boats emerge, rubber dinghies, low in the water. In each one is a crouched figure, paddling. Expertly, the paddlers draw the dinghies into the shallows, and step out, holding the boats against the hungry current.

At the whispered command of the guide, the people move towards the boats. The water is cold, strangely fibrous in its feel, like gossamer. It seethes at their legs. The sand turns to silt, then mud, and sucks at their toes. The old woman refuses to move and is picked up by a man, carried out.

As they pass him, the guide divides the group between the two dinghies, one to the left, one to the right. The boats rock as the people climb on board, provoking more consternation. Then a moment of confusion, rising almost to panic, when a young woman tries to change boats to be with her children. She is shoved back. The boats fill. The last passengers are squeezed into place.

Two men are selected in each dinghy, and given paddles. There are more instructions. 'That way. Paddle quickly. Don't stop.'

The first craft is pushed into the water. The current catches it and with a swift swirl it drifts downstream. 'Paddle,' the guide calls.

Then the second is pushed out, the people it holds clinging to each other as the water grips and the boat gives a lurch. Behind them, the guide and his two companions turn and scramble back to the bay, where they congratulate each other for their success and with a brief shake of the hand dissolve into the trees.

Out on the river, the first dinghy has disappeared – whether to the sea or across to safety on the far bank, who knows? On the second, the two men who were given paddles dig them into the water with all their might. The flow drags at the boat, threatening to overturn it, or snatch it and whisk it away to the sea. But somehow the men find new strength, and, as one shore slips behind them, another slowly looms. Then, somewhere in mid-stream, a log bangs against them. The boat bucks; the rubber tears. As the water seeps in, the dinghy grows heavier. The men's efforts cease to have any effect; the boat drifts and spins until, with a careless toss, the river flips it upside down. People spill out. Few of them can swim, and in the strong current their frantic struggling is in vain. Some manage to save themselves by clinging to an overhanging tree; others drag themselves onto the small islands that line the shore. But, when it is over, only seven of the twelve people on the dinghy have survived.

In the darkness, they wait, hoping that others will appear. None does. As the sky lightens, they turn inland and start to walk. They walk for an hour, through dense woodland, untidy asparagus fields, and in the early dawn arrive in a small village, with a single rutted street, lined with rough wooden houses. There, they rest for a while, hoping for help when the village awakes – perhaps news of the other refugees. Instead, two vehicles suddenly roar down the road in a cloud of dust and grit. Men leap out, wearing blue uniforms, guns at the ready. The refugees are herded together, pushed into the vans. Then they are driven away.

This is the story that Ahmed told Zarrin. She had met him and his small band of followers when she was four days out from Istanbul, still heading for the border. They were coming the other way.

'Where are you going?' the man leading the group had called from the opposite side of the road.

'To Greece,' she shouted. 'To Europe.'

'Don't bother,' he told her. 'Go back. The Greeks don't want us.'

Then, he beckoned her across, and sitting beside her in the scant shade of an olive tree, while the others rested, he introduced himself and told his story.

'What happened then?' Zarrin asked. 'After you were arrested.'

'We were taken back to the river,' Ahmed said. 'There was already a huge crowd of other people there, a hundred, perhaps two. Syrians mainly, but Afghans and Iraqis as well. They were shouting, arguing. I watched as the police picked out the leaders – the ones causing the most trouble – and beat them. Then they rounded us up and forced us into small plastic boats. They threw in the men they had beaten; they picked up women and children, and threw them in too. Then they towed us out across the river, and dumped us on the other side.'

Zarrin was silent. 'I thought they would welcome us,' she said at last. 'I thought they'd understand.'

'No one wants us,' Ahmed retorted. 'No one understands.'

*

That evening, Ahmed had invited her to stay with his group and travel with them. She had been tempted, for she liked Ahmed and knew that there was a resilience in him which she could trust. But she knew, also, that travelling in a larger group would restrict her freedom and slow her down, and she was impatient to move on. Instead, she wished him good luck, bade him goodbye.

Whether that was a good choice, she couldn't at first tell. Travelling, now, seemed difficult, progress haphazard and slow. It was as though the whole world had turned against her and Elend, and no one wanted them – not Greek, nor Turk, nor any of the drivers that thundered past them on the highway, showering them with grit and dust. Then it started to rain, and the world became a churning mist. She sought shelter in a small hut, long-ago abandoned, its roof leaking, its window broken, one wall entirely gone. She was cold and wet, and yearned for the comfort of a fire or a bed, or just a dry corner where she could lie down and sleep. Elend felt cold, too, and she feared for his health.

But the next morning dawned with silken skies of grey and gold and pink, and slowly, in small staccato movements, she edged north. At first, she pushed Elend in the old buggy, but then, one evening, as she crossed an area of wasteland looking for somewhere to sleep, one of the wheels fell off. After that, she won lifts with truck-drivers, gradually learning the art of making them stop. Where best to stand, in what sort of stance, how to make eye contact.

She crossed the border into Bulgaria in the back of a truck, hidden amidst a load of hides. In the darkness, she listened to the litany of noises that was involved. Cab doors banging, the growl of a forklift truck. Voices. Dogs barking. The tarpaulin being pulled back. Feet clumping in the trailer somewhere nearby. Light crashing between the pallets, seeming to rake across her, swept away. More shouting. Then the tarpaulin was thrown down and there was silence and she and Elend were alone, and some time after that – how long, impossible to know – the truck trailer jolted, lurched forward, bumping on the rough ground, paused, moved on once more, and gained speed. Bulgaria? Europe at last?

Later, when the truck stopped again, and the driver invited her into the cab, she asked that question.

The driver laughed, spat into the dust. 'Yes. Can't you tell? It smells of pig-shit.'

After her cramped, dark space amid the hides, the rest of the journey felt like a procession into a new world. Ahead of her, the sky slowly lightened, disengaged itself from the land; forest and field emerged, river and lake and rock. Then each of those, in turn, becoming textured and patterned, as if dressed for the day. Their first European dawn. A restatement of life.

She cradled Elend to her, kissed him on the forehead, whispered his name. His life, his day.

In early afternoon, on the outskirts of Sofia, the driver stopped. 'I stay here. No more driving.' He touched a black box that sat on the dashboard of the truck. 'In Europe now, eye in sky watching.'

But before he left he directed Zarrin to a truck stop, on the other side of town. There, late that evening, she found another lift. From a group of drivers huddled around an open fire, one rose and came across to her. She saw the other men watching, glances exchanged.

'You want transport?'

'Yes.'

'You have money?'

She nodded. 'A little.'

'Where are you going?'

'Romania. Bucharest. Can you take me there?'

'Two hundred,' he said. 'Euros. I don't want any of that Turkish crap.'

'I don't have that much.'

The man looked at her, said nothing.

'One hundred,' she said. 'That's all I have.' Not true, but she was afraid to gamble every cent on one journey.

Again he was silent, then he nodded. 'OK. But you know the score. One hundred on account, and I'll help myself to the rest later.'

For a moment she didn't understand, but a movement amongst the other men told her. Nudges and smirks.

'No.'

He stood, regarding her, his message clear. *You're worthless; you have no choice.*

One of the men at the fire called out.

'Go on, lady, take it. It'll be over in seconds. You'll hardly know he's visited.' The other men laughed.

She gave a quick, small nod and he held out a hand. 'Money first.'

She turned away, lifted the hem of her cloak, eased the money out. He took it, then thrust his face forward, close to hers, as though inspecting something he might buy. 'Yes,' he said. 'I look forward to second instalment.'

She huddled with Elend amongst the pallets in the trailer, exploring their roughness with her hands. For a while she sat awake, alert, but slowly the motion of the truck lulled her, and she dozed. She lost track of time. Where she was, which country, which part of her life she was in. Syria, Turkey, Bulgaria. Asia, Europe. Weren't they all alike? The same drag of travelling, just to reach another place that would be the same. More begging. More walking. More tiredness and boredom and despair. Men, demanding money and sex.

The money, in this case, he already had; the sex he'd have to fight her for.

She was woken abruptly by the sound of his voice, ordering her out. It was dark, still night-time. They were in a forest. The trees framed the sky, a vast tapestry of stars, moonless, crystal clear. Across it, the Milky Way – Darb Al-Tabbāna, the Hay Merchants' Way as she'd known it in childhood – made a pale stripe, like a rent. In that moment, the notion seemed sharp and profound, as though it cut to some inner secret. The world was surely too damaged, too wounded, ever to be whole again. Amidst such hurt, her own pathetic journey, from east to west, now north, seemed futile and bound to fail.

'Leave the child,' he said. 'He'll come to no harm there.'

'Where are we?'

'Near the border.'

'Not yet across?'

'Not far.'

'I said in Romania. Not before.'

'We do it now,' he insisted. 'Then you get payment of being taken across the border.' He grabbed her arm. 'Come.'

His grip was tight. He led her to the cab. 'Inside,' he said.

His hands were on her hips, slipped down her thighs, as she clambered up. Inside the cab, there was a long bench seat. He'd spread a thin mattress along it. Every comfort, she thought with a stab of irony. And then: how often did he do this?

He climbed up behind her, slammed the door. She retreated to the far end of the seat. Already he was unzipping his trousers, pulling them down. She tried not to look at him, kept her hands behind her, hidden.

He came towards her, clumsy, half-crawling. She shrank back.

His face loomed. His hands were under her cloak, pushing it up, rough against her skin. She bit back a scream, braced herself against the door.

He was clawing at her knickers, tugging them down. Though every instinct was against it, she made herself keep calm, still.

He was clambering onto her, his knees pushing their way between her legs. He yanked at her, pulling her away from the door.

She slid her hands down his side as though to support him, as though to guide him to her.

Then she thrust. And thrust again.

The first time, the rusted nail dug into his thigh, not breaking the skin. He howled, tried to draw back.

The second time, she found her target, felt the nail bite deep. He was struggling to get away, legs flailing, screaming with pain. She gripped the nail tighter, forcing it as deep as she could.

He lashed out, struck her a glancing blow.

She kicked him off her, scrabbled at the door, tumbled out. Then she ran to the trailer, grabbed Elend, her bag, and fled into the forest.

She ran with Elend clutched against her, one hand protecting his head. She stumbled between the looming shapes of trees, ignored the brambles, the lash of branches, until the darkness absorbed her, until she could no longer hear the man's wails and sobs. Then she sank to ground, shushing Elend to silence, listened.

For a long time, there was nothing. No shouts, no curses, no sound of pursuit. Then she heard the bark of the engine, the distant crunch of wheels on gravel, and at last, silence again.

The long nail that she had eased from one of the pallets was still clutched in her hand. Her fingers were sticky with his blood or semen – she could not tell which. She threw the nail away in disgust, wiped her hands in the dust and leaf mould, until the earthiness made them feel cleansed. Then, cradling Elend, humming to him, that ancient tune she'd heard in Istanbul, she made her way back to the road.

*

It took her another three days to reach the border to Romania, and then two weeks beyond that to find a way through.

She'd hoped to cross the Danube, though by what means she didn't know. Another truck, perhaps. Or a boat. An unmanned bridge. Yet every way she tried baulked her. At

Ruse, the security at the border was fierce. She watched from a safe distance, talked to other refugees who had tried the crossing or had friends who had tried. It wasn't worth it, she was told. On the Romanian side, in Giurgiu, everyone who entered was questioned, their papers inspected. Cars and vans were emptied, luggage checked. Trucks were directed into a holding yard, where the wagons were unloaded, the cargo searched. Soldiers with guns slung across their shoulders stood by the customs posts or paced the waiting queues. If you had no papers and got caught, they arrested you and locked you up. If you were lucky you were sent back here to Bulgaria. If not, then you were deported to Turkey or wherever else they thought you belonged.

She tried anyway. She went to truck stops and cafés, asked drivers if they would give her a lift. Most simply refused. Those who didn't wanted far more than she could possibly afford. She tried the river, following it upstream in search of somewhere she might be able to steal across. Out in the countryside, she'd been told, there were people who would ferry you if you could find them, and others who would sell you a small raft to make the trip yourself. But, when she stood on the banks of the Danube and watched the sweep and swirl of the current, the story that Ahmed had told her of his experience on the Evros came back, filling her with fear. On her own, perhaps, she might take the risk; with Elend, never.

She needed an agent, she thought; it would be cheaper in a group. Back in Ruse, she asked around, was directed to a small bar in the back streets, told to ask for Christo. When she at last found him, in a dark and airless bar, a glass of *rakia* on the table cradled in his hand, she knew at once how hopeless her task was. As she approached, he glanced at her, frowned, said nothing. She wondered: was he waiting for her to buy him a drink? Instead, she began to explain her need.

He interrupted her after a few words. 'Two-fifty euro. That's into Romania. Another two-fifty to Hungary. You and the child.'

It was more than twice as much as she could afford. 'I don't have that much.'

'Then I can't help. Every day there's more people like you. Every day the price goes up. If you can't afford it, you'll have to earn it.' His eyes rose again, examined her. 'A good-looking woman like you should manage that easily enough. But you won't do it standing there.' He gave a dismissive flick of his head, went back to his drink.

Outside she paused, trying to decide what to do next. Around the door was a scatter of tables, at which men sat, talking; not a woman in sight. She wondered if any were agents, or lone traffickers – whether she might have more luck with one of them. Then her eyes caught words in Kurdish: *Azadiya Welat* – 'Freedom of the Country'. It was an independent newspaper, one of the few that still published in her native tongue. It lay on a table beside an elderly man, who sat back in his chair, staring vacantly into the square. She took a step closer.

'Are you Kurdish?' she asked.

He turned to her, smiled. 'Of course.' He indicated the paper. 'Who else would read this?'

'I need some advice.'

He invited her to pull up a chair, offered her coffee; when he ordered it, added a baklava. 'You look as though you could do with one,' he said. 'And it's our custom. Every guest must eat.'

She thanked him and started to outline her plight. When she told him that she was a refugee, he nodded and said, 'All Kurds are exiles. That's what happens when they take away your country.'

She had a choice, she continued: to risk crossing the border, or go to the police and ask for asylum here in Bulgaria. She'd been told that she would be allowed to do so, if she asked. Did he live here? How did they treat Kurds? What was life like?

The man gave a snort of derision. 'What do you think it's like?' He gave a sweep of his hand, taking in the café, the square, the streets and town beyond; perhaps the whole country. 'Look at it. And it will just get worse.'

'What do you mean?'

'The country's poor. It offers you nothing. Your child there, even less. And for immigrants it's a trap. Here you are stuck. You won't be able to travel outside of Bulgaria. This isn't the gateway to Europe, it's the portcullis, keeping you at bay. You need to get inside the Schengen area; then you can be free. Get across Romania, into Hungary. But you must do it soon. The flood has only just started. Soon there'll be too many to cope.'

'Too many?'

'Too many people like you. Too many refugees. Syria, Afghanistan, Iraq; Somalia and Yemen too, I expect. Ten times as many as we're getting now. Twenty times. Who knows? Already the trouble has begun – the prejudice, the slogans, the hate. The politicians won't have the guts to resist. The next thing, they'll be closing the borders. Building fences and walls. Locking you all up. Sending you home. You'll see. I've been here thirty years – but, then, even I won't be safe.'

Her coffee came, the cake too. She ate it self-consciously, but the man nodded, smiled.

'Good, yes? The one good thing about the whole country. That and the *rakia*. For you and your son here, there would be nothing, believe me.'

'How do I get into Romania, then?' she asked. 'I can't afford an agent, and the river is so wide, so dangerous.'

'The river is bad,' he said. 'Don't go that way.'

'How, then?'

'East. Dobrich province, where the border and the river are separate. You can still walk across there.'

'Do you mean that?'

'I've done it myself. Both ways. It's a long walk; you'll need a buggy for the child. But if you're careful you won't be caught.'

'Then why doesn't everyone go that way?'

He smiled, gently, mocking, then leaned towards her, spoke confidentially. 'Because I don't tell everyone,' he said.

*

As he had warned her, the way was long. She'd stolen a trolley from outside a supermarket, and loaded all her belongings, with Elend, into that. She pushed it most of the two hundred kilometres to Silistra, before it eventually collapsed. From there, where the border swept south away from the river, she walked for another two days through the windswept farmlands of Dobrich to find one of the paths that led north, then for more hours along a dry and rutted track, between untidy fields, towards where she thought the border must be. As she did so, she marvelled at the isolation of the place and its emptiness, and imagined herself walking into Romania, walking perhaps unimpeded to Budapest.

But she remembered the man's words – be careful – and kept her eyes open, scanning the land for anything that moved, or anywhere from which she might be spied upon.

Even so, the sound of the helicopter came as a surprise.

It burst upon her from beyond a low hill, filling the air with its echo, like the bark of a hundred dogs. Instinctively she snatched Elend up and cowered into the shadow of a tree, crouched low, shielding him against the attack.

The helicopter came closer, swept over her, seemed to pause and hover overhead. She could see its shadow on the stony ground, twenty metres from where she hid. It moved, paused again. She imagined eyes bearing down on her through the thin canopy of the tree, binoculars sweeping. Perhaps heat-seeking sensors, as well, stripping her cover away, leaving her body bare, bright.

Then the note of the engine changed. The shadow shifted. It flew on; paused once more above another small cluster of trees and disappeared over the hill.

How often did that happen, she wondered; would it return?

She decided to wait. She huddled down against the bole of the tree, fed Elend, told him the story once more, the story of love and hope.

'Once, long ago, before you were born, or me...'

5

Luck

'Hungary?' she asked. 'Budapest?'

'Cluj,' the man said. 'That's as far as I go. Fifty euro.'

After crossing the border – a strangely anticlimactic event, past a rusted single-bar barrier bearing the simple words *Romania. Do Not Pass*, and done at night – Zarrin had walked for two more days. She had chosen the quiet ways, and the ways that felt unseen. Keeping to the woodlands and hedgerows, avoiding the roads and the villages, for the land did not yet feel safe.

But now, at last, she had ventured onto the highway, and after half a day a truck had stopped. She had run after it, realised too late that it had not stopped for her but to allow the driver to check his manifest. She banged on the window; the driver waved her away. She held up money, watched as the man fought his instincts: disgust and greed. Greed won.

'Yes,' she said. 'Cluj is good.'

She climbed in, sat back with Elend clutched to her, watched the road slip past. They were making progress again.

But less than halfway there the truck started to labour, bucked at the hills. 'Brakes,' the driver said, and swore. 'I knew you'd be bad luck.' He got out, kicked at the wheels of the cab; swore again. She could smell their heat, raw, acrid. 'I'll have to let them cool.'

They sat there for two hours. Here in the mountains, spring hadn't yet come. The sky was clear but the wind was cold, and on the higher peaks pockets of snow remained, like flecks of blank canvas where the picture had not yet been sketched in.

The driver smoked, listened to harsh Western pop music on the radio, asked her about herself, though without real interest, and was satisfied with the answers she gave. But when they started off again they managed no more than a few kilometres before the trouble returned. 'I'll have to call out a mechanic,' he said. 'We'll be here a while.'

To escape from the man's cigarette smoke, she took Elend outside and waited in the lee of a boulder. Beside her, Elend searched for pebbles in the grass, chattering to himself; picked up ones that seemed to attract him in some way, brought them to show her. When he tired of that, she snuggled him against her and pointed out the things they could see. The sun completed its climb. In the valley, cattle moved between the scrub, seeking places where the new grass was sweeter. Larks sang invisibly from the pale sky. It felt almost like happiness – peace at least. She might stay there like that, and be content.

The driver came over, offered her coffee from a metal cup. She drank it gratefully.

'No father?' he asked, looking at the child.

'Dead,' she said, simply.

He nodded. 'I'm sorry. Where are you going?'

'I don't know. Wherever we are safe.'

'Safe?' he asked. 'Are you in trouble?' She didn't answer and he added, 'Perhaps you're right. Nowhere is safe these days.' He wandered back to his cab, sat on the foot-plate, smoking.

Some time in the afternoon, the mechanic arrived. He was young, lean, long-haired, wore a ring in his ear. He laughed a lot, whistled as he worked. The sound of his whistling, of the squeak of the jack, the tap of his hammer merged with the buzz of insects, the chittering bird-song. Zarrin spread out her cape, laid Elend beside her, and sang to him until he dozed. Her thoughts drifted, memories and imaginings weaving into one.

March 20th, Newroz – the day of the ancient Kurdish festival, marking the start of spring and the new year. Later, when she was older, she'd learned what it all meant, and why it meant so much, for in Syria it was officially banned by the government, and as a consequence had become not just a celebration of tradition but a political statement and an assertion of cultural identity. As a child, though, she had known it just as a day of joy, when the whole neighbourhood gathered, and the adult rules of correctness and respect and orderly behaviour thawed a little, and one could dance and play games and receive all sorts of treats and gifts. A bonfire was lit in the village square, and people paraded with torches. In her memory, or in her imagination, she saw herself in a bright green dress, cascading to the ground around her, and she lit a torch and carried it as they marched, and felt at that moment as though she were leading the whole world to some new and undiscovered land.

And another day, when she was older – on her thirteenth birthday – and she had recited a poem to her gathered relations. She'd found it while she was doing her duty of tidying up one of the classrooms, after school, in a book that a teacher had perhaps confiscated from an older pupil (for no teachers would surely read such things), and left carelessly open on the desk. It was called *Exile*, and the first lines that caught her attention seemed to take refuge in her mind, so that she instantly knew them:

I go, I go
till I find a child
and with the light of his eyes
I teach the sparrow to fly again...

She had scribbled the whole poem down hurriedly, afraid all the time that she would be caught, then had written it out neatly at home, kept it hidden in her room, read it and read it again until she knew it by heart. And a few months later, at the gathering for her birthday, she heard the adults talking around her about the struggles in Iraq, and remembered it, and, when invited to give a speech to them, recited it.

It hadn't been a success. The poem was met with stunned silence, shakes of elderly heads. Only one uncle came up to her afterwards, and with a hand on her shoulder said, quietly, 'That is a beautiful poem. I know it well. And I think of it often, when I think of my sons, fighting in Turkey.'

Now, sitting by the roadside in the distant land, with her own son snuggled to her, she tried again to find its words in her memory, and stumblingly, with hesitations and once or twice with a guess at a phrase, she recited it again, beneath her breath, from beginning to end.

A shadow passed across her, and she looked up.

'We've been talking – the driver and me.' It was the mechanic. He stood, looking down at her, framed against the sun, so that she couldn't see his face. 'He's going to have to take things slowly. He said you should come with me instead.'

'I've no money,' she said.

'I don't want any. Nor anything else. But I can take you to Cluj.'

She nodded. 'Thank you.'

In the cab of his pick-up, he asked, 'When did you last eat?'

'This morning.'

'Properly?'

She smiled. 'What is properly?'

He pointed to a box on the seat between them. 'Look in there. Help yourself.'

She thanked him again.

'Your luck's changing. That's what people say when they meet me.' He laughed. 'Let's hope it's true.'

It felt that way. The food was good – breads, vegetable pies, cheese, which he insisted she keep eating, was proud of. She broke pieces off for Elend and shared them with him. The man was proud of the food. All home-made, by his wife, he said: the best cook in the region. 'She's intent on fattening me up.' He patted his tummy. 'She's not succeeded yet!' He talked easily, made her laugh. He told her about himself, his wife, their life together, some of the drivers he had to deal with. 'He blamed you for the breakdown,' he told her, flicking his head back – indicating where they had been. 'A woman in the cab – bad luck.' He glanced at her, eyes twinkling. 'They're superstitious, most of these truckers. They all have their good luck charms – Madonnas and saints and the like. They'd have their cabs full of virgins if they could. Dolls, I mean, not the real thing. You'd have to search hard to find enough real ones for that in Romania!' He raised his eyebrows, a mock apology. 'Sorry.'

She shook her head, dismissing it. Once it might have offended her. Now, it meant nothing.

He told her other stories about breakdowns and accidents he'd attended, motivated by places they passed. Folk tales about life on the road, urban myths. The panther that supposedly sat on a tight bend at night, eyes flashing, scaring the unwary over the edge; the naked woman that hiked along one section, begging lifts from anyone foolish enough to believe what they saw – a witch without a doubt. Gently lampooning confessions about things he'd done himself. The admission that he'd proposed to his wife by email. 'I didn't dare ask her outright, in case she said no. Worse than that, in case I embarrassed her. I knew how embarrassed she'd be, how much it would hurt her to hurt me. So I drafted a message to her, all in rhyme. I wasn't going to send it, meant to delete it, but I pressed the send button by mistake. I felt terrible.' He drove on for a minute, his face a theatre of emotions at the memory. 'She emailed back to me an hour later. *I don't care whether this is spam or not, but it's in writing and the answer's yes.*'

Zarrin laughed. She laughed properly, from deep inside her, instead of just with her mouth. When had she last done that? she wondered. Not since the camp, for months before then. Laughing now was a release, a restitution. The person she had once been, briefly allowed to live again.

When they arrived at the depot, she got down from the cab, thanked him.

'Here, take this,' he said. It was her fifty-euro note. 'I got Basil back there to give it to me, to take you off his hands. He didn't want any more bad luck. It's yours.'

She hesitated and he pushed it towards her. 'Go on. You'll need it.'

She took it, turned to leave, stopped.

'What's your name?'

'Fredrik,' he said.

'Thank you, Fredrik. I'll remember you.'

His face lit up. 'That's good. That's all any of us can wish for.' He gave her a wave, slammed the engine into gear, drove through the gates.

*

She was right, she did remember Fredrik; and he was right, for her luck seemed to have changed. Perhaps he left some behind for her to use.

But luck comes in different guises, and when it reappeared she didn't recognise it at first. The next morning, as she headed out of town, following the highway, a police car cruised past, stopped ahead of her, waited. She hesitated, wondering whether she should turn back and run. But already a police officer had got out from the passenger side, was coming towards her. He demanded her papers; when she showed him her ID card he shook his head as if in sorrow, beckoned her to follow.

He led her back to the car, told her to sit in the back, got in beside her. 'We don't want you jumping out,' he said. 'It makes such a mess on the road.'

They drove off, not to town as she had expected, but out into the countryside. After ten minutes, they turned off the highway, onto a small track, came to a halt. What followed might have sounded like a pleasant conversation – two officers doing their best to help a young woman and her child in need. But to Zarrin it was full of menace and abuse. They outlined the future she faced if they took her to the police station. Detention, the charge of being an illegal immigrant, the invitation to be deported or apply for asylum in Romania. If she chose the latter, the man beside her said, his voice rueful, then she'd be locked up for four months or so, maybe six, while her case was considered. Maybe her son would be taken away for safe keeping. Then she'd be deported anyway.

But, of course, there was an alternative. They could look away for a few moments, or wander away from the car and have a pee. And when they returned, she'd be gone.

'What do you want?' she asked.

The man beside her gave a mock look of shock. 'We're police officers, lady. What are you suggesting?'

But the other man said, 'Of course, if you happen to leave something behind by accident, we couldn't do anything about it could we? You've never been here.'

She reached into her cloak for her purse, showed him the contents: twenty euros, some loose change.

The policeman laughed. 'And in the lining? Or in the hem? Or sown into your knickers. Would we find something there if we looked? Money? Maybe drugs.'

It was an obvious threat, a double one, for no doubt they'd plant drugs on her if they needed to. 'I've a hundred euros,' she said. 'That's all. It's my last money.'

The man nodded.

She pulled up the hem of her cloak, found the loose fold where half her money was stowed, extracted the two notes, held them out.

The man shook his head. 'You dropped them by accident, remember?'

She laid the notes on the dashboard. The policeman smiled, then reached past her, opened the door. As she scrambled out, clutching Elend and her belongings, he called after her. 'Your lucky day, really, meeting us. An honest policeman, if you can find one, would have locked you up by now.'

It taught her something, that experience. Every day did that, she thought, every experience. For even after all this travelling there was so much to learn. She might be in Europe, but without papers she needed to be cautious, to move unseen. As she headed north, therefore, she shunned the busier roads, followed the country lanes as much as she could, walking much of the time, accepting short lifts when she was offered them by locals in their beat-up Trabants and Ladas and Datsuns, and gratefully sharing their invariable offers of food. At the border, she turned north, and, repeating the trick that the Kurdish man in Ruse had taught her, headed for the remoter lands of Satu Mare, where she followed cobbled roads and sandy tracks through the patchy farmland and forest and slipped, with unexpected ease, into Hungary and the borderless Schengen zone.

*

And, even now, Fredrik's luck went with her.

The truck drew up uninvited, as she walked along the road out of Debrecen. The driver leaned across, opened the passenger door, almost barring her way on the hard shoulder.

She stopped in alarm.

'No worry, lady,' he said. 'I not mean to frighten you.'

'What do you want?'

'I offer you lift.'

She hesitated, and he asked, 'Refugee? Yes?'

She nodded.

'Then come with me. I travel everywhere. All over Europe.'

Something in the man's voice, his manner – his round and jovial face, his bald pate, his teasing eyes – made him look safe, almost clown-like, and she wanted to believe him. But life had taught her never to trust.

'No,' she said.

Behind the truck, traffic was queuing; horns tooted.

'Come on,' he said. 'What have you to lose? In Vienna tomorrow. Prague two days after that. You see the world.'

'Why?' she asked.

'Because I need company. Driving lonely on your own. Because I feed you, and your child there, and keep you safe.'

'And what will I have to do in return?'

'Nothing, I promise. Just enjoy scenery. Listen to me chattering. Tell me stories to keep me awake.'

It made no sense, she knew. There was danger in it, uncertainty.

A loud blast came from the vehicle behind, and the truck-driver beckoned with an urgent wave. 'Come on. Please. Otherwise they swear at me all way to border. Overtake on corners. Cause bad accidents. And it all be your fault.' He grinned. 'That joke – not really.'

She laughed. 'Alright. Help me.'

She held out a hand and the driver grabbed it. As she scrambled up, Elend clutched to her chest, the man pulled, gently yet firmly, so that she seemed to rise without any effort. He laughed. 'See – easy really. Now we go. World your oyster now. That what they say.'

She reached for the door handle, yanked it shut. The engine revved. The truck jolted.

'I am Salvador,' the driver said. 'People call me Salvo. What about you?'

'Zarrin,' she said. 'And this is my son. Elend.'

'Pleased to meet you, Zarrin.' Salvo leaned over, shook her hand. 'You, too, Elend. Welcome to my world.'

6

Salvo

Salvo's world was the road. He spent his life on it, seemed to need it for the sustenance it gave – not just the money but a purpose to his life, the feel of the tarmac beneath the wheels of the truck, its long line ahead of him, the constant sense of movement. He was from Slovenia, he told her, and had been driving trucks for years. He had his own one now, was independent, could choose his contracts, go where he liked.

If he had a home in his current life, Zarrin soon learned, it was in Belgium, in Brussels. It was from there that he obtained his most regular jobs, transporting parts for the Audi factory in Forest, or electronics for Bosch and other companies in nearby Anderlecht. He offered what the bigger companies could not: one-way transport, at short notice, at cheap rates, to deal with last-minute demands. He was known to be reliable, and for himself he was confident that he could always rustle up another load that would make the trip pay. And his overheads were low: no bosses or shareholders or living expenses to pay for. Just himself – and, now, Zarrin and Elend. He was rarely short of work, therefore, but his life was haphazard. He dotted around, responding to phone calls, following leads from one client to another, sometimes just scouting amongst the people he'd worked for before to see if they had any contracts coming up.

He had no house to call his own, though in Brussels he had access to a small apartment, in the drab back-streets of Veeweyde, which he would often use. It was a share arrangement, with two men whom Zarrin never met. Slovenians like him, she guessed, for whenever she returned there would be a copy of the *Slovenske Novice* lying on the table and half-empty packets of food by Zito, bottles of Slovenian soft drink, in the pantry cupboard. When he found the newspaper, Salvo would give it no more than a glance before screwing it up for fire-lighting. The foodstuffs, however, sparked a more emotive response, and he would extol their virtues with descriptions of the meals he used to be served as a child, or the way he and his friends would sneak off from school with a bottle of Cockta and a stolen packet of cigarettes, and share them illicitly in a hidden den in the park.

Elsewhere, he had similar arrangements. A tiny basement room, a bare and empty flat, a run-down holiday shack; in Poland an old railway carriage parked in the siding of an abandoned goods yard. Most, he told her, belonged to friends or other drivers; some she suspected were abandoned and unused, places whose owners had died or moved. They were all simply furnished, offered little in the way of comfort. An old red sofa, its springs straining at the fabric. A rickety chair. A rough table made from a disused door laid on four piles of breeze-blocks. In most, utilities were lacking: water came from a barrel, fed from the gutters; lighting was a candle; cooking was done on the Primus stove that he carried in his cab. Heat was won from a makeshift fire in the hearth, if there was one, or they did without. Sanitary needs were provided by nature. To Zarrin, though, their progress from one to the other felt like a royal tour, each place a palace.

Otherwise they lived in his truck. Behind the driving seat was a curtained off compartment across which was slung a hammock; beneath that, stretching the width of the cab, a wooden box in which he kept his clothes. Salvo offered Zarrin the hammock to sleep in, but she refused, so he constructed a bunk-bed for her and Elend on top of the box, and lined it with an old sleeping bag and cushions that he scrounged from somewhere. When she lay in the bed at night, Zarrin loved the sound of the cab. Salvo's gentle snoring from the hammock above, Elend's occasional snuffle from beside her, the tick-tick-tick of the engine cooling beneath its cowling.

As they travelled, Salvo recounted stories. When he'd invited her aboard he'd said that he needed her to talk to him, but that, she soon realised, was only partly true. What he needed more was someone to listen, an audience for his fluid mind. Sometimes he'd tell her about incidental things: the vehicles passing the other way, what sort of truck or car they were, their good points and bad; the landscape and places that lay there, out of sight; the birds, the crops, the clouds and the shapes he could see within them. But such things led him on to other things, and they eventually became a story.

He had a wealth of stories to tell. Many seemed apocryphal, and figured people he knew as their victim or hero, while a few were folk tales of a sort – ancient stories from the mountains and forests of Central Europe, or modern myths with a moral twist. Most seemed to display the weaknesses of men, the stupidity in their bravado. Amongst them, though, were strands of his own life, and from these Zarrin constructed the bigger story of his past and how he got from there to here. Born poor, in what had then been the Socialist Republic of Slovenia, part of the former Yugoslavia. Rebellious as a child, in his own rather placid way – resisting by not doing, by dreaming, rather than open revolt – he hadn't flourished at school, and had left early, worked in a series of unskilled, low-paid jobs, dotting around the Balkans to avoid the war. A mechanic for a while in a small garage in Slovenia, a farmhand in Bosnia, an ambulance-driver in Macedonia. It was then that he developed his love of the road, and earned the qualifications he needed. He'd worked for a haulage company, driving logging trucks, saved his money. When Slovenia joined the EU, he'd taken a gamble and invested all he had – plus a bank loan that he said made his eyes water – to buy a truck of his own. But it had been a good choice. The burgeoning trade across Eastern Europe meant that work was plentiful. He'd long ago paid off the loan for the first truck, had traded it in for a newer and bigger one – his pride and joy.

He was content with his life, he said. He was a free man.

And yet Zarrin wondered how content he was, how free. Beneath his apparent serenity she sometimes glimpsed a sadness, a darkness that lurked. He never revealed it openly, but there were nights when he would take himself away into the town, and not return until morning. And when he came back he would be dishevelled and quiet, and his breath would be sour and his clothes damp as though he'd been walking the whole night, or had dossed down somewhere with hobos and drunks. She wondered, too, whether in those absences he found himself a woman for brief company.

If so, she felt no censure. It was his life, and she held no sway over it. And yet it disturbed her, for it was a reminder of what had happened to her, and seemed in some way to link Salvo with the act.

In return, she talked to him mainly in the evenings, when they sat together in the darkening gloom of the cab, or in their borrowed hut or room. She soon learned what she could talk about and what she could not. The world, the harsh and ugly realities of it – politics, war, economics, crime – held no interest for him. He liked more mundane and material things. Mostly she talked about Elend, or the people and scenes she'd glimpsed while she was exploring this town or that, or just sitting watching the world go by. That was what he liked best, she thought – those half-seen things. They intrigued him, teased him with their possibilities, with the connections they made to all the other pictures he had in his head.

She never talked about her past. She didn't want to, and Salvo never asked. Whether his reticence was for her sake or his, she didn't know, but she knew that it was right for them both. It would merely pain Salvo, and make him feel inadequate for rescuing her too late. And for her, it no longer mattered. She'd conquered it, that past; she'd outflown it, left it behind. She was safe at last.

*

It was a good time. She knew that then; later, it felt even better. She sometimes wondered how it had come to her – what deals had been done in heaven to make it possible. She travelled so far, saw so much of the world. North and south and east and west. To the grey Baltic, the blue Mediterranean, the wild Atlantic coast, the bleak and forbidding forests at the border with Russia. There could be no road, she thought, that they hadn't travelled.

The journeying brought revelation and discovery; more learning, too. She realised how huge, how varied was the continent they called Europe. So much greater than she'd thought. She saw all the types of people there, in all their varied colours, clothes, cultures, communities. So different – yet always, she thought, the same. For the smiles and laughter didn't change wherever she went, nor the kindnesses. Nor the clutter and mess and insults and crime.

Yet, amidst it, she found her favourites. Places to which she looked forward to returning, places that drew her back. She preferred the smaller and older cities, had no taste for modernity or the grossness of tourist hotspots or international centres. Tallinn she loved, with its quiet cobbled streets, its sense of complacency: it seemed happy as it was. Luxembourg, too, for its country-town grandeur; Graz the same. But what she loved best were the mountains. The sweep of green pasture, the crystal flash of snow, cow-bells calling from the valleys, the pale sky. They felt like a haven, far from the reach of either her future or her past, far from the troubles of the world.

She picked up languages as she went. French, enough Italian to find her way around a city, to shop, live; a smattering of German and Dutch and Spanish, too. But the Eastern European languages eluded her; despite Salvo's efforts to teach her, what Slovenian she learned one day she would forget the next. In return, she attempted to instil the Arabic equivalents in Salvo's mind. He tried and failed, never able to shape his tongue and throat in the way the language required. 'Horrible language,' he would often complain, after spitting out the words. 'Worse than Russian. Fit only for camels and mules. Talk to me in English.' So that was the language between them, and, as Elend learned, it became his language too.

Elend flourished in his new life. He grew taller, lost the last of his baby cheeks and pudginess, and now, nearing two, was a slim, self-contained boy. He had none of the clumsiness she'd seen in other children of his age – that puppy-like overenthusiasm that caused accidents, knocked over cups of milk, made messes on the table. He was quiet, watchful, rarely bored, always content. He never cried. As they travelled in the cab, Zarrin would sit him on her lap, or hold him at the window beside her, and point to things that caught her eye. A boat ploughing its way along a canal, a train on railway, the angular derricks of a crane lifting containers at a port; a herd of cattle winding their way for milking, an imperious llama surveying the scene, a family of wild boar foraging at the forest's edge. She'd tell him their names, ask him to repeat them, then she'd explain what they did or why they looked like that. In the interludes between, where there was nothing to point out, he'd murmur the names back to himself, add in words or childish babble of his own. If he saw something he already knew, he'd stamp or bang his hand on the window, and point or tug at her arm. 'Look, look.'

She loved that connection with him, that necessity to share, and realised that weaning hadn't really been the end. Mother and child remained as one.

In the cab of his truck, Salvo kept an old road atlas of Europe. He almost never had need to use it, for he knew the roads he travelled like the back of his hand, and if he ran into difficulties – a motorway blocked by an accident, a flooded bridge – he would wind down the window in a service station car park and ask a fellow truck-driver for an alternative route rather than use his phone or peer at maps. But in the past it had seen good use and bore the scars to tell. It was tattered, stained with coffee and chip-fat, and some of the pages were coming loose from the long spiral spring that bound them. Scribbled over the inside of the back cover, and in blank areas at the bottom of pages, were Salvo's notes to himself: telephone numbers, addresses, codes for this and that, here and there someone's name.

To Zarrin it was a treasure trove. When she first discovered it, she tried to find all the places she had been as she and Elend had travelled north through Europe – the towns and villages, the roads, the blank areas of farmland or forest through which she must have walked. The revelation shocked her. The journey was so haphazard, so lacking in logic or plan, the places often so empty and uncharted. She marvelled that at the end of it she had arrived here, with Salvo, in a life as rich as this.

She used it, too, both to map her life with Salvo, and as a story-book for Elend. Often, while they were waiting for Salvo to discuss business, or pay his respects to some friend, she would take it out and open it on her lap. Then she would sit there, Elend propped against her, and trace the roads they had driven, telling him about them, describing the wonders they'd seen. She'd tell him the names of the towns and entice him to repeat them. Antwerp, he learned to say, and Malmo and Breda, but his attempt at Rotterdam made her laugh. And, as she showed him where the places were and the routes they'd travelled, Elend would reach out and follow the red and green and yellow roads with a finger, or try to grip the edge of the page and turn it over, always eager to move on. Had she already made him like that, she wondered: a wanderer, a traveller? Was that what his life would always be?

7

Syrian Echoes

Sitting in the cab beside Salvo, crossing the continent from west to east, north to south, driving through mountains, across broad and verdant plains, following wide rivers – the Rhine, the Po, the Seine – as they headed inexorably for the sea, Zarrin often felt like a bird, high above the turmoil and travails of the world. Soaring, sweeping, swooping, untouched and unreachable. Or like a feather, weightlessly wandering on the wind.

Yet outside, she knew, there was another world that could not be denied. Sometimes, it reached in on her, stirring memories or doubts or fears.

It did so inconsequentially. As she walked down a street, the fleeting scent of bougainvillea or an exotic spice would bring her old world back. As she sat in a park, watching Elend play, a Kurdish voice would seem to call to her, making her remember. On a country road, she'd glimpse a child watching over a field of goats, and be returned at once to her grandfather's farm, the sun warm on her arms and cheeks, the breeze teasing at her hair. The sight of a mosque or the sound of the imam's call would nudge at her and instinctively her conscience would respond, an echo of her faith, and she'd wonder: had she turned away from it too readily; had she allowed herself too easily to fall? And now and then, she'd hear a name, or mishear a word, that reminded her of Mahmet or Nasr, and for an instant her whole world would lurch. Fear would return, sharp and intense, then linger for days until at last a new place, a smile from Elend or Salvo's sudden laughter banished it again.

But the harshest intrusion into her life was from the war. It seemed impossible to escape that.

Since she'd been travelling with Salvo, her contact with world news had been slight and sporadic. Salvo avoided the news almost as if it were a plague and might infect him. He refused to watch it on TV on those rare occasions when the house they were staying in had one; he'd switch to a different station if the news came on the radio in his cab. He never bought a newspaper. For Zarrin, therefore, information about the world came only obliquely and by chance: from a headline on a hoarding, a snatch of conversation heard in the street; banners or boards held aloft by a small group of demonstrators outside an embassy. *Stop the killing, End the slaughter, Save Our Syria Now.*

Always that, it seemed. Syria, Assad and the war.

Each time it saddened her, and made her shrink away. She didn't want to think of it; she didn't want to know. It stirred too many conflicting memories, too many sorrows and fears. It tugged too much from her past.

But then, in Lille, on a wet December day, she found herself with hours to fill and nowhere warm or dry to go.

She retreated to a café, parked the buggy Salvo had bought her beside a table, ordered a coffee. In the fug and the warmth, her thoughts drifted, settled on Salvo.

She'd begun to wonder about him in recent weeks. What he was, what she was too; what they were to each other. What they might become. They weren't yet questions that disturbed her, but they tugged at her mind. One day, she knew, they would demand a response.

In all the time she had been with Salvo, he had never made an advance on her, never tried to kiss her, embrace her, never hinted at sex. Any physical contact – when he helped her from the truck, when he touched her to wake her in the cab – was gentle, and carefully held back. She was grateful for that, thought of it as some deep trait of chivalry in him, and evidence that she was safe in his presence; that he regarded himself as too old, she too young. She imagined, also, that he might have a wife somewhere – back in Slovenia, perhaps – to whom he would one day return when his work allowed. His occasional night-time roaming was thus no more than what she supposed most lonely men did: a necessary form of release.

Yet, at times, she doubted that easy explanation, and imagined a more convoluted truth: that it was her he was escaping from on those nights – or rather, from the desire she provoked. That behind his careful deference he wanted her, lusted for her, maintained his distance from her solely by an iron act of will, and by these brief forays into the night.

Did he love her; did he, perhaps, imagine her as his wife? And, if so, could she really hold him at bay? Did she have that right, after all he'd done for her?

There was Elend, as well. He needed a father; in Salvo he had one. She could not deny him that.

Did she even want to?

'*Ça suffit!*'

She looked up, startled. The manager of the café stood beside the table, arms folded, indignation scrawled across his face. '*Il est temps de vous en aller! Partez, s'il vous plaît.*'

She started to protest. But the manager insisted. She'd been there too long. Elend's buggy was blocking the aisle. He started to wheel it towards the door.

'*Attendez, j'arrive*,' she cried. She grabbed her coat, hurried after him, snatched the buggy from his grasp. He held the door open for her with exaggerated politeness, closed it firmly in her wake.

Outside, the rain was turning to sleet. She walked the streets, huddled into her coat, trying to avoid the spray from the passing cars, the blustering wind. In the shops, Christmas trees glistened in the windows, Santa Clauses stood in the doorways, carols rang out.

She turned into a small square. Ahead of her, a flight of steps beckoned, leading up to wide glass doors beyond which she could see a foyer, bright-lit. A museum? An art gallery? As the rain gusted once more, a man stooped beside her.

'Here. Let me help.'

He lifted the axle of Elend's buggy, and in a few strides they were at the top of the stairs. She thanked the man, and as the doors slid open, followed him inside.

She stood there, dripping.

'Read me story,' Elend said.

Beside them, on a stand, was a display of books. Ahead of them, beyond a set of barriers, a vast room stretched away, ranked with long shelves.

'*Puis-je vous aider?* Can I help you?'

A woman had appeared. Zarrin gave a shrug of helplessness, uncertainty, taking in not just herself and the state she was in, but Elend, the whole building, the world outside.

'It's horrible out there, isn't it?' The woman smiled. 'But it's warm inside. Why don't you leave your buggy here? The children's area is that way.' She pointed between the rows of shelves. 'Is that what you want?'

Still Zarrin hesitated. Was this place really open to people like her? Was it free?

'Come,' the woman said. 'I'll show you.'

Zarrin was led to the far corner of the library. There, against a window that looked out on a small courtyard, was a play-pen filled with coloured balls, another with toys for children of every age. On the shelves beside them were children's picture books, and along one wall a row of tables bearing computers.

'I'm sure you'll find something to amuse him here,' the woman said. 'If you want any help, just go to the desk.'

They spent the rest of the afternoon there. Zarrin found books for Elend with pictures of animals, and read to him, showed him the pictures, encouraged him to give them their names. 'Efant…gamel…nake.' Going back every now and then to earlier pages when he demanded to see one again. Then Elend clambered down from her lap, went over to the play-pens, pointed at the coloured balls. 'Want to play,' he said.

For a while, she watched him. He burrowed into the mass of balls, popped up again, laughing. He scuffed at them with his feet or hands, throwing them up so they fell about him. He sat, holding them in his hands, studying each one as if it held some inner magic. When he tired of that, he clambered into the next pen, picked up a toy truck, said its name, pushed it along. Later the coloured bricks caught his eye; frowning in concentration, he piled them up. Three, four, five high. Each time, on the fifth, the tower toppled. Each time, he drew his brow tighter, started again. Soon, he was absorbed in his endeavour, oblivious to her presence.

Zarrin looked around, wondering what to do. The screen on one of the computers blinked. Idly, she went across to it, clicked the mouse. A page opened. The *New York Times*. World headlines. Central amongst them, in the largest font, news of the Syrian war.

She flinched at the sight of it, tried to turn away, but found her eyes returning to the page. The latest casualty figures confronted her and with a quick jerk of her finger she touched the mouse.

The next page loaded. A picture of a mass grave.

This is your country, it seemed to say. *This is the place you once loved.*

Despite herself, she scrolled down the page, started to read. More statistics. The dead and the injured and the missing. The numbers of children killed.

The name of a town she knew caught her eye, and, grateful for the chance to escape, she clicked on the link.

New horrors: more images of destruction, more hundreds of people dead. Then another shock: the name of a man she'd once met – a general in the army to whom Mahmet had introduced her at one of the business meetings she'd attended. Chief of staff, now.

And another. The poet, Bawer Gulbahar, who had visited her home at Mahmet's invitation. Killed by snipers.

Other places. Al Hasakah, in the northeast, where she'd grown up. The old souk in Aleppo, where she had walked and shopped once with Nasr in those heady early days, soon after their affair had started and their love had seemed new and pure. Now – like an emblem of their fate – the souk had been devastated, destroyed, proved to be nothing. Only rubble left.

It was too much. She fumbled for the mouse, shut the page down, turned back to Elend.

In the days that followed, Zarrin tried to forget what she'd read. Syria was no longer her concern, she told herself; it no longer owned her. She might still have friends there, her parents, her sisters. Somewhere, in Damascus or whatever was left of her native town of Al Hasakah, there might be records noting her birth, naming her, recording her marriage. But she did not belong there any more. Nor did she want to. What had happened to her – the abuse, the brutality – must have happened in different ways a hundred thousand times in the months since she had left. How could a place like that claim you? How could you love it, owe it anything except your anger and disdain?

Yet a seed had been sown, and she couldn't quite ignore it. She'd been far too unknowing, she realised; too unenquiring. All through her life she'd allowed those around her to keep her locked away from the world. As a child by her parents and teachers; during her marriage by Mahmet; now, by Salvo. Each of them seemed to want to keep her innocent and shield her from the truth. Yet wasn't it innocence that had caused her downfall? The careless indulgences, her foolish dreams of love. Little wonder that she'd been dealt with as she had.

She needed to armour herself, she thought. She needed to know the world, understand it, be prepared for what it might bring.

A few weeks later, therefore, when she was back in Brussels, she found the local library and repeated what she'd done in Lille, sitting at a computer, reading up on events in Syria while Elend played nearby. And, in the weeks afterwards, that became a routine. In each town they visited, she would find a library or an internet café and would spend time on the web, searching for more news from Syria, following the country's sad fortunes. Adding to her knowledge, adding to her regret.

Then, in a small library in Ulm, she tried a different search. Sinjari – Mahmet's family name.

What motivated her to do so, she wasn't sure. Curiosity perhaps, or fear. Or just the need to know. She typed the name tentatively, pausing after each letter, sat for long seconds when she'd finished before pressing the enter key. The page filled with twenty links to the name. Dread flooded her. Each one made Mahmet and his family seem just a touch away. She imagined them watching her even as she sat here, waiting for her next move, ready to snare her, ready to pounce.

Reluctantly, yet knowing she could not resist, she followed a link, then another. With each one, more appeared. The Sinjaris were everywhere, it seemed. Yet she shouldn't have been surprised. The family was rich, had history on its side. They were knitted together with the other major families that ran the country – the Shalishes, al-Hassans, Hamboubas and Makhloufs – even with Assad himself. But somehow she hadn't known; somehow she'd never guessed.

Most of what she found was business stuff, and most of that referred to Mahmet's father, Talor. In such matters, it was clear, he still ruled the family roost. And his companies were doing well, despite the war – or perhaps because of it. The Sinjari empire was built on textiles and chemicals – valuable goods in peacetime, during war even more so. Whatever the family might have lost to battles and bombs had been fully compensated by the rewards of what it contributed to the armed forces; the foreign exchange it brought in from Iran, Russia, China. With that had come political gain. The recent photographs of Mahmet's father were more often of him alongside the Minister of Finance or a general or a member of the Assad family than other businessmen.

About Mahmet there was much less, and she was relieved, though from what she found it seemed that he was slowly being groomed for succession. He held several significant positions in subsidiary companies, ran a charity for orphaned children in his own name. Sometimes, he was seen with his father in the company of members of government. In several of the most recent photographs he had a young woman at his side, though each time a different one: the eligible daughter of a politician, the widow of an army man, a distant cousin. Zarrin was pleased. He had moved on from her, it seemed. He was learning to forget. Might he have forgiven, too?

But then, shocking her with its intimacy, she was confronted by a photograph from her own past. She walked at Mahmet's side, her hand on his arm, as they made their entry into the towering Four Seasons Hotel in Damascus. She remembered the occasion. It was a banquet in honour of Dr Azir Rahif, retiring head of some bureau on arts and culture, of which she'd never previously heard. The food had been lavish. They were treated to a recital by a Lebanese pianist flown in for the occasion. All the people who mattered were there: government ministers, police chiefs, generals, business leaders, many of them related, members of the same tight knot of families who ran the country. She remembered, afterwards, being ushered onto the terrace while the men were left to conduct the real business of the day. There, she'd stood looking out over the city, a tapestry of white and pink and orange lights, black shadows, woven with a tight weft; beyond, the heavier glow of the day gone, arching the hills. A woman had appeared at her side, paused, saying nothing, as if sharing her moments of reflection and peace. Then the woman had said, 'It won't last, you know. They will destroy it.'

'What do you mean?' Zarrin had asked.

'The men.' She nodded back towards the hall. 'With their pacts and jealousies, and their greedy schemes. They will ruin everything. They always do.'

'I don't understand.'

The woman had tilted her champagne glass, drained it.

'There will be war,' she'd said, emphatically. 'Can't you tell?'

About Rohat there was almost nothing, and she didn't dig too deep. She wondered if he had died or gone overseas; whether he might have been disgraced and banished, as she had. The thought gave her hope. But then, in a dull-looking article in the *Syrian Times* – about a business delegation to Europe that would explore ways of improving co-operation after the war – she caught again the Sinjari name in the caption to a photograph. A dozen neatly suited men stood, smiling at the camera. She counted the faces along the row, found the one that was Sinjari, flinched. Was it him: was it Rohat? The photograph was too grainy to be sure, but her heart knew. He had come to Europe.

She searched for other news about the delegation, seeking something that might pin his presence down. But she found nothing. Was he here? Was he looking for her as he moved from one city to another, criss-crossing the continent? Biding his time? Waiting for the chance to strike?

She left the library that day feeling vulnerable and exposed. As she hurried home, scarf tight to her face, Elend in his buggy, she scanned the side-streets and alleys, imagining Rohat there, in every shadow.

On another day, in another library, she searched for a different name. Nasr Hadad. There was a pause, then the results came in. No matches. She did not try again.

8

Dragon-Slayer

On the outskirts of Bremen, she sat in the cab with Elend. Outside, the wind buffeted the truck, making it tremble. Grit from the car park rattled against the door. Now and then, the trailer seemed to jerk. She was glad they weren't driving in this weather, was impatient for Salvo to return so that they could find somewhere sheltered, settle down for the night.

He was late, but she tried not to worry. It had happened before, this lateness. He'd chance upon old friends while he was in town negotiating contracts, get lured into a bar where they caught up on the years of separation, marking each one with another drink. The truck, Zarrin, Elend, would be forgotten. By the time he returned late into the night he'd be drunk, happy, singing – then briefly remorseful as he realised how long he'd been away, before sleep claimed him and he snored his way noisily to a sheepish dawn.

Was that what had happened? She wondered whether to assume the worst and feed Elend, make something for herself. Or did she give him another thirty minutes?

Elend pushed at the atlas on her lap, scuffing up the page. She turned it, and he pointed.

'Italy,' she said, and Elend repeated the word.

'Eatie.'

She guided his hand to Rome and told him the name.

'Wome,' he said. 'Tell me story.'

She tried to think of one, could come up only with the tale of Romulus and Remus, and that vague in her memory. It was a story far too old for Elend, but she started to tell him anyway. And after that, other stories that she dredged from her mind: snatches of history, or folklore, things she'd glimpsed from the cab as they'd driven through the night-time streets of Rome, months before. And eventually, Elend slept, curled against her side. She closed her eyes, let herself drift into a doze.

'Salvo back now. No time to sleep.'

She looked up blearily as he hauled himself into his seat, slammed the door. He was beaming with satisfaction and pride. The tang of alcohol was on his breath.

Elend had woken, too, and Salvo chucked at his cheek. 'Hello, big boy. Where have you been travelling today?'

'Italy,' Zarrin said. 'I've been teaching him about Rome. About Romulus and Remus, and Horatio, and gladiators, and the Pope.'

He laughed. 'You make him like encyclopaedia before he ten, that boy. He already know all the geography and history of world.' Then he grinned more widely. 'He lucky boy. You lucky too. Now, thanks to Salvo, you go somewhere new.'

'Where?' she asked. 'When?'

'Best place in the world,' he said. 'We go day after tomorrow. Soon as I load up.'

She quizzed him: where did he mean? But he wouldn't tell, made her guess.

'London?' she suggested. 'England.'

Salvo laughed again. 'London – not even second best. London big, ugly, too wet, too cold.' He turned up his nose. 'And full of foreigners, no?' Then he looked more serious.

'And Britain no good. Outside Schengen. They not allow people like you and Elend in.'

He made her continue to guess, and she searched the atlas looking for places they hadn't yet been. Vilnius, she tried, Madrid, Barcelona, Lisbon.

Then realisation dawned. 'Slovenia? Where you come from?' She hurriedly turned the pages of the atlas until she found the right one, struggled to pronounce it. 'Ljub...ljana?'

'You see? You know after all,' he said. 'Nowhere the same. Beautiful city. Noble, full with dignity. Like lady, like a queen. Like Zarrin.'

She blushed, turned away, then giggled and turned back. No one had said such words to her for years – not since Nasr. Then, the compliment had felt warm and seductive, yet the memory of it was nothing compared to Salvo's simple words. She reached out, touched his arm.

'I'm not beautiful,' she said. 'And I'm certainly no queen. But you are a saint.'

*

The trip there took two days. South through Germany, across the Alps, into Slovenia. They seemed to be toying with the seasons the whole way. From winter's edge, through a rapidly burgeoning spring with tulips and daffodils, back to snow and a biting wind, then out again into the valleys and plains of Slovenia, where ruddy cattle lay contented in the lush pasture, and the orchards frothed in white and pink.

Ljubljana, when they reached it, was just as Salvo had promised. A majestic city, yet modest in its scale. There were castles and stately mansions, white-walled houses that crouched low beneath the sweep of their red-tiled roofs. The placid Ljubljanica River seemed to idle in the town as though reluctant to move on, knowing that it had a long way to go. There were markets full of spring vegetables and flowers, neat parks, higgledy-piggledy cobbled streets. It felt bright, untrammelled; a place that history had made not by design, not by conquest or royal demand, but by the simple accretion of time. Real people, real events. Chance and fate.

In their few days there, Salvo tried to fill her with his stories of the place – its buildings, its history, its legends and myths. He told her about the earthquake in 1511, which had destroyed most of the town, and how it had been rebuilt in the form she now saw. 'You see,' he said. 'Out of rubble, beautiful things grow.'

He told her the story of the dragon that guarded the Dragon Bridge. 'You know Jason?' he said. 'Man with golden fleece. He steal fleece from King of Black Sea. Yes?'

Zarrin nodded, though doubtful about how much she really knew.

'King very angry,' Salvo continued. 'Hopping mad. Jason stole daughter too. Daughter beautiful – dark eyes, black hair, skin like satin. Fleece only one in world. King not sure which he miss most, fleece or daughter, so he chase Jason all way up Danube. Jason, though, good sailor, go anywhere in his ships. He lead them here. But river become too shallow, and even Jason not able to go any further, so he decide that they take ships apart and carry them across land, to Adriatic. But weather too bad, so he order men to wait there until spring. They build camp, settle down – men with food and beer, Jason with pretty princess on his golden fleece. Then – boom, bang. All hell break loose. Great spitting monster fly over camp, breathing fire. Sailors run off, jump into marshes to save themselves. Half camp burn down. Jason make choice: either kill dragon and live here for while or go back, face angry father of beautiful princess. Dragon easier, he think. So he make canoe, take princess with him, go hunt dragon down. Which way to go? Easy, he decide: where dragon has home, nothing else live, so he go where no sounds, no birds, no animals to be seen. Find dragon in his lair.'

Salvo paused, smiled.

'All true,' he said. 'Not just blah-blah, like stories on news. Not like stories priests and imams tell you.'

He eyed Zarrin mischievously, as if waiting for a reaction. When she offered none, he continued.

'Now come clever part. Why bring princess with him on dangerous venture, you wonder? Why not leave in camp? Maybe not trust other Argonauts with pretty woman, you think. Or maybe because dragon return and take her. No, Jason have better reason. Princess know magic spells. Already used one to get golden fleece. Now he send her ahead, to cast spell over dragon, with her beautiful singing. That what she do. Then Jason creep in and try to slay dragon. But sword not able to cut through dragon-hide. Instead, princess tell him bind mouth of dragon with chains. "And I have chains here," she say. "Just right for job." So he do this, and they flee back to camp. Dragon wake up, all angry and confused from dreams. Chains stop him breathing. He try to escape, but chains too strong. Dragon struggle and struggle, all that fire inside getting hotter and hotter, until – pouf! Dragon explode. Fire and sparks, pieces of dragon everywhere. Bad mess. End of dragon!'

Salvo had told the story as he did most of his stories, with humour and a touch of parody, yet with a sort of reverence too. As though it were oral history, and in telling it he was keeping it alive. Yet, as she listened, Zarrin wondered whether he was telling it, too, for a more personal reason, as if to give her a message of some sort. He as the hero, she as the princess, and what they were together – each dependent on the other, their combined strength. Or about the role that he yet had to play. Dragon-slayer.

She laughed, therefore, but gently – from pleasure rather than amusement – and said, 'Thank you, Salvo. It's a lovely story.'

Salvo wiped his brow, nodded, his face serious. 'See?' he said. 'More than one way to kill dragon, like skinning cat.' Then he smiled again. 'Ljubljana know that. That how it survive, while countries all round fight and invade and try to squash it. Build Dragon Bridge in honour. Have dragon carnival, every year. Big parade, feast, lots of fireworks. Dragon explode all over again.'

On their last day there, he told her more about the place, the personal story. He showed her the street where he had been born, had grown up. It was small, nondescript, part of a village that had been swallowed up by the expansion of the town twenty years before. The house was gone, he explained. It had been both home and business – his father had been a cobbler, like his father before him. Now, where the shop had been, there were faceless apartments.

'And your parents?' Zarrin asked, as they turned and began to walk away. 'Where are they?'

Salvo pointed down, then smiled and glanced upward. 'Or perhaps up there. They wanted that, believed in place. Not like me.' He walked on, then said, 'They old before their time. The old life – the Communists – make them like that. But then, when world change, when wall pulled down and they find that Slovenia in Europe – you know, with Disney and McDonald's and all other American shit – they not able to cope. They yearn for old life again. They die of confusion,

I think, and regret. For not knowing when they happy, or what happiness really is.'

Zarrin nodded, hearing the poignancy in his words. Then she asked, 'Are you the only child?'

Salvo laughed. 'No. We Catholics, remember. Six of us. And sister who died young.'

'Do they live here?'

'No. One sister in USA. She marry Christian man – priest in big church with lots of singing and hugging. She have children – make me uncle. Make my parents proud. Other sister, young one, run away when fifteen. No news for years.' He shrugged. 'Rest, brothers. Like me, not much use. One work on oil rigs. Good money, bad life. One marry crazy woman, slowly go crazy himself. He drink too much, kill himself one day. Other just waster. Not work, gamble away money my parents left.' He shook his head, sadly. 'World better place without us.'

Zarrin had met this sadness and despair in him before, though had assumed that it came from his own experience – the wife that she'd assumed he'd had, and perhaps lost. But perhaps it went deeper, she thought, stretched further, out into the reaches of his family and his world.

'Not without you,' she said. 'You're a good man. You make up for anything your brothers and sisters might have done.' She took his arm, slipped it beneath her own so that she could hold him to her, against her side. 'You have given Elend and me a new life. Not many people do anything as precious as that.'

That evening, he took her to a restaurant: a traditional *gostilna* with low ceilings, rough-plastered walls, heavy furniture; a sense of welcome. He had never done this before, taken her out like this, and she could not help wondering about the motive. At his insistence, she dressed in the best clothes she had. Black trousers, a dark red blouse that he'd bought for her from a market stall in town earlier in the day. A scarf of midnight blue, the token she needed in place of the hijab that she rarely now wore. None of it stylish by any means, and nothing like the dresses that she once would have worn, with their drop sleeves, bright colours, flowing lines. But for that evening she felt as high-born and special as she ever had.

They sat at a table by the window, watching the evening bustle in the small street outside. Elend sat in a high-chair, placed beside her, his eyes bright with interest. Salvo studied the menu alone, chose the food. 'Slovenian,' he said. 'You not understand. You not know what good for you.'

When the waiter returned, he gave the order, and the waiter glanced at Zarrin as he wrote it down, nodded, smiled.

'What did you say to him?' she asked.

'I tell you later.'

When the wine came, he poured her a glass, though he knew that she almost never drank alcohol. Then he said, 'I tell waiter, I bring special lady to his restaurant. She deserve best food in house. She a princess.' He raised his glass towards her. 'Now I toast her. To Zarrin. My beautiful princess.'

Zarrin blushed, lowered her eyes, sipped at the wine. But then she returned the gesture. 'To Salvo,' she said. 'My own dragon-slayer.'

*

That night the weather, which had been calm and balmy, changed. Storms swept down from the mountains, with thunder and hammering rain. They were sleeping in the cab: Zarrin and Elend as they always did, on the bench behind the curtain, Salvo stretched out on the hammock above. The cab rocked in the wind; the rain lashed the roof. Zarrin lay awake for a long time, thinking about the evening and what Salvo had said about his family, wondering what sort of life Elend would one day have. It had to be good, she knew; it had to be worthy. Only in that way would everything that had happened make sense. And, in its way, Salvo's family history gave her hope. Between him and his siblings, every sort of journey seemed to have been made, even though all had started from the same place. It wasn't just biology that decided it, but life itself. Yet within that, where were the decisions made? Could they be seen; were there clear moments of choice, or was it just the track of life, leading you on? A prepared road, or blind wandering and chance?

And what of Elend, she wondered; would this life she inflicted, transient and rootless, give him what he needed, make him good? She did not know.

*

In the morning, they headed north beneath broiling clouds, in squalling rain. The windscreen wipers worked in a frenzy, trying to fling the water away. The highway was almost invisible. They seemed to move suspended within a swirl of raindrops and mist.

Somewhere in the foothills of the mountains, as they approached the border, there was warning of a diversion because of floods or a road-slip ahead. Salvo grunted, swung the vehicle off down a narrower side-lane. 'I know better way,' he said. 'Further, but away from mountains. Out of this rain.'

As ever, his instinct was good. Within an hour they were beyond the worst of the storm, and driving along an empty by-road, between sodden orchards and fields. The clouds had lifted, and the rain lessened to showers and drizzle. Beside the road was a railway track. Zarrin sat, watching its rhythmic passage, as the sleepers and rails slid by. It was hypnotic, strangely soothing. She tried to show Elend, but he seemed unable to see it, and just reached for the teasing traces of rain on the window.

A dark shape flashed past – a control box or piece of signalling. Then another. Then a cluster together. She peered into the mirror, trying to detect what she'd seen. And then there were more. They were people, walking along the railway track. Groups of them, bent against the rain. Workers? Passengers from a broken-down train, plodding to the nearest station? Then realisation struck. They were migrants, refugees. Scores of them. Perhaps hundreds.

She glanced at Salvo, wondering whether he had noticed. But he was staring ahead, focused on the road.

She looked again at the railway. There was no one there. The people were behind them, out of sight. The track curved away, disappeared amidst trees.

She sat, pondering what she had witnessed. Were they Syrians, she wondered; more refugees from the war? Or was this some new wave of migrants from some other disaster that hadn't yet hit the news? Or one that had simply been going on for too long, lost its sense of horror, so that no one bothered to mention it any more. Afghanistan, Iraq, Yemen. Drought in Africa. Oppression in a country she had hardly ever heard of and couldn't place.

She remembered the man's words in the café in Bulgaria, his warning – *ten, twenty times more* – and shivered.

They drove on. The rain intensified. Spray from the road clouded around them. Then the truck lurched. She gave a yelp of surprise, clutched Elend to her protectively. Salvo swore.

Outside the window, at the edge of the road, she saw the blur of another dark shape. She knew at once what it was. Another refugee. As she looked in the mirror, straining to see through the fog of raindrops, the shape resolved itself, became a woman, two children, one holding each hand. They were already diminishing, becoming lost in the swirling spray.

'Stop,' she said. 'Stop!'

'Why? What's wrong?'

'Those people. That woman. They need help.'

'No worry. I missed them,' Salvo said, eyes on the road ahead. 'No thanks to them. Almost invisible in this rain.'

'No, we should help them. Give them a lift.'

Salvo shook his head.

'Why not?'

Salvo shrugged. Why them, he asked; why not all the others? How could anyone help?

Zarrin tried to argue against him, countering that it was a mother and her children, on their own. They needed a lift.

'We almost at border,' Salvo said. 'What then?'

'We could take them somewhere. To the next town?'

The argument became fiercer. She tried to plead on their behalf, but Salvo was adamant. It was too risky. It might be free movement across EU borders, but the police were on the watch. They took no notice of one woman in a truck; a whole group would be different. And, if they found them, they would find Zarrin too. None of them with papers. Every one of them illegal. What then?

'This not Romania,' he said. 'Bribery not work here. Police make money different way – catch thieves, arrest illegal immigrants.'

She continued to argue, even though by then the people she'd seen were kilometres away. But, as they passed into

Austria, she fell silent. There was a tension between them unlike any that she'd felt before.

By the time she woke the next morning, though, Salvo's spirits seemed to have revived. He was moving around the small borrowed room, in his trousers and vest, whistling, teasing Elend with his looks and strange noises, a cup of tea ready for her in his hand. She took the tea, thanked him, tried to let go of her own lingering sense of hurt. She couldn't quite do it. But she managed a smile, a word of thanks, and it seemed to be enough for Salvo.

For the next few days, she couldn't shake the sense of betrayal and disgrace away. She was shamed by what she had witnessed, angered by Salvo's inability to understand, made guilty by her own privilege. It wasn't *why them* that she wanted to know, but why her, why Elend?

Salvo seemed to notice, and redoubled his efforts to make amends. He was solicitous, jokey, prattled even more than usual as if he feared that another silence between them would be impossible to break. Zarrin tried to respond in kind, but the sourness remained. How much was due to what had happened, and how much to the period she was experiencing, and the fatigue of the travelling they'd done, she couldn't tell.

But, in the end, the mood dissipated. Watching the landscape slip past her outside the window, the shapes of the houses change as they moved from one region to another, as the farmland opened out into broad fields of young wheat, then closed again to vines and olive orchards, then changed once more to forest and castle and cliff, it seemed impossible to doubt the timelessness of it all. The permanence of the life she now had. Salvo – her dragon-slayer – at her side.

9

Contract

Almost as soon as Salvo left, Zarrin missed him, and began to pine for his return.

They had been outside Rotterdam, bound for Lille, when his mobile phone had rung. A strident, jangling tune, the device writhing across the dashboard like a tortured animal. Salvo had signalled, pulled over onto the hard shoulder, stopped. The road was busy, trucks and buses and cars streaming by in an endless flow. Salvo spoke in Slovenian as he answered the call – words Zarrin couldn't understand. Then he opened the door, got down from the truck, moved to the safety of the verge. The call went on for several minutes. A police car drove past, slowed. Salvo waved his hand to them, indicating that it was nothing serious. They drove off.

When he got back into the cab, he told her the news. He had a new job, an urgent one.

'How urgent?'

'Start this evening. Straight away.'

'Where?' she asked. 'Where are we going?'

'Not you.' He spoke brusquely. 'Outside Schengen. Not allowed.'

Her face fell. 'How long?'

Salvo shrugged. 'Five days, a week maybe. Not sure.'

The flat in Brussels wasn't available, Zarrin knew; Salvo's Slovenian friends were there. She asked where she and Elend would stay.

'I fix something,' Salvo said. 'After I drop load, I find somewhere, take you.'

He took her to Calais. Zarrin was quiet as they drove there, trying to picture the days ahead. He'd done trips without her before – trips outside the Schengen zone, or when he'd had to work with another driver to complete the trip in time – but then she'd always been able to stay in the flat in Brussels. She'd been in a place she knew, the nearest she had to call her home. She had never been to Calais. Would she like it? She asked Salvo: what's it like?

'Calais?' Salvo shrugged. 'Port. Like all ports; full of sailors.' He glanced at her, grinned. 'So Zarrin be careful. You know what sailors like.' Then he said, 'Town nothing special. Not like Ljubljana. But on a clear day, you see England. White cliffs of Dover. You like that.'

'I'll miss you,' she said.

But Salvo ignored the remark, or didn't hear it. 'You go there one day,' he continued. 'What you think?'

'Go where?'

'England. Like all refugees. England, Eldorado. Land of milk and honey.'

Now she laughed. 'You told me it was too wet, too cold.'

'You become English lady,' Salvo said. 'Become wife of big lord or duke. You think so?'

It was meant as a joke, she knew, and she tried to compose a reply that would match it, but none came.

'You live good life,' he said. 'They say "life of Riley". You be Mrs Riley, Lady Riley, with big house, servants, people touch forehead when you pass. You dream of that maybe?'

Again, she had tried to think of words to disabuse him. That wasn't what she dreamed of, she wanted to say, but the question came: what *did* she dream of; what future did she want? And she couldn't answer it.

'But house I take you to good, as well,' Salvo said. 'Nice holiday home for Zarrin and Elend, while Salvo work. You like that too.'

He was right. As they'd drawn up in front of it, she couldn't prevent a small cry of delight.

It was in Bleriot Plage, a small village, a kilometre or so west of Calais. The rest of the town was unattractive – the land flat and windswept, the centre a few blocks of narrow streets lined with cars, the newer areas just bland suburbs. But here, in the oldest part of the town, were whitewashed terraced houses – fishermen's cottages, perhaps – each with a pair of shuttered windows either side of the front door, tiny dormers poking from the roof above. Each had a painted door of a different colour. Theirs was blue.

Salvo searched for a moment until he found the key, tucked beneath a shoe-scraper beside the step, then stood back to let her in. The door stuck against the flagstone floor as she opened it, and he leaned past her, gave it a helpful push. Inside, the house was cold, damp from disuse, sparsely furnished. But the electricity worked, and upstairs were two bedrooms with simple box-beds. Salvo brought in her belongings from the truck, stowing them in the bedroom upstairs, while Zarrin prepared them a meal on the two-ring stove in the kitchen.

They ate in silence. As soon as they were finished, Salvo had prepared to leave. In the doorway, he hesitated, regarded Zarrin with a look almost of pleading in his eyes. She went to him, reached up, kissed his cheek.

'Go safely,' she said.

Still he had hesitated, as though there was more that he wanted to say. Or perhaps he wanted to take her into his arms, hold her. Then he'd turned, climbed into his cab, fired the engine, and with a quick wave, pulled away.

Now, in his absence, time dragged. To help it pass, Zarrin spent as much of the time as she could out with Elend. Spring had arrived in northern Europe, in a hurry as if late for its appointment. The cherry trees were suddenly laden with blossom; there were tulips and daffodils in the gardens; the ducks on the Watergang du Sud had become noisy, squabbling. Walking through the town, she couldn't help but take pleasure from the world. After life so long on the move, the stillness was a relief, and the time alone with Elend allowed her to study him and almost discover him anew.

When she found the nearby track to the beach, she took him there. As they walked along the sandy path between the dunes, Elend seemed to sense that something exciting lay ahead, and tugged at her hand. She let herself be dragged along. At sight of the water, he let go, took a half-pace forward, stopped.

He'd seen the sea before as they drove along the coast in one country or another, but never so close. Zarrin laughed.

'Come with me,' she said.

She picked him up, took him to its edge, kicked off her shoes and paddled in the shallows, holding him against her side. He wriggled, wanted to be put down. She held him out, let him touch the frothing swash, stood him in the water. He giggled, kicked, tried to break free from her. She released his hand and he stood swaying with the waves. A larger one caught him, and knocked him down. He hauled himself up. Three times it happened. Each time, he got back to his feet, stood there again, defiant. How long he would have stayed there, trying to withstand the waves, she didn't know. She took his hand and, with promises of an ice-cream on the way, led him back to the house.

It became a daily ritual, and he seemed to wait for it, impatiently.

Salvo returned after nine days. He looked tired, relieved to be back. She asked about the trip. While he'd been away, he'd texted often, brief messages telling her little except to confirm that everything was well and he was still travelling. But he'd rung twice. Both times the mobile coverage was poor, so that his voice had surged and faded as if borne on some wayward wind. She longed to hear him talk again, to see him laugh. Yet, now, he seemed drained of words, and there was no smile left in him. It had gone well, he told her. But when she tried to find out where he had been, he was vague.

'All over,' he said. 'Everywhere.'

'And no trouble?'

He shook his head. 'No trouble.'

'What now?'

'Now I rest. Now I sleep.'

'And then?'

He shrugged. 'We see.'

He was home for three days, then another telephone call, late at night. The next day, he went away again. He returned as he had the first time, exhausted and uncommunicative. She imagined him driving huge distances, for long hours, far in excess of what the law allowed.

She chided him, telling him that she didn't like this new work of his, however much it paid.

'No more for moment,' he told her. 'Now life normal again.'

For the next two weeks they travelled together once more, shorter trips into the Netherlands, up to Denmark, then to Paris and Dusseldorf. Once, he stopped by a lake, and sat with Zarrin and Elend on a bench, looking across the steely water to the hills beyond.

All of a sudden, he said, 'Elend is little treasure. You know this?'

'Of course I do.'

'He is like son to me. I love him like one.'

She reached out, touched his arm. 'And he loves you, I know.'

For a long moment she let her hand lie there, while she wondered whether the seal of affection between them had at last been made. Not directly, but implicitly through Elend. Whether Salvo had been declaring his love for her too; whether her own words back had meant the same.

'And you like daughter,' he said. 'Daughter I never had.'

The paradox stabbed at her – son, daughter – and she felt herself flinch. Was that how he tried to reconcile his relationship with them, she wondered; was that the only way he could cope?

She waited for him to say more, to explain, but he remained silent, staring out across the lake. Then, he said, 'I do anything for you.'

She gripped his arm more tightly, leaned her head against his shoulder. She felt the touch of his lips on her head.

Then Salvo stood up, and suddenly light, matter-of-fact again, said, 'Now, road calling. Time to go.'

*

Once more, Zarrin waited for Salvo to return. She was back in Calais, in the same street, in the same house, with the same mist of anxiety around her. Why she felt like this she didn't know. He'd said nothing, done nothing, to alarm her. He was simply doing his job: the job he'd done for years, since long before she met him, and did well. And yet she fretted. Something about the way the work was organised, his hazy plans, the unstated destinations, didn't fit the Salvo she knew. The same with his mood of blankness when he returned. It was as if the trip had sucked his vigour from him, left just an empty shell.

She had hoped that the contract was finished, that his long journeys alone would be at an end. But a week earlier, as they were travelling through France, Salvo had had another call. He stopped the truck, started a conversation in Slovenian, jumped down from the cab. Zarrin watched him as he paced up and down the verge, phone against his ear, in earnest conversation. When he came back, he was frowning, intent.

'Change of plan,' he said. 'Drop this load today. Calais tomorrow. Another big trip.'

'Take us with you this time,' she said. 'Please.'

He shook his head. 'Not possible.'

'Why not?'

'I tell you before. Outside Schengen. Too dangerous.'

She knew that she was being unkind, loading him with guilt, and yet she wanted him to yield: not to take her, for she knew that wasn't possible, but to refuse the job, rescind whatever contract he'd made.

She almost threw his own words at him – that he would do anything for her – had to bite them back.

Their return to Calais had been made in grudging silence. The following morning, early, while she was sleeping, he had left once more. She'd heard his truck start up, outside on the street, hurried to the door, hoping to catch him and call him back. She wanted to hug him, like a real daughter would do. But by the time she got the door open, the truck was pulling away. She had stepped out, waved. Whether he saw, she couldn't tell. Above her, the seagulls swirled in the grey sky, screeching in contempt.

Now, she went through the ritual of busying herself in his absence. She went into town, spent time in the library, took Elend to the beach, walked with him along the Watergang, read to him, started to teach him the alphabet.

She counted the days away, one by one, some days almost by the hour. Texts came, but, as before, they merely marked Salvo's presence somewhere out there in the world, told her no more. She yearned to talk to him, to hear him explain: what he was doing, what was going on. He called just once. He was in a bar, she guessed; she could hear music and chatter in the background. She tried to ask him where he was, when he would be back, but the clamour must have swallowed her voice, for he simply repeated to her not to worry, that all was well.

For the next two days, there was nothing, not even a text. She rang his number, though she knew that when he was working his phone would be switched off: a distraction while he was driving, an unwanted intrusion when he wasn't and was trying to rest. He didn't answer. She left him a message, received no reply.

To divert herself, she spent more hours in the library, searching for news of Syria on the internet.

It was as depressing as ever. In between passing resolutions condemning the violence, the United Nations estimated that the human cost had risen to eighty thousand deaths. There were new claims of the use of chemical weapons by both sides, reports of bombing and missile strikes. Millions of displaced people, living amidst the rubble and terror. Hundreds of thousands of others, fleeing where they could: to Iraq, Jordan, Turkey, Europe.

Especially to Europe, of course. Where else would anyone go if they had an iota of choice? They came, it seemed, by every means possible: via Bulgaria, the way she had come; across the Aegean into Greece; through North Africa, then over the Mediterranean to Italy. Their stories littered the web. Telling of the horrors back in Syria – the bombing and shelling and hunger and disease and abuse. The hardships of the journeys. The obstacles and oppression on the way, the rare bright flickers of welcome and generosity. The boats trying to make the crossing from Africa to Italy, the deaths at sea.

Zarrin remembered the refugees she had seen as she drove with Salvo back from Slovenia. The woman and two children alone by the roadside in the rain. Just the first, she thought; the first of a countless tide.

She tried to double and redouble that picture, on and on, until it matched the scale of this tide – the sorts of numbers that they were quoting, the hundreds of thousands – to picture them, or even some small portion of them, squeezed into the camp in Turkey, limping along the railway tracks, lining the road. She tried to imagine their misery and fear, their hunger and thirst and boredom; to total it up.

But she couldn't. Even with her own experience to draw upon, it wasn't possible to accumulate the suffering of others in her mind. Suffering was always personal and unitary; it added only to the sum of your own life. The suffering of unknown others had no substance to it, and came to nothing.

She thought how lucky she'd been, setting out when she did. One of the first in this vast new migration, and compared to the others, perhaps, one with a more meagre excuse. Just her own life, her own sins – the simple beliefs and cruel cultures of her own people – to blame for it. How lucky, too, to have Salvo.

But then, a shock. As she walked home with Elend along the main street, she passed a shop selling televisions. One window displayed a dozen screens, each playing the same news programme. On each one, a voiceless face talking to the world with earnest intent; beneath it, a quickly changing headline. A Malaysian airliner crashed in Ukraine. More missile strikes in Gaza. Latest stage win in the Tour de France. Then, as she turned away, under the heading 'Breaking news', she caught the name 'Sinjari'. She swivelled around, looked again at the screen, saw the end of a headline, disappearing: '…President of the Council.'

What had she seen? What did it mean? Was Rohat here, in Belgium? Meeting the President of the European Council?

She waited for the headline to reappear. But, with a flick, the channel on all the televisions changed, and the pictures turned to sport.

*

Her phone was ringing. She roused herself, blinked into the dim light of the room, got out of her chair. What time was it, she wondered; how long had she slept?

The journey back from the library had been full of fret and fear. Those glimpsed words on the television haunted her and filled her with dread. She tried to convince herself that she had imagined or misread them, but could not. She just wanted to get home and hide.

She wanted Salvo back. She wanted to travel with him again, away from Calais and Brussels, to a place where Rohat could not be.

Yet her progress was almost instantly thwarted. As if in proof of everything she'd been reading on the internet, Calais seemed to be seething with migrants and police. Halfway down the high street she was warned about it, by a young African man, hurrying in the other direction. The police were coming, he said, checking identity cards. They were making arrests. Doubly scared, she turned back, took a long detour along the canal, through the fields on the south side of town, before heading back towards the coast, and what for now was home.

It was almost dark by the time she reached it, and Elend was unsettled, moody. When at last he was fed, she played with him for a while, then made herself a simple meal, ate it quickly, sat down with him and sang to him, until he dozed again. All the time, her mind went over and over the news she had seen on the television, tried to make sense of it, tried to decide: imagination or fact? What should she do?

She turned on her phone, searched for any mention of Rohat's visit to Brussels, couldn't find any. She turned on the radio, listened to the hourly news summary. There was nothing there, either.

Some time afterwards, she must have fallen asleep herself.

Now, sleep still clogged her mind. She found the phone, puzzled at the number – one she didn't recognise – accepted the call nonetheless.

'Zarrin – it's Salvo. Listen to me.'

Salvo's voice was clear, urgent. She knew at once that he was in difficulties and tried to ask: what was wrong?

'No, listen. I not have long. Listen. Salvo in trouble. Big trouble. Been to Serbia, like on trips before. Police in Hungary stop me on way back. They search truck. They find people in back. Refugees. One very ill. Later she die. They arrest me. Say I charged with murder, go to prison, lose truck. Pay big fine. I say I innocent but they not care.'

Zarrin listened to him in shock, struggling to understand what he was saying. Refugees. Murder. Prison. It made no sense. On the line, there was silence, and she asked the only questions that came into her head. 'How did they get there? Didn't you know?'

But he ignored her, said again, 'Listen. You do as I say. Must promise, and do it now. Promise?'

'Salvo. I don't understand. What were you doing?'

'No time. Just promise. Please.'

'Promise what?'

'You must leave. Go to England.'

'I can't. I can't leave you.'

'You must. They find out about you. Come and catch you. You not safe for long. You go now. Go to England like we said. Promise.'

'No!'

'Please, please.'

'Alright. I promise. But I don't want to. I don't know how.'

'Listen. I give you name, address. Friend. You go there. He help. He take you.'

'No.'

'Café Rudolphe. Guemps. Opposite church. You go there. Ask for Emile. Go tomorrow. He wait until noon. I leave you money in drawer – where I leave tax forms. Take money. Go. Go tomorrow.'

There was a noise on the phone, voices calling.

'Salvo!' she cried.

'You do it,' Salvo said. 'You do it like you promise. Not wait for me. You have good life.' There were more noises, a grunt as if of pain.

'I love you like daughter,' Salvo said. 'Love Elend too. You give him good life.'

Then the phone went dead.

*

What had happened to Salvo, she never found out, though she tried to imagine, guessed. And, with the guessing, the burden of guilt came down like a mountain upon her, making her weep.

He had taken her words to heart, she thought – those words of anger and disdain when he had refused to stop for the woman and two children in Slovenia. He had been burned by them, scarred. He believed that she had lost her belief in him, that he was no longer her hero but a weak and flawed man, no better than the rest. He didn't want to be that, couldn't bear the thought of it. He was her dragon-slayer. She had told him so. And dragon slayers were afraid of nothing.

Somehow, amongst his contacts and friends, he must have had a connection with one of the gangs who arranged to smuggle refugees in, or perhaps just someone who could provide him with a contract that would give him the cover he needed. Maybe he just went there unplanned, and took his chances. However he had managed it, he had got himself to the Serbian border, collected a group of refugees – or turned a blind eye while they scrambled on board – and shut them in. Driven them into Europe.

And one woman had died.

She wondered how it had happened. Had she already been ill? Or had she suffocated, like the helpless people she'd read about on the web? Had Salvo shut them in without any air to breathe?

Not that, she thought; he would never do that.

And other questions, piling upon her, demanding their answers. How many? How many trips, how many people? How much did the police know?

What would happen to him? Did he have a lawyer? Might he be released without charge; would he be fined? Would he go to prison? How long?

Where was he now? How could she help?

She felt herself floundering, close to panic, fought to make herself calm.

She vowed that she would wait for him, however long it would be. She owed him that, for everything that he'd done for her. And for what she'd done to him. Somehow she would get news of him, make contact. She'd beg and plead on his behalf.

But in one breath her hope and determination cracked, and despair flooded in. What influence did she have – an illegal refugee? And she'd read enough about other smugglers caught like this to know what their fate would be. The drivers arrested red-handed on the Balkan borders, the boat-owners on the Mediterranean route. Long months in prison waiting for a trial; when it happened, a quick, arbitrary decision and sentence. The truck or boat confiscated, two years jail at least. For Salvo, it could be more.

What could she do?

His words came back to her. Go. Go to England. Have a good life.

The promise she'd made.

Which was worse, she wondered: to keep a promise that would hurt him, or to hurt him by breaking her promise?

She sat in the aftermath of the call for an hour, while the contradictions inside her raged. Elend tugged at her hand for attention, and she picked him up, cuddled him mindlessly. She lay in bed beside him and stared at the ceiling, her thoughts streaming past her like clouds on the wind. None of them with substance or shape.

At some point, she slept. And, in the morning, she relived what had happened all over again.

Guilt swept down on her once more. It was her fault. She had made him do it.

She tried to undo it by the sheer force of her will.

In some part of her thoughts, she prayed.

But Salvo's words would not quieten. *Go. Go to Guemps.*

She wouldn't…she would…she didn't know how.

She knocked on the door of the neighbouring house, asked the woman there, 'Where's Guemps? How do I get there? I have to go.'

It was out to the east, the woman explained, a dozen kilometres away. It was small, uninteresting. Nobody ever went there. But she gave her directions, nevertheless.

Still Zarrin prevaricated. If she was going, she had to leave immediately. The police might already be on the way. But could she? Could she leave? Could she abandon Salvo and just flee?

Yet, without him, what choice did she have? She felt alone, helpless, lost.

She thought of Rohat, even now perhaps in Brussels. No safety there.

She remembered Salvo's instructions, went to the small chest of drawers, opened it. In the bottom drawer was the satchel, in which he kept his business documents. She looked inside.

Amid the papers, a brown, padded envelope, unlabelled. It contained money – six hundred euros, and a twist of paper.

Wrapped in the paper, a ring. It was gold, looked old. His mother's? His wife's? A ring intended for her?

She didn't know.

Tears welled in her eyes.

*

'Are you Emile?'

The man looked at her, said nothing.

'Salvo sent me,' she said. 'He said you would help.'

The man turned back to the bar, picked up his glass – green absinthe – studied it. She remembered the other man, in the bar in Ruse. Were they all the same?

'I have money,' she said. 'How much do you want?'

He gave a small nod towards the counter.

She took out the wallet, lay it down.

The man drained his glass, held it up for the barman to take, waited for it be refilled. Then he opened the wallet, looked inside.

He flicked through the notes, extracted some, handed the wallet back. 'That's mine. The rest you can keep.'

'Thank you.'

The man looked at her, his eyes hard.

'People like you cause problems. Salvo is a good man. He deserves better than this, better than you.'

She nodded. 'I know.'

Then, with a quick toss of his head, he drained his glass again, banged it down.

'Come. We go.'

10

Camden

London came as yet another shock.

Emile had taken them only to the outskirts of Maidstone, and had left them there. He'd seemed relieved to get rid of them, glad that his part in the sordid business was done.

But he had clearly done this sort of thing before, for he had done it well. Hidden in the depths of his truck, in a false compartment in the trailer, they were invisible to all except the most thorough of searches, and the trip had been without incident. He knew, nevertheless, not to extend the risk of discovery any longer than necessary. On the outskirts of Maidstone he'd left the motorway, driven to an old quarry a mile or so outside the town, ordered them out.

He pointed across the fields, towards the town.

'You go that way,' he said. 'Two kilometres. Good luck.'

Then he'd slammed the door, bolted it, walked to his cab, and was gone.

Zarrin had led Elend across the fields to the town. There, she found the coach station, changed her euros at the exchange kiosk nearby, and took the first express bus. Sitting by the window, watching the road stream by, the tentacles of London take hold beyond the dark fringe of the verge, she'd tried to believe that what they were doing was a leap forward, to some better life – the sort of life that Salvo had joked about, teasing her. But the only thing she could feel was loss.

At the coach depot near Victoria Station, the city bludgeoned her with its sudden clamour and busyness. As she walked away, seeking somewhere they could stay – a hostel or a cheap hotel – she seemed to be engulfed by a forest of signs and streets and traffic. Everything was commotion. Cars and buses came at her on the wrong side of the road. Horns blared. People pushed past on the pavement. Lights and music blasted from the shops.

For the first week, they stayed at a small hotel that she found in the back streets of Shepherd's Bush. She had headed towards the area, following one of the road signs, for no other reason than that the name sounded bucolic and placid, like the place she had grown up in with its pastures and sheep and goats. But, walking around the drab and dark housing estates, the brash shopping areas with their takeaways and pubs and all-night stores, she'd realised how deceitful London was, how nothing was what it claimed. It was the same with the hotel. It was called the Lord Argyll, and enticed her in through a glass-panelled door between two white stucco columns, to a small but brightly lit foyer. Beyond, though, was a different world. Worn carpets, dark stairways, peeling plaster. Her room was cramped, in the basement, almost windowless. Outside, the lift clunked and clattered through the night. And the price she had been quoted – thirty-five pounds a night – was just one part of the cost. Breakfast was extra. She had nowhere to cook, nor to wash or dry clothes. And at weekends there was another ten pounds a night to pay. All too soon, she felt the money Salvo had given her dwindling, and knew that she must move on. She found a hostel, stayed there for three nights – the maximum that was allowed. Another seventy-five pounds gone.

Then she resigned herself to their lot – two more vagrants, two more homeless, making do on the streets. There seemed to be no end of those, she discovered, as she gradually worked out the hidden social structure of the city, and found her place within it. In the day, they sat slumped on the pavement outside shops and railway stations, or on park benches, or huddled in small groups on a patch of waste ground. At night, they gathered under the archways of road and railway bridges, ignoring the rumbling trucks and trains, or rolled themselves beneath their tattered mounds of blankets in dark alleys and doorways, their backs turned to the world. Some were accompanied by demons of one sort or another. They were drunk or high on drugs, muttered to themselves or shouted wild obscenities and accusations, baulked at scenes that they alone could see, coughed, spat at passers-by. But many were like Zarrin, simply lost and with nowhere to go. Old women, pushing trolley-loads of belongings. Mothers with children. Teenage girls. Young boys, some no more than twelve years old, but already hardened to life on the streets.

When there was no choice, Zarrin joined them, finding space for herself and Elend in the places they slept. On other nights she sought a place apart. In the loading bay of a supermarket, using a pile of discarded cardboard as a makeshift bed. On a bench by the river, in a bus shelter, in a pedestrian subway. None of them pristine, each one bearing the marks of previous occupants – but hers and Elend's for a night.

All the time, during the day, she searched for work, wheeling Elend in ever wider circles around the town in an old buggy she'd found in a skip. Hammersmith, White City, Fulham, Paddington, Kensal Green, Notting Hill. Nowhere wanted her. Nowhere had jobs to offer, especially for a woman like her, with a young child in tow. She tried to be rational, to see her predicament from the outside rather than from the dark centre of it where she was held. Yet no answers came. Just more walking, more searching, more knocking on doors.

Late one morning, unsuccessful again, she stood outside a greengrocer's, surveying the fruit on display, wondering what she might be able to afford. A blackened banana perhaps. A bruised pear. Elend was in his buggy beside her. She let her thoughts drift, remembering the fruit she had eaten as a child: watermelons, pomegranates, succulent figs.

She thought of Salvo, took out her phone and rang his number, as she had so many times since she'd fled. There was a recorded message back, in French: *this number does not exist*.

'I hope you intend to pay for that.' It was the shopkeeper. He stood in the doorway, hands on his hips, the classic pose of the outraged.

Zarrin looked down. Elend had helped himself to a peach from a punnet on the stall, was eating messily, the evidence smeared across his face.

She apologised, promised to pay, picked up the whole punnet as proof of her integrity.

'Two pounds,' he said, and then, in Kurmanji, 'One pound to you.'

She smiled, replied in the same language. 'How did you know?'

He shrugged. 'I didn't. But it was a simple test.' He indicated Elend. 'He's a nice boy. What's his name?'

She told him, and he said, 'That's a good name. Daybreak. New dawn. I wish I could be that again, don't you?'

Zarrin nodded as she handed over the money, then, encouraged by the man's kindness, said, 'I'm looking for a job. Do you know anyone who might have something?'

The man looked at her, assessing, but with humanity in his eyes. 'A refugee? No work permit?' He didn't wait for confirmation or denial. 'I don't know of any. But you're doing the right thing. Go to the stores. The ones run by people like me, Arabs, Afghans, Syrians. Someone will help. If not today, then tomorrow, *inshallah*.'

It seemed like good advice, and she accepted it gladly. In times of despair, she reflected, that was sometimes all you needed – a word of encouragement and direction; something to give you cause. The rest of that day, much of the next, she wandered from shop to shop, seeking out ones that seemed to be run by Muslims. Twice she came close. One of the owners knew someone, he said, who was looking for temporary staff in his launderette. He rang up for her, shook his head sadly as he put the phone down. 'Sorry. Just too late.' Another sent her to a café nearby, but when the manager learned that she had no papers he too shook his head, apologised. 'I would if I could,' he said. 'But if I got caught employing you, I'd be dead.'

Again, disappointment welled inside her, threatened to turn to dismay. Then, late in the evening, in a back street in King's Cross, she asked a woman in a Moroccan store, and the woman simply nodded. 'Of course.'

'Where? What?' Zarrin asked.

'At the market. Camden, up the road. They always want people to help. Just be there in the morning, early. Six o'clock. No later. Someone will take you on.'

Early the next morning, she went to Camden and prowled the market halls and streets, approaching any stallholder she could find, asking if they wanted help. For the first hour she was luckless, but then a tall, beak-nosed man saw her talking to another stallholder and called her over. Within minutes she'd been hired; ten minutes later had been set to work unloading the first van-load of produce. After that, while the stallholder stood, his mobile phone to his ear, furrow-browed at whatever tale of woe or excuse or reluctant increase in prices he was being told, she set out the stall, making it as attractive as she could, and then cleaned up the mess of boxes and wrapping and loose leaves and spilled soil. As she worked, Elend played contentedly under the stall, making dens and trains and trucks and beds out of the boxes, burying himself in their midst.

When she'd finished, the stallholder came across, looked at her handiwork, shifted a sign here, a banana there, and said, 'OK. You didn't do so bad.'

It was, she guessed, better than he'd expected of her, better perhaps than whoever had done the work before, because later he asked, 'Can you do this every day?'

Nothing had been said about wages, nor hours, nor even his name. But he'd not asked about papers, either, and for that reason she nodded.

'OK. For now, you can help me sell. We're going to be busy.' Then he held out a hand. 'I'm Dinos. You?

'Zarrin,' she said.

'Sandrin?'

It was close enough. She nodded.

'Yes.'

'And the boy?'

'Elend.'

'Alan. OK, him too.'

During a brief lull in business just before lunchtime, he told her what had happened – why he'd snatched at her help so urgently. Micky, the school-leaver whom he'd hired a month ago, had failed to turn up. It wasn't the first time, but as of now it was the last. He was about to learn that he'd been sacked.

For a moment Zarrin felt ashamed – that she was the cause of someone else's ill fortune seemed unfair. The stallholder saw it, perhaps, for he grinned. 'Hey, Sandrin, don't look so upset. It's not your fault. The bastard should get up in the morning, stop smoking crack.'

As the day wore on, Zarrin found herself more and more left alone. In the early afternoon, as the trade slackened a little, the owner disappeared for lunch, didn't return until nearly three. Soon after that, the place became quiet and she was told to start packing up. While she was stacking the empty crates, sorting out the good produce from the bruised and the bad, he drifted away again without a word. Then there was a new flurry of activity. Elderly women, harassed mothers, refugees like herself, all hunting for those bargains that could only be found at the end of the day – the food no one else would want. Was she meant to charge them, she wondered, as she let them pick through the rejects, or did they just help themselves? But they seemed to know the rules. They held up their pickings, asked, 'How much?' or suggested a price: '10p the lot.' She took whatever they offered; when she had to, named a token price; sometimes, just shrugged and nodded towards the exit. 'God bless you,' an old man said, as he shuffled away with a scabbed aubergine and a wilting lettuce clutched to his chest. But then, as he passed the end of the stall, she saw his hand sneak out and two perfect tomatoes disappear into his pocket from the top of a box.

By the time Dinos returned, it was nearly half-past four. The stall was packed up. The rest of the market, too, was closing. He nodded at her, said, 'OK. I'll sort things out from here,' then turned away. She stood, waiting, wondering whether she was meant to leave, whether she should ask now for her wages.

He noticed, looked back. 'It's alright,' he said. 'Same time tomorrow. I'll pay you Saturday. OK?'

She thanked him, called Elend and left.

For the next three months, she worked with Dinos. He was true to his word, paid her at the end of each week – not handsomely, but enough to seem fair. One hundred and sixty-two pounds for six days' work, nine hard hours a day. It was well below the minimum wage, she knew, but there was no tax, and no questions asked. With the picked-over and battered fruit that she was allowed to take home, like the beggars and scroungers who came at the end of the day, she could live off that. She found a room a few tube stops away in a small maisonette. It was owned by an elderly woman, almost crippled with arthritis, who moved around painfully hunched over her stick. But Mrs Jervais was a kindly soul, and welcomed the company, not just of Zarrin but Elend, too. In return for that – the company – and a few small errands, she kept the rent low, and gladly looked after Elend during the day.

Zarrin enjoyed her work. She enjoyed, too, the buzz of people around her. The myriad voices speaking in different accents, different languages, tongues she couldn't recognise, made her feel at home there, and safe: just one of the many and thus of no special account. As she worked, she watched them and tried to read them, to peer into their lives. The bent Jewish man, who arrived early each morning, before the market was officially open, buying salad for his café in Primrose Hill: always the best, fresh, as untouched as possible; always just enough for his needs – never too much. A boy who came on random mornings, once or twice a week on his way to school, and always bought the same things: two Braeburn apples, a pound of onions, three sticks of celery, one red cabbage. For what purpose she didn't know, and couldn't guess. A trio of well-dressed young women who appeared a little later, looking for vegetables. They ran a soup kitchen, they told Zarrin when she asked, then laughed. 'No, not that sort. Not for the homeless, not for bums and no-hopers, and people like that.' The name was sardonic, they explained – a joke to make their clients laugh. This was a high-class establishment, selling authentic soups, home-made, to busy businessmen for their lunch. Customers texted in their orders and the soup would be ready waiting in returnable earthenware pots, with tightly fitting lids, when they – or their PAs – turned up to collect them at the allotted time. As the day wore on, she watched the harassed mothers who shopped on their way home from work, the single men, self-consciously choosing things that were safe – things their mothers had taught them to cook.

And at the end of the day, she watched out for the 'bums and no-hopers', and did her best to give them some hope, saving for them something special when she could, giving them a little more than they might expect.

She watched the other stallholders, too, and sometimes caught them watching her back. Next to Dinos's pitch, on one side was a bookstall. The old man who ran it seemed either tired or timid, or perhaps both, for after he'd set it out each morning he'd retire to a chair behind the table, where he'd sit, head down, stroking a small ginger cat. He seemed to sell little, and put little effort into the task. If potential customers came, he'd let them browse without the slightest hint of awareness or interest. If they offered him money he'd accept it; if he had to, would scuffle in a tin box with half-gloved hands in search of change. Otherwise, he seemed content to let them go. Perhaps he wasn't there for the money at all, but just to fill his day; to reflect on the life or a wife that had gone, or of either that had never been.

On the other side was a stall offering holistic health products and aromatherapy. It sold mainly soaps and scents and candles, and was run by a colourfully dressed and haired woman of indeterminate age – somewhere between twenty-five and fifty, Zarrin guessed. Her name was Josey or Joycie or something like that, and her selling technique was simple. She would stand in front of her stall and grab the arm of any likely-looking customer and steer them to the display. She liked couples mainly, and if she grabbed the man she would lean against him, nestling against his side as though she were his *amore*, whispering into his ear as she seduced him, no doubt, with promises of what her wonderful products could do. Yet she could work just as well on the women. Then, she would engage in a private conversation, interspersed with assessing glances towards the man. *You've a good man there*, her look might say; *you need to do everything you can to keep him.* Or equally: *you've a bit of a dunce with that one; you'd attract something better with a bit of what I have to offer you at a very good price.*

Opposite, there was another greengrocery stall – O'Farrell's – managed by a family of three: husband, wife and son, or so Zarrin deduced. On less busy days they'd

130

work in shifts, sharing the duties. At weekends, all three would be there, filling the air with their Cockney cries of encouragement and challenge, drowning out Dinos's more throaty calls. As a sales technique it seemed to work, for when she first came they were serving three customers to every two that Dinos's stall might attract.

Once, she asked Dinos about the situation, whether they were bent on stealing his trade, why he didn't fight back. He merely shrugged and said, 'They do things their way, I do them mine. There's room for more than one way of working in this world.' And, when she persisted, he shook his head as if to dismiss the subject and would say nothing more.

One morning, working alone, she resolved to take matters into her own hands. She stood for a while where the customers stood, asking herself what was wrong with their display, what might lure in more people. They were in a favourable location, easy to see, and the quality of the produce was good. The stall was laid out neatly, looked cared-for and clean. Yet it was just another stall for all that, and too easy to walk by.

She thought of the stalls she'd known in Syria, in the markets and souks. So flamboyant, so colourful and full of life. Could she do the same here?

In sudden earnestness, she started to take things off the stall, pile them back in the boxes, stripping the counter clear. The husband from the stall opposite laughed and called out, 'Leaving already? Not before time if you ask me.'

But then, piece by piece, she began to reassemble the produce. She built pyramids with the apples, ziggurats with the oranges, complex flower patterns with the brassicas, butterflies and huge spiders with the display of peppers and chillies and gourds. Soon she had a small crowd behind her, watching. When she'd finished, a ripple of applause rang around. By the time Dinos turned up, there was a queue waiting to buy from her, and apologising for spoiling her display. Each time she laughed and said, 'Oh, there's always more where that came from.'

Over the following weeks it became their trademark, each day a new creation. Often, people would stop and take photos of the stall. Sometimes, they asked Zarrin to pose with them. She always refused. 'I just help here,' she would say. 'Dinos is the artist. He does all the work.' Dinos beamed, and graciously had his photograph taken once more.

After a month, he put up her wages, only by a pound or so a day, but enough to embarrass him at his own generosity. 'Trade's been better lately,' he said. 'Since you came.' And then, to take away any hint of praise, any suggestion of cause and effect: 'You arrived just at the right time.'

Autumn came with winter close on its heels. The mornings, when she started, were dark and misty, the smell of the canal heavy on the air. Evenings arrived early, and quickly sucked the last light and warmth from the day. The stallholders looked like overstuffed ragdolls in their woollen jumpers and scarves, bobble-hats, fingerless gloves. Customers queued in anoraks and overcoats, and stamped their feet on the cold concrete as they marvelled at the display. And from the O'Farrells' stall opposite came the even frostier glare of jealousy and disdain. Comments were made.

'Stuck-up bitch,' she heard from the wife, on more than one occasion.

'Fucking Islamist,' her husband sneered, as he talked to a customer, with a quick glance towards Zarrin.

'Cock-teaser,' the son muttered, pushing past her as she leaned down to unpack a box of fruit.

Again she talked to Dinos about them. Once more, he brushed her concerns aside. 'Leave them be,' he said, then nodded towards their stall. 'That's their world over there. Here –' he tapped his foot on the floor '– on this side, is ours.'

Perhaps he was right, for the next week the atmosphere seemed to have changed. The O'Farrells still watched, talked amongst themselves, but the bitterness was no longer evident, and she heard no more comments.

On the following Saturday, however, there was a sudden commotion behind her. She looked around from the end of the stall where she was sorting out the last few boxes of produce. Dinos had his back to her, standing beside a woman in front of the display.

'It's her,' the woman shouted, peering past him, pointing at Zarrin. 'I know it is.'

'No, no, no,' Dinos said, his voice soothing, almost pleading. 'We're very careful here. Everything is good.'

'It's her fault,' the woman insisted. 'Look at her. You can see she's unclean.'

'No, don't say that. Please don't.'

'I tell you, I was poisoned. The doctor told me. He did tests. Campo something or other. Campo bacteria. It could have killed me.'

An audience was gathering now as customers paused in their shopping, looked around. On the O'Farrells' stall opposite, the family had broken off their trade, and were watching the pantomime. There was amusement on the wife's face, something keener on the man's – excitement, almost eagerness.

The woman puffed herself up, as if in acknowledgement of her role. 'Five days, it was,' she said. 'Five bloody days. I could hardly get off the bog for the bloody squits.'

133

Dinos's head fell; his body seemed to squirm. He muttered something that Zarrin couldn't hear.

'The tomatoes. That's what it was. No argument. She sold them to me. I remember looking at her, wondering when she last washed her hands.'

'I told you, we wash all the time. Look, we have basin there.'

'Not that one. She's an Arab. Or a Turk, or something. They're all the same. None of them wash.'

Briefly, Dinos's sense of honour got the better of him, and he fought back. 'No. You can't say that. It's not true. And it's not legal. If you talk like that again, I'll call the police.'

'Go on, then. Call them. See what happens.'

Zarrin felt a flood of fear. If the police came, they would ask for her papers. Then, everything would be lost.

'Compensation,' the woman said. 'That's what I need. That's what I deserve. Else I've no choice but to report you.'

'Not report, no,' Dinos pleaded. 'That's not necessary.'

'So, how much? Five days off work. Doctor's bills. The pain and humiliation. How much is all that worth?'

'One hundred pound?' Dinos asked, tentatively.

'Two.'

'One-fifty. I can give you that now.'

'Alright.' Then she turned, stabbed a finger at Zarrin. 'But you'll have to get rid of her as well.'

Later, Dinos came to Zarrin, apologised, said that he had no choice. 'But you have to go. I'm sorry. I can't take the risk.'

'It wasn't me,' she said.

'I know.'

'It was them!' She glared across the aisle. 'I can't prove it, but I know it was. They've been jealous of your success. And they hate me – they're racists.'

Dinos nodded, but he looked away, eyes wide with panic. 'I know. Yes, I know.'

'Then why do you let them get away with it? Why don't you stand up to them?'

He spread his hands in supplication. 'How can I? We argue with the woman, and the police come. We accuse them, and they call the police. I make a fuss and it happens again. I lose each time. You do, too.'

She nodded. She knew he was right. She knew that if the police became involved, without papers she'd lose more than anyone. But in that moment she hated him. She hated all the prejudice and hatred in the world, and what it changed people into, herself included.

11

Yaasmin

Dark. Dark streets, dark houses, a deep darkness inside her, too. The whole world seemed dark.

The city could be everything, she realised. It had its own character, its own moods. Those days after she had first arrived, it had appeared broken and contorted, a place with no pattern she could see. Later, when she'd been working with Dinos, she had gone one morning to the hill at Greenwich and looked across its vast stretch and marvelled at how bright it seemed, reflecting back the sky and sun from every roof and window, from the white concrete and silver steel of new buildings, from cars and buses as they plied their way along the roads, the tinsel twist of the river. On other nights, from her room in Highgate Hill, it had been a huge, glowing dome, overlaid upon the scribbled patterns of the streets and shops and houses, like a child's snow-globe, waiting to be shaken. On evenings when she'd prowled the city centre in search of work, it had been full of noise and movement, light that was never still, sparkling, flashing, streaming, blurring, as if the whole edifice of the city was urgently, garishly reforming itself around her.

Now, though, it had turned black and brooding. All light gone. She walked along unlit back roads, past houses that were dark and huddled, between shadowy parks and cemeteries, patches of dark waste ground, a derelict factory, a boarded-up pub, black alleyways and ginnels where anything or anyone might lurk, unseen.

She understood that mood, that darkness, and shared it.

Four months had passed since she left the market, three since she'd been forced to leave her room with Mrs Jervais. The first had angered her and left her bitter, although as the days went by the bitterness had dissipated, and she had let herself accept that it hadn't been Dinos's fault. Instead, she knew, she was the one to blame: for her arrogance in believing that she could make the stall better than it was, and the extravagant way she had done so. An old conceit. The same conceit, she told herself, that had made her agree to marry Mahmet, thinking that she could control him in some way; that had allowed her to become involved with Nasr, imagine that he might love her, and defend her if needed; that later had made her face up to Rohat and pretend she could defy him. The same inflated self-regard that made her think that, even now, she was of such importance to Rohat that he would pursue her, find her, spend months and years tracking her down so that he might finally satisfy his honour. The same arrogance that had caused her to push Salvo to do what he did – and pay the consequence.

Having to leave her room with Mrs Jervais had hurt her more. She'd grown to like the elderly woman, and the feeling was clearly mutual, for when Zarrin told her of her misfortune, said that she'd have to leave because she couldn't pay the rent, Mrs Jervais had waved the idea away. 'Nonsense. You can stay. You can stay as long as you like. And if you feel guilty about the arrangement, then you may pay me in kind – or, rather, in kind-*ness*.' For a month she'd remained there, coming back each day after her fruitless searching for work, or her brief stints in temporary jobs, to sit with Mrs Jervais, talk to her, listen to her stories, do bits of housework when she was allowed, cook a meal. But then everything changed. Zarrin returned one evening to find another woman there, and a tension in the room. 'My daughter,' Mrs Jervais said, in a voice that was tart, shrill. 'She has come, as she does occasionally, to make sure that I'm well.' Then she turned towards her daughter. 'And this is Zarrin, Elend's mother.'

The daughter hesitated, held out a hand, seemed to have second thoughts, withdrew it.

'Yes,' Mrs Jervais said. 'She's Syrian. A refugee. I was going to tell you that.' She smiled at Zarrin. 'And a friend, too, I'm happy to say.'

But Mrs Jervais's feelings hardly seemed to matter. Whatever plans her daughter had arrived with were changed. She was going to stay, not just for a day or two, but several weeks. Her mother clearly needed help, needed to sort her life out. Perhaps she needed to be in a home, for she was obviously losing her mind, inviting people like this into her house, letting them live there for nothing, acting as childminder.

Zarrin heard the conversation – or the daughter's side of it – as she hid with Elend in her room, knew how it would end even before the knock came on the door. When she answered the knock, the daughter stood there, stiff and imperious. She was sorry, she said, but Zarrin had to leave. She needed the room herself. Her mother needed help. The current arrangement was untenable; even Zarrin could see that.

'Now?' Zarrin asked. 'You want me to leave now?'

The daughter was conciliatory. Of course not; Zarrin would need time to pack, and the poor child needed to sleep.

The morning would do. She herself would go to a hotel for the night, but, when she returned, Zarrin must be gone. Was that understood? Otherwise the police would be called.

Zarrin said nothing, looked past the woman into the living room. There was no sign of Mrs Jervais, who had presumably been despatched to her own bedroom to reflect on her sins.

'Do you understand?' the daughter asked again.

Zarrin nodded. 'Oh, yes. I think I do.'

For the next six weeks, she and Elend had lived where they could, in any hostel that would take them. When none did, they slept in abandoned buildings, or in whatever shelter they could find: in underpasses and doorways, under stairwells and bridges, sometimes huddled in the bushes in a park.

How Elend coped with it, she could not comprehend. He had never known luxury, poor child, but in their time with Salvo, more recently with Mrs Jervais, he had always had comfort of a sort, a rough routine, somewhere that might seem like a home. Now he had been thrown back once more into a life of poverty and neglect. Yet he accepted it, didn't complain, seemed still to trust her despite the pain she brought him. She loved him for that.

At intervals, she had found work. For two weeks she washed dishes in a Lebanese restaurant, slaving in a steamy and poorly ventilated kitchen, her arms raw from the water and cheap washing-up liquid that the owner insisted she use, her head filled with the clatter and clamour of the chefs and the waiters, the air pungent with spices and the smell of burned food. Then, soon after she left one night, there was a fire. The building was gutted, her job gone. She had tried to be philosophical. She commented to one of the waiters, as they stood outside the charred ruins, how much worse it must be for the owner to lose everything. The waiter – a languid Caribbean with Afro hair, tattooed neck – had scoffed. 'No way. It was an insurance job. And not the first time, either. I saw it coming. He'll be laughing all the way to the bank.'

After that, on and off, there were other jobs. She was taken on as a cleaner, on a zero-hours contract, would wait the whole day and into the night for a call. Most of the waiting was in vain. Twice she was summoned, and hurried to the address she was given, only to find that there was no work for her any more. Someone else had stepped in and beaten her to the job; it had all been a mistake.

But, at last, she got something. Four days' work, litter-picking in the small public parks and gardens and cemeteries that were dotted around Vauxhall and Brixton. 'Shit-picking,' one of the other workers called it, as they made their way through the scrub at the corner of the park: dog-shit, child-shit, the shit and vomit of the drunk and loose-bowelled; of anyone and anything that had been caught short. Condoms, too, some clearly less than an hour or two old, others the residence of all sorts of wayward or undiscerning wildlife – beetles and woodlice and spiders, slugs. The worst, though, were the needles and syringes, the razor blades, the broken glass that lurked amid the grass and leaves, ready to cut any unsuspecting hand. She'd been given a grabber for picking up dangerous items, and gloves for protection. But the grabber was stiff and made her fingers ache, and the gloves were heavy, hot, clumsy. No one used them. Each venue was timed to the minute, and had to be spotless before they left; bare hands were faster and nimbler – never mind the risk.

In the following weeks there were more jobs, much the same. The place varied, the excuse for it. But the story each one told was the same and was equally depressing.

She knew these people, of course, for she'd lived amongst them, even then inhabited the same world. Watching them, she often saw a strange nobility. People who survived despite the odds, people who made a life much like those beetles and woodlice did, amidst the discards of others. People with unexpected skills: resilience, adaptability, disdain. People who were strangely protected and made strong by their ignorance – their knowledge or memory of nothing else. This is life. Live it.

But here, picking up the dross that framed their world, and which was all they left behind, she saw something else. The empty space where hope should have been – the hope that had long ago deserted them or which they'd never had. The layers in life – that spectrum from good to bad, from pleasant to painful, from right to wrong – which had shrunk almost to nothing, so that all experience was the same. A life so narrowly defined that there was no room for relativity or rules. Just the stark reality of the moment.

Was the same thing happening to her, she wondered: was her life being reduced in the same way? Had it already happened to Elend?

Was there no way out?

Her musings ceased. The debate inside her faded. She was home. She paused on the pavement, glancing round to make sure that she was alone. Then she ducked through the gap in the fence, where the wooden slats were broken, and picked her way across the patch of grass. The building, the scrubby trees were just shadows, the ground rutted and rough. But she made her way to the entrance sure-footedly, for she had been here for over a month now, and knew the topography by instinct.

Inside, there was a weak glimmer of light. She went down the corridor, ducking beneath the broken joist that hung from the ceiling. In the room at the far end, the light resolved into half a dozen flickering points, scattered between the shadows of beams and concrete blocks, old sacks, blankets, sheets of plastic that had been used to divide up the space. Beside each one was a hunched figure, in some cases several, seeming to wax and wane unsteadily in the candlelight. She moved past the first two, saying nothing to the people who crouched there, receiving no recognition in return. Beside the third, a man and a woman, no more than shapes in the dark, were eating noisily.

At the next, she dropped to her haunches beside the pair who were already there, said, 'I'm back.'

'Mummy!'

The smaller shadow opposite rose, scampered towards her, threw his arms around her. She kissed him.

'How did you get on?' Yaasmin asked. She was a refugee like Zarrin, illegal. She came from Somalia but, beyond that, what her history was, Zarrin didn't know. She was Muslim, devout, and dressed in a simple brown kurti and hijab. She was pensive, passive, seemed incapable of anger, ever-generous, always forgiving. But she was withdrawn, too – worn back into herself by the troubles she must have suffered, the constant grind of the life she now lived.

'Nothing,' she said. 'No work.'

'Food?'

'I've got this.' Zarrin opened her bag, took out a small parcel, wrapped in paper, and handed it across. 'It's to share.'

Yaasmin lifted the parcel, sniffed at it. 'Fish and chips? Wonderful. How did you get them?'

Zarrin shook her head. 'The usual way. Begging. He was just closing up. They're not very warm, I'm afraid.'

'We'll enjoy them even so.'

Already Yaasmin was undoing the paper, and Elend, smelling the contents, abandoned Zarrin's hug and moved to her side. 'Ah – my friend now,' Yaasmin said.

'Has he been trouble?'

'No. Not really. Sometimes, though, I wish I could chase after him. He knows I can't.'

As a child, Yaasmin had contracted polio. It had left her with one leg withered and shorter than the other. In a life of comfort she might have made out; in poverty, she was always on the edge of survival, teetering on its brink. That was how Zarrin had first found her. Begging on a blanket outside a tube station, as the rain and rubbish swirled around her. Thin, cadaverous from lack of food, skin grey and cracked from the cold and damp and lack of hygiene. Zarrin had offered her one of the apples she had scrounged earlier that day and they had talked. Yaasmin had told her about the squat she lived in, had invited Zarrin to join them. It was informal, she explained, a shifting population of people like themselves – the jobless, homeless, hopeless. They had walked back there together, a slow, hobbling progress through the darkening streets. Now they shared a corner and had created a small sanctuary for themselves, each helping the other. Zarrin begged, worked when she got the chance, shared any money or food she could obtain. Yaasmin looked after Elend, sometimes begged herself in the nearby streets. There was no comfort in it, little pleasure, but together they survived.

'Has anything else happened?' Zarrin asked.

Yaasmin shook her head. 'There's nothing else that can happen here.'

Zarrin glanced at her, said nothing. That was not true. During the day, like the night, all sorts of alarms and excursions might grip the people who occupied the place, some real, many invented. Insults and threats, wild beasts, ghosts of one form or another; sudden urges or commands of inner voices. Drugs could turn vicious and sour. Fights might break out over the merest slight, an imagined insult, or nothing at all. Sex might be offered or demanded or stolen for as little or as much. And yet those same people could be generous and caring beyond measure. When asked, they might share their last joint or their dregs of meth with a stranger. If someone was having a bad trip, one of the others might sit with them, try to make sure they didn't harm themselves, later might try to calm them or reassure them with a few words. On cold nights, some of the women might huddle together, keeping each other warm.

Zarrin offered the last chip to Elend, watched as he ate it. Yaasmin watched too.

'The forecast is bad tomorrow,' she said. 'Rain all day. There'll be no point begging. I'll try the restaurants on Lavender Hill, early, just in case there's anything there. Then I'll come home.'

She had little hope. At weekends, when the restaurants worked late, there'd sometimes be food worth salvaging in the bins the next day. But midweek there was rarely anything better than swill and mouldy bread. Yet the weather brought compensation. Time with Elend. A chance to rest.

*

'There were over fifty of us,' Yaasmin said. 'Crammed in, with no room, no means of escape. I was terrified. I had no food, hardly any water; I was cold and soaked to the skin. I had a lifejacket, but I knew it would not work. It was nothing, just polystyrene in a cheap plastic vest. We were cheated about that, like everything else.'

Darkness was settling again. Outside, the rain gurgled in the downpipes, and the wind moaned. On their makeshift table, a stub of candle flared and flickered in the draught. Yaasmin sat beside Zarrin, her shoulder close. They might have been sisters, Zarrin thought. In a way they were. Elend was asleep on his mattress. Elsewhere, in the shadows, the other occupants were spending the last of the day in whatever way they could. Smoking, muttering to each other or themselves, groaning in misery or pleasure as their fears and visions took hold.

It was the first time that Yaasmin had opened up like this, talked so freely about herself. What had brought it on, Zarrin didn't know. Just the hours together, perhaps, with nothing other than their own lives to share. But, having started, Yaasmin seemed desperate to complete her story, as if it had to be told before it was too late. She talked about her life in Somalia, her escape, her trip to Europe.

It was the civil war that had done it. Five years ago, her home in Mogadishu had been bombed, her parents killed, her brother abducted or slain. She'd fled with her two younger sisters to Ethiopia, walking for five days. She carried Sadia, the youngest, her withered leg hampering her all the way, and she cursed it. But at last, they'd staggered into Dolo Ado and found refuge in the Kobe camp, crammed in with twenty-five thousand others. They had no belongings, little money, no friends. The climate was dry and hot, water was scarce, sanitation almost non-existent. They were dependent for food on the meagre supplies of aid that found their way to the camp, and those they had to fight for if they were going to obtain enough. With no men to do the fighting, she and her sisters were always hungry. Sadia caught measles, and died. Yaasmin buried the child, and a few days later she and her remaining sister, Aisha, tried to flee. Al-Shabab soldiers intercepted them and sent them back. They tried again, were once more caught and returned. What happened with the soldiers, Yaasmin wouldn't say, though Zarrin could guess.

'We were there for six months,' she said. 'In Kobe. The drought got worse. The rations got less. There were fights every day about water and food. There was malnutrition, illness. Sometimes I counted the bodies outside the hospital. Ten, twelve; one day over twenty. One day I knew it would be one of us – Aisha or me.'

Again they had determined to escape, and this time they'd succeeded. Yaasmin used what money she had to pay a smuggler to take them into Sudan. They spent two weeks travelling across the Sahara, she and her sister and five others – men, women, children, packed tight in an old and battered car. The exhaust leaked, filled the car with fumes; the engine often overheated, so that they had to sit and wait for it to cool. They had punctures, breakdowns, accidents. One of the passengers died when the car rolled into a wadi; Aisha was injured. They buried the dead man, patched up Aisha's broken arm, moved on.

When they reached northern Sudan, Yaasmin had thought the worst was over, but it seemed that it had merely just begun. The men who met them there demanded money, not for the journey that lay ahead but the one just completed. Four thousand dollars, they said. Yaasmin couldn't pay so she and Aisha were held hostage, in a tent in the desert. They were not the only ones. There were thirty tents in all, each holding up to a dozen refugees who, like them, had no money to pay this unexpected supplement. Most of them were from Somalia; the large majority were men. The women had been left behind.

Food was miserable – plain pasta or rice, water that was brown with silt and scum. Most of the time they were roped together to a large peg in the ground. If they tried to loosen their bonds, they were beaten. They were threatened every day, offered a phone with which to call their parents, so that they could ask for money to be sent. 'My parents are dead,' she told them, but they would not believe her. They told her to ring her grandparents or other relations instead. 'They are poor,' she would say; 'they have no money. They cannot help.' Her captors grew more angry. They refused to feed them; their water was contaminated with petrol, a little more each time, until it was undrinkable. They begged water from other hostages, sucked at the canvas of the tent at night, searching for the smallest drop of condensation.

One morning, they were pulled out of the tent. 'Come, watch,' the man said. In a circle of other hostages, two men were being held, kneeling in the sand.

The leader walked up to the two men and went through the same ritual that he went through every day with Yaasmin: 'Ring your family. Ask for money. Make them pay.'

The men shook their heads, pleading that they were poor.

'Then why should we feed you and keep you?' the leader demanded. 'Tell me that.'

The men pleaded: let them go.

'I'd rather shoot you,' the leader said to the younger of the men. He took out a gun, fired once. Not at the head or the heart, but the stomach. Then he did the same with the other man. The men were dragged away, screaming with pain, dumped somewhere in the desert.

During the night Yaasmin could hear their screams, until they faded to a lower tone, wailing and groans. In the morning, there was just silence.

The atrocity emboldened the hostages. Word was whispered to her that they were planning a mass escape. At first, no one wanted to include Yaasmin. With her withered leg she would be a hindrance, slow them all down. But Aisha defended her. 'She's stronger than you think,' she said. 'She'll outrun half of you. And if she needs help, she has me.' Reluctantly they agreed.

Two nights later, Yaasmin and the others in their tent loosened the ropes that bound them, crept out. The hostages in the neighbouring tent were also ready. It was a moonless night. At a signal, one by one, they crept away. Fifty metres from the tents, they started to run. The darkness swallowed them, but they kept running, simply following the vague shadow of the person in front. Yaasmin struggled, limping over the rough rocky surface, through the sand. But she kept up until at last, after an hour, they paused to rest.

For almost a week, they headed north and west, pausing in the hottest part of the day, moving when they could. Their progress was slow, for no one had much strength, and Yaasmin was far from the weakest. They had little water, no food. They scavenged what they could from desert kill, found water in the wadi sands. Not everyone survived; the old and feeble died. But about twenty of them reached Libya, and eventually came to a small desert town where they were given sanctuary in a mosque. From there, Yaasmin and Aisha travelled on alone. A month later, they arrived in Benghazi, found themselves trapped again. A boat trip to Europe cost money, and Yaasmin had none.

She looked for work, was offered money for the only thing men seemed to think women were worthy of: sex. She refused. Instead, she and Aisha begged, scavenged, ran errands for the smugglers, tried to make themselves useful.

One day a man found them and offered to take Aisha to Italy. She refused to go unless Yaasmin came too. 'Not her,' the man said. 'We can't take cripples. It's just the girl.'

Yaasmin agreed, and, despite Aisha's objections, she was led away. Yaasmin never heard from her again. Whether she reached Europe, Yaasmin didn't know. Perhaps she did. More likely she died on the way. Or perhaps the whole thing was a scam, a trick. She might have been taken into slavery, a child prostitute.

'I didn't realise then,' Yaasmin said. 'I didn't know. Everything that happened to me was like something I had to discover, as though it had never happened to anyone before. I felt sometimes that every atrocity was invented just for me.'

Zarrin nodded. 'I know. But the truth's worse. They do these things to everyone. They always have.' She reached out and took Yaasmin's hand. 'What did you do? How did you get away?'

'I got money. I found ways. I paid for a place on a boat.' Then she told about the journey – fifty refugees in a rubber dinghy, no motor nor means of steering. Just four paddles, hardly big enough to drive it when it was empty, let alone when it was full.

'They said they would tow us,' she said. 'And we believed them. Whether we really did, I don't know. You believe with your heart because you want to, even if your mind believes something different.'

'How long did it take?' Zarrin asked.

'On the boat? Over a week. Ten days in total. They cast us off after the first day – just loosened the ropes, and let us drift. We were shouting after them as they left. People were crying, waving. The raft almost turned over then. Some people fell in. They drowned, I think. We never found them, and we couldn't steer the boat. It just went where the waves wanted.'

Yaasmin was silent, and Zarrin squeezed her hand, in comfort, in encouragement – in whatever the gesture could give. Yaasmin looked at her, something like sorrow in her eyes – the sorrow of memory perhaps, or of an intimacy she yearned for, yet knew she could never have.

'We drifted. Some days we saw boats, and we shouted and waved, but they never came. Some people died. Some became hysterical. Fights broke out amongst the men. It's the only answer men seem to have: fighting.' She withdrew her hand, looked at it, as if seeking some mark there of Zarrin's touch. 'The man next to me was stabbed. We pushed him overboard when he died. There was nothing else we could do. Who stabbed him, I don't know, and after a day or two I didn't care. It was just what happened on a boat.'

'How did you survive?'

'We were lucky. We prayed, and perhaps Allah heard us. Perhaps He thought He'd punished us enough. A coastguard vessel found us, took us on board. It was Italian. The men were like angels: Hafaza, Jundullah. They carried us, cared for us. When someone fell, they swam after us and saved us from the waves. They were so good.'

Her voice faded; she stopped.

'And then?' Zarrin asked. 'How did you get here?'

Yaasmin shrugged. 'I was just one,' she said. 'One amongst hundreds. I just did what they did. I walked. I waited. I went thirsty and hungry. I was spat at and kicked and beaten by the police. I was given a helping arm by people I had never met – people who fed us and walked with us for a while. I slept in fields. I did my business there, with hundreds of others. I lost whatever was left of my dignity. And one day

I was put on a truck with forty other people and we were locked in. And we sat in the dark, bumping along roads, rumbling along highways, sitting somewhere waiting. And it was hot and there was no air. And we had no water. Why do we never have that? Why do the men who do these things – who take your money, who make you pay with whatever you have – why don't they give you water? And again, more people died, and some broke down and just cried or shouted, or tried to hurt themselves. And men fought. And one day we were let out. And we were in England. In the countryside somewhere. And so I walked and a few days later I arrived here, in London. And here I am.'

'What will do you now?'

Yaasmin lifted Zarrin's hand, clutched it between hers, bent forward, kissed it. 'I will do what we all do. I will live for another day, and then see what life brings.'

*

At night, as she lay in her small space in the corner, Zarrin could hear the rats. She heard them in the wall cavity. She heard them scurrying across the floor. She could smell them, too: their mustiness, their dank odour of urine or mould or bad breath. Occasionally she felt one, a shiver of movement running across her body, then gone. Once, turning, she had dislodged one from her chest and felt its weight for the first time, heard its squeal of alarm as it leapt away.

She did not hate the rats, did not fear them, but they disturbed her nonetheless. They were a mark of what she was, the way she lived. They were all rats now, she thought. She and Elend and Yaasmin and everyone else in that world around her. They lived there unseen – part of a huge and hidden population of homeless and down-and-outs who eked out an existence in London: in the cracks and crevices, beneath the floorboards, in dark corners, in wastelands and derelict buildings, creeping out only at night to scavenge and steal, and even then moving in the shadows, ready at the slightest danger to melt back into the night. And like rats they were vermin: unwanted, but too numerous, too deeply embedded in the world ever to be removed. Push them out and they would return. Kill them and others would take their place. They weren't a problem to which there was a solution, just a by-product of the world that humans had made. The only thing you could do was accept them, try to ignore them, pretend they weren't there. Hope that they didn't infect you or infect your dreams.

Zarrin's dreams contained other demons. Rohat and his men.

They came to her as he had done then. With his men, like a raiding party, clumping up the stairs to her room. Her room. The one to which even Mahmet knocked before he entered. Not so Rohat. He burst in upon her, even as she fled through the opposite door.

What happened next would vary. The scenes would change from one occasion to the next, or within a single dream. In reality, she had fled to the garden, tried to hide in the stable block. In reality, it had all happened there. But in her dreams it could be almost anywhere. In her room, in the garden, in the desert, in any of the dark and stinking barns and sheds and passageways in which she had taken refuge since. And the men would change, too. Sometimes Mahmet would be there, or Nasr. Mahmet would just watch, saying nothing, a silent judge, counting the punishment away. But Nasr could play any role. Sometimes he'd be her defender, pulled roughly away. Sometimes he'd be there in the background, a helpless witness. But sometimes he would be one of them, doing what they do, taking his own turn.

And sometimes they wouldn't be men at all, but something more shadowy. Ghostly figures of horror. Worse than rats.

Those changes in the way it happened seemed to be a cruel trick of her mind. They didn't just repeat the act, entrench it more deeply, but expanded it, added to it. Multiplied the hurt.

But wherever it happened, whoever was involved, the basic elements would always be the same. The fear, the shame. The clothes stripped from her, each garment another layer of innocence lost. The hard ground beneath her. The smell and the filth. The yank of her legs, opening her up, ripping her body apart.

Rohat's words – always them – 'Who's next?'

It was then that she usually woke, with the echoes of her screams filling her mind.

Whether it would ever happen again, whether Rohat would really come for her, she didn't know. Sometimes she could believe herself free of him. Sometimes her fear seemed just another illustration of her own arrogant self-regard: believing herself so important that he would harbour his damaged honour for so long. But often, it felt inevitable – as if it was already written in the story of her life. For the black world around her seemed redolent with his presence, as much as it was with the rats' pungent smell. He was there in the alleys and underpasses, there in the dark shadows of the trees; around every corner, behind every wall. And if not him, then his influence, his evil, like an invisible web. Spreading out from its dark centre in Syria, through all the places she had travelled, the countries she had crossed, the borders and deserts and seas, spanning the streets and parks, the housing estates, the whole of London, reaching even to the dark corner where she lived.

*

'What's wrong?' Zarrin asked.

Yaasmin gazed past her, said nothing.

In recent days, Zarrin had detected the change in her, worried about it. She seemed distracted, and ill at ease. Why, Zarrin didn't know. Life for her should be better now, for she had work at last. The work was dreary and tiring, Zarrin knew, in an all-night launderette, supervising the premises, operating the machines for customers when asked. The money was poor, and the nights were never easy. Like the squat, the launderette was a haven for everyone with no other place to be. Drunks and druggies, the lonely, the lost, the confused. Yaasmin was vulnerable to all sorts of insults and abuses. All sorts of threats. But at least there was money. They both benefited from that.

'You need to go soon,' Zarrin said. 'You mustn't be late.'

Again, she received no answer, and Zarrin wondered what Yaasmin was thinking, whether there was some secret that she dared not reveal. Had she lost her job? Had she been abused to the extent that she dared not go back?

Then, in a small voice, Yaasmin said, 'I don't want to go. I want to stay here, with you.'

Zarrin smiled. She'd noticed that change in her, too. That dependence. Not just the mutual reliance they both felt – of strength in companionship – but something deeper. Affection. Almost love. Was that what Yaasmin wanted?'

'I know,' Zarrin said. 'But you need to go. You've work to do.'

'I hate the work. I don't want to do it any more.'

'Why? What's wrong?' Zarrin stood up, went across, knelt beside the mattress where Yaasmin lay like a huddled child. 'Is it too hard? Do you need help?'

A small shake of the head.

'What, then?'

Another shake of her head. Silence. Zarrin insisted. 'Tell me.'

'It's a man,' Yaasmin said, at last.

'A man?'

'He visits me.'

'Visits you where?'

'In the launderette. While I'm working.'

Zarrin wanted to laugh. 'What sort of man?'

Yaasmin looked away, as if trying to hide her disgrace, and Zarrin waited. She looked so small, she thought, so defenceless. She tried to imagine what had happened, what trauma Yaasmin had been through.

'Who is he? What does he do?' she asked.

'He's a security man,' Yaasmin said, her voice a whisper. 'He patrols a big depot further down the street. He comes into the laundry. He says it is just to get warm – that the yard where he works is cold, and he has no shelter from the rain or the wind. But I know it's not. He watches me. Sometimes he tries to help me, and he gets too close.'

'Perhaps he just likes you,' Zarrin said. 'Perhaps he really is trying to help.'

'No. No, it's not like that.'

'What is it like? Does he touch you? Does he look at you in some way?'

Yaasmin shook her head, eyes closed again, lips tight. 'I – I don't want to talk about it. I'm sorry.'

'You can tell me,' Zarrin said, gently. 'Just say it.'

'I can't.'

Zarrin stroked Yaasmin's hair, said once more, 'Tell me.'

And at last, Yaasmin did.

What she said seemed trivial to Zarrin, a matter of almost no import. The man came most nights, as he was doing his patrols. He would sit by the door for a moment, watching Yaasmin working, perhaps make some comment about how she looked: tired today, or pretty, worried or happy. When a machine had finished, and needed unloading, he would come over and kneel beside her, and help her take the clothes out. When there were sheets or anything large, he'd help her fold them. If he touched her, it seemed accidental: a brush of his hand, their shoulders grazing each other as they moved. He didn't seem to say anything other than kind words, didn't force himself on her in any way.

Zarrin imagined him lonely, shy, wanting companionship. Perhaps liking Yaasmin for the sort of woman she was: innocent and unassuming.

She couldn't understand Yaasmin's anxiety and fear.

She tried to tell her: don't worry so much. Be kind to him. He's doing no harm.

Yaasmin nodded, said nothing.

'Not all men are monsters,' Zarrin said. 'There's no need to be frightened. And this one seems to be behaving far more honourably than most.' Then she asked, 'Is he a Muslim? Where's he from?'

'I don't know. He hasn't said. I don't speak to him.'

'Do you want me to talk to him? Would that help?'

Yaasmin looked up at her, her eyes unfathomable, sad.

Zarrin waited.

'I do not understand,' Yaasmin muttered.

'What don't you understand?'

'How things happen in this country. What I am meant to do. What is right and what is wrong.'

'Yes. I know,' Zarrin said. 'I know what you feel. I'm as confused as you are.'

'I don't understand men,' Yaasmin said.

Tears formed in her eyes. Zarrin leaned down and kissed them away, as she would with Elend.

'What shall I do?'

'You'll do what you always do. And if he comes tonight, you'll be kind to him, and let him talk to you, and you'll talk to him. Then, maybe, you'll understand what he wants.'

Yaasmin nodded.

'So – go now. And I'll see you when you come back.'

She kissed her once more as Yaasmin left, thinking again: we are like sisters.

But in the morning, Yaasmin didn't return.

Zarrin waited, wondering what had happened to her, imagining that she might have agreed to meet the man after she had finished her shift; even now might be sitting there with him, telling him the story that she had told her. All would be well, she told herself: don't worry. But after two hours Yaasmin had still not appeared. Taking Elend, Zarrin walked to the launderette, stood outside. Everything seemed normal, but there was no sign of Yaasmin.

She went in, asked the supervisor if she knew where Yaasmin was.

The supervisor shook her head. 'She wasn't here. I've had to report it to the management. The place was unattended when I arrived.'

As she walked out, all Zarrin's dammed-up fears broke through. Was Yaasmin safe? Had something happened to her? Had she had an accident? Was she ill?

How would she know?

All day, as she scoured the city for food or work, Elend at her side, she tried to banish the questions from her mind. Despite her disability, Yaasmin was strong, resolute. She had already survived so much.

Yet where could she be?

Wildly, grasping at dreams for comfort, she tried to imagine a happy explanation – the sort of good fortune that Yaasmin surely deserved. She and her timid suitor walking and talking in the park, like the people she could see there any day. Or wandering the streets together, lost in their new-found love.

Yet she knew it was just a fiction. Life couldn't be so kind.

More likely she'd returned to the squat. Zarrin abandoned her own begging and wandering, hurried back early. There was no one there.

That evening, Zarrin went again to the launderette, at the time Yaasmin should have started work. Even before she got there, she could see that something was wrong. There was a small crowd of people outside in the street, a police car, its blue lights flashing. The red and white stripes of security tape.

'What's happening?' she asked one of the people in the crowd.

'They've found a body. Somewhere out the back. It's the woman who worked here at night. The Somali woman. It looks like she's been murdered.'

12

Elysium

Recruiting now, the notice said.

Since that night, Zarrin's life had been hard, almost unbearable. She sorrowed for Yaasmin, missed her companionship and help. She felt burdened with guilt. But for Zarrin, but for the advice she'd given her friend, Yaasmin would still be alive. She, of all people, should have been aware of the dangers, warned of them. She should have gone that night with Yaasmin, been there to help her and protect her.

As she begged and roamed the streets, as she sat at night in the squat with Elend, her sadness would overwhelm her in sudden floods. Tears would run down her cheeks, unstoppable. Anger would well in her, bitterness and remorse.

Another person betrayed, she thought, and in her mind counted through the list. First Mahmet, then Salvo, now Yaasmin. Each of them victims of her own inflated pride.

Lying awake in the night, she thought again of the story Yaasmin had told her, of her long journey from Somalia to here. The strife and the fear and the loss. She railed at the injustice of it all, the vicious irony. To have come so far, to have survived so much, for an end like that. What sense did it make?

She remembered Yaasmin's words: *I will live for another day, and then see what life brings.*

159

This was what it brought, she thought: death. Just an unfair and brutal end.

One afternoon, her mind filled with the turmoil, the sense of guilt, she went to a mosque with the intention of finding the imam, opening out her heart to him, asking him for his blessing, and to help her pray for Yaasmin. But when she got there, her resolution failed. There was far too much unholiness in her to enter such a place, too much for absolution. Yaasmin's devoutness would only be marred by any supplication that she might offer.

She turned away.

And she asked herself: how could anyone honour a life such as Yaasmin's? How could anyone mark it, and give it the monument it deserved? Her answer gave no solace. People like Yaasmin – like herself, too – didn't receive memorials. Just abuse and hate. They left no legacy, not even the space where they used to be.

Yaasmin was right. Their one role in the world was to struggle, to survive as long as they could.

She started back towards the squat. Her mind was dark, her grip on Elend's hand unyielding and stiff. Then motherliness seeped back. Poor boy, she thought, dragged along the streets like this all day. What joy in life was there for him? She saw a playground, with swings and slide, took the small street beside it to find the entrance. Halfway along, on a board outside a small shop, the words on the notice caught her eye. She read on: *Vacancies in the hospitality trade*. There was the name of an agency – London HR Services – a telephone number.

The odds were against her, she knew: the notice would be old, the jobs would be long gone. She knew, too, that even if anything existed, this was the path to exploitation: no agency worth its name would advertise in out-of-the-way places such as this. But she went into the shop, bought a voucher for her mobile phone, dialled the number.

'Have you worked in hospitality before?' she was asked.

'Yes.'

'What did you do?'

'I worked in a restaurant. In Kilburn. Unfortunately, there was a fire recently, and it burned down.'

'And you've references?'

'I'm afraid not. I mean – it was very sudden, and the owners were too upset to ask.'

'Hmm. But you can start immediately?'

'Yes. Whenever you want.'

'Where are you from?'

'I'm – I was born in Syria. But I live here now.'

There was a silence, and Zarrin's heart sank. Not the right answer. Not the one the woman wanted to hear.

'I'm a good worker,' she started to say, but the woman's voice cut across her, curt and matter-of-fact. 'Come in the morning. Ten o'clock. Don't be late.' She gave an address. 'It's for an interview. I'm not guaranteeing anything.'

The next day, Zarrin made her way to the address she'd been given. It was a small office, in a run-down building, shared with other companies that couldn't afford, or didn't want, anything more pretentious. Inside, Zarrin found herself in a dingy corridor, with doors on either side. On one was a sign bearing the name of the agency, the instructions *Knock and Enter*. She parked Elend's buggy in the corridor, told him to be good, went in.

The room was dark, as dowdy as the rest of the building. There was a desk, a single filing cabinet, three chairs. A woman sat at the desk, her back to the door. She didn't turn when Zarrin entered, but waved a hand vaguely, as if in invitation to sit down. Zarrin remained standing, her hands folded in front of her, head level, eyes lowered: the servant's pose. She'd dressed as smartly as she could, and in this setting felt just sufficiently neat. The woman wore trousers, a thick pullover – what might have been men's clothes.

At last, she turned, regarded Zarrin, saying nothing.

'I telephoned you,' Zarrin said. 'Last night. About a job.'

The woman nodded.

'I'm Zarrin Kashlan.'

Another nod, another long stare. The woman pointed at a box on the windowsill. 'Bring me that file.'

Zarrin walked to the window – five paces – picked it up, took it to the desk, handed it over.

The woman accepted the file, but then reached out and took Zarrin's hand, regarded it critically. 'The other one?'

Zarrin let her see it.

'Good.' She released the hand. 'Where do you live?'

'I live in Shepherd's Bush, ma'am.'

The woman gave a thin smile. 'Ma'am! I like it. You learn quickly.' Once more, her eyes ran across Zarrin, assessing. 'You're pretty. That helps. You stand neatly, walk well. What about your English? Tell me something. Something about yourself.'

'I am from Syria. I think I told you that when I telephoned. But I lived in Europe for several years.' Neither truth nor lie, she thought, but that strange area between the two and therefore, perhaps, forgivable. 'I came to England about a year ago. I am honest and reliable. I work hard. I will not let you down.'

'Alright. Enough. Your English is good. And you can work anywhere.'

'Yes, ma'am. If you wish me to.'

'It was a statement, not a question,' the woman said. She opened the box file, sat looking at the contents for a moment, then shook her head. 'But you've no papers.'

'No visa. Just my ID.'

'It was another statement,' the woman said, but her eyes were light. 'Don't worry. It just means that there won't be any bureaucracy.' She closed the box, put out a hand. 'Let me see.'

Zarrin handed over her ID card. The woman looked at it, nodded. 'Sinjari? You said Kashlan. Which is it?'

'I was married,' Zarrin said. 'He died.' It felt like truth now, and came to her lips easily. 'Kashlan is my maiden name.'

The woman handed the card back. 'The hotel will hold that. Just as security.' She regarded Zarrin once more. 'Four pounds an hour, for an eight-hour day, but there'll be overtime. You can make up your salary with tips.' She gave that same, rueful smile. 'It's not much, I know, but for people in your position it's tax-free. If you want, you might be able to have a room in the hotel. They'll deduct eight pounds a day for that. It's worth it; it will mean that you don't have to travel and it's far less than you'll pay anywhere else.' She looked at Zarrin knowingly again. 'And it's more comfortable than squatting or sleeping rough.'

Zarrin nodded, feeling exposed. 'I've – I've a child,' she said. 'A son.'

'How old?'

'Three. Three and a half.'

'Where is he now?'

'Outside,' Zarrin said.

The woman sucked in her cheeks. 'That makes it difficult.'

'I can manage. He won't be a problem.'

Another suck of her cheeks, then the woman said, 'He'll need a kindergarten, though, won't he? Here – try this one.' She selected a card from a small box on her desk. 'A friend runs it. She'll give you a fair price. Tell her that Kerry sent you.' She waved away Zarrin's thanks. 'Any questions?'

'Where is it, ma'am? Where will I be working?'

'The Elysium. Do you know it?'

Zarrin shook her head.

'Old Brompton Road. Opposite the cemetery. Tomorrow morning at seven.'

'Yes. Thank you. Thank you very much. I'm very grateful.'

'Make sure they are too.'

*

'Next. You do it this time. I'll watch.'

Zarrin followed Gabby along the corridor, feeling the soft tread of the carpet beneath her feet. Such luxury. Working here would be a delight. How could she be so lucky?

Gabby had been delegated to show her around, give her a day's induction on what the job would entail. To Zarrin, she already seemed like a friend. She was easygoing, had a quick smile, a light and singsong voice that belied her size. She was built for strength. She had shown that in the first room, when she demonstrated what to do. She whipped off the bedding with a quick flick of her arms, manoeuvred the clumsy hoover as though it were a child's toy; moved the chairs and tables aside with a careless shrug. Zarrin suspected she treated all obstacles the same.

When Zarrin tried to make the bed in the next room, she realised the trickery in Gabby's performance. The work was hard, took both skill and brute force. She would have to learn the technique, toughen up, to last the day.

Gabby looked at the result of her efforts, grinned. 'Shall we have another go?'

They worked on. By the third or fourth room, Zarrin's bed-making skills had improved. Gabby seemed content.

She chatted as they worked. Gabby was pleased, it seemed, for the chance to talk. She was Jamaican, she said, from Montego Bay in the north. She had come to England to study. But she'd had problems, dropped out of her course, and was now working in hospitality. She laughed at the word and said, 'Have you ever noticed – hospital, hospitality? It's no coincidence, if you ask me. This place feels more like an A&E department than a posh hotel. All crisis and calamity. It's a mad-crazy life.'

Gabby paused, regarded Zarrin, gave an ironic smile.

'I've been here six months,' she went on. 'I'm still a junior chambermaid, on the lowest pay – well, except for you now. Though it's not for lack of experience; this is my third hotel in the last two years. I never stay long. Be a moving target, that's my motto.'

'Do you have papers?' Zarrin asked.

'Papers?' She laughed. 'This is the Elysium. It prides itself in being a paperless business. No need for things like that. But no. I'm meant to be a student, aren't I? I'm not meant to work. Not work-work. I'm meant to be studying. What about you?'

Zarrin shook her head. 'No. Not immigration papers. Not a visa.'

Gabby shrugged. 'Well, join the club. Just keep your head down, that's all. It's what I do. You'll be fine.'

The Elysium was old, had history. It had started small, grown big, and with each sale, each new campaign of refurbishment, the place had evolved. New wings had been added, neighbouring buildings taken over and linked until it was as large as the street would allow, a complete block. From the outside it appeared impressive, with its colonnades and covered porticos, its railings and its steps. But inside it was a confusing maze, for it rambled and twisted in every dimension it could find. Floors met at different levels, lifts started part-way up the building, finished before they reached the top. Corridors bucked and turned. It needed a map to find your way around, was a nightmare to tend and clean.

Yet somehow, for its clients, it was regarded as a place of quality, amongst the lesser élite at least. The foyer had been recently modernised, with plate-glass windows, golden crowns, and purple drapes wherever they would fit. On the lower floors, especially those with views of the cemetery across the road, the rooms were large and plush. There were meeting rooms, too, and a wood-panelled boardroom, equipped bizarrely with an ancient wooden throne. But on the upper floors the rooms became smaller, drabber, the carpets in the corridors more frayed, and here and there, on the ceiling and the walls, was the faint evidence of stains where rainwater had leaked in or the plumbing had burst out.

Here, too, the lifts were more basic and travelled, it seemed, according to a timetable of their own.

For the staff, there were two service lifts, one at either end of the building; otherwise it was the stairs. 'They keep you fit here,' Gabby warned. 'The three Fs: fit, frugal and fucking poor.'

'I'm lost,' Zarrin said. 'I'll never find my way back.'

Gabby laughed. 'It happens. We lost one chambermaid for a week. By the time we found her she was half-starved, poor thing; she'd even eaten her mop.'

Later, they stood in the yard at the back of the hotel. Gabby rolled herself a cigarette, made thinly with materials she kept in a leather pouch. 'We call this place The Reef,' she said. 'Because you can hide here and have a smoke.' She saw Zarrin's blank look, and explained: 'Reef – a reefer. You know, like this.' She held up hers. 'Tobacco if you like, or cannabis, usually a bit of both. Half the staff here are on something. Cannabis is the least of it. It's what keeps us going.' She offered Zarrin a puff.

'No, thank you.'

'Good girl,' Gabby said.

She talked about the staff, their foibles, some of the ones to watch. The hotel manager, Dr Plunkett, was a pompous ass. 'God knows what he's a doctor of. Divinity perhaps – he struts around like a bloody god. Luckily you won't see much of him. Only when we have someone important staying here. Otherwise he spends all his time on the golf-course, or in his gentlemen's club, from what I've heard.'

Frau Braunlich was the staff manager – the one who decided whether you were hired or fired. 'Brownbitch, I call her,' Gabby said. 'She's Swiss or German, and young – probably fresh out of college with a diploma of some sort. She's ambitious, officious. Malicious, too. She won't stand for anything she thinks is bullshit or insolence. You need to treat her with respect.'

But Mr Seddon was the worst, she went on. He was one of the floor supervisors, bullied you, undressed you with every look. 'He's a groper,' Gabby said. 'Fingers in every orifice. Keep your distance. Watch out if you ever get listed for the north wing – that's his domain.'

Then she asked, 'Where are you living?'

'In the basement. They gave me a room.'

Gabby looked surprised, and Zarrin explained. It was because of Elend, and because she'd agreed to be on emergency call. She had to pay, of course, and the room was small, but it suited. After her life before, it felt good.

Another quizzical look. 'Life before?'

'Squatting,' Zarrin said.

Gabby gave a nod. 'I see. Well, lucky you. There are girls who would sell their body and soul for that – a room. Or for much less, if they had to. Even so, watch out. They'll have you working every hour of the day and night if you let them. Nothing's worth that.' Then she glanced at her watch. 'Talking of which: time I caught up with myself.' She squeezed her reefer dead, slipped it into her pouch. 'I'll keep that for later. Waste not, want not – that's my motto.'

*

Zarrin's intuition had been right: the work was hard. The beds were heavy, the lifting and bending and twisting and scrubbing hour after hour made her limbs ache.

She had never had to do housework before, not like this. As a child she had helped around the home, doing small tasks at her mother's direction, or just to show that she was being good. But as the youngest she was pampered, seen as the delicate one, a thinker rather than a doer. Compared to her sisters, therefore, her duties were light. What they had made of it, Zarrin had no idea, for she had never bothered to ask. Yet now, she wondered: had they honestly loved her and doted on her as much as they said, or had they thought her selfish and spoiled?

Here, the work seemed unrelenting. The days had a pattern that didn't vary from one to the next. The only change was how long it lasted, how tired she felt at the end.

Each one started with a briefing when the duty lists were handed out and any special warnings and announcements made: important guests in the north wing suite; recarpeting in the second-floor conference room; staff lift number two out of action. After that, the public rooms would be cleaned, the work shared amongst them. And then it would be her roster of guest rooms: a dozen to eighteen depending on their size. Finally, another two hours of work in the corridors, disposing of waste, helping if needed in the kitchen. Eight hours on a good day, when everything went as planned. Ten or more when there were difficulties, which most days brought.

For Zarrin, those days when she worked late caused special problems. With pleading, she had managed to enrol Elend in the kindergarten that she had been recommended, three blocks away, on Dovehouse Street. But she had to pick him up before four-thirty. She would dash there at the end of her shift, still in her work clothes, arrive panting at the door with just minutes to spare, the last to claim her child. If she was late, there was a penalty charge to pay. Then she would listen to whatever tales of disapproval or advice the manager had to impart, and walk him home. When the weather was fine, she would take him to the park. Most evenings she took him for a meal in a café, somewhere, or bought a takeaway for them to share. Sometimes she would eat with him in the corner of the hotel kitchen, forbidden scraps, smuggled to them by the chef. Then she would go back to their room, wash him, read to him, tuck him up in bed.

And even then it wasn't over, for Gabby was right, too. Her small room in the basement came at an additional cost to what she paid from her wages. She was always on call. When a child fell ill, or an adult drank too much and vomited on their bed at night, Zarrin was summoned to clean up the mess. When there was a panic because a guest had lost their wallet or their ring somewhere between the bar and the casino and their room, Zarrin was called to help with the search. Once, when a young couple decided that they wanted to go out to a club at midnight and needed someone to mind their young child, Zarrin had been drafted in as babysitter.

During those times, she had to leave Elend alone in the room. She fretted about him, wondering if he was safe, whether he might wake and wander out and look for her.

And yet the life felt good, and she still gained pleasure from walking on carpets rather than pavements and ill-made wooden floors. They were steps to something better, she told herself – a sign of progress at last. She had a place to live, a job, wages at the end of the week. She was safe; Elend had playmates during the day, a warm room to sleep in at night. If she worked hard, worked well, she might get a promotion. Then she'd be able to save, and they'd be able to eat more healthily.

One day, beyond that, a proper life waited. School for Elend. A flat of their own. A garden, perhaps. Holidays, treats.

A father for Elend, too? she sometimes wondered, though the thought always brought a shudder of apprehension, and she couldn't make it seem real.

All it needed was a tiny twist of fortune, a brief smile from fate. And where better to seek it than here, amidst all these well-paid businessmen, these well-dressed women, the sirs and madams and lords and sheiks that swaggered and slept just a few metres from where she worked, where she lay? Somehow, a small amount of wealth or wellbeing or luck must surely leak out.

Three months gone and it hadn't come yet, that small drop of luck. She moved amongst the wealthy and privileged, she made them comfortable, made their world neat, answered their calls, but she might have been invisible, lived in a different sphere.

The room she had been given in the basement was dark and cramped. A single bed, a chest of drawers, a hard wooden chair, a tiny washbasin, no cooking facilities or toilet. A high sash window that peered through grime to give a slit-like perspective of the pavement above, the truncated lower limbs of the people passing, the dogs that cocked their legs against the railings, the drunks who sometimes slumped there, or peed into the window-well. She made the room as homely as she could. She cut pictures from magazines that she found abandoned in the guest rooms, made mobiles and collages by cutting shapes of animals or people from folded pieces of paper or card. She fashioned ornaments out of tin-foil or from objects they found in the park. But pride of place went to the drawings and paintings that Elend did at kindergarten. Scribbles and random dabs of colour; stylised houses with a starburst yellow sun, sticklike figures of mother and child; more enigmatic pictures that told a story she couldn't see, yet which he would try to explain. The pictures enchanted her, and sometimes worried her with the glimpses they gave of a life she didn't know. He had artistry in him beyond his years, she thought, but then would correct herself, for surely every mother believed that of her child. No – what he had was worldly experience.

On days off, when she managed to get one, and on warm evenings when the hotel was quiet, the room was too small a place to spend their precious hours together, so she would take Elend out. If time was short, they walked in the cemetery opposite the hotel, and she read the names on the gravestones to him, made up stories about who the people were, where they had come from, the adventures they'd had. When she could, however, she took him to Kensington Gardens, for that was her favourite. It was big, seemed like a world on its own, and the people they encountered there confirmed this, for they were of every age and kind and colour. Elend loved those visits, and would tug her hand all the way to the gates, urging her on.

There, they watched the animals and talked about what they did, imagined what it was like to be a squirrel or a rabbit or a duck. They inspected the trees and flowers, and gave them names. They climbed the steps to the Albert Memorial, and she told him the little she knew about who the consort had been, what he had done. They talked about everything: where the wind came from and where it went, the nature of clouds and the shapes that they took, the colours the sun made in the Serpentine and how shadows were made. They talked of ants and spiders, dogs and cats, queens and kings.

In between their talking, she would chase him, or he would chase her, and they would catch each other, and tumble around on the grass, laughing, screeching. Or he would go off on a small adventure of his own, hiding in the bushes, or behind trees, though never quite out of sight, for he knew how much that frightened her.

Sometimes they would meet other people who might exchange a greeting; then, he would stand behind her, his hand on her leg, shy and withdrawn. And occasionally he would encounter another child, and the two of them would stop, eyeing each other uncertainly, neither knowing what to do next, how to move beyond this silent impasse.

She showed him the Peter Pan statue. Elend was entranced by it – the boy with his strange three-pipe flute, and his entourage of fairies and squirrels and rabbits and mice emerging from the plinth below. He peered at the creatures, talked to them, stroked them, ran his hands across the bronze, seeming to feel some deep meaning in the smoothness of the metal. He wanted to climb to the top and touch Peter, but Zarrin forbade it.

She only knew the sketches of the story – the boy who never grew up – but, as she stood beside the statue with Elend, it sparked in her mind the question that always lay there, teasing her with its ambiguities. What would he be? What would he become? And, as always, the possibilities haunted her, with their huge span from good to evil, hero to villain, and all the conflicts of nature and nurture with which he would have to contend.

Later, pondering on the conundrum as they made their way towards Round Pond, she glimpsed the answer – or something that might be one. In a glade between the bushes they came across a family, picnicking on the grass. Mother and father and a young child, perhaps two years older than Elend. It seemed like a timeless tableau. The mother sat on the blanket, spreading the plates and foodstuff out. Father and son played together, making a small kite fly. The kite was lozenge-shaped, with three tassel-tails, coloured in red and purple and yellow and blue. The boy held the strings; the father held the boy with a hand on his shoulder and with the other teased the strings to make the kite stay aloft. It darted and danced, feathered on the fitful breeze, swooped, almost fell, gathered itself and soared. And in her mind it set memories dancing, none of them quite resolved enough to pin down. A pale canopy of blue in which a dozen kites twisted and twirled, each one a tethered bird, about to be let loose. A hawk above the desert, wheeling, ready to take its prey. Skylarks singing from the empty sky, their song falling around her like wedding-day confetti.

She knelt beside Elend, tilted his head, pointed out the kite. *That is you*, she wanted to tell him. *And one day you will learn to fly like that.*

But until then, she told herself, the only one he had to help him was her. Home-maker, teacher, kite-flyer, protector. She was all of those, and would be until the day came to let him go and fly away, free.

*

She moved down the corridor, paused outside the bedroom, listened, knocked. There was no answer and she let herself in. The room was empty. The bed confronted her, almost like an accusation: a disordered mess of duvet, pillows, pyjamas, underclothes. On the table was a wine bottle, beside it two glasses, one on its side. More clothes were draped over the back of the chair; on the floor, another bottle. Beside it, on the carpet, a red stain.

She sighed. It distressed her to see rooms left like this. Not just because of the extra time it would cost her, in a schedule that was already far too tight, but because of what it said about the occupants. The self-indulgence, the disregard.

Yet it could have been her room, once, she thought, or Nasr's. The hotel in Damascus, where they'd first met – had they left their room like this?

Perhaps, for that night, too, had been one of wild abandon and excess, and she'd departed not with shame but with bubbling glee, uncaring of anything except the joy of discovery and release.

She began to tidy the room. She removed the clothes from the bed, folded them, placed them on one of the chairs. Then she pulled off the duvet, stripped off the cover, dropped it onto the floor. The sheet was stained, but she tried not to look at it, simply bundled it into a ball and added it to the pile. She picked up the glasses and bottles, set them on the tray, noticing as she did so the smear of lipstick on one of the glasses. No wife, Zarrin knew, for the room was booked out for single occupancy – to a businessman of some sort, with a company account. A rendezvous with a lover, perhaps? Or more likely someone he'd met, picked up in the bar or out in the town. Maybe even one of her fellow chambermaids, for that happened, she knew, and not all of them yielded to the demand unwillingly.

There was a saucer on the table, a tag of silver foil, blackened by a flame. She screwed it up, dropped it into her waste bag.

This was her world now, she thought, all this sordidness and filth. Compared to what she had dealt with when she was doing cleaning work for the council, it ought to have been less shocking, and yet it shocked her more. Here, in these plush rooms, in this world of wealth and privilege, it betrayed not desperation or neglect, but scorn. Raw and uncaring greed.

*

She thought of pomegranates. She could almost taste them as she worked. The red juice, liquid on the tongue, like jelly in the throat, the tang of blackberry; the crimson seeds, hard to the bite, yielding their own flavour of cherry or cranberry,

175

bittersweet. The elusive aroma of woodiness, earthiness, musk, flowers.

As a child, she would pick one straight from the tree, nibble along the ridges of the husk, then twist it open, suck the fruit out. It was inevitably messy. Juice would dribble down her chin, stain her frock: more trouble at home. But it was worth it. She loved the sensation of opening the fruit, as though taking the lid off a forbidden jar; she loved the feel of the juice on her chin and neck. The taste that seemed to come to her belatedly, as if held back.

Later, in her teens, she imagined something sensual, sexual in the whole process, and it heightened the experience. She wasn't surprised, though she had blushed, when she'd learned that pomegranates had been suggested as the forbidden fruit of the Garden of Eden, and in Armenia were a symbol of fecundity and marriage.

Later still, when she was betrothed to Mahmet, they would share one, lips close as they sucked up the seeds, tongues touching when they licked the husk clean. In fantasies she imagined herself as the fruit, knew that one day soon, it would happen.

Sometimes, too, she thought of figs. Nasr's fruit. Truly forbidden.

It was the hunger that did it, brought back those memories. It was real hunger now, visceral, abdominal, not the hunger of desire.

The hunger, and the bowl of fruit.

That bowl seemed to haunt her all the time she worked. In each room it was the same. It stood on the table in front of the window, caught in the shafted light of the sun. Apples and pears, peaches, oranges, a dozen in total, piled together until the bowl almost overflowed. If any were eaten or bruised or in any way imperfect, she had to replace them. More often, they would stand there like that, untouched, until the guests left. Then, she would have to refill the bowl and the fruits she'd removed would go to the kitchen, be served up later as an exotic dessert salad or poached with honey and mascarpone.

Often, she felt tempted to take one. Who would know? And yet always she resisted. Out of honour and honesty, out of fear of being caught. For there were rules to follow: she had to make a note of how many had been eaten, how many she replaced. Rumour had it that checks were sometimes done, traps set. It was easy to be caught out.

The hunger was new. She hadn't felt it until now. But somewhere in the vast empire of the hospitality industry a butterfly had flapped its wings, and the Elysium had felt the effect. Profits had slipped; shareholders had been ruffled. A new business strategy had been introduced. Economies were needed, the salary bill had to be reduced. Staff hours had been cut.

It was another twist to her employment contract that she hadn't appreciated when she signed. No extra pay when she did overtime, but a pay cut when she did less.

Elend's kindergarten fees, also, were going up. She was trying to be frugal, saving what food she could for him, eating less.

She looked again at the bowl, then at the small stock of fruit on her trolley. Might she? Just one? If not for her, then for Elend.

There was a movement behind her.

'Daydreaming?'

It was the supervisor. He had come in silently, without her noticing.

'No, Mr Seddon. Just checking that everything is correct.'

'Daydreaming,' he said again.

She made no reply, looked down. But perhaps he could sense the contempt in her eyes, or read her thoughts, for he took half a step towards her, until his shoulder was almost against hers.

'Is there something wrong, Mr Seddon?' she asked, her voice demure, innocent.

He said nothing, but reached out, touched her hair, twisting it between his fingers.

She remained still, head down.

'Some people think you're high and mighty,' he said. 'Because you live here, you and your brat. But you're no different really, are you? You have to do what I say.'

'Of course, Mr Seddon.'

Holding the lock of her hair, he moved his finger across her cheek, left it resting against her lips.

'Bite it,' he said.

She frowned, glanced at him from lowered eyes.

'Bite it,' he said again.

She was confused, uncertain what he wanted, what sort of trick he was playing.

He tightened his grip on her hair.

'If I say bite,' he said, 'you bite. And if I say kiss, you kiss.' He leaned towards her, forcing his mouth against hers, still gripping her hair so that she couldn't twist away. His lips were wet, his breath rank. With his other hand he was groping between her thighs.

She wanted to kick him, wanted to fight, knew that if he went any further that was what she would do, whatever the cost might be. But in that same instant he paused, his face close, his hand still between her thighs.

178

'And if I say fuck me,' he said, with a pinch of his fingers that made her flinch, 'that is what you do. Remember.'

Then he laughed, let go her hair, withdrew his hand.

'Nice,' he said. 'A little pleasure while we work. We all need that, don't we?'

*

High summer. Visitors were returning, bookings going up. The hotel was crowded again.

Zarrin did the sums as she worked.

The hotel had two hundred and thirty bedrooms. According to Gabby, who seemed to know such things, for an establishment with this many stars that implied a staff of two hundred and fifty or more. Since its cutbacks earlier in the year, the Elysium had been working on only three-quarters of that, at best. And the deficit, inevitably, was made not amongst the managerial ranks but in the masses at the bottom of the pile – kitchen staff, laundry workers, chambermaids. As a consequence, hours were long, holidays more or less banned and, for Zarrin, her nights repeatedly disrupted by calls for help. It was a rare day when she worked less than twelve hours, a rare week when she got a full day off.

But Zarrin made other calculations as well. Four or five hundred guests on any day, most of whom stayed several nights, but many just one. How many per year: seventy thousand, eighty, a hundred? As many as might live in a small town, she thought, and over half of them from overseas.

She tried to imagine them, those guests, scattered in a wide arc stretching out around the hotel. Each one caught within its strange magnetic force. All across London, all over Britain; in Brussels, in Paris, in Berlin, beyond. Anywhere that Rohat might be. Touching him, beckoning, tugging at him; leading him to her.

*

'Zarrin!'

She hesitated, turned. She was late for the meeting, would already be in trouble. She didn't want distractions – not even Gabby.

'Where are you going?' Gabby asked.

'To the training. I'm late.' She flapped her hand in agitation. 'I can't talk now.'

'No. No, you mustn't.' And when Zarrin started to move away again, 'No. Don't!'

Again Zarrin stopped. 'Gabby, I must. We were all summoned. It's for special training. I told you, I'm late.'

She had come as soon as she could. The meeting had been called for the end of her shift, but, as ever, she had finished late because of the extra work she had to do. She was already worried what penalty she'd have to pay.

Gabby grabbed her arm. 'You mustn't go,' she said. 'Listen to me. I know.' She opened the door next to where she was standing, pulled Zarrin inside. It was a laundry store, small, dark. Gabby felt for the light switch, clicked it on.

'What are you doing?' Zarrin asked.

'It's a trap. I've seen it happen before. I've been waiting for you, to warn you.'

'What do you mean?'

'It's not training. They do it every now and then. They round up all the new staff like this, put them in a room together. The immigration police will be there. They'll check papers – the hotel hand them over; anyone without proper documents will be taken away.'

Zarrin couldn't understand it, couldn't believe what she thought she'd heard.

'It makes no sense.'

'Not to you. It does to the hotel. It's a way of culling the staff at the end of the summer season, without having to fire them, pay them off. The hotel is happy: they get cheap staff while they want them, no strings attached. Immigration are happy: all they have to do is turn up on the day, handcuffs ready. No doubt, somewhere along the line, money changes hands. Bribes or rewards.'

'Would they do something like that?'

'They do. And I doubt they're the only ones. It's just the way the system works.'

'Won't they know? Won't someone come and look for me?'

'I doubt it. It's not personal, just a process – just a scam of sorts. It's not an organised hunt. Stay out of the way the rest of the day. That's what I did, and I'm still here; it worked for me. Let's hope it does for you, too.'

Gabby must have been right. Zarrin fetched Elend from the kindergarten, spent the rest of the day with him in the park, then took him to a café as a treat, walked with him around the streets until long after dark, sneaked back to her room, fearful. No one seemed to be looking for her; everything seemed quiet. But over the next few days she became aware that some of the faces she usually recognised were missing; there were gaps in the rosters; she was given extra work to do. Otherwise, life went on, the same.

*

Zarrin moved through the crowded ballroom as discreetly as she could: not easy with a bucket and mop in her hand.

People stepped aside as she passed, glanced at her with a look of either amusement or distaste. Through the windows at the front of the hotel, she could see the lights of passing vehicles, the dark hulk of the portals to the cemetery opposite, distorted by the rain. There were signs of rain on the guests, too: a gloss on the shoulders of the men's jackets, a sheen on the women's hair; for some an annoying unravelling of a curl or a neatly set quiff, a splashed calf. None had come prepared for that, a sudden April shower, puddling the streets, drenching them as they scuttled from taxi or car to the hotel door.

Where exactly she was meant to go, Zarrin wasn't sure. She'd simply been summoned by reception from her room. A spillage of some sort on the floor of the ballroom where the guests were gathering before dinner, she was told. She needed to clean it up – and be quick. She'd fetched the tools of her trade for mishaps like this, hurried up the stairs.

She wondered what the event was: who the guests were, where from. Business people, she guessed, from their age, their dress. Men in grey suits with club or society ties; a few, mainly younger ones, more casually attired in smart slacks, open-neck shirts. The women in long gowns, or designer-made party dresses, with plunging necklines, slits or gaps to show the flesh; jewellery in abundance – diamonds, emeralds, sapphire, silver and gold. One small stone, she thought, dropped by accident, would be more than a year's living for her and Elend. Double, even triple what she would earn.

She noticed something else. The nationalities. Though most were white and, from the snatches of conversation she heard, British, a proportion were dark: Arabic or Turkish, she guessed. A few were wearing Middle Eastern dress:

Muslim women in kurti or salwar, with hijab and *shayla*, men in *thobe* and *ghutra*. The sight of them, as it always did, brought back flashes of memory, of life in Syria, of her parents, Mahmet. Gatherings she had been to with them. Family gatherings – Newroz, her sisters' weddings. Business conferences with Mahmet, like this.

A space opened up, and she realised she had found her goal. There was a pool of red wine on the floor, broken glass. People had trodden in it, making footprints in the area around, but now they were giving it a wide berth. She put down her bucket near the centre of the pool, and swept the glass and wine towards it with the blade of the mop. Then she knelt down, picked out the larger pieces of glass, dropped them into the bucket.

As she worked, the crowd closed in, their space returned to them now.

She mopped the wine, knelt again to dry the floor with a cloth.

Someone bumped against her, cursed, strode on. A small, neatly dressed man, his kindly eyes wide in his spectacles, thanked her and gave a small bow, hands touching, as if in prayer.

She finished the drying, stood back to check that everything was clean. A sliver of glass gleamed in the light, and she crouched, reached for it. But, as she did so, the light changed with the movement of the crowd, and the glint vanished. She felt for the fragment with her hand. The crowd closed about her. She looked around. Down there, she was like a small creature in a forest – a rodent, a mole, living its own timid life amidst the shadows and the leaf litter. It felt secret, almost cosy. Then, the crowd moved again, and a tunnel opened up. And between the legs and the bodies, the hands hanging loose with fingers splayed, or twisting, turning like leaves in the wind, the dark suits, the flowered dresses, the silken shawls, she saw a man. He had his back to her, stood with one arm folded behind his waist, in his other hand a wine glass, held carelessly at his side, its contents lapping against the rim. And, in that instant, she knew him. She knew that strange stance. She knew, as her eyes followed the line of his arm, the curve of his elbow, the slope of his shoulder, what she would find. The large square topaz cufflink that fastened his sleeve. The sharp line of the collar, the neat, straight cut of his black hair. The curl of his ear.

Rohat.

She froze, staring. Her mind stalled.

He moved his hand, raising the glass to his lip. *To Zarrin*, she imagined him saying. *My brother's pure and beautiful wife*.

He had said that once, and, although it had been meant mockingly, his words had been true. The purity at least – and she had blushed, looked down, embarrassed.

Later, when he said it again, she had looked at him and smiled, hiding what she knew.

Now, he turned and faced her, and for a moment his eyes seemed to settle on her, as though he had already seen her there.

She looked away, crouched lower, head down, weak with terror. The helpless animal, trapped. She felt blood trickling down her finger from the glass shard she'd picked up.

What was he doing here? How did he know? Had he seen her?

Was it really him?

But when she glanced up, through half-averted eyes, the crowd had moved again and he had gone.

She grabbed her bucket and mop, gave the floor a quick wipe where the blood had dripped. Then she fled, pushing her way through the crowd, ignoring the harsh looks, the muttered complaints, back to her room.

13

Fens

She cowered on her bed. Was it him? How could she be sure? How could she know?

It seemed implausible. By what chance would he have come here? What odds might be involved? Yet she remembered the calculations she'd done before – that steady flow of guests sucked into the hotel from far around – repeated them now. She thought of that web of contacts and intrigue that seemed to spread across the world, the six or seven degrees of separation that supposedly divided you from anyone you might know. Didn't that make it possible?

She remembered the picture she'd seen in the *Syrian Times*, in that library in Belgium. Standing innocuous yet proud amidst the business delegation in Europe. It was over two years ago, but had he come back with another delegation? And to London this time? She tried to see again what she'd seen in the ballroom, as she looked up. The shoulder, the elbow, the hand. The ring. The tilt of the glass. That Sinjari stance.

Rohat. Mahmet?

And yet, she knew it could not be.

But she had to know for sure. Her life depended on it. Elend's too.

She picked up the phone, dialled.

'Reception.'

She introduced herself, explained that she'd been in the ballroom earlier, cleaning the floor, and had seen the crowd of guests. She wondered what the event was. Could he tell her?

'Why do you ask?'

'I – I keep a record of the extra work I do at night. I just wanted to get it correct.'

There was a silence, and she could imagine the receptionist frowning, preparing to refuse. Then his voice returned. 'It's the Asian and Middle East Business Forum. They have a conference here on the top floor.'

More than plausible, then. Just the sort of event that a Syrian envoy to Europe would attend. A Sinjari, especially.

'Do you have a guest list?'

'Of course.'

'Is there – is there anyone called Sinjari on it?'

'Sinjari?'

Again, a silence. Was he checking?

'Why do you need to know?'

'I – I know them. Rohat Sinjari, his brother Mahmet.'

She heard the man's intake of breath.

'I don't think the delegates are your business,' he said, 'do you?'

'Please,' she said. 'I need to know.'

The phone went dead.

She could guess what he thought of her, his assumptions. Another slut of a house-keeper with whom a guest must have sought entertainment one night, and who now believed that she might be worth remembering. Such was the burden men had to carry; such were the presumptions of women like her.

She sat for a moment, her mind fogged. Rohat. Or Mahmet, perhaps. Or neither. Which was the truth?

She tried to imagine how she would know them after all this time, how they might have changed. The younger merging into what the older had been, the older – Mahmet – into what? His father?

She tried to decide, once more, what she should do. Whether she should leave; whether she could safely stay. If she fled: where she could go to.

She remembered Yaasmin and shuddered. One mistake was all that it took; one wrong choice. She remembered Gabby's advice. Always be a moving target. There was truth in that.

And yet she resisted the notion. It felt too drastic, too final. It was a submission to endless fear.

And there were all those times before. When she'd thought she'd seen him, heard his voice, heard his footsteps following her in the street. None of them true.

In that same moment, as if mocking the notion, there was the sound of movement in the corridor outside her room. Footsteps pausing rather than passing by. What might have been the slow sigh of someone's breath.

She shrank, froze.

It happened, of course. Footsteps outside. Always innocent, even at this hour. Guests or new night staff became lost, ended up in the basement, following the dizzying maze of corridors. Older staff, too, forgot how the rooms down here had changed their function over time, and might come to the wrong door. More than once she'd been woken by the sound of the door handle being rattled, or a key being tried in the lock, as someone tried to enter in search of linen or spare furniture, or for a quiet smoke.

Still she listened.

Then the footsteps continued, faded. Had they gone? Was it a trick?

She went to the door, put her ear against it, trying to quell the steady thump of her heart. Nothing.

She glanced back at Elend's sleeping figure, the small sanctuary of their bed. He looked so peaceful; her own bed beckoned. But her decision had been made. This place was a sanctuary no more. She had to leave.

This was their life, she thought; it always would be. To run, to hide whenever danger showed.

Quickly, quietly, she packed her belongings in her bag. Then she woke Elend, shushing him to immediate silence as he sleepily rubbed at his eyes and started to ask what was happening.

'We need to go,' she said. 'Don't worry. Just get dressed on top of your pyjamas. Hurry.'

Elend did as he was told, groggy but uncomplaining. As he did so, Zarrin checked around the room once more, snatched up a few items that she'd overlooked, closed the bag.

She remembered her first flight, all those years ago.

'Ready?' she asked.

Elend nodded.

She placed a chair beneath the window, stood on it, turned the latch on the sash. The top pane slipped down, and she grabbed at it, stopped it before it made a crash. The street air rushed in, pungent with the smell of exhaust fumes and dust. The noises of the city, strident.

Outside, there was a shallow well, then a wall, topped with railings, dividing it from the street. It would be a narrow squeeze, she thought, but she could just do it. She lifted up her bag, dropped it into the well. Then she climbed out, stood in the well, turned back.

'Now you,' she said to Elend.

He clambered onto the chair, raised his arms, let her lift him out. She held him up so that he could grip the rails, helped him over. She passed him the bag, followed.

'Let's go,' she said. 'Let's run.'

*

She had no plan in her mind as she fled, other than to put distance between herself and the hotel and whatever dangers it might contain, and disappear into the night. But even the fleeing seemed to be an invitation for notice, with its noise and untimely hurry. She felt exposed, imagined Rohat or Mahmet or any of their spies looking down on them from the hotel windows, already preparing for pursuit.

She ran around a corner, took the next street, turned again at the next. Three blocks away, she paused for breath, tried to think what to do. She wondered whether they could go back to the squat where they had lived before, though she knew that the ghost of Yaasmin's presence waited. Or back to Mrs Jervais. Would she give her shelter for a day or two? Yet everywhere in her past felt more like a trap than an escape, as though it would merely set her on the same course again, life repeating.

Only then did she remember her ID card, still lodged at the hotel. Should she go back, try to recover it?

But it was too risky, she knew. And in any case, what was it to her now? It merely tied her to the person she was. Better to be nameless, to have no past that might define her.

She took Elend's hand.

'Come on.'

She led him to the nearest Underground station, took the first train. It was to Cockfosters, at the end of the line. They stayed there for a while, then took another train back. At King's Cross, they disembarked, and spent the rest of the night in the mainline station, huddled against a trolley near the public toilets, ignoring as best they could the noise and the smell.

For the next two days they roamed the city once more. It felt like a jungle. A disordered and impenetrable world. The traffic snarled at her. Brash youths sized her up as they passed. Young women in their fashionable clothes, blood-red lips, brightly painted nails, stalked the pavements, like hungry cats. On the construction sites, workmen bared their chests, swung on scaffolding, or bent showing their pink buttocks like chimpanzees performing a sexual display.

She felt vulnerable and hunted; trapped.

Then, outside Victoria Coach Station, where she wandered by some instinct, she was confronted by a man. He was smartly dressed – too smart; a pimp or hustler of some sort. She looked away but he called to her in Arabic, referring to her as '*umu*' – mother.

She hesitated, half-turned.

'You look for work?'

She nodded.

'I give you good work. No problem.'

'Where? Why?'

'Because I like you. And your most fine boy here.'

'What sort of work?' she asked, suspicious again.

'Good work. Here.' He held out a leaflet, and cautiously she went to him, took it. The paper was flimsy, the printing smudged. The text was in both Arabic and English. *Farm work*, it said at the top. *Workers wanted now.*

'Where is it? What will it cost me?'

The man laughed. 'Cost? Nothing – no payment to me. Me, I am just the humble agent. You take this. Go to this address. Tell them Fazir sent you. You get this job. I get paid by them. They get a young and beautiful worker. Everyone is happy, yes?'

The address was in Cambridgeshire. She had no idea where it was, how to get there. But it was what she needed. A means of escape.

She found a coach that was heading as far as Cambridge, paid for a ticket, relieved to discover that Elend went free. On the journey, she gazed out of the window, watching the city slowly unravel into housing estates and suburbs, then fields, the streets unclogging, trucks and buses yielding to tractors and cycles and empty, winding lanes.

She marvelled at her luck in meeting the agent, and thought how uneven life was. How it became snagged and stuck on the smallest of obstacles, yet could leap across chasms and mountains with scarcely a missed stride.

She thought again of survival, and wondered what it was. In that, she thought, Yaasmin had been wrong, and her death had proved it. Survival had to be more than simply living to see another day. There had to be a legacy of some sort, a message.

Love, perhaps, or the product that it could bring. A memory at least.

In her case, she knew what it was. Elend. It was for him alone that she survived.

She tried to imagine what waited for them in the unknown place to which they were heading. Whatever it was, she told herself, it must be better than the world they had just left. Away from the city and the prying eyes of police, the squalor, the abuse. Rohat's constant threat. There'd be freedom and distant horizons, if nothing else. Perhaps safety, too. And with that, she might find peace for herself, and for Elend the sort of life he deserved. She tried to cling to that hope.

But as she approached her destination – after more buses, a long walk, a lift with an elderly couple in a car – her spirits sagged. The land daunted her. It was flat, featureless, as drained and dead as she was herself. The sky, too: a grey, flat sheet. As she made her way down the main street of the small fenland town, the wind gusted between the mean buildings, fitful and cold. It seemed to suck the will from her. Too bleak and blasted for salvation.

The office was closed when she found it. But there was a handwritten note on the door: *Back in half an hour.*

She waited two, until dusk gathered and the cold wind filled with sleety rain. No one came.

Had she travelled all this way for nothing? Was it a just a trick?

She found a room for the night in the local pub. It was above the bar and was noisy, smelled of stale beer. The window latch was broken and the wind beat out an irritable timpani as the hours dragged by. The bed was cold and damp.

She cuddled Elend to her, lulled him to sleep with stories and songs. Once, he asked why they had come here, why he couldn't go to kindergarten any more. 'We're going to live in the countryside,' she said. 'There'll be cows and sheep and horses. You'll be able to play in the fields.'

But afterwards she lay awake trying to resolve what she'd done: not just coming here on this foolish errand, but events before. Rohat or Mahmet, out there somewhere, unforgiving. And the things she'd done herself and equally couldn't forgive. What she'd done to Salvo. The innocent woman she had sent to her death.

So many betrayals in her life, she thought. Who would it be next?

*

The morning greeted her with a steely brightness, promising not sunshine and blue skies but resilience. She returned to the office.

'You should have telephoned,' the receptionist at the desk said, when she explained. He was young, hardly more than a boy: a school-leaver, she guessed, stuck for some reason where he didn't want to be. He was surly, harassed. 'I'd have told you not to bother.'

'I didn't know,' Zarrin said. Then, remembering the leaflet she'd been given at the bus station, she showed it. 'The agent in London – Fazir – promised me you'd have something. I came straight away.'

He looked at the leaflet, shrugged. 'What would he know?'

She reached out, touched his arm.

She felt him stiffen, and read a frenzy of emotions in the sudden confusion in his features: anguish and fear and desire. She might have laughed at his innocence.

'Please,' she said.

He regarded her hand, followed it as far as her wrist, seemed unable to force his eyes further. 'Do – do you have papers?'

'No. I'm afraid not.'

'And he – the boy – is he yours?' He glanced at Elend.

'Yes, he is.'

'I don't know.'

194

She said nothing, regarded him steadily, until he looked up. She knew the contradictions he would see. Beguiling young woman, older sister, imperious mother. She guessed, too, the way his mind would use the moment later, imagine it to a different end. She allowed a small smile to appear in her eyes.

He gave a quick nod. 'I'll see what I can do.'

'Thank you,' she said. She squeezed his arm.

He picked up the phone, dialled a number. There was a muttered conversation, interspersed with sidelong glances at her or Elend. Each one, she returned with a smile.

'OK,' he said, as he put down the phone. 'They'll take you. Latimer's. It's asparagus at the moment. Will that do?'

Zarrin nodded. 'Of course. Thank you.'

The boy took Zarrin's details, not noticing, it seemed, her small hesitation as he asked for her surname, and she replied with the first one that came to mind: Pashew. A new identity – and one she shared with the poet she so admired. Who better?

He spelled out the terms of the contract. Two months minimum, half the wage held back until then. The weekly rate, the deductions that she'd have to pay for accommodation, work clothes, insurance. His voice was limp, apologetic.

She smiled once more, thanked him again. She shook his hand to close the deal. Another small squeeze. When did she become like this, she wondered: siren, seductress? Then she thought: I am anything I have to be now. Anything at all.

'Do you have transport?' he asked.

'No. Is it far?'

'It's quite a way. I – I'll drive you if you like. It might be better. You'll need to sort out your accommodation and everything.'

'You're kind,' she said.

He blushed. 'Shall we go?'

He took her to a small van parked outside. The seats were worn; the smell of petrol filled the air. The boy drove slowly, inexpertly, crunching the gears. Each time he did so, he apologised. Once, clumsily, his hand slipped on the uncooperative gear-stick and brushed against her knee.

'Oops,' she said, and glanced at him, her lips pursed, brow furrowed. A school-matron's look.

'Sorry,' he said again.

There was no repeat.

At the farm, he pointed towards the gangmaster's office, didn't offer to accompany her further, drove away as soon as she had closed the van door.

*

'Ready?'

The engine coughed. She gripped her knife.

She had been set to work on a large horticultural farm on the margins of the fens – one of a team of a dozen in a wide expanse of field. Ahead of her stretched long, straight ridges of brown soil, each one topped with a line of green spikes bearing ragged purple crowns. The row seemed to extend to the horizon, out of sight. Away to her right were dozens more. Enough asparagus, she thought, to feed an army; enough to keep the small team of workers busy for months.

'Let's go.'

The supervisor had explained the technique as they waited for the trays to be stacked on the carrier beam behind the tractor. Just follow the tractor along the row, cut the ripe stalks as she went, drop them into the pocket of her apron. When she had enough, she needed to go to the tractor and transfer the stalks from her pocket to the tray, then continue from where she left off. He'd given her a knife, its blade curled, the edge razor-sharp. He demonstrated it to her on a length of string; one swish and it was cut.

While he explained, it had seemed simple, almost effortless. But, as soon as she started, she realised that there was far more to it than had appeared. The whole process was like an ungainly dance, done stooped and bow-legged. She had to walk with her arm stretched, knife ready. Every pace or two, when she found a ripe stalk, she had to bend, steady the stalk, cut it as near to the ground as she could, and at an angle, with a single stroke. Sometimes she dropped some of her harvest, hastily had to regather it. If she put too many stalks into her pocket, they crushed and broke. If she didn't put in enough, she had to dash to the tractor too often. But when she hurried, or didn't pay attention, the ground would trick her and she'd stumble or jolt her knee against her elbow or chin. She seemed to be constantly on the run. The only brief respite was at the end of the row, when the tractor turned, repositioned itself. Then it was off again.

At the start of her second row, the woman next to her looked across, grinned, showing yellowed teeth, a ring in her tongue. 'Keeps you fit, doesn't it?'

Zarrin nodded, indicated the line of trays on the carrier beam. Most pickers were already on their second or third tray; she was still on the first. 'I'm missing so many. I'm so slow. I'm worried they'll sack me.'

'You'll learn, I promise,' the woman said. 'Today will hurt. Tomorrow even more – and the day after that you'll wish you hadn't been born. But the second week is easier.'

Zarrin wanted to ask: did they ever have a break; how long did they work like this? What happened when her pile of trays was so high that she could no longer reach to the top? But the tractor was moving again. They stooped, followed.

After a few paces, the woman beside her called across. 'I'll help you out. Don't worry.'

She needed it, she quickly realised. Her first row had been at the edge of the field, where the crop was sparse. Twenty rows in, the growth was denser. Now she really did struggle to keep up. But the woman beside her was as good as her word. Every dozen metres or so she stepped across, out of her own row, quickly sliced some of Zarrin's stalks, dropped them on the soil. Zarrin just had to snatch them up and add them to her own.

At the end of the row she thanked her.

'I'm Carla,' the woman said. 'You?'

'Zarrin. Where are you from?'

'I'm a Kiwi. I'm travelling, seeing the world.'

Zarrin thought how wonderful that sounded, how free, and told her so.

'That's me,' Carla agreed. 'A free spirit. I live by my wits, never stay long, go where I please. It's just a shame I have to earn enough to eat. When I set out, I thought I'd work in bars and restaurants wherever I went, have free food and alcohol, men to choose from every night. But right now this is all I could get. No alcohol, no men – and bloody asparagus in every direction I look. I even dream about the stuff. Green and purple penises! No man will ever seem serious again.'

As the day progressed, Zarrin could understand Carla's hallucinations. The stalks filled her vision, filled her mind, seemed to infect her. They ceased to be plants, insensate and blind; became human. They could be tall and strong, weak and woeful, slim, tubby, straight, bent. Some gave themselves up willingly to her knife, others resisted. Some stood proud and defiant, some dodged, some wept. When she lay each handful in her tray, it felt like laying a child to rest.

At last, mid-morning, the tractor stopped. For fifteen minutes they were allowed to lie in the grass at the edge of the field, or sit with their backs against the gate, or stand and smoke, drink coffee, snatch a snack, talk.

Carla came across to where Zarrin had flung herself down, stood beside her, a cigarette in her hand.

'How's it going?'

'I'm exhausted,' Zarrin said. 'I don't know how you keep this up.'

'It's hard at first, like I said. But somehow your mind seems to find a space. And then time passes and it's all done. That's what I find, anyway.' She drew on her cigarette. 'How's the hands?'

Zarrin turned her palms outwards. The right one was already blistered from the handle of the knife. On her left were scratches, one deeper cut across the ball of her thumb where the knife had slipped.

Carla tutted. 'Have you got any gloves?'

Zarrin shook her head.

'Here, use this.' She went to a bag that lay beside the fence, pulled out a bottle. 'Tea-tree oil. All the way from sunny Aotearoa. You can't beat it.'

Zarrin sniffed at the bottle, smelled the pungent acidity of the oil. She rubbed it into her hands. It stung, but then came the slow easing in its wake.

'I'll find you some gloves for tomorrow.' Carla looked down, smiled. 'You a refugee?'

Zarrin nodded.

'Legal or illegal?' And when Zarrin did not immediately reply: 'It's alright. I'm not going to split on you. But in any case, I guess your silence tells me.' She took another drag of her cigarette. 'Where from?'

'Syria.'

'How long?'

'Five years.'

'Shit. That must be hard.' Then, 'Is this your first farm work?'

'Yes.'

'Then take some advice. Watch the gangmasters. They'll screw you – and I mean that in every sense of the word. When they shout at you and threaten you, just take it and don't argue. When they start being nice to you, that's the time to worry.'

The same everywhere, Zarrin thought. In every job she might ever find.

They returned to work. The morning slowly went. Each row seemed endless, and was succeeded by another endless row, the same. The march of the crop beneath her seemed like a long litany of words in some foreign tongue, counting off her sins. She found herself counting them, too, until the numbers rang in her head. By lunchtime she was nearing six thousand, and silently repeated the tally to herself, as though afraid that, if she forgot it, she'd have to start again – not just the counting, but the harvesting as well, back from her first step.

That night, the numbers haunted her, and in her sleep dissolved to an endless staircase up which she hauled herself, knowing that she had to reach the top, yet knowing that, when she got there, all she would find was the void beyond.

The next day she hurt, just as Carla had warned her, and the day after was worse. But by the end of the week the toil became less. Her hands hardened, her muscles gained strength. She learned how to walk the rows more efficiently, on pliant legs, knees lowered, so that they didn't jar against her body as much. She learned how to use the knife, scooping it so that she could take the stalk with a single, clean cut. She became adept at timing her dash to the trays so that she didn't miss ripe stalks, nor have to backtrack too far to find them. She no longer needed help from Carla, could do her share, keep up.

And slowly, as her body found its rhythm and adapted to the work, she found time to discover pleasure in her days. The skylark, spilling its song across the land. The sudden scent of cherry blossom, carried on the breeze. The glimpse of a fox. The arch of a rainbow against the clouds, the smell of rain in the air. In the morning, her shadow stretched before her as she worked; in the evening, preceded her as she made her way back to the minibus.

The physical luxury of rest, safe in the enclosing cocoon of the night. Elend beside her, on a mattress by her bed.

They lived in a hostel with fifty or more other workers, all contracted to the same trio of gangmasters but working on different farms. The building, once a rambling farmhouse, had long ago fallen into disuse. The floorboards were bare, the walls covered with flaking and stained wallpaper in patterns of roses and tulips and bluebirds. The stairs were narrow and steep. It was arranged into half-a-dozen dormitories, each holding four or five pairs of rough-made wooden bunks. Downstairs, there was one further room, a large flat-roofed extension which served as dining room and kitchen. Hygiene was primitive: half a dozen toilets out in the yard, a row of shower units fed by lukewarm water. Living was casual and unstructured, suiting the place. There were few rules. Men lived downstairs, women for the most part up, though, for matters of romance or companionship, or simple desire, exceptions occurred. Eating was communal, and the boundaries of ownership were often fluid.

The workers were an eclectic bunch. Poles and Croats, Lithuanians, Romanians, Estonians, Greeks. A Moroccan or two. A scatter of people from Africa, South America, the Middle East. Yet, for all their differences, most were the same. Poor, dour, shrunken by the life they were forced to lead. Amongst themselves the men sometimes squabbled, and competed for what women there were. But to her relief Zarrin seemed to be outside their attention – protected, perhaps, not just by her ethnicity and the religion it implied, but by Elend too. For each of them was a complication that might make any casual predator think twice, and turn to easier pickings. The women, though, were amiable in a detached and workaday way. They liked Elend, and petted him and spoiled him within their meagre capabilities, and there were other children there with whom he could play.

There was, also, Brodie. She was a local girl, hired to look after the children when the adults were at work. She was young – perhaps seventeen or eighteen years old – though with childish ways, a doughy body, a moon-round face. The other women said that she was a simpleton, and suggested Down's syndrome or other disorders of which Zarrin had never heard. She'd not met anyone like that before, and wondered whether whatever disability afflicted her was visited only on Westerners; or whether in Syria such people were hidden away and never saw the light of day. Would she have known? Thus, Brodie's strangeness was a barrier to her, and she was uncertain how to address her, whether as a woman or child, and their conversations together were stilted and brief. But Brodie had a way with children – a natural directness that made them laugh, kept them good, often seemed to lock them in humble silence, spellbound. Elend loved her, and would always run to her when she arrived in the morning; sometimes stand beside her, reluctant to let go, when she left at the end of the afternoon. He enjoyed, too, the company of the other children, and, one of the oldest amongst them, he gradually adopted the senior role: caring for them, organising their games, sometimes sitting them in a circle around him and telling them stories.

Zarrin saw the change in him and was pleased.

The days passed. Weeks became months. They moved from field to field, farm to farm. Workers came and left. After a few weeks, Carla was one of those to go. She did so abruptly, with no word or warning, and Zarrin wondered why. She missed her friendship and ready advice. The crops, too, changed, one succeeding another. Asparagus to cherries, then to strawberries, then to salad vegetables, then to apples and pears and plums. None was without its challenge; each one assailed her body in new ways. The scorching sun. The sweat and flies. Wasps stinging her as she picked the fruit. The ache of constant repetition – cut or thrust or stab or tug. The tedium of long hours spent doing the same thing. But she was adaptable now, and could quickly learn, and her body had the suppleness and stamina it needed for almost any task. And most of the time her work left her mind free to think and remember and imagine and plan.

She thought of Dinos in the market, and found a strange satisfaction in harvesting the vegetables and fruits that previously she had sold, and she wondered whether any of the ones she had handled would find their way to his stall. She thought of Salvo, and hoped that he was free and driving again, and to that wish would dedicate her day's work.

Sometimes, she thought of Yaasmin, and felt a familiar stab of guilt.

She thought, too, of Rohat, and found herself confronted by an enigma. Then and now. The lifetime that seemed to have passed between the two. She'd changed so much. She would hardly recognise herself if she met the woman she'd been then. And he, Rohat? Had he changed? Might he have forgotten? Could he really be out there, still searching for her? Or was she safe, with a new name; here, in this wide and open place, where there was nothing but flat land and blue skies, and where she was absorbed into that nothingness, like a tiny insect, invisible and unimportant?

Was she free?

14

Turkey Trot

Another field, another crop. The seasons passing. Autumn, the mornings cool, dew on the grass, the days mellow, always shortening. Birds on the wing, heading south. Then winter, arriving quickly, with a simple shift in the wind. Workers following the birds. The nights clamped around her coldly, so that she slept beneath a pile of blankets, scavenged from the empty beds, Elend cuddled at her side. In the morning there was ice on the puddles; the soil was hard beneath her feet. Her hands and lips grew chapped by the cold, the dirt set deep in the cracks and cuts in her skin.

Day by day, there were more of those – cuts – for she was harvesting Brussels sprouts. Like all the other crops, they seemed to require a new skill, a different way to wield the knife. Zarrin marvelled at the irony. This work was meant to be so menial, so lowly, that anyone could do it, and for the minimum of pay. And yet it taxed the mind and body, the wits and the nimbleness of touch. She had so much to learn, and had to learn it the hard way – by trial and error. And the cost of failing was severe. With each slip of the knife, a new nick, a new scar. If you were unlucky, it could be far worse. A gash on the palm or the web between forefinger and thumb, which might require stitches, would take weeks to heal. The end of a finger sliced off: more weeks off work, without pay.

Care was the only solution, but care made you slow, and the pocket suffered. Rush the work, and both hand and pocket paid.

Always the victim was blamed.

'He should have worn gloves. That's the rule. You all know that,' a gangmaster pronounced after one such accident. Though the gloves didn't fit, were too clumsy, prevented you from achieving your quota.

'Get to hospital,' another said to a Polish worker as she stood, holding the loose and bloody flap of skin on her thumb in place. 'And don't bother coming back. You'll be no use bandaged like an Egyptian mummy.'

Like the rest of the workers who were left to face the winter in the fields, therefore, Zarrin stooped and twisted and cut and dropped, and carried the baskets of sprouts to the trailer, and tried to ignore the cold, and the soreness of her lips and hands, and the latest slash on her palm. And slowly the rows yielded to her knife, and day by day the small team of workers edged across the field, east to west, as if trying to retreat from winter's advance. Yet each morning the shadows seemed to have moved with them, and each evening they came earlier to reclaim them again.

*

As Christmas approached, and the weather worsened, work in the fields ground to a halt. Zarrin was one of the last to be laid off, but that brought no benefit. By the time she roamed the area, looking for new work, the last Christmas jobs had been taken. And as ever, on her final day, when she had faced the gangmaster to collect her wages – to settle the balance of the bond she'd paid against all the additional charges for which she was deemed responsible – she had received less than she expected. There were so many costs the poor gangmaster had to bear: the childcare, the wear-and-tear on clothes and tools, the consumables involved in her accommodation, the transport and the unexpected increases in insurance and health costs – she was lucky that there was any money left at all. Within days, she was running short. She needed something, didn't know where else to look.

But then, in town, where she had gone in search of anything that might give her shelter and food in return for work, she met Carla, leaning against the wall of a pub, smoking. They hugged, exchanged welcomes, news. Carla seemed embarrassed about her new life, reluctant to tell, but finally admitted that one of the gangmasters had made her an offer she couldn't refuse. She grinned sheepishly. 'I'm his assistant, officially. His *amanuensis*. His right hand.' She grinned again. 'A good term for it, given the things I have to do.'

Zarrin stood, speechless at the news. How could Carla have done that, she raged; how could she sell herself in that way? Yet then she thought of Elend, and what it would mean to him – a home to live in, stability of a sort, the chance for proper schooling. If she had the chance, shouldn't she do the same? Wouldn't it be a betrayal of him not to?

'Not that it will last,' Carla said, and her grin faded, became a vague and distant frown. 'I'm letting myself be used. But, hell, I was man-hungry, and this is sex in a comfy bed for a change, and it's fun.'

Then she asked Zarrin what she was doing now.

'Nothing. Looking for work.'

'What sort of thing?'

'Anything. I'm—' She shrugged. 'You know how it is.'

'Have you been to the factory?' And Carla explained: there was a turkey-processing plant just out of town. At this time of year, it was always rushing to meet the Christmas orders, desperate for staff. She should ask there.

'We've all done our stint,' Carla said. 'Tell them I sent you.'

Zarrin took Carla's advice, was hired immediately.

And so, for the next three weeks, she stood in front of a suspended conveyor track, on which carcasses of turkeys, hung by their feet, paraded past, like something from a Disney cartoon.

Plucking was done to a strict regime. For hours at a time, the conveyor never stopped. Each worker was given an allotted part of the bird to pluck: right breast, centre breast, left breast, back, legs, wings. Zarrin was the last in line and had to do the tidying up. As each bird moved relentlessly past, she had to find all the missed feathers, pull them out before the carcass swung out of reach.

It was tiresome, neck-aching work. The conveyor was set to the average height of the men, but Zarrin was the smallest so worked at the limit of her reach. She tried standing on an upturned crate, but it was too unsteady, and when she slipped off, the carcass would be gone by the time she'd righted it and climbed back on. There'd be reprimands from the supervisors; if it happened too often, a fine to pay. And the carcasses were coy in giving up their final feathers. Some came away with a sharp tug; others clung fast and needed to be eased out. Some simply refused. She never knew which to expect.

As she plucked, she tried not to think of what she was doing – what had gone before. When she'd been recruited, she'd been given a tour of the premises. The stunner where the birds were anaesthetised, the bleeding line where they were killed, the scalding room where they were dipped briefly in hot water to soften the feathers. After they'd been plucked, the finishing room where they were washed in brine, then dried, wrapped. But the stench always reminded her. A sickly blend of blood, offal, damp feathers, warm flesh, brine.

She longed for Christmas. Longed for the work to be done.

She longed, too, to escape from the accommodation unit that she occupied. It was a flimsy Portakabin, shared with twenty others, crowded in one room, men and women alike; another cabin, acting as a communal room, was furnished with gas rings for cooking, a pair of uncooperative microwaves, four long tables, low wooden benches. It was noisy, public, always cold. There were two small washrooms, with toilets and showers, in a separate cabin on the other side of the yard. A coin-fed boiler, which hungrily swallowed any money it was given, yielded its contents of water reluctantly and lukewarm.

For Elend, life was even worse. The only childcare available was in the crèche that the factory ran. Another dull Portakabin, at the back of the premises, supervised by a series of bussed-in women from the nearest town. He was the oldest child, and there was no teaching, few books or toys for someone of his age. He came away from it each evening surly from boredom, restless, anger just below the surface. Zarrin would try to make up for it in every way she could – reading to him, inventing games that they could play, cuddling him to her – but she knew how inadequate it all was. She saw the darkness in his eyes return, that sense of resistance grow. She blamed herself for it, and counted the days until it would be over and they could move on.

At the workers' request, a radio was brought in to lighten the mood, improve productivity. It blared out at full blast over the rattle and rumble of the conveyor, the background hiss of the waterlines, the shouts and calls of the staff. Pop music mainly, raucous and throbbing. Zarrin hated it, tried to shut it from her ears. But the other workers enjoyed it, and would sing along. And as Christmas approached the programme changed, turned to popped-up carols, and ditties about snowmen and Santa Claus and robins. The engagement of the workers increased, became more inventive, more obscene. The tunes and the words lodged in her brain, repeated themselves endlessly day and night, matched by the endless procession of dead and half-naked turkeys.

But, at last, the end came. As the world outside darkened, and the lights in the plucking room took hold, the final turkey swung by, decorated by the time it reached Zarrin with threads of tinsel, a silver star, a Santa Claus hat. The noise of the machinery stopped. The radio blared on, unaccompanied. The workers stood for a moment, bemused by the lack of activity, their arms and hands becalmed, unsure what to do next.

Then a ragged cheer broke out. People hugged. The supervisors came down from their balcony, beaming now, no longer the harsh masters of time and motion, the guardians of brand quality, but fellow workers, amiable friends. They handed out envelopes, wishing each recipient a merry Christmas. Inside, when she opened hers, Zarrin found a corporate card bearing a seasonal message and a voucher for a free meal – a turkey chasseur – at the local pub.

That evening, in the accommodation unit, the sense of camaraderie continued. Food was shared. Toasts were proposed. Someone remembered a dance called the turkey trot, and performed it to much laughter and encouragement. Then they all formed a ragged line and danced it together, weaving around the small room, arms wagging, feet kicked out. Elend and the other children thought it immensely funny, and wouldn't stop. Long after the adults had tired and sat around, slipping back into their usual small ethnic groups and huddles of friends, they continued to chase each other, squawking, screeching.

*

Then it was vegetables again, and rain and wind and clay. She walked to the fields at dawn through a land that looked as if it had been scarred by war. The ground churned to mud by yesterday's assault, the mud frozen, puddles skimmed with ice that creaked and cracked as she passed; abandoned cuttings lying twisted in the soil. And ahead of her the ranked platoons of today's crop sullen, crouched, awaiting their fate.

In that first hour, she was met by dour resistance. The clay was hard, the cabbages and cauliflowers slippery in her hands, the stalks tough and unyielding against the knife. As she worked, the coldness rose up to claim her, clamping her feet in dull pain, so that each step jarred and was taken reluctantly. Her breath became her own, gathering around her, freezing on her cheeks, until it fitted like a tight mask. Every false move brought hurt beyond its worth: the whiplash of a leaf against her face, stub of clod against her toe, the razor-sharp gash of a flint. She yearned for the sun, for daybreak at least, when she could see what she was doing, avoid these taunts. Yet later, as the murky grey of dawn was replaced by the paler grey of day and the land slowly thawed, the pain simply shifted and took on new forms. Her hands became clagged with soil and her boots grew heavy, so that she moved clumsily, like an old woman on tired legs. Sweat, slug slime and sap smeared every exposed piece of skin. Her back ached, knees protested, arms were like lead. The skin on her fingers split, her eyes burned with the cold and the dirt.

And all the time, the wind came, searching for her. It blew from the east, a Russian wind. It carried with it an ancient Bolshevik distrust of anything in its path. By the time it reached Zarrin's corner of the world it had already split boughs, toppled trees, stilled rivers, turned vast tracts of forest and lake and boggy waste into bleak white deserts, felled elk and deer in their tracks. Now it had only her left. It fretted and snarled, frayed the hems of her clothes, the loose edges of her mind, tried to devour her. She hated it, and it hated her in return.

She armoured herself as best she could. On that first day back, she had been given a pair of overalls and calf-length rubber boots. The overalls hung on her loosely, and smelled of damp soil, rotten vegetation, stale cigarette smoke. The boots slopped around her legs and as the day went on filled with clay and grit and the cold mist that dripped from her, and made a prison of her feet. In the days that followed, she acquired other clothes by whatever means she could. One of the other women gave her an old pullover, its sleeves torn and holey – her sister's, she said, before she fell ill and had to cease this type of work. In a recycling bin in the village she found a vest and an assortment of woollen socks for herself, two old pullovers and a coat for Elend. One weekend she learned about a jumble sale in the church hall, in support of world peace. She went along and braved the war of jabbing elbows, grabbing hands, to win a priceless pair of gloves and a sheepskin hat with flaps that came down over her ears, tied beneath her chin. Better than any hijab or scarf.

Then, the weather changed once more. Writhing curtains of rain swept in from the west, wrapping the world in grey, turning the soil to a dark and sticky morass. Then, in February, snow again, making a carpet through which the plants peered like mischievous street urchins, each with its white prayer cap. Then rain returned, and all was slush and mire. Zarrin fell ill, her throat raw from constant coughing, her nose and lips swollen and red. She lay in her small bunk, huddled against the cold, shivering. Her mind became loose and lurid. Dreams and waking fears merged. Rohat, searching for her, Elend wandering and lost; the gangmaster in some strange way co-conspirator with them both. And, in her hallucinating, she and Yaasmin became one, and her body, or Yaasmin's or the two combined, hung before her, naked, from a chain.

After three nights, when the fears and dreams grew too strong, she dragged herself back to the fields, and counted the hours away like days, each one with a morning, a noon and a night.

All this time, since she had returned to the fields, Elend's life had been makeshift. There was no crèche or childcare available now, nor enough workers with children for them to make their own arrangements; no one like Brodie that she could call upon. For Elend, therefore, the day was spent in whatever way she could fix up. Supervised, in a loose and casual manner, by one of the workers if they had to stay around the camp for any reason. Farmed out to a local schoolgirl if there was one on holiday that she could find. If all else failed, with her, in the fields, finding whatever shelter and amusement he could, near enough for her to check up on him occasionally. Sometimes, left for long hours on his own.

He didn't complain. Though what he thought of it, and what he did while he was alone, she had only the scantiest idea, for he would tell her little of his days. She imagined him sitting around listless and bored, or roaming, adventuring, finding hazards that she dared not think about. Once, when she'd left him alone in the accommodation area, she couldn't find him on her return, and he didn't respond to her calls. She searched and called ever more widely and with increasing anxiety, almost panic. Still he didn't appear. She looked in the storage sheds, in the lean-to where the tractors and implements were housed, in the old workshop which contained a startling array of rusting tines and knives and saws and scythes. She went to the pond, and searched for some clue that he might have been there. She stood in the gateway and scanned the road in either direction, wondering whether he had wandered off.

George came across. He was an elderly widower who had taken to an itinerant worker's life when his wife had died, and to most people was known as Jug, because he was rarely seen without a beer tankard to hand. But Zarrin always addressed him more respectfully.

He asked what the trouble was, and she explained.

He nodded sagely, told her not to worry; assured her that they'd soon find the child. As she looked again in the places she had already searched, she heard him from the other side of the yard, calling and whistling, as he would a dog.

And, to her relief, it worked. For Jug suddenly came up behind her, Elend at his side. 'Here he is,' he said.

She grabbed Elend to her, hugged him, then held him at arm's length and asked, 'Where were you? Where have you been? We've been calling.'

'He was up on the hay, in the Dutch barn,' Jug said.

'How did you find him?'

He grinned. 'I let myself imagine where I might spend the day, when I was his age. That's where I'd have gone. It's dark, it's warm. It's a good place to go.'

She looked at the barn. The hay was stacked fifteen or more metres high, almost to the roof.

'How did he get up there?' she asked,

Again, Jug grinned. 'The same way I did. He shinned up the post. That's how I used to do it as a kid. It's a world of your own up there.' He scuffed Elend's hair. 'A boy needs a world of his own.'

She should have found relief in the incident, for no harm had been done, and Jug's words suggested that there might even be pleasure in the life that Elend was leading. But, in her mood of guilt and self-blame, relief refused to come. Instead she added another sin to her litany: what she was doing to Elend. The life she was imposing on him; the world she had brought him to. What had he done to deserve that?

*

'It's not your fault,' she said. 'It's not.'

There were tears on her cheek. She wiped them away.

'I'll make it better for you. I'll find something else to do, something that will give us time to be together again.'

As winter had eased, and the fields slowly turned from frosted white to dung brown, and then to green, she had expected their life to improve. Better weather, longer days, a change of work. And, crucially for Elend, the flood of springtime workers returning, with their chatter and stories and laughter, and their own children for company.

Yet it hadn't happened. This year, the roads remained empty. The boards advertising vacancies for seasonal workers stayed propped against the farm gates. The gangmasters prowled the streets and pubs of town, seeking out anyone who might like a job, or trying to bribe those who already had one with offers of better accommodation, higher pay.

The reason for the whole dilemma was plain enough. It was plastered over the newspaper headlines, on the hoardings outside newsagents, on local and national radio almost every day. It was argued about in pubs and on the street. Brexit. Britain's choice – confirmed now by the government – to leave the EU. The xenophobia that many claimed had led to it all was obvious, too. There was graffiti on the walls, demonstrations where right-wing banners were lofted and waved, counter-demonstrations that often as not led to fights, police arrests. Tales were told by the gangmasters of migrant workers and the farmers who employed them being beaten up, their vehicles and homes torched.

Faced with all that, the workers from Poland and Romania and Bulgaria, who usually arrived in a steady stream at this time of year, had chosen not to come. Who wanted to work in a country like this? Who wanted to take the risks of being abused, deported, attacked?

For people like Zarrin it might have been a godsend: so much work around. Instead, it seemed like a curse. Jobs were plentiful, the wages better than before, but the toil was unending, the targets and schedules impossible to achieve. The gangmasters drove the staff they had to the limit and beyond. Many of the workers who had been recruited were also novices, or students with no great commitment to the job. Mistakes happened regularly, work was poorly done, fuelling even further the gangmasters' ire. For eight weeks, Zarrin had worked without a break, long hours, long days. And each morning there seemed to be yet more to do. She was exhausted, felt bludgeoned and bruised.

Elend, also, should have found the change to his advantage, yet suffered instead. In an effort to attract workers, help out the farmers, the local school had thrown its doors open to any children of migrant workers old enough to attend. Thus, with half a dozen other children from nearby farms, Elend went to school. But the arrangements were ones of expediency rather than educational ambition, and the needs of the children had been given little thought. Whatever their age or language or ability, the incomers were put together in the entry class, left to learn what they could. Elend found the work boring. Thanks to Zarrin's and then Brodie's efforts, he'd already learned arithmetic beyond the level that the school offered, and he'd learned to read the way that they taught him, not in the fancy manner that the school used. He became moody, recalcitrant, began to misbehave. He returned one afternoon from the school with a note from the teacher, informing his mother that he would be barred from school if his behaviour didn't improve.

Zarrin was too tired, too stressed to give it the attention it deserved, simply added her own reprimand to that of the teacher.

Elend sulked.

Today, she'd been summoned to the school, given a final warning. Elend had been caught fighting in the playground. He'd hit a local boy, made him cry. It couldn't happen again.

Zarrin had stood, head down, repentant, as though it was she who'd done the deed. Elend stood beside her, surly in defiance.

As she led him away, she'd seethed with embarrassment and motherly indignation: at the teacher, at the school, at Elend. Yet mostly at herself. It was her fault, she knew. Yet again she had given him too little, demanded too much. For weeks the sum of her attention had been to call him awake in the morning, feed him a hurried meal, send him off; and in the evening to greet him with a quick kiss when she returned, then feed him again, put him to bed. At all other times, her work consumed her.

Now, on the street, she pulled him to her, hugged him against her side. It wasn't his fault, she told him, and promised him that she would make his life better.

He nodded dumbly, something like disbelief or simple incomprehension in his eyes.

She hugged him again. 'I will,' she said. 'I will.' Though how, she didn't know.

15

Choices

Was this the answer? She closed the door behind her, paused for a moment on the step, her thoughts in turmoil. What should she do?

The gangmaster had summoned her that morning – 'My office, after work, six-thirty sharp.' A summons like that spelt trouble, without doubt, and she'd wondered what mistake she'd made, who had complained about her. What sort of sanction she faced.

She steeled herself for the worst.

The gangmaster had been sitting at his desk when she went in. He was unshaven, had unkempt hair, the manner of a man with no time for the niceties of life. When he indicated, Zarrin had sat in the chair opposite, avoided his stare, looked at the desk.

Despite his busyness, he seemed to be in no hurry. For some moments he said nothing, until at last she looked up.

'We've not talked before, have we?' he said.

She shook her head.

He asked about her work, about the accommodation, about Elend. She wondered what his motive was, whether he was probing her for some hint of dissatisfaction that he might use against her or one of the other staff. She answered neutrally.

'It can be hard, can't it?' he said, in a voice that might almost have been affable. 'That's true for every one of us, I know that.'

She nodded. 'It can be.'

He grumbled about the life he led, telling her about the difficulties he was facing at the moment: the lack of labour, the problems with the weather earlier in the year, his concerns about the weather to come. The pressure that was on them all. 'People think me a cruel man,' he said. 'I'm not really like that. It's just the job that gets to me.'

She offered bland words of sympathy.

Then he said, 'It's difficult doing this job alone. That's what I've discovered. It was easier before.'

'Before?' she asked.

He gave a dismissive wave of his hand. 'Before your time.' He indicated his desk – the scattered papers, the half-smoked cigarettes, the stains of food and sweat. 'It wasn't like this then.'

'No. I can understand.'

The gangmaster leaned back. 'So, I've made a decision. It can't go on like this. I need a helping hand. Do you get my drift?'

Again, she nodded, uncertain.

'A foreman of some sort,' he continued, then gave a stiff, apologetic smile. 'Foreperson, I suppose I should call it, under the circumstances.'

Another small nod.

Someone to supervise the workers in the field, he told her. They needed someone with an eye for detail on them; they slacked too much. And to help organise the work-teams, to take responsibility for recruitment, to help with the accounts as well. What did she think?

'Yes,' she said. 'I can see that makes sense.'

He regarded her steadily, as if expecting her to say more; when she didn't, said slowly, as if talking to a simpleton, 'I want it to be you.'

She looked up at him in surprise. Did he mean that? She tried to read his eyes, see what lay behind the offer.

He seemed to take her silence as a form of bargaining, and said, hurriedly, 'It would mean more money, of course. And better accommodation. You'd welcome that, I'm sure. That child of yours too.'

'Elend,' she said.

'Yes, Elend. He's a nice boy. He deserves a proper home.'

'Yes, he does.'

'A proper school, too,' he said.

'I know.'

He stood up, went to the window, looked out.

'These days,' he said, 'good people are like gold dust. Workers – women like you.'

'People like me?' she asked.

He turned back to her, smiled. 'I've had good reports about you. You're reliable, bright. Congenial. That's what I'm told.'

She bit at her lip, abashed, looked down. He came across to her, stood close.

'We'd work as a team,' he said. He raised his hand as if he was going to pat her on the shoulder, but let it lapse. 'We'd make a good team, you and me. Don't you think?'

She remembered Carla, the choice she had made. *Sex in a comfy bed*, she'd said. And what was the phrase she'd used? 'Amanuensis', his right hand. She remembered, too, her own reaction. Shock, then realisation: she'd do the same thing if she had to. For Elend's sake.

Would she? Could she? What other choice did she have?

'Well?' the gangmaster asked, and then, as she still hesitated, he gave her shoulder a clumsy pat, let his hand lie there.

She tried not to flinch. 'I need to think about it,' she said.

'Yes. Of course.' He patted her again, and with what seemed like reluctance, the smallest brush of her neck, removed his hand. 'You do that.'

'Thank you,' she said. She stood up, turned to go.

'You won't keep me waiting too long, though, will you?'

'A day or two,' she said. 'That's all I ask.'

She felt his eyes follow her as she walked to the door, opened it, stepped out.

*

'They're swimming,' Elend called.

It was a week later and she'd not yet given the gangmaster her answer, or not quite. But earlier that day he'd cornered her again, asked: had she decided yet? Almost, she'd told him, and given him a small, encouraging smile. 'It's a big step. I just need to be sure.'

This evening, she'd taken Elend out for a walk. She wanted to think, a chance to convince herself one more time. It was the right choice. The only choice. And in the scale of men she'd known, was the gangmaster so bad?

But the evening seemed unfitted for such matters. The air was heavy, the land warm from the day's heat, the sky slowly darkening to cobalt and burnished pewter. From the fields came the gummy munch of cows chewing their cud. Rooks squabbled above a line of oaks; in the distance, an early cuckoo called. Elend had walked at her side, one hand in hers, the other clutching a long stick with which he swished at the verge, making the moths dance, the pollen rise. There was the scent of parsley and musk and honey.

Then, suddenly, he had pointed ahead to where the road rose over a little hump-backed bridge, its bricks fire-red in the lowering sun. He let go of her hand, ran down the road, hauled himself onto the parapet, peered over.

'Careful,' she'd called.

'They're in the river,' he'd shouted back. 'Look.'

She assumed that he meant ducks. 'I'm coming,' she said.

But before she reached him he jumped off the parapet, was scrambling down the bank at the side of the bridge.

'Where are you going?'

'I want to play with them.'

By now, she could hear the voices. She reached the bridge, looked over. Below, in the stream, was a gaggle of children, paddling, splashing beyond the fringe of reeds. Elend was standing on the bank, kicking off his shoes, pulling at his socks.

She called him to stop, but he ignored her, yanked off his jeans, gave a yell, stepped into the water. There was a moment of hesitation as its coolness gripped, then he plunged forward. Within seconds he was lost amongst the other children, welcomed into their midst.

She stood, watching, laughing at the children's antics, and at Elend's bubbling happiness. It seemed halcyon, this scene, like an Impressionist painting of an innocent world long-gone. The smooth bodies of the children, with their haloes of shimmering spray. The water, rippling away from them in folds of greens and blues and reds. In the distance, the trees, delicately dipping their branches into the languid flow, making it swirl. Swallows swooped and kissed the surface. A kingfisher flashed past, a brilliant turquoise gem.

'It's lovely, isn't it?'

She turned at the voice, startled. A man was standing behind her. He was short, stocky, had brown curly hair. But it was the way he was dressed that surprised her. Over shorts and T-shirt he was wearing a long apron, ornamented with bright yellow daisies.

She felt flustered, out of place. 'I – I'm sorry. I didn't mean to intrude. But Elend – my son – wanted to go in the water.'

The man laughed. 'Why not? It's not our stream. And even if it was, he'd be welcome.'

Zarrin nodded, wondering what to say next. She glanced over the bridge. 'Are they all yours?'

'Heavens, no. There's half a dozen of us. They're shared.'

Another silence. She turned to look at him, but the apron drew her eyes.

He noticed, grinned. 'I'm sorry. I assure you I don't always dress like this. But I'm cook tonight. I was just checking on them.' He hesitated, then said, 'You could join us, if you like. For a meal, I mean. We'll be eating soon.'

'I – I can't.' The offer was tempting, but she didn't know how to accept, nor whether it was even genuinely made. Yet nor did she know how to end this encounter; how to extricate Elend from amongst his new-found friends; how to turn and walk away.

The man came, stood beside her, looked down. 'Actually, I don't think you've any choice. Unless you're prepared to go in and haul him out by the ears.'

She laughed. 'No, I wouldn't do that.'

'I'm Doug, by the way.' He held out a hand.

'Zarrin.'

'Pleased to meet you, Zarrin.'

They shook hands.

He led her to the path that ran along the bank. Within fifty metres, around a corner, the small stream joined a larger one. Beyond the confluence, two canal boats were tied against a ramshackle wharf. The cabins were painted in intricate patterns; the windows were adorned with small flower-boxes and curtains; stove-pipes protruded from the roofs. On the cabin-top and the deck at the back were an assortment of bicycles, boxes, sacks, buckets, rolls of canvas, lengths of wood.

In the clearing in front of them, a small fire was glowing within a circle of stones. Above it a thin wisp of grey smoke curled, questioning the still air.

Doug went to the fire, picked up a pair of tongs, poked them into the flames.

'Trout,' he said. 'Baked in foil in an open fire. My speciality. I hope you like fish.' Then he turned, pointed. 'The others are down there. You could go and join them if you like.'

She followed his gaze. Shadowed beneath a line of willows, the water seemed to churn. In the sharp contrast of light and dark, she couldn't make anybody out at first, but then the patterns in the water seemed to coalesce and became figures – five or six people, swimming. They swam well. Their arms swept the water aside; their feet seemed to reform it in their wake. They might have been otters from the way they moved, the smoothness of the action.

Then one of the figures separated from the others, swam to the wharf, gripped it with a hand. A man, she realised, as he paused there and gave a flick of his head to clear the water from his eyes. He reached up, braced his arms against the wharf, and with a quick twist of his body hauled himself out. His blond hair lay lank against his neck; the muscles on his arms caught the gold of the sun. He was completely naked. Zarrin blushed, turned away.

'That one's Jamie,' Doug said, grinning. 'He's a commie bastard, but don't worry about that. I'll introduce you to the rest, when they come out.'

*

Doug and Melanie and Pal and Blaise and Lara and Julie. Plus Jamie. As she ate, she recited their names to herself, and tried to assign some feature to each of them that might fix them in her mind. Doug, the leader insofar as they had one, steady, calm, his northern accent an echo of the land. Blaise, matching her name, sunny and radiant, with a mop of blonde hair that seemed to take to itself the colours of the fire. Pal, Dutch and tall, a calm and saintly demeanour. Lara, dark, mysterious, and, Zarrin guessed, with hidden moods. Julie, sharp in every way: face, voice, wit. Melanie, small, imp-like, never still.

And Jamie, the communist, of course, though when her eyes settled on him that first glimpse of him, rising from the water, came back to her and she felt herself blush once more.

Then the children: Ben and Corrie and Jazz and Sasha and April, and Ben again – was that the same one or different?

'There are two Bens,' Doug explained when she asked. 'That was a mistake we should have avoided. But it's a nice name.'

She'd never remember them all, she knew. But that wouldn't matter. For, when the meal was finished, she'd take the long walk back to the farm and to her decision, and never see them again.

Now, Doug was telling her about their lives. They were travellers, he explained. Travelling players, but travelling workers as well. They lived on the canal boats, moved from place to place, stopping where the opportunity presented to perform a play, entertain the local children, collect whatever takings they could raise, then move on. In between, they did itinerant farm work, any other jobs that came up. They lived communally, shared everything, took turns to be cook and teacher and nurse.

It sounded carefree and idyllic, and Zarrin envied them.

'What sort of plays?' she asked. 'Shakespeare?'

Doug laughed. 'Not quite. Things we write. Pal's the writer. The rest of just spout what he gives us, and pretend to act.'

'What are they about?'

'The plays? Comedies mainly. About life, the world. Sex.' He grinned. 'If Pal had his way, they'd all be about that.'

Not so saintly, then, she thought, and blushed again, covered it with another question. 'Are you doing a play here?'

'No. Just passing through. We've been working down near Whittlesey. Next stop is Bugbrooke, on the Union Canal, for fruit-picking and to earn some real money. After that, we go south.'

Again she felt a pang of envy. Such freedom.

'What about you?' Blaise asked. 'What's your story?'

'My story?' she echoed, and thought: is that what life is to them – a story? But then she said, 'I'm like you, I suppose. I work on the farms, move from place to place.'

'No home?'

She shook her head.

'Are you a refugee, then?' Lara asked, and, when Zarrin nodded, 'Where from?'

She told them: Syria.

'How did you get here?'

'Like most refugees,' Zarrin said. 'Walking, begging. Other people's kindness. More than my share of good luck.'

Blaise was intrigued, wanted to hear more, but Doug hushed her. 'Only if Zarrin wants to tell.'

She didn't really, but they were being kind to her, and were owed some sort of story at least. And as she started – telling them how she'd fled Syria, made her way to Turkey, her time in the camp – she realised that they had drawn closer around her, were listening, intent.

She told them about Elend's birth, then her escape from the camp. The long trek to Europe. Sometimes, someone would ask a question. Once or twice, when she paused or faltered, Blaise would encourage her to go on.

She told them about Salvo, and the travelling she had done with him. How he'd been arrested. Blaise gasped.

She described her time in London, at the market, in the squat, later in the hotel.

She told them about her time on the farms.

She told them something else – her real name: Zarrin Kashlan. Why, she didn't know, except that it felt right, to be the person she was. She wanted them to be able to trust her, and she knew that she could trust them.

Once or twice, she glanced at Jamie. Of them all, he said the least, and seemed separate, sat a little apart. Why was that, she wondered; was he a stranger amongst the group, like her, or was he just shyer than they were, more reserved? Covertly she tried to sum him up. The blond hair, tied now in a knot at the back of his head. Spare frame, long face, aquiline nose, a small, apologetic tuft of beard. He looked monk-like, ascetic, yet there was wildness in him, too. She could imagine him striding the hills, arms flung out, proselytising some ancient creed.

'It's our fault really,' he said, cutting into her thoughts.

She turned towards him, surprised.

'What do you mean?'

'Britain, the West. We laid the grounds for it. Now we make profit out of it by supplying the weapons.'

He meant for the war, and she could have agreed with him, though she'd have argued that the issue was more complex than that. But his words exposed a lie, too. Her lie. For, as ever, she'd let them believe that it was the war she'd fled from, not the punishment that she'd brought upon herself. It was a deceit, now, that she could not permit; if no one else, then these people surely deserved the truth. She started to explain – 'No, it wasn't really like that—' but Blaise interrupted.

'You're amazing, Zarrin. You put us all to shame. You're so brave.'

'I'll second that,' Doug said.

The others nodded.

There was silence then. Just the crackle of the fire, the murmur from the children where they were gathered at the edge of the glade, playing. The distant trilling of a blackbird. Zarrin tried to accept Blaise's words, tried to think of herself like that: brave. But the word wouldn't fit. Rather, the opposite: always frightened, on edge; ashamed. She wondered if that would ever change, whether she'd somehow find a path to peace. If not somewhere safe, then at least a place where Elend could have the sort of life every child deserved. Perhaps then she'd lose that sense of guilt.

She thought of the gangmaster's offer. Was that the way?

To break the silence, and move the subject away from herself, she asked about the names of the boats. One was called *Aphrodite*, the other *Gaia*.

'*Aphrodite*'s mine,' said Doug. 'Well, I'm the elected captain. She's the Greek goddess of love. Need I say more?'

She laughed. 'Probably not. I know about Aphrodite. But what about *Gaia*?'

'That's Jamie's. He can explain.'

She turned to Jamie. He shrugged. 'Another Greek goddess,' he said.

'Of what?'

'The Earth. She's the Earth Mother – the mother of all life. And she's a philosophy, too. Have you heard of it?'

She shook her head. 'No.'

'The Gaia principle. It's about the unity of Earth and the life it bears, including humans. The need for us all to live in harmony with nature. That's what we try to do here.'

'Yes. I can see.' And it made sense to her that here, in their small group, they could live like that, in harmony with the world. But in the wider world that she'd known, the notion sounded fanciful and simplistic. Again, she wanted to challenge him, put his idealism to the test, but courtesy held her back.

Then laughing, Pal said, 'Please. Don't start him on philosophy. We'll get the full lecture on Nietzsche and Marx and Engels and the rest of his friends if you do. Let's have some music.'

'Wrong philosophers,' Jamie murmured, almost to himself. 'I'd start with William Morris. But yes, let's have some music.'

Already, it was happening. From the other side of the fire came the sound of a penny whistle. Melanie was playing, and within a few moments was being echoed by Lara on a flute. A sad and simple tune. To Zarrin, it sounded like an elegy for the story she had told, somehow adding the parts

230

she'd not said. And perhaps it was also a statement of their collective response, for, as they played, the others sat, staring at their hands, nodding. Doug took the flute, played some Irish melodies, and passed it back to Lara, and a guitar appeared, joined in. There were more songs, which everyone sang, children included. Zarrin listened, spellbound.

'Jamie's turn,' Pal said.

Jamie shook his head.

Pal thrust the guitar at him. 'Captain's orders.'

Jamie shrugged, started to strum as if checking that the instrument was in tune, or searching perhaps for something to play. Gradually, a pattern formed, soft and lilting, and as it formed, he started to sing. His voice was a light tenor, not pure but rough and authentic. Zarrin couldn't catch all the words, but there was a phrase that repeated, about being taken by the hand and walked through the streets of London, which felt like a message aimed at her.

She and Elend had done that, she thought – walked the streets of London, his hand in hers. She glanced again at Jamie, wanting to acknowledge his choice of song, but his head was raised, his eyes closed, and he did not see.

'Do you sing?' Blaise asked, when he'd finished.

Zarrin shook her head.

'I bet you do. You sing to Elend, I'm sure.'

'Sometimes,' she admitted.

'Sing us what you sing to him. A lullaby. Sing for the children.'

Still she demurred, but then Pal said, 'You should. We'll be offended if you don't. We've even managed to get Jamie to sing.'

She sang. '*Lay, lay*' – Sleep, sleep – telling them that everyone in her country knew the song, because every mother sang it to their children. After the first time, she was made to sing it again, and Melanie picked up the tune on her penny whistle, and Pal followed, humming softly, a wandering melody that wove its way between the notes. And she felt herself suddenly let loose so that the words seemed to spring from her, like fledglings, and fly into the night.

And later, as others sang and talked, and even the blackbird paused its song to listen, and Elend came and snuggled against her, she tried to imagine a life like this for the two of them. Not just for this night, but for all the nights ahead. The days, too. Days of travelling and working together, life simple and free. And the thoughts felt like a dream, more real than life could ever be.

Then Blaise came and knelt beside her, and touched her knee.

'What do you think?' she asked.

'What about?'

'About us.'

'I think you're lucky. It's lovely here. It's been one of the happiest evenings of my life.'

Blaise nodded. 'I'm glad you've enjoyed it.'

'Elend's already asked me whether we can come back.'

Blaise laughed. 'We'll be leaving tomorrow.'

'Yes. I told him.'

For a moment they were both silent, gazing into the fire. Then Blaise said, 'So you haven't long to decide.'

'Decide what?'

'Whether you're coming with us.'

16

Travellers

Zarrin walked alone. It was a strange sensation, this solitude, and one she enjoyed. Aloneness without regret or guilt. She'd left Elend with the others, lost amongst his bevy of friends – where he spent most of his time now. She'd left Blaise and the others, too. If she'd asked, Jamie might have come, because he was, she guessed, a rambler himself, seemed to enjoy spending time out in the countryside. But she still wasn't certain how to approach him, whether he even wanted her company; wouldn't have known how to read his refusal. Shyness, or matter-of-factness, or disdain? For his words to her often seemed brusque. She wondered as she walked: should she persist? Should she try harder, or back off and leave him to himself? Another thing to ask Blaise.

It was a month since she'd joined them. Though it seemed improbable now, she'd not accepted their offer immediately. Instead, she'd anguished over the choice she had to make: the gangmaster's offer of what felt like security and solidity, or the wild uncertainty that the travellers seemed to represent. She felt trapped by the commitment she'd already half-made to the gangmaster, didn't know how to go back on her word. She worried about the way that Doug and the others would expect her to live – like them, loving freely – and that they would take from her those last moral strands that tied her to her past. She worried that they might even want her to be part of their plays.

She fretted, too, about what it would do to Elend. Would he become wild and feral?

Thus, for days she'd prevaricated, each morning fending off the gangmaster's increasingly urgent advances, her own fading dreams.

Then Elend had asked, 'When can we see our friends again? I liked them.' And her doubts had crumbled, turned to dust.

'Tomorrow,' she'd said, with a certainty she did not quite feel. 'We'll go tomorrow.' And overnight the certainty had hardened, became determination like steel.

In the morning she'd told the gangmaster her decision. She felt a stab of guilt as she did so, for he was clearly saddened, shocked. He tried to dissuade her, but when that failed his anguish turned to complaint and then to anger, so that he refused the balance of pay that she was due. Then she gathered her belongings, put Elend in his buggy, and set off to Bugbrooke.

It took them two days to reach it, and all the way she'd wondered whether they'd arrive in time, or whether the travellers would have moved on; whether they would remember her, and still want her. She needn't have worried. As they walked down the lane towards the canal, she'd seen the boats parked beside the lock, heard the shouts and laughter of the children playing in the evening sun. Then they were spotted and one of the children let out a squeal – 'It's Elend!' – and they were greeted by a horde of small figures running towards them up the road. Then Blaise and Doug, warm with their welcome, and the others emerging from the boats, some half-dressed or half-washed from their evening ablutions after a day in the field. Jamie the last, diffident, a book in his hand.

'I knew you'd come,' Blaise had said. 'Doug didn't believe me, but I told him.'

'Hoped, but didn't quite believe, I admit,' Doug said. 'But either way, I'm glad she was right. I'm glad you're here.'

After the greetings, the explanations – what took her so long, had they really walked the whole way? – she was shown to her quarters.

She'd been given a berth in Jamie's boat. It was small yet surprisingly comfortable. Two bunk beds, a built-in cupboard, a chair, a tiny desk, the entrance curtained, a rag-rug on the floor. It was in the middle section, partitioned off from the galley and saloon on the forward side and the space occupied by Lara and Julie towards the aft; Jamie's room was in the bow. Whether the berth she'd been given had already been vacant, or the others had moved around to make the space, Zarrin didn't know and was too embarrassed to ask. But it seemed to have been prepared ready for them, felt fresh, aired, even held a collection of books and toys for Elend. Blaise's work, she guessed: a talisman to her conviction that Zarrin would come. Zarrin was grateful. It made her feel as though she was there by right rather than as a guest. And she loved the room, basked in its cosy simplicity, added small features of her own that made it truly hers. On windy nights, when she lay in her bed, she felt the slight rock of the boat and was lulled by it; on bright nights, moonlight would shaft through the small window and make dancing shadows on the walls. On dark nights, it was like a cocoon, safe.

Even so, in those first days, she'd felt awkward and ill at ease. Not that she didn't belong, but that she didn't know how to make the belonging work. There was so much that was strange to her and undefined, so much that she couldn't quite understand. What they wanted from her, what role she had. How they lived. Who slept with whom, which child belonged to which mother, who the father was. Whether the sweet scent she sometimes caught in the evening as they sat on the canalside, chatting, was apple wood or pear wood on the fire or something else – cannabis?

Eventually, in desperation, she'd sought out Blaise and asked her advice.

'Are there things I ought to know? Am I doing alright? I keep thinking I'm making a fool of myself. I feel so – so lost.'

Blaise had laughed. 'You're doing fine,' she said. 'Don't worry. What is it you want to know?'

Zarrin had shrugged. 'The rules?'

Another laugh. 'That's easy. There aren't any. We thought you'd realised that. Well – just one maybe. Be yourself.' And then, as Zarrin frowned. 'OK, and in your case, maybe another: enjoy being it.'

Zarrin knew that it was said honestly, yet it left her feeling stranded. She needed a foundation, a map, expectations at least. She tried a more indirect route, asked about the children. Again, Blaise laughed. Yes, it was a bit complex, she admitted; she could see why Zarrin was puzzled.

'I sometimes think they don't know themselves any more,' she said. 'They treat us all as their parents.' But then she explained: Corrie, Ben the elder and April were all Melanie's and Pal's; Sasha was Pal's and Lara's. 'Though – ' Blaise looked at Zarrin quizzically, as if expecting some reaction ' – as you've no doubt guessed, Lara's with Julie now.'

Zarrin nodded, though she hadn't guessed. Not quite. She'd worked out that Lara and Julie shared a berth but had imagined that it was just convenience, nothing more; or the opposite, an inconvenience – part of the reorganisation that had happened to make room for her and Elend. She'd felt guilty for that, and grateful. But now she felt betrayed. Less by them than herself. By her own naivety.

'And the others?' she asked.

'They're mine. Ben two – the younger one – was with Doug. Jazz was with Jacko.'

Again, Zarrin nodded. Who Jacko was, she had no idea, but it all added to her sense of bewilderment.

And that still left Jamie. She asked about him: where did he fit in?

Blaise shrugged. 'Oh, Jamie's just Jamie.'

'What do you mean?'

'Don't be put off by him,' Blaise said. 'He can seem, I don't know, remote, stand-offish. He's had his troubles, poor guy. But he's a good man. You'll get used to him.' She seemed to see Zarrin's frown and laughed once more. 'Don't look so worried. You'll get used to us all. You'll see.'

*

'Oh, unhappy world. Oh, unhappy life. I am undone.'

'Then pull your flies up,' came an exaggerated whisper from offstage. The audience laughed.

'Who will save me?'

More laughter as Zarrin peered from behind the tower of bales, wand in hand, waved it.

'Where is my fairy godmother, my sprite, my guardian angel?'

Zarrin stepped out, stopped, bent down and retied her shoelace.

'I said,' Doug pronounced, his voice louder, 'where is my bloody guardian angel?'

As he looked desperately around, Zarrin held up a hand, twiddled her fingers, gave a plastic smile.

She was part of the troupe now. Pal created small characters for her. She was rarely given much to say, for she felt self-conscious and afraid that she'd fluff her lines. But she could mime. Her large eyes, pliant face, the easy way her limbs moved seemed to give her no need for words. Expression, gesture could do it all.

She stood up, ran towards Doug, stopped, went back for her wand, returned beaming, waved it in his face.

The performance was a morality play. Most of Pal's productions were. Though the moral choices were less about godly issues than issues of justice. Not very deep down, the politics were socialist, the ideals rather like the ones that governed their own lives. Most of the plays had a contemporary edge. World leaders, bankers and film-producers, and others of a similar ilk, appeared often, personified as monsters or devils of one sort or another. Those on the side of virtue were usually women, children, innocent, poor and environmentally aware. Pal and Jamie and Blaise played the evil roles; Doug, Julie, Melanie and Zarrin shared the good. Lara, with her dark eyes, her capacity for swift changes of mood, could be either.

They performed to whoever would have them. They'd arrive early and tie up beside the farmyard or field they'd been offered, then set up the simple stage and seating area with whatever materials they had. A few props they brought with them: all-purpose pieces of scenery, basic lighting that could run from the batteries on the boats. But the rest they improvised. Bales of hay or straw, a branch or two cut from nearby saplings, an abandoned piece of farm machinery or chicken hutch, an old gate. Most things could be made to serve a purpose, and the plays were adaptable. The night before the performance, a ready-made sign would be placed at the gate. On the evening of the performance they would wait impatiently for the first of the audience to arrive, nervous in case this time no one came.

That never happened. Wherever they were, people would drift in: small family groups, gaggles of chattering children, an elderly woman alone, a pair of red-faced men straight from the village pub; embarrassed teenagers, laughing, giggling, diverting their own eagerness into egging on the others in order not to look too uncool. Sometimes tourists who happened to see the sign as they passed by, entering timidly: can anyone come? Then Blaise would step forward into the makeshift stage and introduce the performance, give a hammed-up announcement about what to do in an emergency – an earthquake or a fire or an alien invasion – and with a clap of hands set the entertainment off.

Now, the three villains rode on-stage in what was meant to be an expensive sports car. Pal had a large shell on his head, and was wearing red and yellow overalls emblazoned with the company's name. Jamie was dressed as a banker, in pinstripes and bowler hat. Blaise was a lady of young fashion in designer clothes, still bearing their price labels.

They made a brief pantomime of extracting themselves from the car, then descended on Doug and grabbed him.

Zarrin rushed to his defence and waved her wand furiously at them, to no avail. Eventually she turned, frowned at the audience, shrugged dramatically and, turning back, kicked Jamie on the ankle, jabbed Pal in the stomach with her wand, beat Blaise over the head with it. Then, grabbing Doug by the scruff of the neck, she hurried him off stage.

It wasn't the first time she'd rescued Guy Greenland in the play, and wouldn't be the last. She'd had to rescue the young maiden, Melanie Mustlove, several times too, and still had to contrive to get hero and heroine together in a state of paradisal and sustainable bliss. But with the help of Lara and Julie's Environmental Elves she would no doubt win out.

It was jolly, unsophisticated stuff, and the audience lapped it up as they always did. Many, it seemed, got the not-very-hidden messages – and there'd been ample booing whenever the members of the secretive clan CGC – Corporate Greed and Consumerism – came on-stage. But at the end there would be leaflets with a more serious message about the climate crisis and habitat loss and encouragement to support various causes dedicated to saving the world. Here in this idyllic corner of Warwickshire that might not seem necessary, but that was the point, and one that would be rammed home in Melanie's closing soliloquy: innocence like this was too precious to lose.

Not every one of their plays was so innocent. When they thought the audience might accept it, they performed something more serious, or bawdy, even licentious. When Blaise gave the introduction, warnings might be given about the language or allusions that were involved. Recently, though, Pal had started working on a new play that he wanted to perform next year. He'd not revealed any of it yet; he never did until the writing was done. But it was inspired, Zarrin knew, by the story she'd told them, of her travels across Europe, her experience as a refugee. She worried about it: whether the audience would like it, or find it too dark. And she worried about the way it changed her – from the newcomer, the welcomed invitee, at the edge of their group, with no real claims upon it, to someone who was there at the heart, and around whose experience they converged.

Did that not reify too much what had happened to her, set it in amber? Didn't it make her something she was not? A symbol for the world?

She was worried, too, that she'd deceived them all in the way she had; not by lying but by what she hadn't said. They knew about her journey, the events along the way, how she had survived. Other people's heroism, too. But she hadn't yet revealed what had happened before – the cause of it all. Her marriage, her affair, the punishment she'd been dealt. She wished she'd told them; she wished she could find a way now, but it seemed too late.

'Your cue,' Doug whispered.

She nodded, held out her wand battered by misuse, put on her bright, inane grin, ran on-stage once more to try and save the bumbling hero and his witless heroine and bring the play to its proper end.

*

Zarrin sat on the cabin-top, legs pulled up, head cradled against her knees, her hair loose. The high sun was warm against her forehead, almost like the sun of old – the sun she'd known in her childhood. The brush of moths against her arm, the bleat of sheep from the meadow, added to the memory from those days. This, though, was wheat country. On the other side of the canal, beyond the ragged fringe of nettle and Canada balsam, the golden fields slid by, ready for reaping. Now and then, on one of the higher fields, she'd see a cloud of dust, billowing behind a combine harvester.

It was late July. They were travelling north, a three-day trip to their next job. She loved these intervals. The peace and the quiet, and the relaxation after the long days of work; the early mornings, the journey to the fields, the hours of toil, the jabs of twig and thorn, stings and bites of insects. The sweat, the aching limbs. It gave her body a chance to recover, and her mind to empty again. It gave her, too, a chance to spend time with the others, get to know them better.

She'd made progress on that, just as Blaise had promised she would. She felt at ease with them, knew she fitted in. She took her turn at cooking, cleaning, being teacher, operating locks, wielding the boat hook, even steering the boat. In the evenings, she sat with them, talked with them, sometimes sang. And as her confidence grew, she'd begun to swim with them when they bathed in the canal or a nearby stream. Not naked, as they often did, for that seemed a step too far; but no longer embarrassed by the way she might look, the flesh she exposed, nor by the glimpses they gave of their own bodies. And with Blaise's help her swimming was improving, so that the act became more effortless, and she no longer felt afraid to venture out of her depth.

A moral for her new life, she thought.

Only Jamie eluded her: stiff, distant, strangely unresolvable; so many different men. The one she sometimes watched as he worked in the fields: stripped to the waist, labouring all day, relentless; so pared down and so supple as to seem unbreakable. The one she glimpsed when he was alone: self-reliant, wholly self-contained. The one she saw when he was with the children: part of their games – a grown-up child himself, and one in whom they clearly delighted, for they would chase him, mob him, clamber over him, tumble and torment and tease.

And another version, the political one – socialist, idealist; the messianic one she had caught sight of on that first encounter – angry at the world for all its injustice, and its unwillingness to listen.

It would break out, sometimes, as they sat in the evenings, talking. After a long interval of silence, at the edge of the group, he'd interrupt with a challenge or denouncement. A wrong he must have been brooding on and couldn't hold back any longer. If he could, he would provoke them to debate on the matter, bombard them with quotations from his favourite polemicists and decry their lack of reading. When they tired of such serious discourse, and joked or teased him, his frustration would show. He'd grow surly and retreat to silence again, or hector them all the more. Though, invariably, Doug or Julie would prod and parody him until he at last relented and laughed.

The previous evening, she'd encountered that version again.

Pal had been talking about his play – the one inspired by the story she had told that first night. Blaise had asked him how it was going.

He'd written about half of it, Pal said, but he was struggling with the rest.

'How will it end?' Blaise asked. 'It's happy, I hope.'

Pal laughed. 'Of course. All my plays are. That's the point, isn't it? Life can be good if you give it a chance.'

Zarrin had smiled to herself, grateful for what felt like his gift to her future.

Then Jamie said, 'Not this one.'

Everyone turned.

'Why not?'

'Because it shouldn't. Because it's a lie.'

Blaise asked what he meant.

'It plays to the neo-liberalist myth, that's why.'

'Here we go,' someone said and there was laughter, but Jamie cut them short.

'I mean it. I'm serious. It just feeds the notion that being a refugee is some sort of luxury – just a shortcut to an easy life. One that you don't deserve. Believe that, and the solution's easy. Just put up the barriers, keep them out. Problem solved.' He shrugged. 'Isn't that what the racists and fascists want us to believe?'

'But it's just a play,' Melanie said. 'A fairy story. And fairy stories always have happy endings.'

'Yeah – well fairy stories aren't always socially moral, either.'

'More Marx, less Hans Christian Andersen. Is that the answer?' Doug suggested, and when Jamie glared at him he gave a shrug of innocence, hands splayed. 'I'm just asking.'

'So, what do you think should happen?' Melanie asked. 'In Pal's play, I mean.'

Jamie scowled, inspected his palms, and Zarrin felt herself tighten, as if her own future might depend on his reply.

'What happens in real life,' he said. 'She should get beaten, disappear, suffocate in the back of a truck, drown; or just be caught and deported.'

Zarrin let out a small gasp, snapped her hand across her mouth in an effort to stifle it, condemned by his words.

'That's what happens, isn't it?' Jamie was staring at her, his eyes insistent.

She nodded. 'Sometimes.'

'And does the world care? Does anyone do anything about it?'

A small shake of her head. 'Not often.'

'That's the truth, then. That's what people need to realise. That's the way the world works.'

'It didn't happen to Zarrin,' Lara said.

'Zarrin was lucky.' Jamie stared at her again, defying her to disagree. 'Weren't you?'

'Yes,' she said in a small voice.

Blaise came across to her, put an arm around her shoulder, perhaps seeing her hurt. 'Zarrin got what she deserved,' she said. 'She escaped. She and Elend. They found us.'

There was silence. No one seemed to want to look at Jamie, as if they were ashamed of his words. He sat, his features chiselled, his hands clenched. Zarrin felt small and shrivelled. Not deserve, she thought. She had deserved the abuse and the hardship – she couldn't deny that. But not this happiness. Jamie was right.

Then Blaise continued, 'Well, I don't think our play should end like that. I think she should fall in love and live happily ever after. On a houseboat, with a bunch of really nice people and a grumpy old communist. That's how I would end it.'

They all laughed, and even Jamie gave a stiff smile, and with that the mood changed. Melanie picked up her penny whistle, started to play. The others joined in.

But Jamie remained apart, and seemed to sink back into himself, alone and bleak. Zarrin wanted to go to him, try to draw him back into the group, but didn't know how. He felt too withdrawn, too remote. He was still there, slumped and brooding, when she went to her room.

Now, sitting on the cabin-top, Zarrin tried again to get into Jamie's mind. He was like a man who carried his darkness with him, she thought. He was too hard on himself, allowed no room for forgiveness or escape. She wanted to find some way into his cold and dismal logic, so that she might find its weakness, pick at it, pull at it until it fell apart.

The world is harsh, it said; impartial about who wins and who loses. And it used her own story to justify its claim. While thousands upon thousands of innocent refugees failed – remained trapped in the place from which they tried to flee, were caught and returned, were maimed or killed – she'd been allowed to escape, to survive, and somehow offered redemption here, with these travellers. What had she done to deserve that?

And yet, she thought, didn't her own story tell more? All the other people involved. Could you ignore them? Not just the traffickers who cheated you, and the soldiers and police who exploited you and beat you, and the racists who simply hated people not like themselves, but all those people she'd met who'd been kind to her and tried to help. Fredrik and Salvo and Dinos and Mrs Jervais and Gabby. Yaasmin. And the people whose names she did not know. The man who'd given her the eye-bead, the man in the square in Ruse, the people who'd responded to her outstretched hand with a small donation; the drivers who'd offered her lifts; the countless others whose deeds she'd long ago forgotten, but whose legacy she carried simply by being here. Shouldn't they be in the story? Shouldn't they be part of Jamie's world? Didn't they give him a reason for hope?

She got down, went into the kitchen, made a cup of coffee, took it to the helm. Whether she could convey any of that with a cup of coffee, she doubted. But it might make a gesture. An oblique apology for the despair she seemed to have loaded on him, and her own inability to help.

Jamie looked up, as she approached, offered no greeting. She held out the cup. 'Coffee,' she said.

He took it and nodded his thanks, said nothing, just stared past her at the canal ahead.

She lingered for a moment, unsure how to break the silence, how to leave. She felt unnerved by his indifference. Had she failed again?

Then he said, 'Bridge.'

Puzzled, she half-turned and felt rather than saw the looming shadow. Then a hand was on her sleeve, tugging. She ducked down. The mottled brickwork of a canal bridge slid overhead, light dancing on it from the reflections in the water. His face was close to hers, and the same light stroked across his skin. In his eyes, she glimpsed a message that she couldn't quite read. Query, perhaps, or pleading; the look of a drowning man. Or just an echo of her own vague notion: we're in this together, you and I. Then he blinked, and it was gone.

She returned to the galley, a small smile emerging. She felt light-hearted and vindicated, as though she'd tested an unlikely hypothesis and been proved right.

From then on, when they were travelling, she made that gesture into a daily routine. The cup of coffee, a few words. Whether he welcomed it or not, at first she couldn't tell. Sometimes he thanked her; at others he almost ignored her and when she went back later the coffee would be sitting there, undrunk. But, gradually, the time she spent beside him on the helm lengthened, and they would exchange comments about the morning, the places they were passing; gradually they learned to talk. When he seemed unwilling to do that, she sat on the gunwale for a while and just watched.

Once, as she sat there, he said, 'I like it when you watch me. It makes me feel – real.'

Another day, she asked about a small church that they were passing on the canalside. It was so small and squat, looked so humble and primitive, she marvelled at how old it must be.

He told her. 'Norman, I'd guess,' and explained the reasons. The arch around the door, with its chevron decoration. The heavy masonry, the low-pitched roof, the undivided windows, deep set.

It felt rather like a lecture, and he seemed to realise, for he apologised when he'd finished. 'Sorry. Me, preaching again.'

'You seem to know a lot about churches,' she said.

He grinned, embarrassed. 'A bit.'

'Are you religious?'

He shook his head – a quick, dismissive movement – but then grinned. 'I had a book about them once. A school prize. Betjeman's *Guide to English Parish Churches*. I learned from that.' He paused as he navigated a loose mat of vegetation in the water, watching it slide past. 'I should have been, though,' he continued. 'Religious, I mean. My father was a preacher and tried to make me love his God. Instead, he made me hate him.'

God or father, she wondered; which did he mean?

He apologised again. 'I'm sorry. I forget.'

'Forget what?'

'You believe, I suppose. You must be a Muslim.'

She shook her head, looked away. 'I don't know what I am any more.'

In their wake, a damsel-fly hovered, its wings a flickering blur.

'I didn't know,' he said, and, after a long pause, 'It never leaves you, though, does it?'

A week or so later, feeling that she'd made progress with him, and that some sort of kinship had been established at last, she tried to tell him about her past. That might help, she thought: if he realised that what had happened to her had been, in its way, deserved. Punishment for what she'd done.

Wouldn't it show him that the world wasn't entirely unfair? There could be justice in its cruelty.

And she wanted to tell him for another reason. Because she wanted him to know.

She came prepared; she'd rehearsed the speech during a sleepless night, and now tried to repeat it to him. But she did so clumsily, and in a rush of words.

'I want to tell you something. About what happened in Syria – what I did.'

He stared past her along the length of the canal boat as she babbled on. Then he cut her short with a fierce wave of his hand, as if swatting a fly away. 'I don't want to know,' he said. 'I'm not interested in your past.'

Not interested in her, she thought he meant, and clamped her mouth in silence.

'We've all got history,' he said. 'But I'm not interested in that. Only the future matters.'

Again she struggled to make sense of his response, couldn't tell whether it was a reprimand or statement of philosophy; or a clumsily made apology for all that the world had done to her. But later, when she was alone, the thought came: was that where his darkness came from? Was he a refugee like her, struggling to escape from his own past?

*

November, and at last the weather yielded. Clouds towered on the horizon, like a spectre from some ancient myth. Then rain swept in. Within days all work had stopped, the fields churned to a quagmire, the rivers swollen. Gales followed, flinging the wake of the boats back at them as they crept along the canal. The bloated rivers spilled into the fields. What was canal and what was not became a matter of debate. As if by some strange irony, they were in danger of becoming stranded by the floods.

Shelter and survival were the only priorities. Like a good shepherd with his flock, Doug led them to safety. Standing on the bow deck, hunched against the wind, coat blowing, a mobile phone clasped to his ear, he telephoned friends to ask about weather and moorings ahead of them, and about other travellers for whom he was concerned. Then, through a wild and squally night, he prodded a way between the fallen trees, the floating logs, the misleading expanses of water by the dimmed headlight of his boat.

Late the next morning, tired and tense, they arrived at their destination. It was a small basin off a section of the Kennet and Avon Canal in Wiltshire, between two short flights of locks. On three sides, trees sheltered it from the winds; on the fourth, a rough slope led up to a low rock wall, once perhaps a chalk quarry, now little more than a shelter for huddled sheep. They tied up the boats, set up the tarpaulins over the decks, gathered in the cabin of Doug's boat, and hugged, laughed, patted Doug on the back, thankful, almost exuberant that the ordeal was over.

They stayed there for two months, through Christmas into the New Year. For most of that time, they lived quietly. Outside, the rain was relentless. Milky runoff poured from the hillside; the canal seethed and spat. All day, the wind howled above them, and the trees whipped and lashed in torment and shed their torn tears onto the roofs of the boats each night. Inside, they hunkered down, retreated to their own pastimes and berths. Pal to work on his plays, Melanie to her music, Doug to mending and sharpening their tools, Blaise and Lara and Julie chatting together while they sewed, darned, polished the cutlery, prepared food for Christmas.

Jamie, as far as Zarrin could tell, spent the days reading, or went off to walk alone. When the weather permitted, she took Elend out; at other times, she helped with the chores or played with the children.

After the travelling and work and busyness of the summer, it was a relief to be still. She found that she could happily sit for hours and let her mind drift, memories merging with imaginings, past and future mixing. Sometimes, covertly, she watched Jamie, and wondered about him, and sometimes she wondered about herself. She was changing, she thought, moving on at last from the woman she'd been during those years of struggle when she was always braced, always tense. She was learning to relax again, to do as Blaise demanded; to be herself.

For Christmas, they decorated the boats with garlands of ivy and holly, bracken and fern fronds. Under Julie's tuition, the children made candles of beeswax, scented with honey and herbs. Blaise showed them how to cut origami shapes to make paper chains, and the saloon became a spider's web of dancing fairies and cats and astrological signs. On Christmas Day there were no presents – a capitalist plot, Doug explained with a sidelong look at Jamie. But on Boxing Day, the correct day for present-giving, tokens would be exchanged – things found on their travels, things they had made.

Zarrin thought long and hard about a present for Elend. He deserved so much; she had so little to give. She searched her childhood, trying to picture something there that might serve the purpose, and be possible to find or make. She remembered the games they played: Blind Goat, which in England they called Blind Man's Buff; and Long Donkey, which they knew here as Leapfrog. But toys she couldn't remember. Did they not exist? Had life been so serious?

Then she recalled the scene in Hyde Park. The boy with the kite. And with it came the memories that had eluded her then. A lunch party, out in the countryside, when she was thirteen or fourteen years old. The village boys had been there, laughing and chasing, fighting the way all boys did. But, when they tired of that, they had sat together and made kites. She had been intrigued by what they were doing, stood nearby, watching.

Could she remember how to do it? Could she make him one herself?

She found the materials: a sheet of brown paper for the sail, a plastic bag for the tail, string and some card on which to wind it, sticky tape. She folded the paper, refolded it, making a dart shape. She taped the sharp corners to strengthen them, cut the plastic bag into strips, tied them on; added the string. She'd had no chance to try it out, but it looked right.

The next day, when Doug at last announced that the time for tokens had come, she gave it to Elend.

'What is it?' Elend asked, as he unwrapped it.

She told him. A Devil's kite; where she was born, they were known as *Seytan ucurtmasi*.

'What does it do?'

'Come, I'll show you.'

She took him outside, and, with a silent wish, tossed it in to the air. The wind caught it. The kite lifted, bucked, twisted as though trying to decide which way to go.

'It flies,' Elend cried.

Soon the other children joined them, demanding a turn. Dutifully Elend consented, but in between insisted that he have another go himself.

Later, Elend came to Zarrin, clambered onto her lap.

'This is for you,' he said, and kissed her on the mouth, held his lips there until she tickled him and made him withdraw. But as he got down she realised that there was a small gift, lying on her lap. It was a fossil, one or two centimetres in width, curled like a snake. The stone was dark brown, tinged with blue, almost metallic to the touch. On the surface was a delicate tracery of swirling lines.

She called Elend back, thanked him with another kiss, asked him where it had come from.

'I found it,' he said. 'Up there – in the quarry. Jamie helped me. It's an – anam – an ammonite.' He spoke the word carefully. 'It's made of ...' He hesitated, turned to Jamie.

'It's pyrite,' Jamie said, and Elend repeated the word. 'Fool's gold.'

She laughed. 'I'm a fool, am I?'

Elend shook his head emphatically, and she kissed him. 'It's beautiful,' she told him.

She glanced at Jamie, gave a tight-lipped smile of complicity, fondness, thanks.

17

Coronation

'Adieu,' Jacko said. 'Until August. Don't forget.'

He'd appeared on New Year's Eve. He'd come unannounced. Just the crunch of gravel in the parking area beside the wharf, the toot of a horn.

Zarrin had looked out from the saloon of Doug's boat, tried to make out what sort of vehicle had driven up. Then Blaise had leaned past, already excited. 'It's him,' she said, 'It's Jacko.' She turned, yelled down the boat. 'Jazz, Jazz, it's Daddy.'

Within seconds, woman and child were racing up the gangway, onto the deck. Zarrin felt the slight lurch of the boat as they leapt onto land, heard their cries. Then others followed. Pal, dropping his cooking utensils in the kitchen, striding out. Lara, with a little squeal of excitement. Children, it seemed, from everywhere.

'You'd better come,' Doug said. 'He'll want to meet you.' He led her onto the deck.

In the car park was an old Bedford bus, its livery blue and white; behind the windscreen an indicator board bearing the label *X33 Bristol and Bath: Semi-fast*. On the step at the open passenger door, a man stood. He had broad shoulders, a bushy beard, black hair swept back, a wide grin. Jazz was in his arms, clung to his neck.

Blaise stood below him, her head against his side.

'Douglas!' he bellowed, as Zarrin and Doug emerged. 'Season's greetings.' Then he saw Zarrin. 'And someone new. A most delightful addition to your crew. She must be Jamie's, yes?'

Blaise nudged him with an elbow, said something Zarrin couldn't hear. Jacko laughed. 'Oh, once I get my magic to work, that will soon change. You'll see.'

He beckoned Zarrin, stepped down to greet her. She held out a hand. He took it, looked her up and down, and then, with a practised movement, all charm and unexpected grace, raised it to his lips, kissed her wrist. 'A pleasure to meet you, Zarrin,' he said. 'A pleasure indeed.'

From that moment, until he left, everything changed. The whole balance of the group shifted; the atmosphere became edgy, anarchic. Jacko sat in lordly pomp at its centre, in the saloon, while the children buzzed around him like excited flies, and the adults cooked his meals, fetched his drinks, served his every need. He joked, told stories, scolded the children, flirted with the women, all in a booming bass voice. He organised their activities, was gamesmaster, umpire and judge. He wasn't interested in competition, Zarrin realised, just in being in command. The president, the king of all he surveyed.

He handed out kisses as prizes. To her embarrassment, Zarrin seemed to be awarded more than her share. She wondered, too, how much further his affections went. While there, he slept with Blaise, she suspected; others too? She imagined that he would do the same with her if she gave him the chance, and accordingly received his kisses bashfully, on her cheek, remained prim. Sometimes, at that moment of contact, she would glimpse Jamie from the corner of her eye and think that she could see him stiffen. Jealousy, she wondered; or something else – irritation, contempt? Or was it just her own imagination?

On New Year's Eve, as midnight approached, Jacko took charge once more and ordered everyone to form a ring while they counted the seconds down to the tinny chime of his mobile phone. On the last chime, a cheer rang out, and then 'Auld Lang Syne' was sung as they all pumped their hands and swayed.

The lights went out. 'Ten seconds to find your perfect partner,' Jacko yelled. 'For your first kiss of 2018.'

There was a chaos of stumbling, feeling, grabbing, laughter. Zarrin searched for Elend, imagined Jamie, feared it would be Jacko.

When the lights came on, she was standing next to Doug.

'You and me, then,' he said. 'I'm the lucky one.' He hugged her warmly, kissed her on the lips. He winked as he let her go.

Now, Jacko was leaving. That morning, though, as they'd gathered to wish him farewell, each receiving their parting hug and kiss, Jacko had issued one last command. They had an appointment to keep. Heritage Farm in Kent, in August, for the hop-picking festival. Everyone was invited. Everyone was instructed to come.

He leaned out of his bus, said again, 'Hop-picking in Kent. It's a must.' Then, laughing uproariously at his own obscure and inaccurate joke, he crunched the vehicle into gear, and pulled away.

*

After another ten days, they too moved on. Through the rest of that month, into February, the weather was cold, still. At night Zarrin could hear the canal crackling as it froze around the boat, and when she woke in the morning she scraped ice from the window above her bed. Rime built up on the trees, turning the world to crystal, like a fairytale scene. A soft dust of white powder sprinkled itself on the boat as it passed beneath; later froze to a slippery skein that made any movement on the decks and cabin-top hazardous. The fields were ghostly pale.

They took work where they could find it. For several weeks they picked winter vegetables in the Fens. Hard, back-aching labour, like the work Zarrin had done the year before, performed in a dumbstruck landscape of cold black clay. But now, with friends around her, a place to call home, it seemed more bearable. Then, orchard work and vine-pruning, before more vegetable-picking in early March, with its deceit of a false spring. Bright days when birds sang, daffodils nodded in the breeze, butterflies danced at the edge of the canal. Harsh days when the wind snarled at the boats, seeking every unguarded entrance it might find.

Then spring again. Warm and honest. And suddenly Zarrin realised that it was a full year since she had met the travellers, and she was repeating those heady first days. The same journeys, the same villages, the same farms.

It felt like an affirmation, that reconnection with the places it had started – her entry point, her rebirth – her life relived. And with every familiar step she felt the change consolidate within her. Not just strength and oneness with this life, but something else. Something that seemed to be beyond her, just out of reach. A future?

Love?

Was it that? It seemed improbable, yet she wondered whether Jamie felt it too. For his manner seemed to have changed over the months. He seemed to notice her more, make an effort to reach her. He'd give her a greeting in the morning, with a nonchalance that felt forced. He offered her small kindnesses – a book to read, a helping hand at work – then seemed embarrassed by the act. Sometimes, she thought, he tried to manufacture time with her alone, though when he succeeded he seemed unsure quite what to say.

She was touched by his behaviour, and amused, and couldn't deny that she found pleasure in his stumbling attention. But love? The thought disturbed her.

She told herself to be more sensible, to remember the lessons of life that she'd so painfully learned. She feared, as well, seeming to lead Jamie on. Encouraging him, only later for panic to set in, so that she would turn and flee.

For that reason, and to give her own thoughts space to settle and take shape, she tried to avoid him at times. She deflected his tiny advances. She placed herself close to one of the others – Blaise or Doug or Pal – when they worked or sat on the canalside in the evenings, didn't invite him to accompany her when she took Elend for a walk.

And yet she knew it was happening, and knew that, in the way of love, her attempts at evasion made it happen all the more. Enticing him with her demure denials. The lover's trail.

Sometimes, she wondered if the others knew and watched, perhaps talked about it wryly when she wasn't there. And the thought came: had that always been their plan? Was that why they had invited her to join them? And with that came other possibilities, too confused to unravel. That Jamie had known and was party to it, or hadn't and felt tricked. That each of them was being manoeuvred like characters in one of Pal's plays. That Doug had a sweepstake on the outcome:

how it would end, when. If so, she mused, might Jamie have a ticket?

Even Elend seemed to have sensed that something was going on, for one evening, as they were out walking, he asked, 'Will you marry Jamie one day? Will he be my daddy?'

She laughed, feigning humour rather than shock. 'Why do you ask that?'

He shrugged. 'I don't know. I just thought.'

'Thought what?'

Again, he shrugged, looked down, kicked at the ground. Then, still avoiding her eyes, he said, 'I wouldn't mind. And I don't have one, do I? Not like the others.'

'What, a father? Of course you have a father. But I told you, he died, when you were a baby.'

Even as she said it, she felt the pang of uncertainty: was it time to tell the truth?

'I know,' Elend said, then regarded her gravely. 'Was he a bad man? Did he do something wrong?'

She shook her head. 'He gave me you. That's the best thing anyone could do.'

'So, why did he die?'

'People do,' she said. 'You know that. It's not always fair, but they do.'

He was silent, seeming to dwell on her words, look for some logic in them. For a moment she thought he had finished and she should turn the conversation to something else; but then he said, 'I'd rather have Jamie.'

She knelt down, took both his hands. 'I think that's up to Jamie, don't you?'

In any case, despite her strategies, she couldn't avoid Jamie completely, nor did she want to, so slowly she permitted him back into her presence. One evening, arriving late at the fire, she sat beside him at his feet, without a thought, and as the evening wore on she realised that she had let her shoulder lean against his knee for support or companionship.

And another evening, as she sat in that same way – an accepted arrangement now – she admitted to herself that she enjoyed the touch of him against her, that it gave her comfort, brought no fear.

And sitting there, as she watched the flames reach out and search the darkness for the dust of their thoughts, she acknowledged: it would happen. Not tonight, but one day. And she knew that he knew it, too, yet was content to wait. For he loved her, and he knew that she felt love for him in return. Love, and gratitude – and guilt.

Sometimes, in the weeks that followed, she tried to imagine it. That giving of herself. That reopening to a man. She tried to feel what she would want to feel – anticipation, tenderness, passion. She tried not to feel sordid and scared.

Yet that was how her mind reacted, phobic of the thought.

Sometimes, she wished that he would just do the deed himself. With no preamble, no negotiation or chivalrous concern. Just take her. Have it done. And yet she knew that, if he tried, she would panic and try to fight him off, and that would be the end of it.

And, with a sudden insight that surprised her with its strength, she knew that he never would. There was no physical ferocity in him like that. Only fierceness of his mind, the anger of ideas. He wanted to persuade people, win them over, not own or destroy them.

It was what he wanted for her – perhaps had been seeking from the start.

And she wondered: when will I be ready? How long will it take? Weeks, months? Another year?

Could he be that patient?

Poor man. To have to wait so long.

*

In August, they headed for their appointment with Jacko, in Kent.

As they made their way through London, edging along the river between the tangle of bridges and flyovers, the stooping cranes, the toy-brick blocks of offices and warehouses and flats, Jamie found her sitting at the table in the saloon, alone. He sat down opposite and said, 'I hope you're ready for this.'

'What, London?' She grinned. 'London always surprises me.'

'No, not London. Where we're going. The hop farm. The festival.'

'Why?'

'That might surprise you too.'

He told her about the couple who ran it. Betty and Thijs Vandenberg, she a woman of Kent, whose family had held the land for generations and laid out the fields at least a hundred years before; her husband a Dutch businessman with money to spare and a maritally induced passion for hops.

'For traditions, as well,' he said. 'They run the farm the old-fashioned way. The hops are grown on trellises of pole and string, without pesticides or fertilisers. They're harvested by hand.'

For the occasion, he told her, a dozen or more women came down from the East End of London, keeping up family traditions of their own. To supplement the workforce, itinerants were brought in. To be invited was a privilege. He'd worked there once before, several years ago; he'd never had a chance since.

'Is it Jacko's doing?' she asked. 'Did he get us invited?'

Jamie nodded. 'Everything's his doing,' he said. 'You know Jacko. That's what he does: rules people's lives.'

They arrived at the farm late the next day. It lay on the banks of the Medway, on a low slope of land, burnished by the season and the afternoon sun. Jacko and most of the other workers were already there. Camp had been set up, a collection of twenty or more camper vans, caravans and tents loosely arranged beside a big, creosoted wooden barn. The women from London were already well in evidence, sitting together around a large table, their voices ringing across the field.

As they tied up the boats on the long wharf that fronted the farmyard, Jacko strolled across, languid, lugubrious. He shook hands with Doug, kissed Blaise, regarded Jamie and Zarrin for a moment as they disembarked, as if trying to read something into their appearance.

'Welcome to hop heaven,' he said with an expansive sweep of the scene; then, addressing Zarrin, 'You'll enjoy this.'

Later, Zarrin took Elend's hand and they explored the site together. Everything had been prepared for the workers, it seemed. Benches and tables had been laid out in front of the barn, and along one side was a row of sinks and work surfaces, half a dozen gas cookers. Further away, in the shadow of the trees, stood a cluster of portable toilets, cubicle showers, two open-air baths, a spa-pool. All possible needs and lifestyles catered for, she thought, with a wry smile. She led Elend through a gate, into the next field. The smell of the hops was rich: musty and sweet. They hung from the strings three metres above their heads, like green cones, beckoning, begging to be touched and picked. She reached up one of the stems, squeezed a fruit. It was papery, light, seemed like a personal thing, shaped to her hand. It yielded when she squeezed, yet as she let go it sprang back into shape, filling the void in her palm.

In the evening, she joined the large crowd of workers who had gathered at the tables in front of the barn. Many of them knew each other, and there were enthusiastic reunions, introductions, a few moments of embarrassment as names were dredged up and mistakes made. The children ran around, shouting, chasing a football. Soon, food appeared, and was passed along the table. On a bench by the barn, a vat of beer had been set up on a shaky trestle bench, and a queue quickly formed as people helped themselves. Zarrin accepted some bread, cheese, went to the water tap, filled her glass, drank it thirstily.

Behind her, a cheer rose. The owners had arrived. They walked through the throng, shaking hands like returning heroes, which was perhaps what they were. Then Thijs Vandenberg jumped up onto one of the tables, called for quiet, and welcomed them. They were helping to keep alive a tradition, he told them, and he was grateful. The pay was poor, the work hard, the owners were tyrants; but they should all be proud of what they'd do in the next two weeks. They should enjoy themselves, too, for that was the purpose of life; there was surely no other. His statement was roundly applauded.

*

They did; they enjoyed themselves, and the days went quickly. The work, as Thijs Vandenberg had warned them, was tiring, muscle-knotting stuff: Zarrin toiled for hours with her head twisted, her arms stretched up as far as she could reach,

263

balanced on a ladder. But the scent, the sensuous feel of the fruits, were like a salve, and it was only afterwards, when she lay in bed, that the aches and pains caught up with her, and were like hard stones in her shoulders and neck.

It affected everyone the same. In the mornings, as they stood stretching on the wharf, they would exchange jokes and complaints about what had been done to them overnight, the knots they'd been tied into, the need for a Boy Scout to undo them and set them free. Only the Londoners were immune. Many of them had brought along stilts, inherited perhaps from their parents or grandparents who had harvested the same land half a century or more before. On these, they tottered between the hop-lines like circus clowns, and with the same comic effect. But their work seemed effortless, and they sang and laughed as they cut free the hop-vines, lowered them down, or picked the first-year fruits, while, below, the children ran around playing tag and hide-and-seek, or other less structured games of their own invention.

All too soon the fortnight had gone, the hops picked bare. Already, the strings were being taken down in preparation for winter. On the final day, after the last load of hops had been carried away, trailing the bittersweet scent of must and cedar and lemon in its wake, the owners of the farm reappeared, and declared it party time. It was another tradition, it seemed. The tables were lined up in a long row in front of the barn, and beyond them a large square was marked out with straw bales. There, they took part in games and contests that locals and travellers in Victorian England might have recognised: tug-of-war, quoits, British Bulldog, races of various sorts, piggy-back jousting. For the children there was clock golf, apple-dipping, conkers, Red Rover and Grandmother's Footsteps. At midday, the trestle tables were loaded with food: warm breads, cheese, pâtés, bowls full of apples and pears. There was fresh fruit juice, home-made beer, a richly fragrant fruit punch. As the afternoon wore on, someone started playing an accordion, was joined by a fiddle, a flute, and there was singing and dancing.

Zarrin watched it all with fascination and awe. As part of his delicate courtship – if that was what it was – Jamie had started to lend her books to read. The first had been *The Ragged Trousered Philanthropists*, and she'd found it hard going, and had persisted solely to avoid offence. But the next was a collection of short stories by D.H. Lawrence, and these had been easier, and one of them – a tale about the man who loved islands – had touched her, for it seemed to speak of her own life and her search for somewhere she might feel safe. The latest had been *Tess of the d'Urbervilles*. She'd just started reading it, but already the story had gripped her. She loved the writing, the poetry in the words, felt drawn to the characters, could picture the Wessex that they inhabited. And here, watching the antics around her, listening to the music, it seemed as if the story had become real, that the book had leapt out and absorbed her, or that she had willingly stepped in, and that they were all living in Hardy's bucolic world.

Yet she knew, too, that there was darkness in the book, and felt empathy with Tess for her experience. Rape, she thought, wasn't a crime that was contained within the act, one which could be sealed by the simple passage of time. It left its mark. It hung over everything that followed. It had consequences. Would Tess resolve her life in some way that brought happiness? Could she?

The bell-like chime of a spoon on glass interrupted her musings. Thijs Vandenberg had risen to his feet, was calling for attention. Gradually, the music died, the chattering stopped. People moved towards the table. There was silence. Even the children's voices were quelled. A tension seemed to settle over the scene, as if everyone knew that something important was about to be said.

Thijs let it stretch, become tauter, a small smile on his lips.

'Ladies and gentlemen,' he said at last. 'Friends. It has been a good year again. Kind weather, a good harvest, and an enjoyable few days of your company. I thank you all.' A cheer went up. He quietened it with raised hands. 'Many of you, I'm pleased to see, are regulars here; some of you have been coming for many years, and your parents before you. That is a tradition we are proud of.' Another cheer. 'But I have to say, we like also seeing new faces here – not just the usual crop of new children, but new workers, visitors from overseas. I hope you have felt welcome. I hope you will come again.'

'You bet,' someone shouted.

'Try and stop us,' someone else called, earning laughter.

'But now,' Thijs went on, 'we come to the moment you have been waiting for. Another tradition. Our crowning of the King and Queen of Hops.' He waited as a ripple of anticipation went around the crowd, then continued, 'As you know, it is our prerogative to nominate two of you for this honour, and, subject to your acclaim, they will be duly crowned. Are you ready?'

There was a fierce cheer of accord.

'Then I will ask Betty to announce our nominations and ask for your confirmation.'

He sat down, and Betty Vandenberg took his place. She, too, played the moment, looking around the gathering as if waiting for the last pair of eyes to engage her, the last murmur of chatter to cease. When she had won the attention she sought, she spoke firmly and slowly. 'Our nomination for the King this year is one of our regular friends, and is in recognition of the pleasure his presence has given us not just this year but every year, all, men and women alike.' Again, she paused, letting the tension rise. 'We nominate Jonathan Oliver. Known to you, I think, as Jacko. Do I hear your acclaim?'

'Aye!' was the shout in reply. 'Jacko is King. Long live the King.'

Betty waited until the noise abated. 'And for the Queen,' she said, 'we wish to recognise a new friend amongst us: someone who has come a long way to join us, has worked unceasingly while she has been here, and is surely fit in every way for the honour of Queen. We nominate –' she held out an arm, as if in invitation ' – Zarrin Kashlan. Do you all so acclaim?'

'Aye! Zarrin is Queen. Long live the Queen.'

For some moments, Zarrin sat there dumbly, not understanding what the words meant, what they implied, while the cheers rang around her. Across the table she could see Jacko, standing, beaming, his hands raised in recognition of the award. Should she be doing the same, she wondered: was she meant to say something, make a speech?

Then Betty's voice rang out above the din. 'I invite you to prepare the King and Queen for their investiture.'

Someone grabbed Zarrin's arms. It was Blaise, laughing, her face flushed. 'Your Majesty,' she said. 'Please come with me.'

'What's happening?'

'We're going to dress you for the occasion. Come on.'

For the rest of the afternoon, long into the evening, Zarrin felt all sense of control of her own destiny, of decorum or choice, slip away. Suddenly, she was public property, to be handled and manoeuvred and arranged and arraigned as the crowd might wish. A bevy of women gathered around her, chattering, laughing, excited by what lay ahead. They led her into the barn and then to one of the small byres at the back. As the door closed behind her, she caught a glimpse of Jacko likewise being ushered into a room by a group of men at the other end of the building. Inside, it smelled of hops, of hay, creosote, and a softer, darker fungal scent, like rain on dry soil.

'Clothes off,' one of the women said.

'No!'

'It's alright. We're going to dress you. You'll be fine.'

Zarrin looked around, feeling trapped, panic beginning to rise in her stomach. 'I don't want to.'

Blaise touched her arm. 'It's alright, Zarrin. Honest. We're just going to dress you in hops.'

'I can't—'

'Trust me.'

Hesitantly, reluctantly, Zarrin unbuttoned her shirt, slipped it off, clutched her arms across her chest.

'And the rest,' someone said.

'Just the jeans,' Blaise told her. 'That's all.'

Zarrin turned away, took off her jeans, stood, feeling shrivelled and exposed. A ragged waif, laughing stock to everyone around.

But then, as she stood there, they started to dress her. From a pile of dry hops in the corner they selected strands, draped them over her, weaving them together, fixing them when necessary with small loops of thread. A bodice slowly appeared, then a skirt. She began to enjoy the attention, the sensation of being waited on, like the royalty she was about to become. She laughed as hops were laced into her hair; when bracelets of them were tied around her ankles, giggled as the crisp yet soft flowers tickled her skin. She lowered her head to allow a garland to be hung round her neck, then lifted it to her nose and sniffed deeply, almost intoxicated by the heady aroma.

She sneezed in the dusty air, then sneezed again, and for a moment couldn't stop, so that everyone laughed, and one of the women was sent out to bring her fruit juice to soothe her throat. It tasted rich and velvety, and she asked for another cup.

A loose waistband was fashioned from more hops, then other flowers were added – lavender and thyme, petals of red and white roses.

She was shown her reflection in an old and dusty mirror, and stood regarding it, transfixed by the transformation that had taken place.

She felt giddy, happy, entranced. The innocent child again.

They led her out of the back door of the barn, where the rest of the women were waiting. She was greeted with a cheer.

With Zarrin at the head, accompanied by Blaise as her handmaiden, they processed around the barn. In the area in front of the main doors, two thrones had been fashioned from straw bales, draped with cloth, cushioned – inevitably – with hops. The owners stood behind them, waiting. She saw Jacko emerge around the other side of the barn, the men in attendance.

The two processions met in front of the thrones, stopped.

The accordion started to play, an ancient, teasing tune – half-anthem, half-jig. When it ceased, Thijs read off a long list of names, of all the kings and queens who had been crowned this way before. Then the crowd were asked again to affirm Jacko and Zarrin, which they did with gusto and laughter, long applause.

Betty took Zarrin's arm, Thijs took Jacko's, and side by side they were led to their thrones, invited to sit.

They were asked to choose attendants – a lady-in-waiting for Jacko, a squire for herself. Jacko chose a young, dark-haired woman, with Spanish features, whom Zarrin didn't know. Zarrin looked around in momentary panic, not sure who to ask. Then Jamie took a half-step towards her from the front of the crowd, and she called his name.

Betty and Thijs positioned themselves behind the thrones, waited once more for the crowd to become still, nodded to the accordionist who stood nearby. The music started again. A simple, slow rhythm, hardly music at all; more like the breath of some primordial beast. Zarrin sat, her body taut, wondering what would happen next. A hand touched her neck. Something brushed her hair, slid down, pressing it to her head. It became heavier. A crown, she guessed, though with the weight of something heavier than silver or gold. It nested upon her, its rim pressed against her forehead. She reached up, touched it, exploring its shape. The surface was smooth yet pitted, aluminium perhaps, or copper. A fool's crown. It was straight-sided, but then seemed to bow out on either side. A teapot, the spout to her left, the handle to her right. On the top, no doubt, was a lid. She glanced at Jacko, trying not to move too sharply for fear of dislodging her crown. His crown was a kettle. She laughed.

She was handed a mug of a dark and steaming liquid, told to drink it. For an instant she hesitated. Was it alcoholic? But the smell was the same as that of the juice she'd drunk earlier in the barn, and that had been good. Again, she glanced at Jacko. He downed his in one. She did the same. The liquid was warm on her throat, tasted of fruit and herbs and some other flavour that she couldn't place.

Thijs came around the throne, took her hand, indicated for her to rise. Betty did the same with Jacko. When they were facing each other, Thijs said, 'You may now kiss.'

Jacko grinned, his face triumphant, his eyes bright. He took a step towards her, lifted his hands to her shoulder, let them rest there. Involuntarily, Zarrin half-turned, looked at Jamie, her eyes beseeching. Jamie's face was stiff, but he gave a small, affirmative nod.

She bit back her panic and dread, waited.

Jacko drew her towards him. She felt the teapot on her head wobble, reached up to steady it. His face was close to hers, looming, threatening. She shut her eyes.

The metal of their makeshift crowns clashed. His lips enclosed hers, seeming to seal her to him. His hand slipped down her arm, crushing the hops against her skin. She wanted to turn, scream.

The crowd cheered.

And then she was free again, and it was just a game, and everyone was clapping and laughing, and Jacko was grinning at her, and the kettle on his head was absurd, and Elend had run up to her and was clinging to her legs, tugging at her and telling her she looked silly and asking why she was wearing a teapot.

For the next hour or so, Zarrin sat on her throne, watching the scene around her, feeling regal and smiling at all that went on – the flirting and fawning, the dancing, the foolishness. Jacko was soon whisked away by admiring partners, and, to let Jamie join in with the fun, she persuaded him to relinquish his duties as attendant for a while, and sent him off into the throng. She noticed Blaise amongst the crowd, videoing the proceedings with her phone. At intervals, people would come up to her and take selfies, pressed to her side, laughing. Children would clamber up beside her on the throne. Now and then, a jug would be placed at her elbow. That same rich and fruity drink. She sipped at it, savouring the taste, and needing the liquid now, for the evening was clammy and hot. Several times, too, she was asked to dance. Each time she quietly refused.

Then Jacko returned.

'My queen,' he said. 'It's time we danced.'

His voice was slurred, his features flushed, his breath heavy with alcohol. She felt a shiver of consternation.

'I'm tired,' she said.

'You cannot deny your king.'

She nodded. He was right. 'Of course.'

She removed her teapot-crown, thankful for the excuse to rid herself of its weight, and laid it on the throne, then followed him onto the field. The music was slow, a country waltz. He took her arm. His hand was firm yet his fingers felt gentle. Pleasant or unpleasant? She couldn't tell.

They danced. To her surprise, he was a good dancer, confident yet attentive, and, despite the alcohol, sure of foot. He held her closer than she liked, but it felt safe like this, in his arms. She might have enjoyed it. Why not?

He bent forward, whispered a small compliment – she danced like an angel – and she laughed.

His hand shifted. For an instant she felt his fingers on her skin through the loose strands of hops, and stiffened. Perhaps he noticed, or perhaps it had been an accidental touch, for he moved slightly away from her, and his fingers left her waist. She should have felt relieved, yet the loss left her disturbed, as if suddenly more exposed.

But, as the music played on, it was impossible not to be drawn closer together, and this time she did not resist.

How should she feel, she wondered, dancing with a man like this?

At the edge of the circle in which they danced, she saw Jamie, watching, and tried to send him a smile. Whether he saw it, whether he could read it correctly, she didn't know. Jacko drew her tighter, buried his face in her hop-laced hair. 'Heaven must taste like this,' he sighed.

The music paused, then restarted. They danced again.

When, at last, it stopped, he stepped back, smiled. 'There. That wasn't so bad, was it?'

She shook her head, thanked him. He leaned forward, gave her a fleeting kiss.

'Now, my queen, go forth and mingle with your subjects.'

One of them was already waiting. 'May I?' Doug asked, as she turned.

She felt that same flutter of anxiety, stifled it with a smile. 'My pleasure,' she said.

And after him, others. Pal, Thijs, men she didn't know. One, a young man, from Morocco or Tunisia, who held her as if he owned her, talked to her in the same terms. She quietly refused his request for a second dance.

Then Jamie.

He approached her tentatively, and she could see the struggle in him. The uncertainty, the desire.

'Yes,' she said, before he'd even asked the question.

The music started: another waltz. Yet even so, he seemed to hesitate. Then stiffly, he stepped towards her, allowed her into his arms.

They danced clumsily, neither fluent enough to take the lead. But she didn't mind. Having him hold her felt like a homecoming after long years away. She leaned a little against him, enjoying the small motion of her body against his. She let the movement carry her, closed her eyes.

The question came: was this it? Had she found her haven at last?

Had he found her?

With the thought came a flutter of apprehension. There were so many things he didn't know about her, things she hadn't managed to explain. She ought to tell him; not to do so would be a deceit. But time was running out?

The music finished. They waited for it to restart.

She wondered: was now the time?

But this world was too joyful for stories like that.

A new tune began, slow and languid. They moved together again.

He bent his head to her, said something that she didn't quite catch, and she asked him to repeat it.

'I asked if you learned to dance like this in Syria,' he said. 'So light, so smooth.'

She laughed. 'Not like this. Kurdish dancing is different. You'd be whirled off your feet.'

He gave a chuckle. 'I can manage to do that in a waltz.'

'You'll have to hold on tight, then,' she said, and was surprised at her own bravado.

Then he asked, 'Do you miss it – your life in Syria?'

'I miss nothing,' she said. 'I'm happy here.'

'You must miss your family.' But in the same moment, he seemed to remember what sort of place Syria was and apologised. 'I'm sorry. I just assumed they were still alive.'

She said nothing, danced on, feeling calmed and intoxicated by the warmth of his chest against her face.

But he insisted. 'Zarrin?'

Not now, she told herself. Not tonight. And yet the words came anyway. 'My family disowned me.'

His step faltered. 'Why?'

It was the question of an innocent; anyone less so would surely guess. But she didn't reply, just nestled closer against him, tried to shut the past away.

He asked again.

'Why on earth would they do that?'

She stopped dancing, stood back. 'Do you really want to know?'

His eyes fell from her, though not before she glimpsed the doubt within them. 'Only if you want to tell me.'

Did she?

'Not here. Somewhere quiet.'

She led him back to the place where she'd been enthroned, sat there on the lower bales. He sat beside her. She reached for his hand, stroked his knuckle with her thumb.

'I should have told you before,' she said, felt his hand stiffen, stroked it again.

But tell what? Still, the battle raged inside her. Did she want to tell? Should she? And how much, how should she do it? Even now, could she change her mind and keep her secrets to herself?

'I was married,' she said, the words coming almost involuntarily. 'He was an important man – a member of one of the big families. It was a family arrangement, as is the way there, in Syria. Though I admit, it was my wish, too. I thought it was a dream come true. But then – then I met someone else, and we fell in love.' She bit at her lip, and quickly corrected herself. 'I fell in love. I was – I was young, innocent. I thought…' Yet she didn't know what she thought, and stopped.

Jamie said nothing.

'His family found out,' she continued, her voice low. 'That's why my family disowned me.'

She looked up at Jamie, a swift glance, hoping to see understanding and forgiveness in his eyes. All she saw was confusion.

She paused again, searching for the words that she might use; ones that might tell him, yet somehow spare the understanding. 'They punished me,' she said at last. 'They did what they do in Syria, to people like me. They set my husband's brother on me. He and his men. They caught me, beat me. They – they raped me. They would have killed me if I'd let them. That's why I fled.'

She fell silent, waited for him to say something: outrage, sympathy, disbelief. She waited for him to turn back to her, take her into his arms, let her bury herself against his warm chest.

Instead, he remained unspeaking, didn't move, until – with a power and swiftness that shocked her – he pulled away from her, and her hand fell.

He sat twisted, as if contorted with pain.

Sorrow and sympathy flooded her. She raised her hand to his shoulder. He flinched.

'I wanted you to know,' she said. 'I wanted you to understand.'

He nodded, said nothing.

'I wanted to tell you long ago. But I couldn't.'

Still no response.

'You don't hate me for it, do you?' she asked, her voice pleading. 'Please don't.'

He made a sound, half-groan, half-sob, and she moved to place herself at his feet. His head was in his hands. She reached up, pulled at his arms, trying to open them so that she could see his face. 'Jamie, please.'

'Hey! You two have made it at last, I see.' Jacko's voice, resounding.

She swung around. 'Don't—'

'About time, too. I thought I was going to lose my bet on this one.'

Jamie curled away again, so that his back was to them. She threw her arms around him, but his body remained unyielding and stiff.

From behind her, Jacko said, 'Sorry! Is this a bad time? Do you want me to go?'

She turned back to him. 'Yes, do that. Now!'

In that same moment, Jamie dragged himself to his feet, broke free. She grabbed at him again. 'Jamie!'

He stood above her, hair dishevelled, face pale and deformed – a man distraught. Jacko stood opposite, features frozen in horror. Beyond them, the party went on: bodies cavorting and swanning and swaying; light and shadow dancing; music filling the air. A wild, Satanic scene.

'No.' Jamie's voice, almost a wolf's howl. He glared at Zarrin, then swung towards Jacko, then seemed to lose all control and flung his hands to his head. 'No, no. Just – just leave me. Just fuck off. All of you. Fuck you.' Then he turned and lurched into the crowd.

She moved to follow him, hesitated, called after him, 'Jamie.' He didn't look back.

'What the devil was that about?' Jacko exclaimed.

She shook her head, screwed up her eyes. Jamie's words rang in her ears, though who they were meant for she didn't know: her or Jacko, or the whole world. 'You and your big mouth,' she spat.

Jacko nodded. 'Yes, probably.' Then, 'But what happened before?'

She gave a moan, buried her face in her hands.

'Tell me,' Jacko said.

'It's none of your business. Leave me alone.' Then despair flooded her and she leaned against him, wept.

He stroked her head, told her that it would be alright.

'It's my fault,' she sobbed.

'I don't think so.'

'It is! I shouldn't have told him. I thought he'd understand.'

'Understand what?'

She fought against her tears, tried to recover herself, but seemed to lack the strength. Why? she asked herself. She'd been so strong for so many years. Why such weakness now?

'Understand what?' Jacko asked again.

She drew in her breath, tried to tell him. The things she'd said, her confession, the way Jamie had responded.

When her words ran out, he sat for long moments in silence, his breathing heavy. Then he eased away from her, turned to regard her, his face grave.

'You told him that?' he said.

She nodded. 'What have I done?' she groaned.

From out in the field came an explosion, like a gunshot, and startled, she looked up. The fireworks had started. There was crackling and fizzing, then a rocket burst, showering the sky.

'How much do you know?' Jacko asked.

'About what?'

'About Jamie? How much has he told you?'

She shook her head. 'Nothing. That's the trouble. I know nothing about him.' Then, as if in defiance of her own thoughts, 'I know he's a good man. I know that.'

'Yes. He is. But he's other things, too. He thinks too much. He cares too much. He makes his own life hard.'

She felt a flare of indignation, fierce in Jamie's defence. 'You can't blame him. That's too easy. I won't do that.'

'Do you know about Leisha?'

She started. 'Leisha? No...'

There was more commotion from the yard in front of the barn, as a group of firecrackers was let off, echoing around the field. When she turned back it was to see the agony in Jacko's eyes.

'She used to be on the boat,' he said, his voice heavy. 'She was Jamie's – Jamie's lover. He doted on her. He'd have gone to hell and back for her if he'd needed to; if she'd wanted.'

Her mind lurched. Did he love someone else?

'She didn't, though. She didn't want that.'

'What do you mean?'

Jacko sighed. 'You know Jamie. You know what he's like – the sort of guy he is. How serious, how committed. He doesn't fit in with all this.' He swept his free hand, indicating the party in the field, its noise and turmoil. 'He thinks he's a radical. Maybe in politics he is. But, inside, he's tight and tied. Maybe it's the religion that did it to him, the childhood he had. All that Scottish Presbyterianism. I don't know. But for whatever reason, he's way out of his time. He believes in loyalty, trust, true love, one woman for life. Leisha didn't. She wasn't like that. Whether Jamie just didn't realise, or knew and thought he could change her, I don't know. But...' He shrugged. 'The inevitable happened.'

Again, he was silent, and Zarrin's mind ran back, seeing again her glimpses of Jamie in the fields, in their camp, on the boats when travelling. Seeing what she'd missed before: a man rejected, a man deceived.

'Leisha did her best,' Jacko said. 'I'm not saying she didn't. She tried to change – to be the sort of woman that Jamie wanted her to be. But she couldn't. You can't be what you're not.' He gave a sigh, wry, resigned. 'She was too much like the rest of us – Doug and Blaise, Pal, me. The world's too small for people like us. We need space and freedom.' He waited as more fireworks went off and for the ensuing cheer from the crowd to fade. 'It was never going to work... We all saw that. All except Jamie.'

The story fitted, of course, and Zarrin knew it. Jamie would always give his utmost, assume the best, be the victim of his own expectations and hopes. Wasn't that what had happened with her?

'I tried to warn him,' Jacko continued. 'I wasn't the only one. But he wouldn't listen. He wouldn't hear a thing against her from anyone. Certainly not me.'

'When was this?' Zarrin asked.

'About eighteen months ago. Anyone else would have got over it by now, moved on. Not Jamie.'

She stared into the field. The children had been given sparklers and were running around, waving them, making elfin dances in the darkness. She closed her eyes, wanting to blank the scene out. She wanted to blank out Jacko's words, too. It was already obvious where the story was going, where it would end. She didn't want to hear it, yet knew she must. What she wanted, she realised, was a fiction: just to live in a make-believe world.

'What happened?' she asked.

'What was always bound to happen. Leisha cheated on him, had an affair. It was brief. I doubt it meant anything much. Just fun and sex, a bit of – light relief. But, when Jamie found out, he couldn't take it. It destroyed him, poor guy. He raged at her, threatened her, told her to leave, begged her to go. In the end, that's what she did.'

Zarrin pictured him again, as he sat beside her and she made her self-seeking confession, unwittingly stabbing at him with every word.

'I wish I'd known,' she said. And she remembered what she'd done to Salvo, Yaasmin. Now Jamie, too. 'Someone should have told me,' she cried.

'Perhaps,' Jacko said. 'I thought like that once, but it doesn't work.'

There was pathos in his voice, and another realisation dawned. She let out a gasp. 'It was you, wasn't it?' she said. 'You told him.'

He nodded. 'I thought I had to. I was his best friend, after all. Isn't that what best friends are for?'

She gave a whimper, as new tears spilled, fresh and raw. Not just for herself, but for Jamie and Jacko as well. There seemed no limit to the obstacles and traps life could set for you, no way you could avoid them and run free.

'I wish I knew what to do,' she sobbed.

'You need to talk to him,' Jacko said. 'You need to talk to each other.'

*

She lay in bed, sleepless. Shame seemed to consume her – shame and regret.

What had she done?

Outside, from the field, the sound of the music and laughter continued, though more muted, appetites almost sated.

Where was Jamie? Where had he gone?

Earlier, she'd looked for him – to explain, to apologise, to try to put things right, though how, she did not know. But he was nowhere to be seen. She'd asked Blaise, Pal, Doug. None of them knew. All were too lost now in the haze of the night's excesses to care. Had he gone to his room to weep and sulk? Had he walked off into the night alone?

Had he found one of the other women as compensation?

She'd listened at his door, but could hear nothing. She'd knocked, but he hadn't answered. She searched for Elend, asked him: had he seen Jamie?

Elend shook his head. 'Why?'

'I need to see him,' she said.

'I can look.'

She thanked him. No. It would wait until morning. 'And anyway,' she said, 'it's time you were in bed. Ten minutes. No more.'

Soon afterwards, she went to bed herself.

Yet an hour later she was just lying there, brooding. Going over again in her mind everything that Jacko had said, its implications. The foolishness of her own behaviour – her maidenly attempts to tease Jamie, lure him, lead him on. The crassness of her confession, revealing herself as what she truly was. The very embodiment of the woman who had once broken Jamie's heart.

There was nothing worse she could have done, to frighten him away.

She remembered, too, his hesitancy: afraid to trust himself again to a woman's wiles. How right he'd been.

Poor Jamie, she thought. Poor man. She turned over, buried her face in the pillow, wished she had tears left to weep.

Then out of all the misery, a memory formed. Fredrik, years ago, in Romania. The laughter as he'd told her.

She got out of bed, found her mobile phone.

If Fredrik could propose to his wife by email, she could at least tell Jamie she loved him by phone. She rang. There was no answer. She left a voice message. 'Jamie. It's Zarrin. I need to speak to you. I – I love you.'

*

She seemed to rise from a dark pit. She must have slept. Dreams fell away from her like a burden heavily shaken off. It was quiet, now. No music. The night was black. But something had wakened her. What?

She heard it again. Her name. Whispered so softly that it might have been an echo from her dream.

'Zarrin.'

Elend? Imagination?

Then the rustle of movement in the corridor outside her room.

Memory flooded back.

'Jamie?'

Silence.

'Jamie? Is that you?'

She started to get up, stopped.

'Elend found me. He said you wanted to see me.'

She took a slow breath, trying to compose herself. 'I left you a message. Did you get it?'

Silence again, then, 'Yes.'

'I do,' she said. 'I do love you.'

A small sound, like a sob or a sigh. She imagined him standing there, features screwed tight as they had been when she'd told him what happened, as she stabbed again and again at his heart.

Then, in a small voice, he said, 'I think we need to talk, don't you?'

They were preparing to move on. The boats had been packed. Farewells had been said. Kisses and hugs exchanged.

Everyone wanted to kiss Zarrin. Each time, she glanced at Jamie, received a smile in return. No jealousy any more. No doubts.

Jacko was the last. He hugged her to him, said quietly, 'Do you forgive me now?'

She grinned. 'Of course.'

Then he went to Jamie, shook his hand. 'Look after her,' he said. 'She's too precious to lose.'

'I know.'

They cast off, and with a growl from the engines, echoed by the water, moved away.

Zarrin settled on the cabin-top, waving until the last figure on the wharf had disappeared, watching as the roofs of the farm dissolved amidst the hedgerows and trees, taking a quick look now and then at Jamie, where he stood at the helm. Exchanging unspoken messages of love.

For an hour, they travelled like that. A languid passage, past fields of golden stubble, fresh-turned soil where gulls wheeled above the plough, pastures where cattle stood at the edge of the reeds, tails swishing against the flies. Squares of oak woodland, touched now with September's rust. Behind them, the water fanned out like fingers, trailing a last goodbye. Swallows gathered on the telegraph wires, waiting to see her pass before they left.

It was all for her, she thought. That was how it seemed. How could she be so blessed?

Mid-morning, they tied up briefly for a rest. Blaise came on board, eager to talk to her, her mobile phone in her hand.

'Look at this?'

Zarrin took the phone. There was a video playing, though what it was at first, she couldn't tell. The image was dark, chaotic. Shadows, flashes of light. Music, shrieks of laughter, cheering.

'What is it?'

'It's you. You know I filmed the party the other night, you being crowned and all that? I put it on Facebook and YouTube and Snapchat. It's gone viral. It's had over ten thousand hits already. There's more every minute. People love it – you know, Kurdish refugee crowned Queen of the Hops.'

Zarrin gasped, shook her head. 'No. You don't mean that.'

But Blaise nodded, laughing. 'Yes. The whole world knows about you now. You're famous.'

18

Return

She sits by the window, looking out. Her arm lies on the seat-rest, parallel to his, their fingers just touching.

Below her, the land stretches and unfolds in slow waves. It feels strange, flying like this. Moving effortlessly across the vast expanse of the world. Each minute of suspension gobbling up long months of her past, whole chapters of her life, erasing them in a few breaths. It devalues everything that happened. The journeying and suffering, the boredom, the pain, the cold and the blistering heat. The constant nag of hope, never letting her go,

She peers down, searching for places she might have been – towns that she might have visited with Salvo, roads they might have driven along. But it's all too muddled, too hazy. Just a drab patchwork of greys and greens and browns, like the faded brushwork of an old painting. Its colour and meaning lost.

She wonders where they are, how long they have been travelling, how much further there is to go. What waits for her when she arrives.

She closes her eyes. So tired. And yet so far from sleep. Too many memories, too many thoughts jangling in her mind. Voices, images. Things done, things left undone. Words said and unsaid.

Jamie and Elend. Yaasmin. Salvo.

Mahmet and Rohat.

The man who had caused it all, whom she had thought she loved beyond anything else, could give up her life for. Had, in fact, done so. A face and a body she would have to reach for, now, if she wanted to imagine them again. A name, too. Nasr. Was he worth all this?

Never, she thinks, none of it.

Nor if he were a thousand times more.

Yet, out of it, goodness has come.

Elend. Jamie.

She has known that.

The thoughts well up again. Dissolve to what might be dreams. Fragments. Fact and fiction, jumbled. All time and sequence lost.

*

Blaise's voice. 'You're famous.' The brightness in her eyes. Excitement, pleasure. Sharp and piercing as a dagger.

Her own voice, like a wail, the bleat of a frightened lamb. 'Oh, Blaise, what have you done?'

Later, after she'd explained, Blaise's face, crumpled, pale. Tears bubbling in her eyes. 'No. That can't be true.'

'Yes. Yes, it is.'

*

They came for her two weeks later. She knew they would; it was just a matter of time.

By the time they came, she'd made her plans. She did what she had to.

She'd thought of fleeing, trying to hide once more. But she had no will for it. Not now; not now that she'd found Jamie.

Jamie had said the same: let's go. She'd refused. She couldn't inflict that sort of life on him. Nor did she have the strength for it any more. It was too crushing, too hard. She'd rather take what days she had with him, and trust the rest to fate. Nor could she go for Elend's sake. He was happy here. He was living a child's life at last.

But she told Jamie what he must do. He mustn't get involved; he mustn't try to protect or save her. He just had to get Elend away, keep him safe.

Jamie had argued, refused, but in the end she'd made him promise. And in his heart, she knew, he didn't believe it would happen – that life could work in such ways. For all his philosophy and logic, he believed in fate's justice, that good would win out. That was why Leisha's deceit had hurt him so much.

That was why she loved him as she did.

So he gave her the promise she demanded. And she knew she could trust that.

In return, she made a promise of her own. 'I will be back.'

They came for her one Sunday, in a small village in Warwickshire in the middle of a play. It was the last of the season, and the same play as her first. This time, as defence of a sort, she was heavily made-up, wore a blonde wig. But at some point, while they were there, someone must have recognised her. Someone who had seen Blaise's video, felt it their duty to inform. Someone who didn't like immigrants or Muslims, who considered their country to be facing some alien, existential threat.

They appeared at the back of the audience: three men, immediately recognisable and out of place. Too burly, too assured for the world they suddenly found themselves in. Not playgoers, for sure.

She saw them as she made her own entrance, wand in hand, ready once more to set the hero free. She felt no fear, hardly even dismay. Just resignation. It would happen, as she'd known it would. And one question at least had been resolved. It would not be at Rohat's hands – not yet.

She didn't falter. She played her part. She waved her wand, and the hero survived.

And afterwards, Jamie and the others played their part, too, according to the script she'd given them. Blaise spirited Elend away. No mention of him was made. Jamie kept apart, didn't try to save her. She was interviewed in her old berth, by then cleared of Elend's things. They would not find him. They would not know.

The men confronted her, with their badges and walkie-talkies, their smart uniforms.

'We're from Immigration Enforcement,' the leader said. He showed her the video. 'Zarrin Kashlan. Can you confirm that the woman in this recording is you?'

*

But the thought of Rohat sticks, and memories swirl again, engulf her. For she's not yet free.

The hard floor of the stable, where they had caught her, trapped her, done their deed. The muck and the filth.

A detail that she'd forgotten until now. A chink of light in the roof. And there, framed within it, the red blush of a bougainvillea flower, tossing gently in the breeze. She had watched it, clung to it, tried to be that flower, smiling and above it all. She had hated it, too.

Then the next man had grabbed her, thrown her over, so that her face was against the floor, and, as he entered her, a cheer had run around the room.

The holding centre, where they took her first.

In the corner, a woman screamed. The cry penetrated the room, seemed to hang in the air even as she drew breath. Then it came again.

On the bed beside Zarrin, a young woman sobbed. She held herself tight in a foetal position, choking back her grief or fear, releasing it only in sudden tremors. Opposite, two women – mother and daughter, Zarrin guessed – clung together, hijabs drawn close across their faces.

The whole place was fear and misery, she thought; despair. There seemed no room left to add her own. She felt divorced from her past, from her life, whatever emotions they had left her with. Just an empty shell, from which all feeling had been torn away and cast to the wind. An 'illegal', waiting to know her fate.

*

Another room, no more than a cell. Its bare walls painted in a pale gloss, the colour of curdled milk. Two plastic chairs, opposite sides of a square table, Formica-topped. She'd spent long hours there already, just sitting, waiting, staring at her hands, at the pattern on the table, the smears and marks that other people's hands had made. Looking up at intervals when someone entered, asked her a few questions, left.

It might be her world, she thought, her life reduced to this. Just to sit and wait and repeat the same information over and over again, to one person, then another. Who she was. Where she was from. The names of her parents, of her husband. Her age, the date she was married, the date she was born. That might be all there was now – the facts, the statistics. The living itself spent.

*

'It's a letter.'

The man handed it to her.

'We've opened it, of course. Just in case. I'm sure you understand.'

The envelope had been sliced neatly, along the fold. The straightness of the cut shocked her, almost as though it had been her own flesh. So sharp, so clinical. Whereas she would have torn it open desperately and raggedly in hope, for she recognised the writing. Jamie.

When the man had gone, she took the letter out. It was brief, the words carefully chosen to be ambiguous, bland. He had heard that she had been detained. They were thinking of her, and would do what they could to help. If she needed money, she should let them know. Everyone there was well.

There was a mobile number – a number she knew she could never use, in case it was bugged.

The letter was signed: *J*.

That single stroke of the pen seemed to contain more meaning in it, more love, more loss, than the rest of her life put together.

She cried.

*

The drone of the engine, of the wheels on the road, was like a drug. Sucking her into oblivion. The journey was the same, for she knew that there was no going back. All gone now. Just the bureaucracy to go through. The detention centre. More interrogations. Waiting for a decision to be made.

How long would it take? One month? Two? They said it might be six or more. Did it matter how long? The end had already come.

She tried to feel regret, self-pity. Or anger or bitterness of some sort. She felt, instead, something like satisfaction. Grim and hard.

What was happening to her now had no meaning in it, nothing she could assign. It was just cold logic, playing itself out. But, though fate had claimed her as it always would, she had defeated it nonetheless.

Elend was free. He would have a life.

*

A man entered, sat down opposite her. He was her lawyer, he said. It was her right. Friends of hers had arranged for him to come and to help her with her claim. He was here to talk to her.

He was an Arab – Moroccan, perhaps, or Tunisian. Young – hardly old enough to have trained as a lawyer, she thought. He had a thin, reedy voice, and his English was poor, so that at times she struggled to understand him and had to prompt him with corrections or suggestions of words. His manner was earnest and intent. He leaned across the narrow table, too close to her, so that she could feel his breath, taste it on her lips. Tobacco – *mu'assel* – the sweet fruitiness of molasses. Something else, more flowery, which she could not place. Orris or mace, perhaps, or some artificial ingredient of cheap aftershave that he used to cover up whatever other odours or fragrances he might exude. He never looked at her directly, kept his eyes down, directed at the table or her hands; now and then ventured a brief foray further up her body, towards her breast.

He told her what she already knew. Her rights. What would happen. What the possible outcomes were. She wanted to ask: had he defended asylum-seekers before, had he been successful? But she did not want to embarrass him. He seemed too fragile, too vulnerable.

He asked her what the basis for her asylum claim would be – whether she had been persecuted or threatened, and if so, by whom? Hesitantly, trying to save him from the details, she told him that she had been raped by her husband's brother and his men.

'Gang-raped?' he asked.

'You could call it that.'

'Was this – was this just once? Or did it happen regularly?' Her look betrayed her shock, and he blushed.

'It makes a difference,' he said.

'I didn't stay to give them a second chance,' she told him, and was surprised to hear that there could still be irony in her voice.

*

She thought of Elend. Imagined him with every ounce of her will, until he seemed to be there, real. But in the moment he came, he vanished. She could not hold him.

Jamie the same.

She might have cursed them for their infidelity. Why would they not come to her in her thoughts? Instead, she told herself that their absence was right. This was not the place for them, in a barren cell, trapped. Nor could there be any place for them in her mind. For there they would taunt her and test her with every breath she took. There, she might betray them and mention their names to someone who would take pleasure in hunting them down.

Memories were danger, she knew, and torment. Memories just magnified her loss. Better that she forget them, leave them free.

Free, she thought, from the prejudice and hatred of the world. Free to live their own lives, to roam and wander and wonder, to find happiness, to be themselves. Free to forget her in the same way.

And yet she hoped they would remember.

She hoped that they might look for her, come after her, might one day find her and take her back.

But then, that countervailing thought, fierce and strong. Brute satisfaction. Pride. She'd achieved what she had set out to do. She had given Elend his future. Jamie would look after him; he was safe and free.

*

'Please. Sit down.'

A man and a woman sat at the table. The woman indicated the empty chairs, gave a brief smile of encouragement. The man nodded.

'This is a formal interview,' the woman said. 'You understand that. We are here to help us determine the validity of your claim for asylum. So please understand, also, that we need you to tell the truth. If you don't do so, it will damage your claim. Do you understand?'

Zarrin nodded.

'Say it, please. The interview is being recorded.'

'I understand.'

'And this, I believe, is your lawyer.' She indicated the man who had sat beside her. 'Mr Osmali-Baba. Have I pronounced that correctly?'

The lawyer nodded, held out a hand. It was ignored, and he let it rest on the table, a redundant appendage, forgotten.

'Let's start with the basics,' the woman said. 'Name. Date of birth. Nationality.'

Zarrin gave them, as she had a dozen times before to different people. They hardly even felt like hers any more. They had been taken from her, become just labels, a strange code that gave entry to this world.

They asked about her childhood – where she had been brought up, who her parents were, what they did for a living; whether she had any brothers or sisters. Whether she had been married.

'Yes. I was married.'

'Mahmet Sinjari. Was that your husband?'

'Yes. It was.'

'Was or is? Did you get divorced? Or did he die?'

She hesitated. 'No. We never divorced. Whether he's alive or not, I don't know.'

'You've not seen him since you left?'

'No.'

More questions about Mahmet, about his family, his businesses. Where he stood in Syrian society; whether he had any political role.

'He was known to the government, I think. Anyone in business would be. And his family ran several big businesses.'

'But you don't know the details?'

'No. I was just – just his wife. I went along to dinners and meetings sometimes, but was not involved. I was there for – for protocol. For show.'

A change of tack. When had she left? How?

She tried to recall the date, found that it eluded her. Not just the time of year, but the year too. It seemed so long ago. Another life.

She remembered the man, branding her wrist, and looked down at where the stamp had been, imagined that she could still see the mark.

'It was April,' she said. '2011.'

The interviewer repeated the date. 'What made you leave?'

She didn't reply, and he prompted her. 'You need to tell us.'

'I was abused. By my husband's brother, Rohat Sinjari. And by men of his.'

'Abused? In what way?'

'Beaten. Attacked. Raped.'

'Gang-raped?'

'Yes.'

'And did anything special motivate this act? Or was it spontaneous?'

Again she hesitated.

'We know this is difficult. But we need to know.' The woman looked at the lawyer for confirmation, received a vigorous nod.

'I had an affair,' she said. 'My husband found out. He set his brother on me as punishment.'

'I see. It was – it was a matter of honour, then?'

'They were going to kill me,' she said. 'This – this was just a sort of – taster. Advance payment for their services. Call it what you like. That's why I can't go back. They still will. They'll kill me if they find me. That's what is done.'

*

The look in his eyes.

He had always looked at her like that. He had done so when she first met him, when Mahmet had introduced her, so full of himself, so full of pride. Look what I have captured. Aren't you jealous?

Rohat was, she knew.

He'd looked at her like that – with jealousy, lust – every time he saw her, even when Mahmet was there. A signal to her, to his brother. *Beware.*

He'd looked at her like that when he toasted her: *to my brother's beautiful wife.*

He'd looked at her then, as he took her, and afterwards, as he set his men upon her and watched, egging them on. Yet not quite the same, for jealousy had gone, was replaced by triumph. Then disdain.

And he had looked at her that way ever since. With lust and triumph and disdain. Staring at her from the recesses and shadows of her mind, always lurking, waiting for the moment her defences weakened, her attention slipped. In her dreams sometimes emerging to confront her, face to face.

Body against body.

Now, another layer to add to the rest. Expectation.

*

The journey. They wanted to know about that. How she had escaped, the route she'd taken, what she had done between then and now.

She told them about that day, afterwards, as she hurriedly grabbed her belongings, fled the house. The details surprised her – the things she could remember, the small and irrelevant decisions her mind had made. Her blue comb, lying beside the jewellery box on her dressing table. The strand of hair caught in its teeth, curled like a question mark. She had taken the comb, not even considered her jewellery, which would have been worth money on the road. The row of shawls hanging in the closet. Blue and red and russet. She had flapped through them, seeking the one she wanted: beige, camel hair, in a fine, open weave, embroidered at the edge with gold. Had she chosen it for its strength, or for its connections – she'd been given it by her sister – or for its looks? For whatever reason, a good choice. It had travelled with her, survived. She had it still. She had grabbed it again, along with her eye-bead, when she was arrested.

'And no one saw you?' they asked.

'No. If they had, I wouldn't be here.'

She told them about her journey through the desert, always afraid that she was being pursued, about hiding from the army as she went.

'There was war then?' the man asked.

'The beginnings,' she said. 'I saw the tanks and armoured vehicles. I heard the fighting.' The smallest of deceits, and one for which she could forgive herself. If war hadn't reached her, it wasn't far behind. Even days later would have been too late.

She told about crossing the border, the camp. She told about Elend's birth, too late realised her mistake, stopped.

'You have a child?'

Her mind raced. She pictured them searching the canal boats, sorting out the children, struggling as she had done, to fit them to their parents; sneering at the confusion which only added to what they already knew – a veritable house of sin. She pictured them finding Elend, dragging him away.

Yet if she denied the child, would they find out anyway? Would they contact the refugee camp where he had been born? Could they trace her, find evidence of the birth?

'Had,' she said. 'He died on the way.'

'Your husband's? Or your lover's? Or one of the men that raped you?'

'Not my husband's,' she said.

'How did he die?'

She remembered Yaasmin's story, her sister's death. 'Measles,' she said.

She told about the journey, about Istanbul, how she got to Bulgaria, about living in Europe for over a year. She said nothing about Salvo, but made her time with him a dozen different journeys, in one truck or another, haphazardly taking her north.

They returned to the details of her entry. Where in Bulgaria she had arrived from, which road she took, whether she'd stopped at the border on the way.

'Why did you not request asylum then? That's the rule – at the port of entry.'

She shrugged. 'I didn't know the rules.'

'Ignorance is no excuse,' the woman said.

Zarrin shrugged again, said nothing.

'Tell us, then, about getting into Britain. How did you manage that?'

'I hid on a truck.'

'You had an agent?'

'No. I was just lucky.'

'Tell us the details.'

She made up a story. It sounded contrived, unlikely, but they didn't challenge it.

'And since?'

The same mix of truth and untruth and something between – truth made of shadows and possibilities, rather than the solid and resolved substance of fact.

She admitted to having worked in the Elysium – that the hotel employed illegals was an open secret, she was sure. She talked about her work on farms, blurring the names and dates and places, without too much difficulty, because to her, now, much of her life was that – a blur. She had been a vagrant, too, in London, she said: squatting, begging. Just another amongst the homeless and dispossessed. But she did not mention the people who had been kind to her: Dinos in the market, Mrs Jervais who had given her a room.

'And these people we found you with. The travellers. What about them?'

'They took pity on me,' she said. 'They gave me a lift. They were working on the hop farm, so I stayed and worked with them. The farmer didn't know. I was just one of the group. After – afterwards, they offered to take me as far as Oxford. That's where we were going next. They were just being kind, that's all.'

'You weren't in a relationship with any of them, then? This man you were videoed with. Jacko.'

'No. He wasn't with them. We'd hardly met. We just got picked on that day as king and queen. I don't know why. I've not seen him since.'

'But he wrote to you. He signs himself "J". I think he is paying for your lawyer.'

She tried not to show surprise: at their misapprehension, at what they knew. She wondered whether to correct them, tell them about Jamie, decided not to. The less they really understood, the better.

'I didn't know that,' she said. 'About the lawyer. I assumed that he was just part of my rights.'

'But you aren't in a relationship with him – this Jacko?'

'No. But I'm grateful for what he's done.'

At the end, the woman sat with her, asked her if she had any questions to ask in return. It was a ploy, Zarrin guessed, seeking further clues, hoping for some unintended admission. She asked what would happen to her. Whether they would approve her claim.

The woman shrugged. 'I can't say yet. But you have to be realistic. Statistically, the odds are against you. Less than a third of people are accepted.' She regarded Zarrin for a moment, her face grave. 'I don't know which way it will go. It depends how your answers check out, what else we discover. But on the surface there's nothing special about your story that would single you out, might offer hope. The rules are plain. Refugees should seek asylum in the first port of entry to the EU. If you aren't deported, you'll probably be returned there. What happens then, who knows?'

'I'm from Syria,' Zarrin said. 'It's a war zone. They can't return me there.'

'I wouldn't count on that, I'm afraid.'

*

Another letter. Another message.

Be strong. All's well. Pal's play is finished. It has a happy ending. We're with you every day.

J.

*

The woman was right. War zone or not, it made no difference.

'But I've some news for you,' the woman said, when she told her.

Zarrin regarded her stonily.

'That brother-in-law of yours. Rohat Sinjari. We couldn't contact him. We know why now. He was killed in a bombing raid, three years ago.'

Zarrin nodded. She should have felt relief. Instead, she felt cheated. All that fear for nothing. The imaginings proved false.

The woman smiled. 'But it means, of course, that you've less reason to fear going back there. We thought you'd like to know.'

*

The sound of the engine changes. She feels the plane bank.

Next to her, the man moves. The handcuffs tug at her wrist.

Then sleep claims her again.

*

More dreams. Jamie calling.

Elend coming towards her, no longer a child. His body strangely bloated so that he walks stiffly, as if hardly human at all.

'It is for you,' he says.

But she is shouting at him: 'No. Don't. Don't.'

Then she hears the roar of the bomb, feels the shock wave buffet her.

*

'We're here.'

She looks out onto the tarmac, the terminal beyond. Will Mahmet be there somewhere, waiting?

Her guard pulls again at her wrist. 'Time to go,' he says, his voice quiet, not unkind. 'Welcome home.'

Epilogue

And there is another story. It is a story of one person, and it is a story of thousands.

In the middle of the Mediterranean Sea, a boat drifts. It is heavy in the water and moves sluggishly, like a drunken man, staggering. It is an old boat, was built in Malta in the traditional style, as a *luzzu*, for coastal fishing. But since then it has had countless reincarnations. Drifter. Cockle boat. Pleasure boat. Makeshift ferry for passengers who could not afford the real thing. For a long time just a beached hulk against which the fishermen sometimes leaned as they mended their nets, and in which in summer the children played, and in winter the rain gathered and the algae grew. It is made of wood, the planks fitted carvel-style, edge to edge, and painted yellow and blue. Happy colours, meant to bring joy to the heart, the yellow picking out the tops of the gunwales, the line of the prow and the keel. Once, there would have been a pair of eyes at the bow, for luck. But the paint is flaked now and faded, and the boat is blind. The eyes were lost many years ago; perhaps the luck, too.

In its new incarnation, it has an outboard motor attached to the stern – a small, flimsy thing, that looks inadequate for the size of the vessel, and has proved itself so. It is silent, hangs limp. The only source of movement is the sea itself, and the wind that seems to stir its surface, taunt it, make it restless.

When it set out, there were some sixty people on board, though no one had counted accurately. The men who were organising it all on the small jetty did not bother with such things, for everyone knew that whatever capacity the boat might notionally have would be far exceeded. But when no more people could be squeezed on, despite the pleas of those who waited, the leader leaned down, yanked the starter cord on the motor, and at the fifth or sixth or seventh attempt, with much blaspheming, managed to get it running. Then the other two men used boat-hooks to push it away from the jetty, point it roughly perpendicular to the shore, and, erratically steered by one of the passengers – a young Ethiopian who had never been in a boat before – it headed out to sea.

For the rest of that day it ploughed its way north, struggling against the tide. The men on board took it in turns to steer. Away from the sheltering arc of the headland, the sea grew rougher, the waves became white-topped. As the boat bucked and slewed, the women keened, men cursed or prayed. Many were sick. When the engine coughed, someone filled up the tank with diesel from a plastic drum that had been placed in the stern. Then it was started again.

Night came. For half an hour the sea flamed with the reds and oranges and yellows of the setting sun. There was something that felt like peace on board. But almost suddenly, the colours merged and thickened to liquid pewter and all was dark. The boat continued, climbing unseen mountains, descending into unseen valleys; and at the tiller the men argued about the readings from the compasses on their phones or about which constellation was which, and where the Pole Star lay. Long into that night they motored on, until the moon peeked between the racing black clouds and briefly splashed the sea with silver. Then darkness again.

In that darkness, the first deaths occurred. An old man, who simply disappeared, either fallen or pushed overboard. A child, already sickly when he set out, whose crying slowly subsided, and whose body turned stiff and cold in his mother's arms. He lies there still.

As dawn broke, grey across the sea, the engine stuttered once more. The men at the motor added the last of the diesel – a litre or so, grainy with the dirt in the bottom of the drum. The engine fired, though reluctantly, ran for a short while, faltered, stopped. It has not worked since.

For the next day, and the night that followed, and now for most of one further day again, the boat has been at the mercy of the elements. It has wallowed and slurred, sluggishly turned, like an old cow grazing. Whether there is any overall direction to its motion, no one any longer knows. The sea seems to take it one way, the wind another. Cross-currents twist and tangle everything to confusion. And nowhere is there any fixed point. Grey cloud above, the waves shifting and chopping discordantly. No land. No lights. No other craft. The boat and its human cargo are alone in the world, drifting.

The passengers huddle together, talking in low voices. Now and then, for no obvious reason, a cry goes up, a wild wailing. At prayer times – or times that are deemed to be that – the devout seek the eastern horizon and in their narrow spaces bend, bow, try to prostrate themselves. In the times between, arguments break out, threats are issued. But even the arguments have become listless, and, like the boat, go nowhere.

The waves slap against the hull. The wind whistles softly, as if in warning. Light fades once more.

There is hunger and thirst aboard. The food they all carried has gone. The water too. They'd been told the journey would take one day, two at most, not three or four. And no one was allowed much in the way of possessions: no room for such luxuries. The salt spray that has been lifting all day from the restless waters has etched people's faces, made sores on their lips, around their eyes. Their wet clothes have chafed them in every fold of their bodies. Many are stained with vomit or pee or shit.

The people there are from all walks of life, and of all ages. There are Iraqis and Afghans and Nigerians and Ethiopians, Somalis and Syrians and Yemenis and Kurds. They flee every sort of danger and abuse. War, terrorism, persecution. Drought and floods. Famine and starvation. Family abuse. A few do not flee but are drawn by something stronger than fear. Love of a man, a woman, a child; someone who waits. Many have tried the journey before. For some, this is their third or fourth attempt. Yet the destination they each head for is the same. Not a place in geography, but a dream. A place where hope still flickers.

A wave, larger than those before, catches the boat, making it lurch. A tremor of anxiety runs through the passengers, erupts as a low moan. Into the silence that follows, a man's voice rises, as if reaching to heaven: '*Allaahumma hawwin 'alaynaa safaranaa haathaa watwi 'annaa bu'dahu, Allaahumma 'Antas-saahibu fis-safari, walkhaleefatu fil-'ahli.*' The traveller's prayer, offered now in fear and desperation. *O Allah, lighten this journey for us and make its distance easy for us. O Allah, You are our Companion on the road and the One in Whose care we leave our family.*

As the prayer fades, the sound of the water changes, as if in defiance of the imprecation. It strikes the hull with a deeper thud, seems to suck more hungrily as it falls back. The wind, too, alters its tone, has a growl in its throat. And in the failing light the sky seems to grow heavier; the clouds sag. Near the prow, where a woman sits, wrapped tight in her cloak, the bucking of the boat feels wilder and the spray leaps higher, stabs at her face. There is a storm coming, the woman thinks; though the journey has already been hard, there is surely worse to come. She knew when she boarded that it would happen like this, that the boat would not survive the crossing. She'd heard the stories, read the reports, could work the chances out for herself. Three quarters of attempted passages failed, those who tried had told her. If you were lucky, within a few hours – a day, maybe two – you ended up back where you started. If you were unlucky, you capsized, drowned. She'd seen the evidence as she waited for a passage. The broken boats. The bodies. She saw it, too, in the eyes of the agents she'd dealt with, careless of any consequence. She saw it in her first sight of the boat. Too small. Too flimsy. Its outboard motor under-powered.

She'd taken the precautions she could. She'd bought herself a good life-jacket – one that was made of strong nylon, proper foam – although it had cost her almost half the money that she had left. She had a torch to signal for help, had written a contact number and her name on her wrist in indelible felt-tipped pen so that she could be identified if she drowned. Such things you learned. You had to.

She carries, too, the small charm that she was given years ago. She does not believe in its magic, but its familiarity comforts her, and it contains, she imagines, a residue of all the kindnesses and companionship that she has received on her journeying. She smooths it with her thumb. An instinctive action. Like a prayer, like a kiss.

She tries to sleep. Take it now, she thinks, for later when the storm comes there will be no chance.

She winds her wrist more tightly into the grab-rope that runs along the gunwale – the boat's only gesture to passenger safety – slumps lower, seeking some core of warmth within her body. She tries to find rhythm in the movements of the boat, and let her body go with it. But the sea is playing a complex tune, and the boat dances to it – a *czardas*, a tarantella, drunken and disorderly. With no warning, the prow falls away beneath her, and belatedly she follows it, meets it on its return. Her hips jar. Her neck jerks.

A few minutes later, it happens again, and soon after that once more. The crash of the wave, the lurch of the boat, the pitch of her stomach, jolt of her body. Soon, that is all that happens, and there might be no end to its occurrence.

Her mind goes where it always goes, as escape from these moments. Into imagining. That she is running through grassy pastures, leaping over rocks, flying above verdant hills. That the sea is the land and she is a bird and what she hears is the rush of the wind as she rolls and turns and dives and soars. A lark, a kestrel, a hawk, an eagle.

A kite on a string, tugged back by a child's eager hand.

The boat lurches again and the dreams fracture, become bright shards of crystal white.

Lightning rakes the sky, and an instant later the darkness rumbles, like an old dog. Like all the hounds of Hades, angry.

She's fully awake now, and tries to take in the scene; tries to separate in her mind its different elements, give it meaning. It's a futile endeavour, for there is no sense to be made. Just a world in frenzy. Chaos in negative form. Black sea, tinged white with froth. Black sky, crazed by lightning. Black shadow of the boat, with its ragged cargo of passengers, tossed with every lurch.

Everyone is screaming, now.

The boat slurs, judders. The wind gusts as if to aid it in its task. Sea surges. She feels herself lifted, almost as if weightless; torso and limbs move as if detached. Then her arm yanks, and she feels the rope cut into her wrist.

Above her or below her, she cannot tell which, she sees the dark shape of a body, thrown free.

The sea seizes her. She spins, falls.

Something solid lands upon her, knocking the breath from her lungs so that she gasps. Water rushes in.

She coughs, chokes, turns, thrashes, feels the tight grip on her wrist. For a moment all is black. Then somewhere, far away in some other world, there is a flicker of light. It seems to diffuse around her, as if seen through some strange and shifting gauze.

It brings a moment of understanding. She tries to wriggle her wrist free from the rope, kicks against the upturned hull, tries to push herself away. The rope still holds her, the press of the water around her grows, all-consuming.

She twists once more. Her hand slips free. She kicks again. She swims.

*

In those long moments of wave and wind and darkness, people come to her.

Some she finds floating, or swimming, or clinging to whatever flotsam they have found. One or two she manages to help for a while. A woman whose head she supports, until a wave snatches them apart, and she cannot find her again. A youth she swims with, encourages, until her own strength fades and she drifts away.

Others come more numinously, and as if in judgement. A man, her husband once, anger spilling from him. Not for her leaving, but for her coming back. He thought her dead, wanted her so, has no wish to meet again the woman who deceived him.

A father, the same, blank in his rejection.

A mother, whose eyes tell a different story – yearning, sorrow – yet stands there, and will not speak.

Sisters, torn in the same way between their affection and obligation. Then they fall upon her, hug her as the sea does, in their fierce embrace. Wanting to hold her, keep her, make her stay.

And somewhere, at the edge of it all, two figures roam. A man. A son. Waiting. Fading.

And the bird above her, again. Flying, free.

And for an instant she seems to fly, the same.

The waves lift her. Let her go. She flies. She glides.

She lets herself fall.

The water retreats. And all is still.

*

In the sand is an eye. It regards her, unblinking. Beside it she sees the curl of her hand.

Something passes across the sun. Shadow falls on her. She lies, held in its silent grip.

Then a voice. Words she cannot understand.

A child's voice. Is it him? Has he come?

She looks up, tries to call his name, but her lips are bloated, her throat is raw. All that comes is water, salt and sour, bubbling. She coughs, chokes.

And in any case, it's not him. Just a child, seven or eight years old. He stands in half silhouette against the bright sky. His hair black, curled, his face thin. Conjured from all the children she has ever seen, ever known.

'*Hai bisogno di aiuto?*'

Sounds that mean nothing, yet slowly translate in her mind to a question: do you need help?

Yes.

'*Sei ferito?*' Are you hurt?

Is she? She doesn't know. Her body is no longer her own. But the boy speaks again. '*Di dove sei?*'

Another question that she cannot answer, her thoughts too dull and slow. Where are you from? She thinks of the boat, of the vastness of the sea. Beyond that there is nothing. Is that where she comes from?

But the boy's attention has shifted. He points. '*Cos'è quello?*' he asks. What is that?

It's the eye-bead, lying in the sand.

She moves her arm, closes her hand around it. It's not for him.

For an instant there is an impasse. The boy stands, frowning. She lies with the bead tight in her palm. Then she feels a quiver of guilt, so deep she could cry. She should give it to him. It's just a small charm.

But the boy asks, '*Tu chi sei?*' Who are you?

Once more she struggles to find an answer. Who is she? She amongst all the bodies crowded on the boat. She amongst all those who swam and drifted, who struggled, drowned.

She amidst all the other thousands who have tried to make this trip before.

But a name comes, and perhaps it is hers, though when she tries to speak it she manages no more than a croak.

The boy crouches, and his large eyes travel across her, as if completing a journey of their own. Face, body, arms, hands.

He smiles.

'*Sei tu?*' Is that you?

He reaches for her, touches her wrist, traces the letters inscribed there with his fingers, lightly. Pronounces the word they make.

'*Zarrin*,' he says. '*Sei Zarrin.*'

Acknowledgements

My sincerest acknowledgements, as ever, go to my wife, Ann, not only for her tolerance and encouragement and her invaluable editorial comments, but also for the many hours of discussion about the plot and the characters and how to make the story work. If for any reason it still does not, the fault is mine, not hers. But the fact of its completion is due to her.

My thanks also go to Clare Christian and Heather Boisseau and their colleagues at RedDoor who have been so supportive in making the book a reality, and who have always been a pleasure to work with. Thanks, too, to Kari Brownlie for designing the cover and to Charlotte Chapman for the proofreading. Likewise, I thank Lucy Popescu for her invaluable advice on the matters of sensitivity that a story like this inevitably evokes; and a special thanks to Linda McQueen for her assiduous editorial contribution, which has not only greatly enhanced the text but entertained and instructed me in the process.

While this is a work of fiction, many of the experiences of the characters described here are based on the true events recounted by refugees and migrant workers. I have adapted these events to suit the narrative, have changed names and in some cases locations, but the essence of their stories remains the same. Yaasmin's story of her flight from Somalia is based on the report 'Inside the Deadly Pirate Corridor Where Migrants Escape to Europe' by Michael Scott Moore

(*Bloomberg Businessweek*, 22 February 2017, corrected 4 March 2017). Ahmed's story of crossing the River Evros into Greece is based on the article 'Syrian refugees turned back from Greek border by police' by Rebecca Omonira-Oyekanmi (*Guardian*, 7 December 2012). Events in the Elysium, including the annual round-up of illegal workers, draw upon stories told in the excellent yet harrowing blog *Maid in London* (last updated in 2016). Descriptions of life in a refugee camp on the Turkish border were informed by the report 'Syrian refugees flee across border to Turkey – in pictures', in the *Guardian* (9 June 2011).

Information on conditions for asylum-seekers and refugees in European countries has been drawn from the invaluable pages of w2eu.info, which offers much-needed services to refugees. Other sources of information on the experience of refugees in Europe included: Andreas Ulrich, 'Illegal Immigrants in Greece: At the Mercy of the People Smugglers' (*Spiegel Online*, 24 May 2012); Patrick Kingsley, 'The Journey – the story of Syrian refugee Hashem Alsouki's flight to Sweden' (*Guardian*, 9 June 2015); Nevin Sangur: 'Escape to uncertainty. Turkey opens its doors to refugees, but few are allowed to stay' (*National Geographic*, 8 June 2013); Lorena Luciano and Filippo Picopo's TV documentary *It Will Be Chaos* (HBO, 2018). Information on the procedures for dealing with refugees in the UK is drawn from Migrant Help's *Asylum Advice*.

For information on Kurdish life and culture, I used: Tuija Saarinen, *General cultural differences and stereotypes: Kurdish family culture and customs* (PhD thesis hosted on various websites); Jenna Krajeski, 'Inside the life of the Kurds' (*Smithsonian Magazine*, June 2015); Loring Kasso, 'Let's dance for Newroz' (*Hikayetna*, 14 April 2016).

After I had completed the story, as I was doing the long series of supposedly 'final' edits, I came across Ismail Yigit's article 'Survival Tactics of Waste Paper Pickers in Istanbul' (*Journal of Ethnic and Cultural Studies*, Vol 2, 2015). I was somewhat disappointed to find that Zarrin's survival technique in Istanbul, which I thought she had cleverly invented (with a little help from me), was already a reality. But validation of one's imaginings is always comforting.

The extract of 'Exile' is taken from the poem of Abdulla Pashew, translated by Mahsn Majidy and the Poetry Translation Workshop and published by the Poetry Translation Centre. The words of '*Lay, lay*' are based on the translation of the recording of *Azerbaijani Children Songs* by Sövkət Ələkbərova. Those of '*Nami, nami*' are based on the recording by Azam Ali.

Special thanks also go to Frank Anello of Project Worthmore for permission to use the poem 'Where I Am From' as the Frontispiece. Project Worthmore (https:// projectworthmore.org) has the mission to provide programmes that foster community, self-sufficiency and increase quality of life among Denver-area refugees, and this poem was written by one of the people it has helped – a nineteen-year-old Syrian refugee.

Author's Note

Zarrin's story is based on a harsh reality faced by far too many people in the world: the desperate flight from their homeland in search of safety from war and starvation and exploitation and abuse. Their story clearly needs telling and telling again, for, all too often, refugees still encounter indifference or hostility or rejection from those who they turn to for help.

It is clearly inappropriate and unethical for an uninvolved author such as myself to make money out of such suffering. For that reason, I have pledged all author royalties from this book to a charity for refugees – Refugee Action – with the hope that it may have some practical benefit for their work. I hope, too, that in reading this story others may understand that suffering better and be stirred to care a little more.

*

Refugee Action exists to support refugees and people seeking asylum to rebuild their lives in the UK. Their vision is that refugees and people seeking asylum will be welcome in the UK. They will get justice, live free from poverty and be able to successfully rebuild their lives. You can find out more on their website, refugee-action.org.uk.

LONGLISTED FOR THE MICHAEL GIFKINS PRIZE

THE CLAIM

DAVID BRIGGS

'A beautifully written and gripping novel.
A rare talent indeed.'
Mark Thompson, author of *Dust*

If you enjoyed *Zarrin*, you may also like
David Briggs' debut novel, *The Claim*.

Read on for a taster...

One

'You guys must be born optimists,' the man in the store had said. 'All you prospectors. What else would make you do that sort of thing other than belief – blind hope?'

He meant more than the words implied: that people like Evan were loners who lived off their own company, didn't need the stimulus of a partner or a wife to keep them going, didn't need the earthly chances that normal people relied on. But he was right in his way. You had to defy probabilities; you had to have hope.

The storeman had recognised him as soon as he walked in: a regular customer, even though his visits were a year apart.

Evan had called there on the way in, as he did every year, for a last cup of real coffee, to fill up with fuel, buy a few provisions that he'd forgotten to pack. After the long drive across the Canterbury Plains, the Alps shimmering in the distance, refusing to draw near, then the slow haul over Arthur's Pass down to the coast, Silverstone was the last place that might claim the title of civilisation, and it only just merited that. A scatter of houses, a store that served as a café and fuel-stop as well, a tiny white church offering services the third Sunday of every month. Beyond that there was nothing. No internet or phones or radio. No duties or demands. Just the mountains, the river, the bush. His claim, solitude. Escape.

Then the man had said: 'Maybe that's the secret really. Maybe you have to believe to have luck. That's where I've gone wrong, perhaps, not believing.'

At the time, Evan had laughed. 'Luck's luck,' he'd said. 'I guess we all get our share.'

But whatever it was, belief or hope or just unseeing chance, his seemed to have run out. When he arrived, all seemed to bode well. The cottage had welcomed him, with a creak of the door, the familiar smell of winter mould and dust, two ten-dollar notes neatly folded on the mat. A few days later, when he'd set out to his claim the auguries had stayed good. On the drive up to the saddle the land looked fresh-spruced by the winter rains and spring snowmelt, the sky stretched, the air soft. On the walk from the car park, the fantails danced for him, bums out, tails splayed, while tuis sang and clucked and burped from the bush. At the claim, the stream wove between the gravel bars, beckoning him with its gentler song.

He'd tidied up his camp, stowed his gear, and the next day started panning. He began as he always did, at his favourite spots, exploring the riffles and pools and pockets of sediment that had formed since his previous visit. At first, no gold appeared, yet he did not worry. It was there somewhere; he just had to be patient. He was simply glad to be back, alone and free. In Christchurch, loneliness could be a torment; here it was a salve. And even now, two years after Juliette had left, he still needed that: the solace of solitude. So he had extended his search, remained content, and on the third day his patience and endeavour had borne fruit. His first finds. Bright flecks amidst the black iron and tourmaline sand.

Two days ago, he'd picked a target, a bed of grit and gravel, caught in the curve of the stream thirty metres below the camp. He'd set up the dredge, got to work. Soon, gold was coming out. Nothing dramatic, but a little more every time he paused the pump, checked the trays. Enough to justify the optimism that the storeman had talked about, to promise a good summer ahead. All he needed now was favourable weather and time.

Time, he had. Another eleven weeks before he'd have to leave, go back to work. The weather, though, seemed less accommodating. There was a storm brewing, and it was going to be a ripper. When it arrived, there'd be no more dredging for a while – not until the rain had eased and the river had forgotten it, subsided again. By then, the deposit he was working would have been swept away, the gold dispersed and lost.

He'd seen the storm approaching several hours ago. White wisps of stratus pulled out like combed wool. The change in the sun, losing its brightness, becoming pale and curdled. Later, the pillows of cumulus growing above the ridgeline away to the west. He might have called a halt then, scuttled back to the cottage while he could. He was due to do so in the morning, anyway; it was time for a rest, to replenish his supplies. But he wanted to grab what he could while he had the chance. So he'd kept going, even though he knew the cost. A wild night under tarpaulin, out here in the bush. All the discomfort: the last dregs of his food, damp clothes in the morning, a soggy trip back to his truck.

But now it was time to stop. In the last hour the sky had soured, turned grey and liverish. The birds were silent. Only the mosquitoes were left, riding the heavy air.

He felt for the fuel line, switched off the generator. The thrum and throb of the pump, the rattle of stones on the sluice, ceased. All became still.

He looked around, whistled for the dog. He'd last seen her half an hour ago. Then, she'd been sniffing around in the undergrowth, absorbed in some trace only she could detect. She wouldn't have gone far. She was a good dog, knew her legal limits, would be listening for his call. He whistled again.

She should have been a collie, or a huntaway, that's what friends who claimed to know had told him. They were the dogs you needed in the hills, they said: they had stamina, were fast, could track and catch rabbit or pig or deer – whatever you needed. They were quick to learn as well, could live outside. Instead, he'd chosen a spaniel. A springer, black and white, small, sinuous, with a coat like silk. A rescue dog, though what she needed rescuing from or why anyone would have failed to want her in their life he couldn't imagine, for she seemed to be everything a dog should be. Companion, friend, defender against unseen perils, source of constant amusement and affection. When he'd bought her from the SPCA, at fifteen months old, less than a week from being put down, she was called Molly. He didn't like the name; it was too girlish, too human. For days he tried out different names. Then, one evening, he told her: 'I'm giving you a life. You're going to help me with mine.' So he called her Viva – for life. And it was a private joke as well: Viva the Spaniel.

Once more he whistled, waited. Still she did not come.

In the distance, there was a flickering flash, lightning above the hills. In that same moment, he smelled the rain coming. A muskiness, an earthiness, fungal, hormonal, almost like the smell of sex. He'd misjudged; he had to be quick. Never mind the dog – the rain would bring her back. Right now, he needed to get the dredge and sluice to safety, his tarpaulin pegged down, everything under cover.

He worked feverishly. The water could rise almost as fast as you could move in a river like this. A half-hour respite while the canopy of the bush wetted, the trees soaked the rain up, and then the ground would start to darken, runnels would appear; they'd stretch, reach, join like fingers feeling for each other for comfort and strength. Runoff would drip, seep, surge into the channel. The stream would grow brown with silt; its whole tone would change. No longer a gurgle of laughter, a rippling song, but a thunder, a roar. The banks would sag and slump. Boulders would shift. Even twenty metres away you'd be able to feel the water's anger, its primaeval force.

He lifted the generator, heaved it up the bank onto the higher terrace, carried it across to his shelter and tucked it beneath his tarpaulin. He did the same with the dredge, hauling in the hose, coiling it up, stowing it in the hollow he'd dug under the trees. He broke up the header box and sluice, stacked the trays, tied up the struts and put them alongside. Then he paused, whistled again for the dog, listened.

For a moment, he thought he heard her – a quick yap – but though he strained his ears, it did not repeat. Just the sound of boughs creaking in the wind, or the wind in the boughs, or his own imagination.

Then the first drops of rain started, large, heavy. They beat on the ground, making craters in the silt, splashed on boulders and spat back at the air as if in spite. There was another lightning flash, a roll of thunder, only ten seconds apart. The storm closing in.

He looked around, checking that he hadn't missed anything, was leaving nothing to the elements. A spade stood, stuck into a sandy bar, in mid-stream. He cursed, waded out to it, grabbed it as the heavens opened.

He ran for the shelter. By the time he reached it, he was drenched. He threw the spade down, pulled the flap of the tarpaulin behind him, tugged off his sodden shirt, slumped onto his bed. Just the dog to come now. Where was she?

Half an hour later, and she'd still not returned. He started to worry about her. He crawled to the opening at the end of his shelter, peered out.

The world outside was dark. Not yet the darkness of night, but of something more threatening, more consuming – a world in turmoil. Pattern and shape had been destroyed. Mountains, sky, trees, stream were all as one, just a torn and torrid muddle. Colours had fused. What had been green, blue, white, ochre was all now grey and brown. The only relief from it all was when the lightning flashed. Then, for an instant, the old world would fizz and crackle again, and shape would emerge, a world in negative.

He called again, but his voice was lost to the blustering wind. He ducked back inside, lay on his bed.

The shelter was rudimentary, just a tarpaulin strung in the shape of a tent from two branches, in the lee of a mossy bank. He made some food, a simple meal: a handful of rice, a sachet of dried vegetables, some spices to give it all taste. He ate it, squatting on his bed, a bottle of beer to swill it down. When he'd finished, he put the pans by the entrance, donned his spare pullover to keep himself warm, called once more for the dog. She did not come, and he curled up inside his sleeping bag, fretful, trying not to imagine life without her.

*

When he woke, it was dark. The true darkness of night. He reached for his head torch, switched it on, checked his watch. Gone ten. Still, no dog.

He crawled to the entrance, looked out. The storm had retreated now, settled amongst the mountains where it grumbled and glimmered with evil intent. Here, there was just the rain. It came steadily. The river rumbled and roiled.

He whistled, called the dog by name: 'Viva. Viva.'

The thunder growled back.

He got up, took a few steps into the clearing, stood, listening. At first, there was nothing. Just the instruments of the storm, in irritable disharmony. But then, amidst it, he heard a yap – or thought he did. It was faint, strangely distorted, as though the wind had grabbed it, ripped it apart, reassembled it again. Then the wind billowed, and he knew that he had just imagined it. He was too good at that. Hearing what he wanted to hear. He turned back.

It came again. Not once but repeated this time. High-pitched, short. It was the bark she gave when she'd found something that she could not deal with, something that didn't play by the rules – a hedgehog that refused to uncurl, an injured bird that wouldn't fly, a possum that sneered at her from the safety of a tree. He went out into the clearing, whistled, though knowing that it was pointless, for the wind caught the sound and tossed it behind him.

Another yap. She must have found something out there, he guessed, be guarding it. A pig carcass perhaps, or a deer. He'd leave her to it. She'd come back in the morning, reeking with its smell, belly full, repentant.

Or she lay injured, was calling for him.

He sighed, went back into the shelter, pulled on his coat, put the head torch on. 'Bloody dog.'

He crossed the clearing, down to the stream, started to work his way along it, heading for where he thought the sound had come from.

It wasn't easy. The main path was on the other bank. On this side there was no real trail, thick bush. In the humid air, his torch fogged, so that he could hardly see. The ground was slippery with rain, boulder-strewn. There were fallen trees, logs, patches of gorse and broom, long vines of supplejack blocking and tangling his way. Once, he called, and thought he heard a brief, answering bark.

Slowly, stumblingly, he veered towards it. He splashed through a channel, knee deep. He squelched through mud. He ducked beneath a low branch, received a slap in the face. He found himself in a gully, called again.

The dog yapped. She was somewhere above him, up on the spur. He started to climb. She barked again. Nearer now, the sound distinct, her tone urgent.

He reached a small clearing, paused for breath, moved his head slowly so that the beam made a sweep of the darkness.

Two pinpricks of light gleamed back. Just the reflection of raindrops? Or the dog's eyes?

They disappeared.

He shone the torch again, searching. All he could see was a tangle of shadows, shapeless and shifting in the relentless rain. 'Viva!'

As if in answer, the world was lit by another lightning flash, and in its aftermath he saw her, as if imprinted onto his eyes. She was standing next to a large boulder, head low, looking down.

'Viva,' he called again. 'Here girl.'

But instead of coming, she gave a whimper, then turned, disappeared. He ran in pursuit, felt the ground steepen beneath his feet. He slipped, tried to catch himself, and slithered, half fell down a dark and muddy defile. A rock jarred against his shoulder. He swore.

Then the ground levelled, and he came to an ungainly halt. He crouched there panting, scraping mud from his torch. As the light gathered itself again, the darkness shrank back to reveal a strange and ghostly scene. A wide slab of rock forming a flat bench, ridged and runnelled by weathering. Beyond, the pallid shapes of cliffs, looming above him. Black crevices, hunched trees.

In that instant he knew where he was: at the edge of the gorge, halfway down his claim. It was an area he rarely came to, for the stream here was deep and ran on bare rock, no place for fossicking. In the daylight, the area had a sense of portent and mystery; now, in the rain and the night, it seemed like the gateway to Hades itself.

He took off his torch, played it across the bench. Viva was standing ten metres away, her body rigid, nose extended, tail feathered. He shone the light past her, trying to see what might have drawn her to this place. What her game was, what prize she wanted to show him – what, in her canine view of the world, was worth all this disobedience and discomfort.

There was nothing. Just rock, boulders, the dark shape of flood debris piled against a low outcrop.

The dog wagged.

He got to his feet.

And the dark shape became a bundle of clothes. A human figure. A woman.

About the author

After a career in universities in England, during which he published a number of academic books on geography and the environment, David Briggs moved to New Zealand in 2009. Since then, he has focused on creative writing. *The Direction of Our Fear*, his first novel, was published by BMS Books, in 2016. *The Claim*, which was longlisted for the Michael Gifkins Prize and shortlisted for the New Zealand Booklovers Award, was published by RedDoor in 2019. *Reflections*, a collection of poems with photographs by J.F. Robert, was published by Copy Press in 2021. David now lives in Mapua on the north coast of South Island New Zealand, with his wife, Ann, and their two dogs.

www.davidbriggs.site

Find out more about RedDoor Press and sign up to our newsletter to hear about our **latest releases, author events,** exciting **competitions** and more at

reddoorpress.co.uk

YOU CAN ALSO FOLLOW US:

 @RedDoorBooks

 Facebook.com/RedDoorPress

 @RedDoorBooks